Rhapsody of Blood

Volume Five—Revelations

Books by Roz Kaveney

Author

Fiction

Rhapsody of Blood: Volume One—Rituals
Rhapsody of Blood: Volume Two—Reflections
Rhapsody of Blood: Volume Three—Resurrections
Rhapsody of Blood: Volume Four—Realities

Tiny Pieces of Skull, or a Lesson in Manners (2016 Lambda Award Winner)

Poetry

Dialectic of the Flesh (2012 Lambda Award Finalist)
What if What's Imagined Were All True
Catullus
Ballads: Nightsongs and Neckverses
Selected Poems 2021
The Great Good Time

Non-Fiction

From Alien to The Matrix: Reading Science Fiction Film

Teen Dreams:

Reading Teen Film and Television from "Heathers" to "Veronica Mars"

Superheroes!

Capes and Crusaders in Comics and Films
with Jennifer Stoy
Battlestar Galactica: Investigating Flesh, Spirit, and Steel
Nip/Tuck: Television That Gets Under Your Skin

Editor

Tales From the Forbidden Planet
More Tales from the Forbidden Planet
Reading the Vampire Slayer:
The Complete, Unofficial Companion to "Buffy" and "Angel"
with Mary Gentle
Villains!
with Neil Gaiman, Mary Gentle & Alex Stewart
The Weerde Book One
The Weerde Book Two: Book of the Ancients

Rhapsody of Blood

Volume Five—Revelations

A Novel of the Fantastic

Roz Kaveney

Plus One Press
San Francisco

Plus One Press

RHAPSODY OF BLOOD, VOLUME FIVE—REVELATIONS. Copyright © 2023 by Roz Kaveney. All rights reserved. Printed in the United States of America and the United Kingdom. For information, address Plus One Press, 45 Bridge Road, Novato, California, 94945.

www.plusonepress.com

Book Design by Plus One Press

Cover artwork by Judith Clute, copyright © 2023 by Plus One Press

Publisher's Cataloging-in-Publication Data available on request

ISBN-13: 978-0-9977453-2-0
ISBN-10: 0-9977453-2-0

First Edition: August, 2018

10 9 8 7 6 5 4 3 2 1

In memoriam
Rachel Pollack and Graham Kent,
two close friends of mine for 50 years

Acknowledgements

First and foremost, Deborah and Nic Grabien for believing in and committing to a project so ambitious, and to them and Jacqueline Smay for knocking five books into shape in the most trying of circumstances. Also my cover artists, Amacker Bullwinkle, Graham Higgins and Judith Clute.

Next all my beta readers, listeners down the phone, technical advisors and resolvers of problems when I was stuck on plot points— among them Simon Field, Lesley Arnold, Charles Stross, Simon Bradshaw, Robert Irwin, Jennifer Stoy, Shana Worthen, Tanja Kinkel and Neil Gaiman.

And the insightful critics who made it all worthwhile—among them Jo Walton, Liz Burke, Sophia McDougall and Jonathan Thornton. Also, John Clute—the hours we spent discussing the tropes of fantasy for The Encyclopaedia of Fantasy planted many of the seeds that grew into this.

And Paule, the love of my life.

Finally there are so many writers to whom I owe debts—Roger Zelazny for poetry and a rather different Shadow, Catherine Moore and Joanna Russ for sarcastic warrior women, Ursula leGuin for a sense of how magic might work and Mike Harrison for a sense of its cost, David Gemmell for making me feel the weight of a sword, Clive Barker for the terrible vulnerability of the flesh, George McDonald Fraser and Dorothy Dunnett for how to make history do the work for you, Geoff Ryman and Angela Carter for moral seriousness and turning tropes on their heads. And so many others.

Revelations

"All that is solid melts into air: all that was sacred is profaned."
—K. Marx.   F. Engels

"I will survive."
—G. Gaynor

Measure for Measure

Former Hell, 2004?

Emma stopped time—she hadn't hitherto been doing it just to get around, or to spy on people, because it felt slightly frivolous to do for personal convenience something that she was using to be the Queen and Judge of Hell. Then, getting around and spying on people seemed to be a part of that job.

There was clearly something she needed to see and the formerly damned were going to be on their best behaviour with their Queen and Judge visibly around.

"It really is the sort of thing you disapprove of." Tsassiporah perched on her shoulder and hissed in her ear. "Personally I can't see what all the fuss is about, but I used to be Lucifer's bird and his company was clearly what you would consider bad for my character."

Birds cannot make air quotes with the tips of their wings, but this one clearly didn't need to.

1

Emma walked briskly but attentively along one of the long avenues that Aserath had set up between orchards of fruit and fields of crops and plots of vegetables. The air was thick almost to soupiness with the scent of each plant she could see and many that were not actually present.

Aserath, Emma thought, is a lot more industrious in her own way than she likes to pretend, and a lot more systematic. Once you got away from the office building that was her and Judas' contribution, the former Hell was just as geometric in its way as the old one, only rather more of a garden city than a gallery of horrors.

The first village they came to—well, there was nothing much to see at first. Elegant little cottages laid out in a grid system, with strips of flower garden between them and then a central square. The child Joseph was there playing cheerful tag with other children of various colours. A bunch of men and women were stomping grapes in a big wooden vat while a couple beat out a rhythm on a drum. Emma was ready to stride on to the next village, except it was clear from the excited way that Tsassiporah was breathing in her ear that they had spotted something that she had not. She stopped, and made herself look again, at all of it.

The children were reaching out and tagging each other not with their own hands but with small severed ones that had the claws of a young demon.

In among the grapes Emma could see the living heads of demon women being trampled into vintage.

The skin of the drum had an anguished living demon face on it. Woman or girl, it screamed silently.

Emma had enough access to Sof's memories that she could not help but take all this personally. "Are they doing these things in all the villages you visited?" she asked the bird.

Its chirrup was more like a chortle. "Oh, some of the villagers are much more imaginative than this, and others are just enslaving, starving, hitting with sticks—you used to be human. You know the drill."

2

Emma had thought that becoming a goddess meant that she never need feel sick again or feel that utter self-contempt that goes with vomiting profusely. But perhaps she was more human that she thought because bile rose in her throat and her cheeks burned fire with blushing.

She should have known; she should have foreseen. The formerly damned were people who had been imaginatively tortured for hundreds, in some cases for a couple of thousand years. They had been whipped and burned and torn apart and eaten alive and put back into the flesh to be tortured some more.

And now here they were back in the flesh, but most of the demon males of fighting age had died—in the explosion meant for her and Aserath, or torn apart alive by Simon so that he could rebuild himself into a nightmare. And the few that were left, and their wives and their children, had become targets. Just because most of the damned had been more or less innocent of damnable crimes when alive, did not mean that they were not capable of making up for lost time here and now.

They were after all human.

What had she and Aserath done without thinking? Through indolence or idealism or just being naive.

Emma had never been someone who ran—it had always struck her as one of the more pointless forms of exercise—but now she wanted to be away from her thoughts for a while and perhaps running from them would help her.

It did not. She ran faster and faster and soon the red bird was having trouble keeping up with her. She almost resented that she could not tire, that her feet could not blister, that she would never feel out of breath or cramped by a stitch or panting with thirst again. There was an orchestral allegro somewhere in the back of her head, full of brutal plucked cellos and snarling brass. It was vaguely Russian. It accompanied her mood and helped her run.

She stopped a second so that Tsassiporah could catch up with her. "Go back to my office. I need to be alone for a while."

3

The bird nodded sulkily and fluttered away.

She was angry with herself, angry with her partner in rule, angry with all the gods and godlings who had created this mess, angry with the formerly damned, and with the whole damn universe.

Emma ran.

She needed to clear her head and she especially did not need to be told by Caroline that she should have seen it coming, really she should, or have Aserath and Morgan not see any especial problem with it all, or hear Vretil sniff one more time, or have Judas look at her sorrowfully and ironically and tell her that now she knew what it was like to make bad choices for good reasons.

Emma ran.

And she really could not face Josette, when she heard about it. Or have Dawn look at her with eyes of disillusioned hero-worship.

In each village she spied on, it was the same, or maybe worse or maybe not quite as bad but still awful. After a while she could not bear it any longer. Emma thought of raining down horror and vengeance that would echo the desolate anger in her soul, but she could imagine the smug look on Jehovah's face, or Lucifer's, and she would find a better way of being a god.

She also thought of Josette and Mara. Our elders, who may not be our betters, are important because the thought of disappointing them, of being disapproved of by them, keeps us from doing stupid things.

She avoided villages and sped through the new fertile Hell that Aserath had grown, acre after acre of garden and field and orchard and vineyard and flower-bank and it was all a little the same and she did not recognize any of it. The Hell she had arrived in so long ago in her own subjective time was gone, all of it. It was all so damn flat and fertile and healthy looking—she almost missed the surreal disgusting madness she had found when she first got here.

Except it was not gone, not quite all. She saw something glinting in the distance and picked up speed and raced towards it.

It suited her mood entirely—it was the Cliffs of Regret. Some things never go away.

She stopped running and walked towards them so that they slowly towered over her—the places where they had been shattered by falling angels had healed over and the fragments left on the ground from that shattering had lost their lustre and just become dull slates of forgotten memory. And of course some of them had been taken away by Simon to use as a weapon, and had failed him. Other people's regrets, a weapon that will always turn in your hand sooner or later.

Whereas, she realized as she saw more and more of what the cliffs had to show her, your own regrets are a scourge but also an instruction. The cliffs showed you the worst things you had done and that you had seen done and that had been done to you—they were your past and that was a torture for the damned and a catharsis for those whose accounts were, in the end, mostly clear.

Perhaps they needed the Cliffs of Regret in Heaven as much as in Hell—in old Hell they had just been a torture whereas now perhaps they could be a curative. She made a mental note to discuss this with Jehovah next time they met, or perhaps to suggest it to Mary. After all, Hell needed some sort of economy and she really ought to pay for borrowing Vretil.

It would never do to owe Jehovah.

Yes, she had been culpably naively hopeful, and people under her charge had suffered as a result, but this was Hell still, however she had tried to change it, and good intentions were still something of which one needed to beware.

In the fragments of mirror, she saw, not Caroline's awful first death as she had the last time she was here, but the atrocities she had already seen and the atrocities that she had seen before the damned were in her charge and which she should have foreseen would be requited. Over and over again.

So, right. First thing, she needed to make sure that this became a place of pilgrimage—every person in her charge needed what she needed, a bracing reminder of their imperfections as well as a chance to do better. But how could she bring this about? She turned her face away from regret and sat down with her back to the cliffs and then, because she was suddenly a little tired in spite of her divinity, she lay prone and looked up at the purple sky of Hell, where something glinted that was not, that could not be, a star.

It was too long, and thin.

She got up and walked around—something was prodding her memory, and a few minutes later she stubbed her toe on it where it lay half buried: the broken filigree door and burned and battered sides and back of Lucifer's elevator.

This is going to be easier than I thought, she thought. To walk in Shadow is to feel your way through all directions that come out of order, but there is one direction which precedes all others and it was the one Mary had taken without let or hindrance. Presumably flight is part of the divine package.

She willed herself into the purple sky.

Where, at a height of about sixty feet, she found herself cloyed to nausea by the red dust and made so dizzy it was all she could do to lower herself gently back to the ground without going into an embarrassing tail-spin.

So not as easy as all that, then. Whatever this dust was, and she doubted it was anything natural, whoever had planned it and made it seemed to have thought of every way to isolate Hell from Shadow and, more importantly, from the Mundane.

And large parts of the forces of Good from each other.

She needed to bring people to this part of Hell and she needed to do what Lucifer, for all the proverbs, had never done, and she needed to have a way to get back to the Mundane world and deal with whatever mischief the adversary was working there that he needed to keep his inadequate enemies well away from...

Also, she reflected, she needed to help all those demon women and children who had been treated so badly and persuade them to trust her, after she had not helped them when they needed her.

For a moment she registered her shame that she had not thought of them first.

Above all, she needed to talk to Mara. Someone needed to heal Morgan. And she herself needed not to be distracted, either by lust or jealousy.

So much to do. And Phlegethon was in entirely the wrong direction if you had to walk there…

Why had Lucifer placed his personal lift so very far from anywhere else in Hell, not least far from his Citadel of Dis? It made so little sense if he was in a hurry. And why here particularly?

Set aside all the myths of rebellion and fall—they had never happened back when the legends said. (Even though, as she knew well, they had come due in the end, largely thanks to her…) Lucifer had not struck her as someone who regarded regrets or introspection as other than self-indulgence.

Presumably his lift came down here simply because it was somewhere very few of the damned would ever come voluntarily, so he could keep it secret.

If he could not trust his subordinates because he ruled by playing them off against each other, he could not afford to have his comings and goings observed.

She had been brought to Hell, and shown around it, by Josette, but perhaps Josette had not known, or told her, everything.

Emma walked along the cliffs a little way, trailing her fingers along the shiny surfaces rather than looking at them. After five minutes she felt a thin crack which, when she looked at it, was not part of the damage inflicted by the war or by Simon. It was a straight line.

Oh please, she thought to herself, let it not have a password or a magic key. Let it something as simple as a handle.

And, fortunately, it was—though an invisible one that she only found because she was working by touch and not sight.

Inside a rock that most of the damned would not care to look at— not the worst place to hide something, she thought with respect.

She summoned her godhood around her, pulled the door open and entered. A pendulum blade swung at her and she seized it mid-swing and snapped it with a flick of her fingers; three silver arrows bounced off her; she looked up and caught a descending piece of ceiling as it fell.

If she had not been a god, these things might actually have hurt her. "That all you've got?" she said aloud, and tried the first step of the winding stair that she found herself looking down with her own light.

The place she found herself in was vast—the stairs were only just pitched at a level she could walk down and the darkness around her echoed with each step as if there were halls beyond halls. What did he keep here? she wondered, and then reflected that sometimes what is built reflects the builder and not the client.

She had wondered why the Titans were imprisoned alongside their former enemies the Olympians, but she supposed now that, well, if you are having something secret built, you need to keep its builders secure... She really should have talked to the Titans and the Olympians when she freed them—but she had too much on her mind at the time.

She reached the bottom of the stair and found herself on a dais on which there stood a gong and its hammer. Around her, in all directions save that of the stairway, tunnels stretched in a multitude of directions.

Lucifer had his own private underground railway? she thought. Well, that wasn't in Dante. And clearly none of the Dukes she had interrogated had known about it.

She struck the gong, the usual three times, and she waited.

I could just head off down a tunnel and see where it takes me, she thought, but that would be amateurish. Let's assume that whatever this is, works.

In the distance she heard a rush of wings and a fast heavy tread and the rumbling of wheels. On the dry wind of something travelling fast she smelt civet and blood and horsedung. The creatures that drew the carriage that pulled up by her platform had bodies covered with yellow fur spotted with darkness, but they had many legs, some insectile and some like those of fast horses and some the muscular racing legs of the great cats they might once have been. From their

8

backs there stuck out the wings of eagles and of dragon-flies—and where the stitches had once been, there welled blood and the pus of open sores.

And their faces were the faces of men that hung slack-jawed and wept tears of more blood.

She recognized the handiwork—after all, she had killed what their creator had made of himself.

On their heads were crowns glittering with rubies, diamonds and gold, but inverted so that the rim of spikes pressed downwards into their heads. The crowns were attached by swathes of silver chain to the interior of the carriage, so that a passenger could tweak if he wished more speed or merely to cause pain.

They were creatures in, at best, discomfort but it looked like something that rather worse than agony. These poor beasts had depended on their creator to stay clear of fester and rot, and Emma had killed him.

They whimpered and there was nothing she could do for them here, save kill them, which would not be especially convenient and might be unjust. Like so much else, though, they were her responsibility even if they were not her guilt.

Her next stop, she hoped, was a place where—if anywhere—she might fix them.

Emma addressed the creatures even if they could not hear or understand her—she hoped that her godhood would make it so, but she found it impossible to know.

"Do me this service and I will give you surcease of pain if I can, and death if I cannot."

It is part of godhood to make your every statement an oath and part of your nature.

She climbed into the carriage and sat in the well-padded seat, not caring to speculate where the leather for it had come from. And then, she felt a wetness on her neck and a gentle tickling that was far from unpleasant yet somehow nauseating—she craned her neck around and saw that two large eyes had opened in the part of the seat she leant on and that lashes were butterfly-kissing her.

"I am sorry, poor beasts, poor carriage. I fear I must travel with you at least once, but know that I gutted and then utterly destroyed the one who did this to you. And I will try to make it right. At the Blood Vats of Phlegethon. Where things are made new."

It never hurts to repeat your promises, over and over.

And the human voices ululated and whinnied and snarled and gave the cry of kestrels and suddenly the carriage was off, down the cyclopean tunnels in a darkness that she could have illuminated with a wave of her hands but chose not to, for she had seen too much already.

It was a journey that seemed to last forever because Emma was in her own mind during it, going over regrets and plans over and over again. The crying of the beasts and the darkness through which they rushed was something she could have changed, if she chose. But she chose not to, and to endure. Godhood makes some things into choices rather than necessities, she thought. Is awareness of that part of the process of ceasing to be human?

Simon had made this railway for his former master, whom he had then betrayed. The tunnels had been built earlier—cyclopean, she thought—and that was the right epithet for them because they were the work of Titans, twice over if she guessed right. Built once under Tartarus for some purpose of Hades and then their builders thrown back into the lowest part of Hell. Only once again to be promised and betrayed by Lucifer.

The tunnel ended and drew up at a platform lit by Hell's purple daylight. Emma alighted and stroked the neck of one of the beasts. It was silky to the touch and yet very slightly sticky so that she needed, not to wipe it for that was no longer a necessity for her, but to will the taint away.

"I will do something for you, poor beasts," she promised, though she feared that all she might be able to give was the rest of death and annihilation.

There was a great roaring tumult in her ears, whose source she could not at first discern.

The platform beneath her feet was made of great stone flags and there was no staircase at the end of it, but rather a viewing platform. Beneath it lay, cradled under great mountains that were—she knew this from one of the maps in her office—the boundaries of Hell in all directions, a river that flowed red and stank of rust and iron and salt. A river that was not like the canals filled with flame and worse things that she had seen when first she came to Hell as it was, but yet reminded her of it in its redness and its stink of death and worse than death.

It was a river of blood above which floated will of the wisps that would suddenly ignite, flare red for a moment and then die away again, and there were patches of something pink and disgusting like debris in sewers or shoals of blind and leprous fish and this she realized was the stuff of which hell-flesh was made after being caught in the nets that she saw hanging from a cable that travelled all the way across the river and back. The nets cycled continually from the river to the shore and back out again empty on the higher cable—she could see where they deposited their loads, in great iron drums that sat on wagons to which great and amorphous beasts, like a crude model of a horse modelled in clay, but not clay- were harnessed.

The drums on one wagon were full and the beast that drew the wagon pulled it away and another took its place—some of the pink and grey detritus of the nets fell between the wagons and onto the broad back of the beast of burden where it lay in a pool for a moment and then drained around and into its side, leaving it even more misshapen than before.

She knew that the blood and bones of her beloved were made of the stuff that this liquid, this near-jelly, turned into, and that the plans she was forming, a lattice of ideas and speculations in her mind, depended on it to a large extent. She had been placing the formerly damned into bodies made of it for subjective aeons and she could not afford the mild disgust that she saw when it came from. It was worse, far worse, than knowing how sausages are made.

11

And for a second of disgust she thought of it as meat, as a meat that one might eat, and then that second was over.

A breeze came off the water and sprayed water and worse against her face and then she looked up at what she had thought a cloud without paying it due attention, and it was the source of all the roaring.

To her right, the river narrowed and dwindled to it source, a waterfall that fell, not from the mountains but from somewhere far above them, from the purple sky. Phlegethon was a river of Hell but it had its source elsewhere—draining blood and flesh and sweat and death from, Emma surmised, the Mundane world, because where else would Hell gets its river of life from?

She walked along the viewing platform which became a dock at which a skiff was still moored. An old man with a beard lay in the bottom of the boat snoring—Emma did not wake him but she was reasonably sure that she knew his name.

At the end of the dock was a paved way which led up and over the mouth of the tunnel she had arrived by and there, on a great throne that looked out over the river, was a dais and throne made of black basalt and steel stained with a red that was not rust. In it there sat a god—sometimes you know a god when you see one—who wore a dark robe that covered so much of him that he might almost have been made of the rich lush velvet save that underneath it there was a coiled strength that spoke of flesh.

From inside the hood of the robe two red eyes flashed, and above them a crown of rubies and black opals set in a metal that glistened like gold's dark twin. She recognized the metal as the Adamant, one of the stages of Sof's Work which later generations of scholars had misunderstood and called Alchemy.

She had not seen anyone who might be him among the Olympians in Lucifer's oubliette and had wondered where he was. And now she knew.

"Great Hades." She spoke with courteous deference, though she knew that she was now his mistress and was slightly embarrassed by that fact.

He nodded, lowering his head, still almost unseen within its cowl, as a great king to a greater. "You would be the new co-sovereign of my former realms." His voice was deeper than bass. "The former mortal turned goddess on merit alone whom men call Emma, in the new-fangled Saxon tongue. Which I have never learned because I cannot move far from this place." And indeed, Emma realized, under his robes and lying in great coils about his buskined feat, were lengths of chain. He could walk down to the dock and talk to his former ferryman if Charon were ever awake and perhaps a little way to the building that loomed behind his throne, but hardly further.

It was a serviceable and ugly block, with no attempt at beauty— bricks, or were they blocks of lava? For there was something sulphurous and burned about them. And windows and doors that fitted snugly but had nothing else to recommend them.

Clearly there was no thought of beauty about this place—or perhaps those exiled here to work with blood and flesh saw no point in sugaring the pill.

She spoke, aware that her voice had a hint of thunder in it, as Queen to tributary King. "I have favours to ask from you. And your freedom from those chains would be but the first instalment of my payment to you for those favours."

Hades stood up. He was more massive than his cousins the Titans whom she had only seen in a subinfernal darkness that was hardly darker than the robe that covered him.

"They tell me of you, Queen Emma. They say you are wise and merciful. And I see that you are merciful, but are you also wise? To offer me freedom in the realm that was once mine before Jehovah and Lucifer stole it from me, and before you and the courtesan goddess Aserath took it from Jehovah as his vicereines when Lucifer proved false."

"The labourer is worthy of his hire, and I ask work of you for which you should be paid. And your freedom would not be part of that payment, but merely a gesture of my good faith, so that if you wish to go from this place and not assist me, that would be your right."

He had every right to resent her, she thought, but seemed from his tone not to. Formal speech was nonetheless that right approach until she knew him better.

Hades reached up and threw back the hood and underneath, though still red-eyed and crowned, was the face of a young boy with curly black hair. He kicked the chains away from his feet and laughed, and suddenly he was, or appeared to be, of a normal size.

Emma could probably have told which was the illusion but felt it impolite to use her powers for such a purpose unnecessarily.

"I have been free, if I chose, for many years. But it was not expedient, for where in the worlds would I have gone? Lucifer had placed an overseer over me from whom I was safe as long as he thought me cowed. You killed that overseer, Emma Jones—the beast of a man called Simon—and I owe you favours for that. I am a god, but I feared that man enough to wait out his time and hope that one day he would over-reach." He shuddered.

"He is gone from the world forever, from both Shadow and the Mundane. I used one of the weapons of our secret enemy to ensure that." Emma shook her head. "There are some beings so vile that they need to be gone, though none of us should rush to a judgement on that and I am famous for my mercy."

"We are of one mind on that, then." The boy Hades swung himself down from his great chair.

Emma nodded her thanks for his agreement and continued, "There are beasts, part of which were once men, who were, I think, Simon's creation and which are dying now that he is not there to maintain them. I do not know where they should be stabled, so they remain in harness below, in Lucifer's tunnel."

Hades nodded. "I will have my servants see to them. For the moment. Simon made a salve from the flesh that floats in the river Phlegethon that cures the living of most ills just as the flesh and blood re-embody the dead."

"How unlike him," Emma said, "to do something of benefit."

Hades laughed. It was not a pleasant laugh.

"How else could he keep his experiments alive and suffering? He hated letting them escape into death, even if he could put them back into hell-flesh and start over again. And besides, some of his alterations to himself—well, he needed to be certain that those would heal. I don't think he ever did anything that was not selfish."

"Well, he is done with now," Emma shrugged.

Hades looked at her, his eyes serious and his jaw set. "But the carriage beasts, you know, do you not? That in the end there is only one answer to their pain."

Emma nodded, reluctantly, and he went on.

"The part of them that was once men is gone beyond recall, carved to mush—Simon was trying to create something more debased than manticores, but what he produced were creatures that are perpetually on the brink of death for all their speed, and that is perhaps that they wish at once to run from death and run towards it. In any case, a kindness for what is left of a human brain in them would be a bolt through it."

She nodded again. "I will be guided in this by you. And your servants?"

She saw a group of men—or were they gods?—gather tentatively at the door of the building behind the throne. Hades gestured three of them forwards and they bowed to Emma.

One was a man of mature years who wore a circlet of gold on his brow and a serious expression below it; the other two were obviously father and son from the strong resemblance between them, a man aged by sorrow and a youth with the expression of one who knew joy but had known great pain as well. They wore leather belts slung with small hammers and screwdrivers and various devices for measurement—their eyes, as well as pain and sorrow, had the look of joy she had seen in mathematicians.

"And in musicians, too," whispered that part of her which was still Berthe von Renssler.

"Men, this is Emma Jones, of whom you have heard, her majesty the new co-queen and principal judge of what was Lucifer's Hell and is now under the governance of her and the Canaanite Aserath. Emma Jones, these are my artisans who keep the blood vats running. Most of their names will mean nothing to you, but you will have heard of Minos, once a king in Crete and then your predecessor as judge, though not as ruler, down here in my day. And his former prisoners and servants, now free craftsmen again, Daedalus and his unfortunate son, who fell straight from the clouds to here, where the sky is not an escape."

Emma smiled. "Minos," she nodded in acknowledgement of a colleague, and aware that good administrators are not easily come by and she might have trouble convincing Hades to pass him over to her.

She walked over to Daedalus and his son. "It passes my expectation—though not my desire—to find you so readily among the hosts of Hell. I have tasks for you that will challenge you as much as anything in your Mundane pasts such that you will laugh aloud when I tell you."

She sighed with relief, because one at least of her projects now stood some chance of coming to fruition with these two, and Judas, at her side. If only she could find Nimrod, that arrogant hunter of men—perhaps the Dukes of Hell could be prevailed upon to tell her where in Hell he was to be found. And Aserath had mentioned Malevich—he too would suit her purpose. But no, Aserath had mentioned that his palace for Lucifer had not worked out so well, which would also argue against Nimrod.

The man who had built the Labyrinth—he might be useful.

And so, back to Hades. "Hell is surrounded by mountains—am I right in assuming that over them lies the rest of Shadow, and that for all its reputation and particular attributes Hell is no more than a place in Shadow and not a realm of its own?"

She felt stupid only just to have realized this—it was clear to her now that it was something so obvious that the only reason no one had ever told her was that they assumed she knew.

He smiled and nodded. "Not a point that either I or subsequent managements ever stressed—we wished to discourage both escapees and tourists."

Emma explained about the dust of confusion. "We need to establish communication with the rest of Shadow, and with the Mundane world, and this will take time, ingenuity and sweat. Leave Minos here in charge in this place—I know his reputation as a man of trust. Load up dray wagons with the salve and with barrels of hell-flesh. I have a set of problems to deal with, of which I will tell you, but also a plan."

Wounded

Shadow and Valhalla, 2004

I could not go further up; the dust-infused ice impeded me.

Nothing can harm me. Nothing can poison me. Yet the dust in my lungs felt like lead weighing me down. Worse, I was not used to anything standing in the way of my will. Anger at this is a fault, I admit.

Perhaps I could go down—the mountains of Hell and Shadow should be as passable for me as the mountain I had slept under in the Mundane world those few years before.

I took a step into the rock and at once found myself confused and lost as if the rock had become fog, thick choking fog like that of great cities in which you cannot see your hand before your face and every raised paving stone, every loose cobble, every deep puddle becomes your foe.

I cannot turn my ankle or graze my knee, but I have, on occasion, known what it is to trip, if not in the end to fall.

Arrogant, I persisted, and suddenly I had no footing nor any sense of where light and breeze could be found—I was trapped in my own confusion and vertigo as if the rock through which I moved were spinning round me, up and down and around.

I have no need of air but I am nonetheless accustomed to breathing and it was a discomfort to me because I am not a goddess and I do all things that pertain to humans and there was a dryness in my throat and a pressure in my chest and, choking, I coughed and felt again on my tongue the red dust that I had breathed in all unknowing.

I was not used to the possibility that anything I consumed might confound me.

This was the thing about which Emma had speculated, for which we had come to shadow to search, a sort of dark alchemy, a magic or a technology that worked by different rules to those we knew.

We had suspected that Odin might be trafficking in such stuff, and our suspicion was right, for he had done more than traffic—he had tried to use it and it had undone and used him, had refined him into another form of itself.

The dust that confounded us had once been the Aesir, who turned to dust, which Odin consumed so that it would transform him, but not, it proved, as he had wished. And when the woman Mary Ann had finally slain him, he became yet more dust, another stage in this new darker form of the Work.

Yet again we had need of my sister Sof but she was gone from us into the Mundane we could no longer reach—Polly had to be saved, and yet with Sof on that mission of mercy...

Once, when I was a mere girl in a waystation in the hills, before power came to me, my sisters and I had tried the sour milk mash that we served to travellers. Sof disliked the taste and spat it on the ground and Lillit took two mouthfuls and then simply sat on the ground, her knees under her chin, rocking gently from side to side until she sprawled on the ground and giggled. I though took a third and found the ground shifting under my feet and the air harsh in my lungs and my stomach churning from the mash and the giddiness until I struggled to stand and fell on the hard ground.

It was like that now, except that I was in darkness and I tried to pull power into myself and it came only as a trickle that should have been a flood, and I flailed my arms and my legs for what seemed an hour with no sense of how I could find myself again.

I was trapped, both in the rock and in a moment of dread and despair such as I had not known in centuries, not since the Witch of the Wood cursed me with panic.

At every turn we were outwitted and outplayed, and I feared we were already caught in the Enemy's endgame.

Then my left hand found its way into vacancy and I felt the warm breeze of shadow on it and I thrust the rest of me in that direction and first my right knee and then the rest of me emerged back into the light.

One of you cawed gently at me. "We would not have done that, Huntress. We are glad that you were only gone a minute because we would not have known how to retrieve you, had you not retrieved yourself..."

I ran down the slope finding footings as I ran and glorying in my speed and balance as one does when one has had a moment of helplessness.

I ran back towards Valhalla; the dust did not, at least, impede or slow me on the ground. You matched my pace, which surprised me a little. I noticed almost casually that you stayed a mere ten feet or so above my head. Running was at least an exhilaration into which I could place myself and not need to think for a few minutes, a few score feet-thumping hard-breathing miles.

You fluttered down and settled on my shoulders. I looked into one pair of beady eyes and then turned my head slightly and looked into the other.

"You have something to say?" I asked.

"The dust is everywhere," one of you cawed. I did not know whether it was Thought or Memory; one day I might learn to tell you apart but it did not seem necessary at this point.

"More than a few feet up," the other went on, "it becomes so thick that it will choke anyone who rises into it, as well as leave them hopelessly confused and distracted."

I found myself thinking of all the birds of prey, all the skylarks, all the ocean crossers who would perish if they could not rise on the air and plunge down.

Either I spoke or you could see my thoughts. "It is right that you think of such things," you said in unison, "for the Queen of Shadow must take care of all her creatures."

"I am not the Queen of anything. I am the Huntress."

But even as I spoke, I remembered Cernunnos and how he had talked to me of the responsibility of all who hunt to the creatures that might be my prey or might join me in the hunt.

I realized that, perhaps, that the Huntress was no longer who I was, for I no longer hunted alone.

"Shadow needs a ruler now," one of you cawed.

"It needs a goddess—but we are your loyal servants who defer to your feelings and say Queen."

"Queen," the other echoed.

I paused in my running to think about what you said, and that pause saved me, though not from pain.

We were on the plain across which the river that bounded Valhalla took a meandering course, but there were rocks and scrub and hiding places enough. I confess that the millennia had made me arrogant in my sense of safety—nothing could harm me and so I took little in the way of precautions.

And you were, perhaps, not paying attention, because even Thought and Memory can be distracted. I say, perhaps, because I did not wholly trust you. I lived in a new world now, where this was folly.

In that moment of all our inattention, a crooked beam of darkness jagged out from behind an ordinary looking clump of Shadow's large and heavily flowering variant of heather.

Mostly it missed me, but if I had not broken my stride, it would have cut me in half and I would not have survived. As it was, it removed the skin, and some of the flesh, from the lower calf of my left leg and I screamed. I had never known such pain, either at the start of it, nor as it continued.

I have talked of the fire that went into my making—I lied to Crowley, though not completely—and that was a pain that braced and awoke. But this was a pain that left the taste of vomit in my throat and it continued, slow and sure as a glacier, but not clean like ice or stone or flood. It was a pain of unmaking and undoing.

Nonetheless, I did not fall because not being used to pain did not mean that I gave in to it or broke my stride. I reached and pulled a knife from my hair, a small steel blade whose weighted and balanced hilt meant that it flew true.

I still could not see my assassin—perhaps they were invisible— but I do have some skill. Even in my pain, the choked off scream from behind that small bush gave me grim satisfaction. I do not like to kill, but at such a moment, not even Josette when she was younger and less hardened could have begrudged me that tiny modicum of spite.

I found myself almost afraid, almost shamed, to look at the wound. It was so small to cause so much agony. Yet, as I stared at it, I could see it growing, as slow and inexorable as lichen on rock, and knew that it was my death. Which I would face as I had faced the freeing of Sof from her agony by using That Which Devours—at worst facing this dissolution as bravely as she had hers would be my payment to fate.

Nonetheless, I had responsibilities and there was one near at hand who might heal me.

I turned to the one of you who fluttered nearest at hand. "Bring Josette," I said. "I fear that there is little she can do, but I am Huntress not Healer."

I lay still and looked at the red-tinged sky of Shadow and then at the purple and mauve grasses among which I lay. Presently the small hungry blue mice of the plain crept out and sat on their tails watching the slow decay of my flesh and pondering whether there was anything there that they could eat.

I let them be, because they do a service to the cleaning of the world and there is a sense in which every one of us is carrion on parole.

The one of you that was with me, though, fluttered down and took three of them at a gulp—the others were gone back into the grass in a second.

There was nothing more I could do until Josette arrived and the pain was more than I chose to bear. I could not sleep but I cast myself into memories of other times, early ones, when I was content because I did not know the world of time and chance.

I am devoted to the protection of the weak against the strong, but there have been moments of pleasure along the way. The heady scent of lavender; a song I once heard in Carcassonne and another in Merv that was almost its twin; the taste of honey cakes and of flat bread fresh from the hot stone.

Such things could distract me, but only for a while. I came back to myself and the pain when I felt a soothing gloved hand on my shoulder. "We should talk." Her voice was mellow as cleansing herbs.

I opened my eyes and almost at once looked down—the dissolution had spread and deepened. There was bone visible in the lesion, bone that was blackening and dissolving as I watched. My courage does not fail, and I do endure all, but nonetheless I looked away.

Josette shook her head. "Lillit, or what she has become, healed Aserath when she had such a wound, but that was a matter of Lillit—as I understand it—being the Quintessence that the Work seeks and the three of you achieved between you. And she is not here, and is even more certainly not now. Without her, I am not sure what I can do—most wounds I can take into myself and cure. This—"

I seized her wrist. "I have seen what the healing of ordinary injuries does to you, and how close mortal hurt comes to killing you."

She smiled. "You have not seen me heal anyone for two thousand years, Huntress. I am better at it now than I was then… Nonetheless."

"This is a wound of unmaking rather than of death alone."

"I have faced the darkness once, and you brought me back. I will try if you wish it, but--"

I shook my head. "I am done, I think. No point in dragging you into death with me."

She looked a little relieved and then smiled sardonically. "There would be," she went on, "obvious measures were you not so wrapped around with invulnerability. Normally, I would sever the wounded part of your leg—above the knee to be completely safe, but if we could cut soon, that should not be essential—but there is no blade I know that could cut you, unless…"

She reached up and took the sword from her back. I looked at her and smiled because I thought I could follow her thinking.

"My sword, as I think I have told you in passing, is called Nails and Coins, because when the blade was forged, I had the iron nails of my crucifixion beaten into the steel of the blade and the coins paid to my brother for my betrayal hammered into the hilt. You were there at that death and you brought me back from it. My sword is connected to that death, intimately. As are you. Perhaps…"

She took the sword in both her gloved hands and raised it high above her head for a swift stroke.

"Be clear," she said, "even if this works, I do not know for certain that I can stop the bleeding, or make the flesh of what is left heal properly. We do not know about these wounds of unmaking and how they affect such processes—I do not know the nature of your immortality. And you will be maimed."

24

You both flew up from my shoulders, but your beady eyes were fixed on what was to happen. After all, the death or maiming of the Huntress was a sight that you would wish to fix in your minds forever.

She was not soothing me, but she did distract me for a second so that when she brought the blade down in a fierce sweep, I did not flinch.

And her sword remained in the air, a hairsbreadth from my leg, and could not get further purchase. She winced from the shock.

"Well, that didn't work." My voice was lighter than my heavy heart.

"It was unlikely," she agreed. "But worth trying."

We were both silent for a moment, as were you, where you hovered a few feet above us. I think we would in any case have heard the cough from behind my left shoulder.

It was my sword, the Japanese blade I had named Needful, back in that blood-soaked Paris summer. Its tone was gentle, firm and polite.

"Needful you called me, saying that it was the name of all swords given in a moment of need. I have served you since, loyally, because you were my mistress, but also because you trusted me in spite of your histories with blades such as I. Trust me now, because I am your sword Needful and there is a truth in names and you have never needed me more than at this moment. Take me in your hand and trust me."

I reached up and took the sword Needful in my right hand, and made to pass it to Josette, my surgeon and saviour.

"I am your sword," Needful said reproachfully, "and I answer to your hand and your need and not to another's."

It was fitting, I supposed, that I maim myself for I had been wounded, yes, by the malice of the Enemy but also by a moment's inattention. A weaker person might have forgiven themselves for a moment in so many years, but fate had not been so kind and nor would I be.

I crooked my arm slightly. It would be a difficult swing, but I had strength and to spare.

Needful twisted slightly in my grip. "You have kept me sharp for so many years, even in decades where you had no need of me. Press me gently to your leg and I will carve as softly as I can. It is not your strength we need, but mine."

Josette took a leather strap from the small satchel at her belt and cinched it loosely around my leg, just above the knee.

"I shall try to staunch the flow of blood as quickly as I can, but it is best to have a tourniquet to hand if your body does not listen to my entreaties and start to heal itself."

Then she took a second strap, and offered it to me. I shook my head. I was bearing the agony of dissolution in silence; I could bear more.

"Take it between your teeth, Mara, and bite down hard," she said impatiently; "it will distract you by giving you something to concentrate on." When I still showed reluctance, she went on, "While I am sure you will manage not to scream, because you are just that pig-headed, both I and your sword need to know for certain that you will not, because we have work to do that needs concentration."

Then she took a firm grasp of my left foot. "I shall have to pull it clear once it is off," she explained. "And keep the corroding part well away from you, even before I try to staunch the flow of blood."

I had seen her heal before but not, as she had pointed out, for a long time. She had learned to explain what she was doing, to make her patient a party to her cure. It was disconcerting to see an old friend—an old pupil if you will, though she was Sof's far more than she was mine—in her mastery. It made me realize, far more than before, how much I had missed her for two thousand years.

I had seen her fight and noticed the ease and grace she had now, her confidence in her womanhood—but fighting was not what she was most interested in. I had seen her persuade and command and—which is as great a skill—assist; I had met Emma and Caroline, who had been her servants and pupils. But healer was who she was, far more than fighter or ruler or teacher.

I watched the eloquence of her hands and was soothed, and, soothed, I pressed the blade to my leg and let Needful do its work.

I felt the slow slicing through skin and flesh and sinew; I felt the slight resistance of bone and the delicate severing of nerves and arteries and veins; and it was agony, I do not deny it, but it was also the cessation of that greater agony of dissolution and corruption. But, yes, it is no light thing to lose a part of oneself and all that wisdom in the dance of combat that was spilling on the ground with the gushing of my blood.

I felt Josette pull the severed part of my leg aside and heard the thud as she threw it some yards away. And I knew that a part of me was gone forever.

It lay there some feet away and I fixed my gaze on it as Josette worked—once it was off, it was as if I had been keeping it from dissolution because the black blank emptiness devoured it in mere minutes, and the sandal on the foot too.

There were things I had done daily for thousands of years that I would never ever be able to do again; there were, out there in the world and Shadow, people who would die in a greater agony than mine because I would not be able—maimed—to save them. And as the sword cut and as Josette worked on me with those practiced fingers, and knowing that she would save my life if she could, and that I would have to live in the world and find new ways of service, I turned my face aside, and bit down harder and harder on the leather, because my silence was a boon to me for that there were so many things for which I would have to find words, but need not now.

Josette had tightened the tourniquet for a while and now she relaxed it. "The blood vessels are sealing themselves off," I heard her say. "We're not out of the woods yet, but at least you won't bleed to death."

And I wept, for myself and for others, and for my friends Josette and Needful, who were doing what they must to save me, but knew also what they were taking from me in that act. And I wept too for you, birds whom I had accepted but did not yet trust, who had been betrayed by their master and had had to watch him corrupted and changed and sublimated into dust.

I had not thought of your feelings before—my dislike of your parent was still that strong—and now thinking of what your grief must be was a relief from my own desolation.

Nonetheless, there were things to take care of.

"Birds." I spoke gently to you—I had perhaps been harsher earlier, and resolved to watch my tone in future. "At some point I will need to be back in Valhalla and for the moment, at least, I had best be carried there. Ask someone to organize a litter."

"That would be for the best," Josette added. "While the extent to which the wound is healing now it is free of the corrupted part of your leg is remarkable, you will need to rest, and I would not want you to think you can adjust to a crutch quickly. Not even you, Mara."

She patted me very softly on the upper part of my leg and I realized that I was hardly in pain any more, just a slow steady ache deep in the bone. I have heard that for many people there is a constant pain in these circumstances, that the absence of part of a limb does not stop one feeling pain or an unscratchable itch from the missing part. Whether because of the virtues of my supernaturally enhanced condition, or because, where it lay, the severed part of the limb was slowly consumed into nothingness, I have not had this experience.

All that I can report is, that once I had gone through the process of being cut, the agony I had been experienced faded away, and was not replaced. I appreciate my good fortune in this and know that it is not typical.

I looked down at the stump—as she had promised, I had kept a part of my lower leg, a couple of inches below the knee. "My thanks to you, my friend—and to you too, Needful, my sword and companion."

Josette smiled. "It's what I do; it is a part of who I am."

Needful sounded almost embarrassed. "You named me—and by naming, saved yourself. I am the weapon of your hands, as are so many. You wield us in justice and love, and we serve."

And I was content to take the service of my weapons, because I too serve and have served. Whether, maimed, I would ever be able to use them as well again—well, that was an open question. I had seen men fight bravely with worse wounds—of course I had—but…

These were selfish thoughts, though, I realized. I looked, really looked, at Josette in sudden concern. She looked fine—not drained or pale at all; I could not be certain though—she was after all capable of putting a good face on things.

She caught my glance and guessed the reason for it. "No, Mara—I hardly had to exert myself at all—an ordinary healer would have done as much. Once we had removed the infection, your body healed itself, as much as it can. I don't think it will ever go so far as growing you another leg, of course—too much to hope for. A smaller injury perhaps—I have never understood why Morgan has done nothing about her lost eye."

"I think, perhaps," and suddenly I realized that I should have spoken to her long ago about this, "I think it is her penance for the death of a man we knew. She was engaged in one of her complex intrigues and he died -" I turned to you "- struck down by your sibling which also took her eye. I spoke harshly to her about his death—she may have thought…"

I fell silent for a while, considering the possibility that I had been unjust and unfeeling—there has to be a term to my anger with someone who has truly repented of past crimes and errors, who has worked—most of the time—for good without any probability of a reward for her labours.

But I did not have a chance to pursue this thought for very long because suddenly you returned, rather earlier than I had expected, with a number of Alexander's troops—a scouting party, it turned out—and the man John Knox.

He looked down at my leg with a sharp intake of breath. "That's a pretty piece of field surgery, whoever did it. Where has the surgeon gone? I would congratulate him."

Josette looked at him pityingly. "There was no surgeon but myself, who am not surgeon merely, but one who heals, body and soul and world."

"That's a wondrous set of claims from a mere girl." His voice was harsh. "There was a time when such boasts would be dealt with, with bridle and tongue bore."

And she still did not lose her temper, though I came close, sick as I was. "John Knox," she used what I thought of as her most commanding voice—little did I know—"my old friend Alexander sees something in you in spite of your obstinate obtuseness. You have ideas about the proper stations of men and women and others—discard them or you will find your time in this realm of Shadow as unpleasant as your late sojourn in the Hell of Lucifer. For the moment, carry the Huntress back to Valhalla—she has narrowly escaped death and needs to rest."

He drew himself up to his considerable height. "You cannae talk to me like that, Missie… It is not the place of any woman to--"

And suddenly she blazed in glory and spoke in thunder—truly she was her father's daughter.

"John, do not try my patience. Know that your Redeemer lives, and I am She."

"Blasph–" and the word choked in his mouth, for of a sudden he knew that she spoke true. She took the glove from her right hand and pressed the bloody hole in her wrist to his forehead, where it left a mark. A mark which I suspected time would not remove.

"Know, John, once and for all, that much of what you have believed to be true—and believed in what was once my name—is utterly false and wrong. But I forgive you, as I hope you will forgive me for forcing truth upon you like this."

He knelt in worship. It was really quite embarrassing. She raised him up with a reach of a hand that was suddenly wearing a glove again. "Now,"—her voice was gentler again—"I hope we won't have to mention this little chat again. Not everyone listens—I will not tell tales out of school but Tomas de Torquemada made another and a regrettable choice."

He looked at her, his face full of wonder and a certain amount of lubricity.

"You tell me -" he faltered "- that so many things I thought unlawful are allowed…I thought them temptations that came to me as a test…"

"Yes," she smiled. "If you want to let Alexander fuck you, you have my blessing. If he wants you, of course, which I rather think he does."

I interrupted. All this was fascinating enough but there were urgent matters to attend to. "There are things you need to know—I will announce them when we get back, but you may as well know now. The red dust has done something to the ice in the high passes between Shadow and Hell. It has thickened and become impassable—worse, those of us who have breathed it in, which by now is probably most beings in Shadow, can no longer travel through the air or into the living rock, nor, as Loki showed us, travel to other realms. Our adversary has used dark alchemy to outwit and maroon us."

While we had been speaking, two soldiers had slung a network of ropes between two poles and then placed a blanket over it to create a litter. They and two more of their comrades took this by the ends of the poles and Josette and Knox helped me rise and then climb into it. "Before we return to Valhalla," I added, "I should like to see the face of my failed assassin."

You fluttered over to the bush and the litter bearers followed your lead. The corpse lay where it had fallen. It stank slightly—he had died instantly yet soiled himself in dying.

I sat up on the blanket—I had hardly needed to see his face for he was yet another copy of the man who had killed Sharpe, as I had come to suspect. Still, the knife stuck inches deep through his skull and into his brain was one I should be loath to lose, so I reached down and retrieved it. Annoyingly, I could not wipe it on his over-styled black uniform so I contented myself with cleaning it on the piece of the blanket which hung over the poles.

I looked around in case his spirit had lingered, but there was no sign of him.

These black-garbed thugs believed themselves to be doing Nameless' work, so presumably when they died, they hastened to Heaven to get their reward. I needed to speak harshly to him about that.

"How came this man here?" I asked Josette. "I can believe that his catching sight of me and shooting at a venture was mere misfortune, but…"

She examined the pack he had with him. "Binoculars, good ones. He was keeping a watch on Valhalla, would be my guess." Then she picked up a rectangle of plastic. "And what's this?"

We all stared at it and passed it one to another.

In an earlier age we would have thought it a magic mirror—it was glossy enough that we could see our faces in it, darkly. John tidied his beard a little and tried momentarily to remove the mark that Josette had left on his forehead.

I realized that it reminded me a little of the screen of Emma's computer—she had mentioned that there were portable ones. And the small phones people carried around—it was a little like the tiny screen into which people typed numbers. I had seen them do it and thought them deranged for a little as they talked by themselves in the street, until Emma and Caroline had explained it to me.

"Mercenaries get the newest and best of everything," I suggested.

Several of John's companions muttered that this was not the case in their experience. I stared them to silence. "I should say," I added, "expensive elite mercenaries, which is what the men of Burnedover are by all accounts."

I held the small piece of black plastic up. "This tablet -" I thought that would be a good name for it, "is probably like a very small computer. Or perhaps a phone. Or perhaps both."

Most of the soldiers looked blank, but Josette knew what I was talking about because she was living like me, in the twenty first century.

She explained, "It's a device for talking to people at a distance, writing down your thoughts, checking into a far-off library. Reckoning your accounts."

John narrowed his eyes. "Useful, but unholy."

Which was as it may be, but I explained, "No more magic than an abacus or a mill-wheel."

He did not look convinced until Josette took it from me and ran her finger along its side. She found a small button and pressed it— the tablet made a small whining noise and lit up, with a blank space at its centre and a picture of a keyboard. "Someone might be able to guess its password," she said, "but that would be someone cleverer than me, like Emma."

I thought a second—after all, Emma might be very clever, but neither I nor Josette were exactly stupid. "Try 'God Wills It'," I suggested. "All these Burnedover people seem to say it a lot and I don't think they have much in the way of imagination or independent thought."

"Might as well try that," she nodded. "Sounds plausible."

She tried it. Nothing happened.

"Latin?" I suggested.

She typed again and the tablet gave a welcoming beep, followed by a despairing whine.

A small picture of a thing with wings flickered in the corner of the screen.

"Oh look," Josette smirked, as she ran her eyes down the icons. "He was controlling a drone as well, but it seems to have crashed."

"A drone?" John looked confused—I was too but chose not to show it.

"Small flying machine—you use them to watch people, or kill them. I don't imagine that the red dust does their little jets or propellors or whatever much good." Josette thought for a second more. "So there is less of an overall plan to all this than we might think," she concluded, "because they wouldn't all be here with no way to get back and no way to watch us with their little flying toys and no connection to whatever satellite someone has set to watch Shadow. Polly probably…"

"All?" I butted in.

She pressed another icon which had the numeral 9 overlaid on it. It showed a map with eight little soldier icons scattered on it. All centred on Valhalla except for Number Two.

Josette sniffed, "Clearly they don't think my Just City all that worth watching." She turned to Knox and showed him the map. "Not necessarily their current positions, but he had not moved and so quite probably they have not. Can your men be stealthy? These are armed with those filthy weapons, so taking prisoners is not as much of a priority as preventing a small well-armed hostile force from regrouping in our territory. A prisoner or two would be handy of course."

He walked over to where his men were waiting and tapped seven of them on the shoulders. I was impressed and saddened that Josette, who had died so that she might not apply the lessons she had learned from Alexander, had nonetheless acquired an easy confidence in condemning people to death when needful.

She caught my gaze. "What cannot be helped, cannot be helped. And I cannot save them all. It was you taught me that, Huntress."

"I remember."

"That boy died on the cross, Huntress. That boy was always a lie. You taught me what women do."

"And what is that?"

"What is necessary." She pointed to my stump. "What is needful." She pointed to my sword.

She nodded to John's chosen men and they crouched into the grasses and were gone. Then she picked up the gun that had fallen from the dead man's hand and passed it to me.

"One of us needs to have possession of this," she explained, "and it had better be you since you are less able to fight than you have been."

I looked at its side—there was a handy slide with SAFETY embossed into it in Chinese, Arabic and English, and I checked that it was engaged—and then stuck it into my belt.

She looked at me with concern. "Relax, now. You need to rest because it will make it easier for these good men to carry you. John and I will make sure you travel safely."

And I let myself sleep for the time it took for us to return to Valhalla.

Trusting and tired, I let myself sleep long beyond that, and so soundly that, when I awoke, to the touch of Josette's finger on my elbow, it was to discover that I had been placed on a raised day bed , or reclined chair, with support for my stump and the weapons from my back and belt and hair neatly placed in my easy reach in a sort of rack that formed one of the sides of what, since it sat on the high dais of the throne room of Valhalla, one might almost call my throne.

Whether I had chosen to rule or not.

Leaning against the rack was a carved and gilt staff which might be a sceptre but which I chose to think of as my crutch, until some better could be procured.

I looked about me. Alexander stood ready at my right hand, Josette at my left, and Mary Ann sat at Josette's feet, her petticoats around her and naked ankles dangling off the dais as if she were mudlarking in Shadwell. Loki and his more human-looking children sat at my feet, as did the terrier and the wolf, while the horse and her child flanked the dais on either side. They did not kneel to me for I could not have borne that, but they stilled their conversations and inclined their heads when they saw I had awoken.

You cawed, the pair of you, "All hail to Mara, Queen of Valhalla and High Queen of Shadow." And every person, god and beast in the room echoed your call.

"One might almost say Conqueror of Shadow," Alexander noted, "but that would be a promise yet to keep, and as things are, you will have to let us conquer it for you."

"Why conquer?" My voice was mild because the alternative would have been to lose my temper and who knows what would have happened then. "I thought that we would send emissaries out and ask."

"Politely,"—Josette was mocking me a little—"what the various peoples and principalities of Shadow know or might know of the late Odin's alliances, and the source of his armaments and drugs of power, and where the workshops of dark alchemy are."

"To ask such things of the proud—and most of Shadow is ruled by proud beings—is to tell them that you are entitled to ask," Alexander continued. "It is to say that you are set in authority over them, which you are, or will be."

"But why me?"

"Because who else?" said Josette.

I looked round at the friends who had set me above them and felt at once flattered and betrayed. "I am a reformed character, in many respects," Alexander shrugged, "but my reputation is such that I had better be your subordinate, than all the rest of you be mine. As your lieutenant, I add to the lustre of your rule—no one would believe that you served me."

"But surely you--" I turned to Josette. I caught the note of pleading in my voice.

"I choose not to reveal myself yet, because I am not ready even now to have that conversation with my father." Josette's expression was as inscrutable as her words. "All most of Shadow knows is that I helped create the Just City and give counsel there—I do not rule it and its peoples rule themselves and seek no dominion over others. You are our best ruler because you have no wish—any more than I— to be one."

"Which is all very fucking well in ordinary circumstances," Mary Ann cut in, "but this is a by your leave fucking emergency. Yank soldiers wandering around shooting people's fucking legs off as if they owned the place; dust in the sky and in our lungs; plots and plans and all sorts of fucking connivances. We needs a queen, and who better? I speak as ambassador of the Just City and we will have no other queen than you. At least for the moment."

Josette smiled down at her as a teacher whose pupil might one day excel her, then turned back to me, serious again. "It is time, Mara, past

36

time. If Emma can take on responsibility, as she has, what of you who are older if not wiser? If we are to fight both the old enemy and these new soldiers who may or may not answer to him, we need someone to take charge. And you, my dear, are for the moment incapable of hunting or fighting. It is time you gave ruling a go."

I turned to Loki and his children. "Valhalla is yours. Are you content that I rule here?"

"We are the last of the Aesir." Loki's fluid gesture included Brünnhilde and Heimdall as well as his children. "Doubtless if we chose we could breed more, but I doubt that time would be on our side, or that of any children we might have. My brother's actions have dishonoured us; none of us choose to inherit his legacy. But we wish revenge on the one who corrupted him and made him kinslayer—and who better to lead us to that revenge than the one who has pursued the corrupter for seven thousand years?"

Josette placed her hand on my shoulder. She smiled a crooked little smile. "I would not ask this of you, old friend refound, but you taught me what was necessary and what was needful. Who can be trusted with power but one who does not want it? Who can draw the peoples of Shadow together but one known to all and trusted by almost all? You will rule and you will do what is needed and your dearest wish at every moment will be to cast that rule aside, to cease to be needed."

I have been cursed by many in my time, and few of those curses have stuck. Here and now I felt myself cursed by many of my dearest friends and the worst of the curse was—I knew that one day I would be free of it, the harder I worked at the burden that had been placed on me.

Wearily, I nodded my head. I wore and would wear no crown and yet I felt the weight of one upon me. I must start to do one of the things I hate most in the world, which is give orders rather than do things myself.

I turned to the first of them. "Alexander, in a while some of your men will return with captives or corpses; others will not and by their number you will know how many soldiers of the army of mercenaries called Burnedover we have at large armed with weapons like the one which took my leg. Until all those mercenaries are accounted for, treat Valhalla as under siege; bring their weapons to me and I will place them beyond reach."

The Macedonian looked a little disappointed. I waved down any protest he might have been inclined to make.

"We cannot use what we cannot understand," I explained, "And further, it is possible that such things have a contact with the enemy who ordered them devised. Emma has no such concerns, it is true, but she is young and trusting."

I perhaps was doing her an injustice—I failed to see how the Enemy could communicate with what she seemed to have placed out of space and time, and how did she do that?—but we could not assume anything.

"Meanwhile," I continued, "take counsel with my bird Memory here—once you march out of this place to scout for our main enemy's workshops you will need the best maps we can make. Memory, you and Thought have overflown much of this land; tell him everything he needs to know—which is everything because he is a general, and you are not, so do not assume you know what he needs. And when Knox returns with prisoners or the dead, bring him and them to me—I would have words with any of them that survive."

He saluted me and turned to leave—with too little in the way of comment, I thought, and so I called him back.

"It is not just for what they can tell us of what they are doing in this world, you understand. One day we will find a way of communicating with Polly Wilde, or she with us, and these men may have things to tell us about their organization in the Mundane world. Remember, because I know you of old, that I do not look kindly on torture. Ask them questions until they are deathly tired—and then let them sleep—and then ask them questions."

Alexander nodded. "I have learned patience since you knew me. First in the lands of Spice, then trapped in Josette's mind and then in the mountains of Hell. You are right to question my methods, though, because you knew me when I was young and rash and drank too much."

Alexander saluted me again and this time I let him leave without reproof.

I turned next to the fire god and his children. "We need force here, but we also need guile and someone who knows how the once golden hall of Valhalla used to work in earlier days. I need—what, a chancellor, a master of coin?—and I can think of none better. I know and trust several of your children and so I must, I suppose, trust you, for good children usually come from good parents, in spite of appearances."

Loki looked at me suspiciously. He was one who could deceive with a straight face and I doubted that he had any tells at all. I noticed, though, that his son, the serpent, flickered his inner eyelids a second, confirming what I had already guessed. "Well, we have no treasury. Odin's gold is gone, transformed with him into the dust that is so many of our problems. I know not how we can make any of this realm a going concern."

"All of his gold?" I asked, because I wished to be sure.

"Every coin, and every ingot, that he possessed." He looked solemn.

"That he possessed?" I smiled.

Loki's face did not move, and my smile grew broader.

"But not of course the gold that Odin had mislaid, because possession, as thieves so often say, is the real law. I had wondered for what crime Odin had you shackled at his feet, or of what crime he suspected his brother, Loki Lightfingers, Loki Mantlewearer, Loki Deceiver."

He shrugged and smiled. His smile was broad, but not as broad as mine. "I admit nothing, but if gold I had, my younger brother's portion you might call it, if such gold there were, where?"

I am a straightforward and direct person who does not practice deceit, but what I am not, is stupid. The thing about trickster gods is that you need not know their tells to guess what their move has been—it is always something so clever as to be transparent.

"Your son, the Serpent, is here in his manshape, as earlier he was your snake-shackle, but he is, is he not?, in his other aspect the earthwyrm, who girdles the world and drinks the ocean."

The Serpent shrugged. "She knows," he hissed.

"There are empty cellars beneath us," I pointed to the stair. "I am sure none of us want to see precisely how you will disgorge—but I would like to see those cellars filled. At your convenience. As my friend Vespasian once remarked, it does not smell."

The former goddess of Death looked at her brother disappointedly, as did the Dog and the two Horses. The Wolf shrugged his heavy shoulders and started to clean between the claws of his right front paw with his massive lolling tongue.

Hel tutted at the Snake, "With father, it's just a compulsion, but you shouldn't let him drag you into things." Then, to me, "What must you think of me? Of us all?"

I shrugged. "What I always thought. I trust the trustworthy; the faithless I use if they come to my hand." I turned to her father. "I had hoped you as trustworthy as most of your children. I can't say I am disappointed because hope is so often a liar. But I have my answer."

"To what question?" said the fire god.

"The one I asked myself. Whether I should expect you to act according to your nature, or transcend it. I still have work for you, because you know these lands better than any—but I shall set your daughters and your sons to watch you and supervise you. Now to the cellar with you and you too Snake, and do not return until every scrap of what you took from Odin has been put back where it belongs."

I clapped my hands in dismissal and they left, the Snake with a languorous sullenness that was almost bad grace, his father almost jauntily.

I was not sure which of us had passed, which one had failed, a test.

I had told his daughters to supervise him; Hel continued to stand stiff and silent where she was—Sleipnir winked at me and followed her brother and parent down the ramp into the cellarage.

Lastly, I turned to Josette. "I would have you at my side—I trust you more than any here, even the Horse and the Dog, but I appreciate you have other responsibilities. Go to your Just City and do what you need to do there, but I would welcome it if you could return as soon as possible. And bear them my greetings—if I am to rule Shadow, they must come to an accommodation with me."

She smiled. "I am sure, Mara, that your yoke will be light, but I have to ask them to accept it and advise them that it is for the best."

"And I'll tell them it's a fucking emergency," added Mary Ann. "And that all that was done to us by the late fucker Odin—what I saw to—was done by the orders of some Supreme Fucker that you will bring down in his fucking turn. They'll listen to the pair of us— the folk of the Just City are stubborn and independent, but they are not fucking stupid."

Josette smiled down at her ambassador. "I have healing to bring there, not just of the body but of the mind." Her smile faded. "And I need to make my amends to people. I had told them they would be safe after lives when they were not, and when they lived in dread of what came next. What Odin did to some of them, over and over, was what they had expected in the Hell I kept them from. I was not there to save them from him—I was busy with other business as I always must be, but that is a fact, not an excuse."

She wept, angry tears that Brünnhilde reached over to wipe from her, and the cloth came away bloody.

"Don't you go fucking meddling with my fucking Lady." Mary Ann walked over and struck at the Valkyrie's hand with her own bony one. "So, perhaps you didn't fucking know what your bastard father was fucking doing, and perhaps you did fucking know. But I don't trust you, for all that you seem to be my Lady's frig tart."

Brünnhilde towered over her and glared like the fire in which she was once believed burned. "You are my love's emissary." Her voice was sharp as fiery death. "I respect you for that, and for that you slew the thing my father had become, which was a mighty deed and not unworthy. But do not touch me twice."

Mary Ann bristled—for a moment I could believe that, if it came to it, she had some gutter trick that would take down the Valkyrie if it came to more than harsh words.

"Your fucking bastard evil father? Yes, and you say you knew little of what he was doing to me and mine. Well, that's fucking convenient, ain't it? And you know nothing about them files the Huntress is looking for. Neither you nor the fucking doorman. Only two left of the fucking Aesir, apart from him over there, and he can't be trusted but at least he doesn't pretend otherwise."

Brünnhilde glowered but made no move. The horse Gram trotted over and stood at her mistress's shoulder. "You should trust her because I say she should be trusted. I am her horse and twice went through fire for her."

Mary Ann looked sceptical, but she reached into a pocket of her smart jacket and produced a sugar cube, which she offered to the horse. Gram reached out her tongue and took the sugar from her.

They stood there, the Valkyrie and the smaller wiry woman over whom she towered, and Josette reached out and took each of them by the hand and smiled and it was like the sun driving away mist because the three of them laughed and walked away together, Gram trotting beside them, and I suspected that Mary Ann would not go to an empty bed that night.

I had been awake but a few minutes—half an hour or so at the most—but I was already yawning. Hel snapped her fingers and a full glass of water appeared at my side.

I looked at her and she smiled. "I am a goddess of death—it is the task laid upon me rather than who I am." Her voice was husky with amusement. "If I wanted to kill, I would have no need for poison but, as it happens, I have no power over you. I think, Huntress and Queen, you underestimate just how much power you have accumulated and hoarded down the years. I have a sense of these things and I cannot reckon it."

She shook her head.

"I never glimpsed the adversary—if he visited Odin rather than merely whispered in his ear from afar, none of us saw him. The only person who has is, I hear, your friend the young judge of Hell. If there is a being more powerful than you, it would probably be him—but even he, if grievously wounded, would need to rest, as do you. Sleep, and I and my brothers the dogs will guard you. Because it is not fitting that the Queen of Shadow sleep unattended. And we are the children of fire; we are death and the wolf of the ending and the loyal dog our brother who chose to serve you."

I yawned again, but not at her words, and I leaned back into the padding of my chair. When I started awake, Hel's hand on my wrist and the wind of her breath in my ear, the hall was lit by torchlight.

"Alexander's scouts have returned," she said. "Just now, Heimdall sounded a blast on his horn and they will be with us shortly. With their prisoners."

She snapped her fingers again, only this time what appeared at my side was a cup of strong coffee, which I sipped. I had not hoped to find a brew this strong in my new realm.

Hel caught my sigh of gratitude. "Not all the wealth of Valhalla was in specie. We took a tax on all the trade of this part of Shadow, or to put it another way, my uncle extorted ransom from all traders; you may not know this, but the boundaries of Shadow and the Mundane were thin hereabouts, which placed us athwart routes. How we shall do now those ways seem closed is to be guessed at, but for the moment we have luxuries enough. And my father has a particular taste for good coffee even if he does not need it to sharpen a wit that was oversharp already."

"And where is the Trickster?" I asked her.

"Still in the cellar with my brother, who is still vomiting up their stolen gold. I looked in on them some little time ago, and the cellar is almost full again. It is as if the gulf of his stomach has fathered more gold than they stole."

Her laugh was kin to the sardonic barking of her brother, the neighing of her half sister. I had come to know both sounds well, and now they made more sense as the shared amusement of members of a family. An amusement more often than not directed at their untrustworthy father.

But she cut her amusement brief and looked at the end of the hall, as did I, for there came the brusque step of John Knox and the men of violence he had taken with him after the scouts from Burnedover, two of whom he had with him.

As I had seen in London and been told by Emma, they were so alike that it was as if they shared a soul—by design rather than through the vagaries of time and chance—and there was a deadness in their eyes.

I started to wonder if they really were creatures that had been designed—Emma had told me of the Reverend Black whom she had helped bring to his death, and how his minions were his less sharp twins.

"We took these two sleeping," Knox explained. "The others, their brothers, turned their pistols of unmaking on themselves rather than be taken, or give us a fight. And once they had blasted themselves, the pistols too fell away to nothingness."

"So, these two?" I asked him. "What do they have to say for themselves?" I leaned in closer. "And I notice that one has a split lip and the other a torn ear. What have you to say?"

I had instructed him not to use torture, but this looked like mere venial brutality.

Knox caught my glance and was anxious to display that he had not significantly disobeyed. "They prated at us that they would tell nothing to heathens, that they were the elect of God and soldiers of Christ."

He was indignant- how dare anyone not of his sect claim such a title?

"Now, as you know, Huntress—or should that be your Majesty?"

On his lips, the latter word had a bitter edge.

I shook my head at the latter title to indicate that I shared his repugnance.

He started again, repeating. "Huntress, then… As you know, it is always best to engage men in conversation if you wish them to tell you something and so we asked they what they meant by the elect. It is, after all, a topic which I and my men have found ourselves considering at length since we found ourselves in what appeared to be Hell, among the preterite."

He looked at his prisoners scornfully. "So we asked them, politely, to clarify these matters—after all, we hoped that in several centuries theology had developed a little. As it may have done, but not for these blockheads to whom Election was just a piece of jargon and the worthy name of good John Calvin unknown. And when we tried to instruct them, they talked of us as goddam cultural Marxist intellectuals, whatever that might mean. And they proceeded to tell us that we were godless sodomites, which they meant to be fighting words, and so we treated them as such."

I laughed because the behaviour of men quick to anger does not change across time and chance, and turned to the prisoners. "What have you to say for yourselves? One of your companions—your brother, perhaps, for he strongly resembled you—took my leg, and you were all of you spying on this realm of Valhalla which is now the strong-holding from which I will rule all of Shadow, in a while. Tell me—are you at war with me, undeclared?"

There was no answer they could make which would put me in a biddable mood, but they did not even try. They looked at each other at first in consternation and then blankly, and reached out their hands to each other, and drew themselves into a hug that had nothing in it of the friendly or of the erotic, but rather, of a sudden obscene blending and melding into one flesh, a sphere from which ribs and arms and leg bones protruded bloody and raw and sharp, and spines whiplashed out like cobras in a frenzy.

"Back," I shouted quite unnecessarily, for Knox and his men, crossing themselves, were already stepping back in double time.

"Pikes," he cried, and faster than I could quite have expected pikes were to hand to fend the vile thing off, though as it spun faster and faster, and grew more blades and protuberances than could be accounted for from the bodies of which it had originally built itself, I started to doubt that Knox's men could hold it back.

And that damned voice came from it on cue. "Huntress," he said, for it was the adversary again, Berin or Browning or whatever he was calling himself now. "I have taken your leg from you, and how will you fight me now? I shall take your friends and servants from you, one after another, starting here and now, and how will you stop me now? How…"

And whatsoever he was about to say was stilled as one great arrow pierced the flailing ball of bone and flesh to the floor of my throne room, and another great arrow that flamed like the sun as it arced through the room split the first and set the creature the men had become ablaze with flames that warmed the room like the sun yet created no stench of burned obscene magic but rather a fume that cleansed and purified.

And at the end of the hall he stood, vast as his statue in his home and temple of Delphi in his aspect of triumph, my former and perhaps again friend, the archer, the curer, the purifying Sun, Apollo the Glorious.

As he walked forward, my friends bowed their heads to him in respect, but not in worship or fealty.

"What in Hades was that?!" he asked. "Huntress, do you have enemies I need to know about?"

"That is a long story, best told feasting. But you did not come here for that story, or to rid me of vermin, welcome as that is. Let us be brusque."

He laughed, a laugh I remembered from when he was young and before he was a god. "I came as herald. The Gods of Olympus are returned to freedom and seek a place in the world. We had hoped to seize the throne of Valhalla, because Zeus my friend and brother has an old distaste for Odin One-Eye. Yet you sit in his place and I know you too well to try conclusions with you, even with the small force you have at your disposal." He looked around the room. "Yes, even with the Titans at my disposal, as they are, I would prefer not to risk it."

His smile was sweet as the honey of Hymettus. "Come, let us reason together."

And then I knew that I had a problem.

Healings

London, 2004

Sof hadn't known quite what to expect.

It was a long time since she'd been taken through or into Shadow, and much of that time she'd been in agony or mad with betrayal and grief—but Shadow was always a gradation, a journey of steps that you saw happening even if the pace was fast. When Emma travelled with Tom, she'd just killed someone and was more upset than she realised: that memory was all of embarrassment at sudden public vomiting…

In fact, travel with Tom was a mere moment of discontinuity: one moment they were in Valhalla, then, before you could blink, they were here, in a room that smelled almost imperceptibly of the clean chemical twenty first century.

Like it or not, she was here for the foreseeable future so she had better get used to it.

Tom's wheelchair thudded gently into the thick red and gold carpet at they arrived. Sof, who was conscious of her weight bouncing against his withered legs, instantly got out of his lap, stood up and walked around in vague wonder. Seeing things in Emma's memories really was not like being here yourself. Even in borrowed hell-flesh, it was all so bright and strange…

Not to be critical, she found herself wondering how Emma got through her day always too busy thinking to notice things.

"You didn't need to get up." Tom's tone was gently mocking of her solicitude. "It's not like I could feel anything."

At a desk at the other end of the room, a woman with her back to them was talking into what memory told her was the device for speaking at a distance, the phone.

And how strange to think of Greek, the language she had watched spread in some lives and had spoken as her mother tongue in so many more as an almost forgotten quarry of etymologies. Far speak—telephone—and, inevitably vulgarly, the phone.

"Yep, an American hot, thick crust, extra cheese," the woman said. "Company arrived. Make that two."

Though Sof had Emma's memories of being in this vast room full of screens, tables and books, a room which she knew, factually, to be the office of Polly Wild, being there for the first time herself was different, was vivid and new.

It was partly the musty smell of the old leather-bound ledgers on the shelves of a far wall and partly the carpet seducing the soles of her feet with comfort and partly the raucous music that was coming from speakers on the wall.

The screens too—they showed what looked like random scenes from the entire vast world—busy traffic and empty desert and rolling grassy hills and people. She had not seen so many different kinds of people in a single glance since she had last been in Alexandria. Not even in Hell.

And then one whole bank of screens went a sort of muddy red and then grey, with occasional random sparks of white.

It was not, she realised a moment later, meant to do that.

"What on earth? That's Hell and Shadow gorn down, all at once." She turned to face Tom and Sof, revealing a round young face framed by a blonde pixie cut. "Anything I should know about, young Tom? And hello, whoever you are?"

Sof knew, of course, who this was in spite of shorter hair and fewer clothes. The attitude and voice had not changed in two centuries. "We've met, Polly," she said.

Polly scowled, obviously disagreeing. "Never forget a face, me. Part of my occupation, ain't it. Spy mistress or beggar queen, always remember everyone. Goes with the bloody turf."

"I was mad at the time," Sof went on, "and possessing your great-grand-daughter's body. I only had her face so of course you wouldn't remember mine. Mara's sister."

"Fair enough," Polly shrugged. "Makes sense. So where have you been since, then?"

"Asleep inside Emma, who's my avatar. But she woke my memories and decided she didn't want me hanging around inside her longer than could be helped."

Polly gave a weary nod. "Ok, then," she said in the tone of an immortal whom nothing can surprise any longer. That was the difference, Sof reflected, between even a few centuries of continued existence and her own many births, childhoods, lives and deaths, but that made her think of Mara and so she thought about something else.

"Now about these screens?" Polly continued.

Tom drew in a sharp breath, hesitated and then plunged on. "Well, when they were sort of rusty burgundy, it looked a bit like this dust that happened in Shadow just before we left. We'd just killed this dragon that the God Odin turned into—long messy story -and he sort of dried up and blew away. It looked a bit like that. Maybe it's just buggered up all of your satellite cameras --"

Polly shook her head. "Nah, some of those cameras are in walls, all over the place. So maybe you're right but we can't assume anything or anyone in Shadow is still there to be seen." She gave the heavy sigh of someone who has lived to see too many of the best and brightest die before their time. And at her behest. "I always looks at the dark side because I'm often right and I'd rather be pleasantly than nastily surprised."

Sof did not let herself think about what it would mean for Mara, or for Emma, her other self, to be gone for good. She was here on business and there was one life at least that she could save.

She adopted the professional tone she'd used in various lives as herbalist or exorcist. "So, Miss Wilde, I gather you're having alchemical problems. As possibly the greatest exponent of the Work, or rather a couple of them, I am here to help. A dud batch of the elixir from what I can gather?"

Polly slipped instantly into patient mode. "Well, it was all OK for the first three hundred years. And after what happened with m'daughter and granddaughter the moment they tried it, I thought, oh well, that was awful, but I'm still all right so that must have been just bad luck. I mean, Newton wot made it, well, he was too much of a fricking coward to take it himself and he said it was probably all a matter of attitude."

Sof clicked her tongue against her teeth. "This Newton? Working from manuscripts? I gather that later ages got everything we did wrong. Surprised his elixir worked at all. Still, clever man, did things with numbers that I never thought of, and worked out the motions of the planets better than I managed, so can't expect him to think of everything... Show me."

Polly held up the transmuted paper cut on her arm and rolled up her sleeve to show the patch of ivory there. "Mara did say I needed to be careful of my flesh, but I didn't have a problem till now. I gather it can be a lot worse? Mr. Gibbon reckoned he knew why you was mad and told me not to trouble my mind with what would only upset me? So I didn't ask, and I didn't look it up in his bloody big book. Spose I should have really, but I don't always want to know the worst..."

Tact, Sof noticed slightly tetchily, was not Miss Wilde's forte. She let Polly chatter on nervously as she touched each of the mis-healed wounds in turn, noticing that slight pressure went unnoticed, and a little more made Polly flinch.

She sat down on one of the many chairs, tented her hands and smiled reassuringly.

"It could be worse" she consoled; "it's mostly superficial and none of it goes very deep." And, a little sternly (did Polly flinch a little? Good), "Just, don't ever again go messing around with things you don't understand concocted by amateurs. It rarely ends well. I was the first woman to ever achieve the first four substances—and the fifth was made from me—and I have hard experience behind my advice. This can be fixed, easily, here and now, by me—but you are very, very lucky…"

She reached into her loose garment and produced something that glistened so bright Tom and Polly could hardly bear it.

"Behold,"—and it didn't sound pompous at all, she hoped— "behold the goal of so many generations who died seeking knowledge in all the wrong places and for all the wrong purposes—the Stone, the mother, the panacea."

She touched it to Polly's forehead and then to the palm of her hand, which shone bright with its light for a second and then faded back to healthy flesh.

"I don't need to touch the other wounds," she explained. "Part for the whole and all of that. You shouldn't have any more trouble but let me know if there's anything. And I should probably have another look in a century of so—try to stay in one piece because the alternative, well, I would not wish it on you…"

And she was done.

"Great bedside manner you have there." Polly was clearly embarrassed to be thankful. "Learned at the feet of Hippocrates hisself, no doubt."

Sof laughed. "The other way around, my dear."

She turned and faced Tom. Her face grew grave. She'd noticed his body when sitting in his lap but now reached over and touched him, feather-gently. His throat, the back of his neck, his right hand, his left wrist, his thigh—strong pulses but a wrongness beyond even the gifts of the Stone.

"As I'm sure you've guessed, there's not much I can do for your—ah—condition. It's too bound up with quite nasty blood magic and a number of deaths." She flicked through Emma's memories for a few seconds.

"Nasty… Not really a strong enough word, is it? It's amazing what people have found to do short of the Rituals, so as to avoid the wrath of the Huntress. Kin betrayal—that's got its own powers—and, no, I don't meddle with magic, never have. The work is enough in that line of things for me. Saw where that leads with my first death."

Tom looked at her expectantly, waiting for more—death was after all his professional area of expertise—but she was not forthcoming and he looked away.

She had always hated giving patients a moment of hope followed by bad news. It was the worst part of being a healer, which was why she had devised the Work to begin with. Her own moment of hope and her own disappointment.

But suddenly the two others' attention was away from her and at a screen where a nearly naked brown-skinned young man with electrodes attached to his nipples, blood pouring from one nostril and patches of raw flesh across his stomach was being dragged down a corridor by two men in well-tailored and pressed black uniforms.

His face was familiar to her from Emma's memories.

"Excuse me, ladies," Tom said and vanished, returning seconds later with the nearly naked man. "Miss Sof, if you'd be so kind—"and disappeared again, only to appear on the screen, shoot the two torturers in their kneecaps, and return a few more seconds later with a silk dressing gown.

"Never leave a friend behind," Tom said. "Or even an enemy's enemy in this case."

"At this point, given they were about to bloody shoot me," the young man said in a thick Yorkshire accent, "better say friends, because I don't have many others left."

The good thing about healing, Sof remembered with relief, was that for the ones you cannot help, there are always the others that you can. In moments she was already applying the Stone to the man's stomach, face and chest—she took the electrodes, tossed them in the air and they were solid gold before they landed.

Tom caught them, held them until the man had wrapped the dressing gown round himself, and then tossed them to him, once he had a hand free. "Call them a souvenir, or a first instalment if you like. Now, young Syeed, what have you been a doing of to get yourself in trouble with those bastards from Burnedover again?"

Syeed wandered over to the water decanter that stood on a nearby table, poured himself a glass, drank it, and then said, "Sod bleeding haram" and poured himself a whisky from the other decanter next to it.

"Nowt new," he explained, sitting down on a sofa. "They've been looking for me ever since Iraq—as tha' knows, it weren't me saw to Reverend Black but from what they were saying Emma is kind of above their pay grade these days. Queen of bleeding Jehannam, they tell me—all right for some I suppose. Which leaves Muggins to carry the can, of course. And foocking Students sold me out, didn't they? Sectarian bastards. Just because I didn't see the point in going after Ahmadis—I mean, they may be heretics, but they're our heretics."

He leaned back and watched his former torturers and probable executioners on screen as they bled and writhed. Smirking just a little.

"S'like, Tom. I note you didn't go full whispering death on those two. Fellow kaffirs, am I right?"

"Tom works for me, now." Polly straightened her back and instantly acquired a scary amount of authority, Sof noticed, impressed. "My rules of engagement. I'm at war with bloody Burnedover because they killed Sharpe and tried to kill me and the way to hurt them is not killing off random foot-soldiers. Crippling them means paying for 'ospital care, and re'abilitation and that all costs—private enterprise means balance sheets."

On the screen, an officer walked into view, took a look at the two crippled men and shot them in the head with his side-arm, one and two.

Humanity never gets less ruthless, Sof thought sorrowfully.

"Oh well," Polly shrugged. "And sometimes that 'appens instead. The which at least don't do wonders for their morale…"

"Magic clones, Emma reckoned," Tom noted. "So morale hardly applies. Always more."

Polly wasn't going to back down from her point without a struggle. "Yeah, they still have to make the new ones."

"And Emma killed the original, didn't she? Or was he already a copy?" Sof found this all quite fascinating. "So any new ones will be copies of copies. I used to be in charge of the Museion's scriptorium, and that's when the errors really start to kick in." She riffled Emma's memories a little more and found what she'd been looking for. "Oh, you have these things called xerox machines. Same analogy applies."

Syeed shook his head, his expression shocked. "That's all pretty bloody cold."

"Sweetie," Polly said, not even pretending not to assess his body under the dressing gown, "when you've been in the death and dying and not getting killed business as long as I have, a degree of chill goes with the territory."

"Sorry." Syeed caught her gaze, preened a second and then remembered his disapproval. "You'd be? And the sister over there?"

No matter who they are, or what the dire circumstances they just escaped from, Sof reflected, attractive people meet and at once they start to flirt…

"She," Tom looked at him pityingly, "is Miss Wild."

Syeed looked surprised. "When they briefed me about her, they said Miss Wild had been roonning things since forever. She's young, can't be."

"Alchemy, sweetie." Polly smiled with a lot of teeth.

"What's that? Some sort of face-cream only posh people can afford? That works. Or you mean all that old stuff, lead into gold and all that. That your lot stole from us…"

Sof cut him off, vaguely irritated and her voice perhaps more haughty than she intended. "As you know perfectly well, Arabs called it the Egyptian thing, and we created it. Mostly, I created it—and then men misunderstood it and wasted a millennium on getting it wrong."

Syeed looked a little baffled.

Tom sighed and adopted a tone halfway between an official briefing and a friendly gossip between old acquaintances.

"Right, we'll go through it all again. You know Emma, right. Recognize the attitude? And the explaining? That's because this is Sof, her first incarnation, because that's a thing for some people, whatever they told you. And Sof here is the Huntress' sister from before history, and if you can imagine that family, and Emma's brains. And before you start assuming she's your sister in faith, she's from what you lot call the Time of Ignorance and she doesn't even care for Christians very much."

Syeed looked surprisingly relaxed at this explanation—clearly his world picture had been subjected to many other revelations over the years and he had started to accept it.

He laughed ruefully and then explained in his turn. "That's the other reason I got sold out… After Iraq. The Sheikh weren't especially impressed by what I said when they debriefed me. My son, he says, your experiences have driven you mad. 'E believes in djinns because they're in the book—but creatures like that dead god thing—'e wasn't having it. Said the kaffirs had poisoned my mind with drugs. So they never trusted me again, and sent me off to the Students."

He looked at once sorrowful and relieved. "So that's it for me and the glamorous fooking world of jihad, because there's no bloody point if your own side is trying to kill you and the other side isn't anything you'd care for."

He laughed, and grinned at Tom. "Same as you, from what I hear. Is it true you stuck a gun under Blair's nose and made him wet hisself?"

"Pretty much," Tom shrugged. "Not as if he's not been asking for it. But also, someone turned a blind eye when Burnedover were running round London killing my boss Mr. Sharpe at his retirement party and taking a shot at Polly here. And doing odd pieces of wet work for the real Enemy."

Syeed's eyes widened and then narrowed. "The Real Enemy?"

"The one who killed me and my sister before history began," Sof said. "The one the Huntress has hunted ever since."

Polly walked round, perched on the arm of the sofa and patted Syeed on the shoulder.

"Don't overthink it," she said consolingly. "Sooner or later we all have to learn that the world is not as we once thought it. I've had to go on learning that for three centuries—you never quite get used to it. Go with the flow, as people used to say in the Seventies."

He bristled for a moment at the unwarranted intimacy, and then relaxed—after all, she was his captain now, rather than someone he thought of primarily as a woman.

"There is a war to fight," Polly said, "and you might call it holy if you wanted. And you've been in it since Iraq. Welcome. The Enemy is some guy, and we know almost nothing about him after thousands of years, though your friend Emma got to kick him in the goolies once. And he shows up from time to time going bwahaha from the shadows, when something very nasty has gone down. He has many names and we hardly know any of them. And whoever Burnedover think they're working for, it's mostly him, which means he wants you dead. If you need motivation."

"What happened in Iraq was his," Sof added. "The dead god in a jar and all that. He's developed some sort of equivalent of the Work that unmakes rather than making."

"I'd guess," said Tom, "that he's looking to end the world. We're against that. You in?"

Syeed still looked a bit confused.

Sof thought she'd better smooth his troubled conscience a little. "If it worries you, my sister the Huntress knows the Prophet—on whom be blessings—and she says he's relaxed about all this. He and the other prophets don't seem to be very interested in getting directly involved, but they and their boss are on the right side in all this, for what it's worth."

"Just not their priority for some reason," Polly said. Which is why it's the likes of Emma who standardly end up saving the world. Someone has to... Emma's running Hell, which seems to have disappeared, by the way. So, now Tom and I have been cast adrift by the British state the which I have served loyally since 1730, it's time we put our mind to the important stuff a bit more. We could use a likely lad like you, Syeed, and we'll regard your past in international terrorist conspiracies as useful back story."

"Right now," Tom added, "we need all the help we can get. And you'll do nicely."

He jumped his chair over to where Syeed was sitting and proffered his hand. After a second's hesitation, Syeed took it.

"Like you say, I've been in this since Iraq and the dead god, I just didn't know it. Sounds like you need my help, and like my imam back in Beeston always says, the true jihad is to put yoursen on the path of righteousness. Which I haven't been sure I was for a while now." He sighed, picked up the half-drunk glass of whisky, looked at it sadly. And put it aside. "Which doesn't mean I approve of you or the fooking British imperial war state you've spent—just how many years—upholding. It's just, well, you didn't have to save me, and the Yanks are worse and whatever's behind them is worse. So you'll do until I find something better. And I'll let you know what that is."

"Fair enough," Tom said.

"I started off as the queen of beggars," said Polly. "So I know we can't be choosers."

Sof kept her own counsel, as one does when everyone else in the room is having a private conversations with complicated contexts. She could doubtless work it all out from Emma's memories, but really could not be bothered.

Just then, a doorbell rang.

58

Polly walked over to her desk and looked at a small intercom screen, then back up at the others, clearly impressed and surprised. "Ain't we the fancy ones? What on earth is she doing here?"

An elegant woman in early middle age, in a business suit whose lines were so sharp they hurt the eyes, strutted into the office as if she were walking a kind of red carpet to which she was rather more used.

She looked round her—at the room, at the screens, at the semi-naked Syeed—in what might, in a lesser mortal, have been confusion or dismay, and then flung herself dramatically in the general direction of the wheelchair and bent over to peck Tom on the forehead. "Tom, darling, who are these people and why are you here at what is supposed to be my twelve o'clock, but is clearly something else entirely?"

"Well, that's a bleeding good question," Polly said. "I don't appreciate former ingenues turning up here thinking they've an appointment with someone else entirely."

Sof waved languidly. "You're Elodie," she announced. "I have Emma's memories of you and you were too good for her."

Syeed just gaped for a moment, then he said, "A lot of the brothers are huge fans, not sure you'd want to know that. The Sheikh always told us that you had an innate purity which one day would lead to you the right path to submission, but I think he just fancied you."

"Hi, Elodie," Tom smiled, warm but puzzled. "What made you think you had a twelve o'clock here? This is where I work and it's supposed to be top secret and not the sort of place people turn up at by mistake after getting a letter."

Elodie frowned. "There was a note on my desk. A message left with my secretary just before she left the office last night. I didn't get it until nine this morning."

"Which is still before Sof and I turned up unexpectedly to see Polly, let alone before I rescued Syeed here from torture and execution…"

Elodie fluttered a hand in his general direction. "I think that's all I care to know, sweetie. Back when I was dating Emma, she used to feel she had to explain everything all the time. Back stories I wasn't terribly interested in that usually went away a day or so later to be replaced by some other problems."

Sof liked this woman: definitely too good for Emma.

"Speaking of problems–" Tom began.

"It's almost as if someone knew in advance that you were going to be here," Polly said. "Which is impossible."

At which all of the screens went dark, and when they turned on again, they all showed parts of a silhouette: a man in shadow, or rather made of shadow, in whose face nothing could be seen except deeper darkness where there should have been eyes, and a lot too many very, very white teeth arranged in a way that was wrong. And he was laughing.

"I had help," he said. "I have always had help."

It was the sort of voice you hear in dreams before the corridor starts to constrict around you like a python and the wainscot are teeth and running is like sticking to the air.

Sof had heard that laughter before, thousands of years before. Just before she died in torment for the first time.

"She persuaded me not to kill you. Why waste perfectly good hostages, she said. And I said, because this is the start of the end game and the time is coming when I will need no hostages. And she said that she knew the future and I did not kill you and you were essential to final victory and she never sets me wrong. So I overcame my preferences."

He barked another laugh.

"So consider yourself on borrowed time. You won't be leaving here any time soon. Tom, don't even try—my dust doesn't work on you as quickly as it would work on someone who walks through Shadow but by now I still wouldn't advise it. The god Odin is my servant in death. No one enters and no one leaves."

Polly snarled, "Who are you to come on to my screens in my place without a by-your-leave? I have a lord who-"

That laugh again—it sounded like dread.

"Your Lord of Cliffs and Shores? And the Border Agent? And all the rest? Gone where dead demi-gods go, into nothingness and

60

annihilation. I removed them; from now on borders are opened and closed at my will, not in the name of your games of reason and humanity. You have no Lord. I devoured him."

And then all the screens turned off, and back on again to reveal all the usual scenes of the world that was now untouchable.

Polly broke the stunned silence. "So, that's him. Suppose we should be honoured for the interview, but I'd rather not have been…taken hostage, at my time of life, what a bleeding liberty. And my poor Lord and his friends, made a meal for tyranny. And what I want to know is, who's this she? The cat's mother what drowned er own kittens?"

A space opened up on the far side of the room and someone silver was walking towards them down a long corridor that seemed not only in space but in time.

"That would be me."

The last time Sof had heard that voice, it had screamed in torment along with her own and then one or both of them had overcome the pain and said, "Farewell, sister."

And now here she was, remade as the Fifth Thing, and still sister. But not friend.

She looked around her. "Miss Wild. Mr. Rahmaoon. Miss Grafstein. Prince Thomas. Sister."

She walked over to a far table where a chess-board stood ready to have a problem solved. With a deliberate hand she tipped over one at a time both the white knights, a white bishop, a white castle and the white queen. Then shook her head.

"Obviously," she shrugged, "I learned long ago that I should play for the other side."

Tom pulled a small pistol from a pocket and fired it point blank at her. She shook her head like a nursemaid with a naughty child, held out a hand, showed him the bullet she had snatched from the air and then absorbed it into her palm.

"Really?" Sof's voice was gentle as a silver harp string. "And when did you decide to do to help the man who had us tortured and killed

? When they broke your hands, or when they tore apart your feet, or when they took my tongue, or…"

"So long ago." Lillit sighed and the room echoed to that gentle sound. "That day in the spring of the world when Mara took it on herself to protect the weak, and you chose to know the workings of time and chance, and I asked to set aside the workings of time and chance, to dance down the ages breaking those rules. And Mara learned that she cannot save us all. And you learned that to know is to be helpless and die over and over. And I learned…?"

Sof stared at her with a mixture of compassion and hatred. "That there is no setting aside time and chance. That things will be as they are. That the game is fixed. And there is no choosing."

"Precisely." Lillit's voice dripped like slow poisoned honey. "You understand everything you know, sister, and you are the mistress of oh so many arts. But I have known, ever since the time we died that first time, all of the workings of time and chance. And everything I do or have done for good or for ill. And because I became the Quintessence, I always was the Quintessence. Because the Elixir works around time and the Adamant resists time and the Alkahest imitates time and the Stone transcends and completes and repairs time. And the Fifth thing—the Fifth thing is eternity, is its own perpetual moment. And it was made from your agony and your madness and your body and your blood, but it was not for you to own. So I took it from you and became it."

Sof walked over to her and Lillit upturned a silver cheek for her to kiss. Which Sof did, and then slapped her once, twice with her left hand and then her right and then reached out again and ran three sharp nails down her sister's cheek, breaking and tearing the mirrored flesh so that it sprayed golden blood for a moment before repairing itself.

Lillit's cheek smelled of lightning and felt like icewater.

"I do not forgive you," Sof said.

"I never asked you to." said Lillit. "But don't say I never do anything for you." She flicked a finger and yellow dew started to collect on all the flat surfaces. "See you, somewhere near the end."

And she diminished and thinned and was gone into time or space.

Sof ran a finger through the dew on Polly's desk. "Manna," she sniffed. "Never liked the stuff, but at least it will keep us going."

Polly laughed. "I think we can do better than that. I've never been one as leaves things to chance. There's cellars under here with freezers the size of this room—their own generators and spells of stasis too—there's probably even stuff as you can eat, young Syeed, which I laid down when the Turkish ambassador was my particular friend back in Boney's day. And good wines too, for those of us inclined."

"I doubt my sister does anything that will not someday serve a purpose," Sof said. "If she gave us manna, it will doubtless come in useful. Sooner or later."

Tom looked at Sof, sympathetically. "I've had family troubles of my own, as you know. But that must have been rough."

Sof picked up a paper knife from Polly's desk and turned it over, looking at her hands, her fingernails. "That remains to be seen." She turned to Polly. "If you'd be so kind, I need—oh, a small clean glass jar. Or, Syeed, now you've finished the whisky, could you pass me your glass? It doesn't need to be especially clean. These things purify everything they touch anyway."

He passed her the glass and she scraped under her nails with the knife, wiping golden blood and small fragments of torn golden skin into it.

"My sister always loved a little bit of theatre, even before such a thing was invented. I doubt he was watching, but she managed a little bit of deniability just in case. Polly, this seems to be an extraordinarily well-supplied sort of place... You wouldn't have a small laboratory I can use, about the premises? This being the centre of some vast intelligence operation and all that."

She paused a second in thought. She wanted to do the Work as efficiently as possible, with tools she had used before, but also didn't want to look like a hidebound old fool in front of these modern children.

It had been a millennium and a half since she last set foot in her workroom, two since she had actually carried out operations in the Work, but, she realized with pleasure, she still knew exactly what she

63

was going to need. Agony and madness had not left her mind permanently blunt.

"Nothing too modern or fancy, for preference. I'll be working what you young things would call Old School and I'd rather not have to spend time with instruction manuals just so I can do things I invented two thousand years ago."

The others looked at her questioningly.

"Lillit is the Quintessence, I have the Stone, and Polly has the Elixir in her blood and her spittle and her other fluids. Spittle will do nicely. I won't need That Which Devours or the Adamant for this, I shouldn't think—the Work was completed seven centuries ago with my own tortured flesh, so I don't need further spiritual exercises. Just a work bench, some glassware and some flame."

She did not want to think about either of her sisters, but work had always been the best way to occupy her mind. The worst thing about having been mad was the perpetual distraction and distress of having a mind too busy to think.

Polly smirked. "There's a room with all the 'fancy modern stuff,'" she made air quotes, "and in my little Black Museum we has the workbench of bad Mr. John Smith, hisself, the which some of you know of as the Ripper. Which my young friend Mr. Herbert Wells used when we was hinvestigating the 'orrible murders alongside your sister Mara and the late god of the Hunt. I think you'll find it has everything you need."

She paused as they all heard a clip-clopping on the wooden floor of the hallway, and then a small bearded and horned face stuck his head round the door.

"Two American Hot," the faun said.

"Hallo, dear," Sof said. And rushed over to hug him. She had gathered that he was alive and awake in this age but it was glorious to feel his taut inhuman shoulders under her hand, run her fingers through his tousled hair.

He was at once a safe masculine force and the child she had never chosen to have.

"'Ang on," Polly said, "I thought as how his Nibs said no-one could enter or leave."

"Clearly," Sof said in the voice she had used in various lives spent teaching recalcitrant students things they were not especially interested in learning—"clearly the Adversary didn't bother taking non-humans into his calculations. Odd that he should have forgotten my friend here, who was the start of Emma's career and such a part of my own story."

"Everyone forgets about me." The faun clearly had a grievance. "Emma wakes me up, gets me a job in the catering trade and that's the last I hear of her, except some dryads tell me she's a goddess now or something. I never found out how she woke me, come to that."

"She's me, sort of," Sof explained. "Which meant she could undo what I did without even knowing she was doing it, because I was asleep inside her mind at the time."

"Oh," said the faun. "Doctrine of like identities. Why didn't you say so? You taught me all that back in the Museion."

"Sorry," Sof apologised, "it's been a while."

"Anyway," Tom interrupted, "nice as it is to see old friends meet up—and Emma always speaks very well of you, faun, she's just been pretty busy these last few years. Anyway, this not being human thing—"

He disappeared and was suddenly close up in one of the screens for a second—on a street in Buenos Aires, it looked like—and then instantly back.

"So either being a mutant makes me not human," he mused, "or I'm a mutant elf."

Sof nodded. "Either of those would make sense, but now we know you can do it, perhaps best not to do it too often. Clearly he thinks he has us totally bottled up and so not worth killing—let's not change his mind unless we have to."

"As a civilian," Elodie said. "I may not have a vote, but I'm all in favour of not being killed."

The faun nodded enthusiastically.

65

"Inshallah," Syeed added, "But I'd rather I died usefully rather than as collateral bleeding damage, if that's an option still."

Sof looked round with an inclusive 'We're all in this together' smile that she realized a second later might come across as a little patronizing, but never mind.

"Besides, there's important things for us—well, me—to do here, and I'd rather not disrupt them. And I'm sure that you'll be able to help—take notes and things…"

"Do tell," Polly butted in, "if you're prepared to share with lesser mortals."

Sof smiled.

"For a start," she said, "A couple of you are mortals, more or less, so we may as well fix that. Elodie, Syeed—"

"Hang on," Polly cut in anxiously, "what about my daughter and granddaughter? They took Newton's elixir and it did for them quick as you like."

Sof brushed her words away reassuringly.

"Impurities. I told you before Newton was careless. I won't pretend that you don't have to take care of yourself, but that kind of instant change and death shouldn't happen. I don't suppose you have any of his version left—I'd really like to study it. It might be a key to something…"

She thought a little harder, excited by the puzzle of it. "It might be part of the answer—look, the crucial thing is that we understand the dust. It's supposedly keeping most of us here and it's probably keeping Mara and Emma and the rest of them bottled up in slightly less well-appointed prisons. It's the Work's darker twin and a version of the Work that's imperfect sounds like a good starting point… After all, it's not like we've got anything better to do."

Here they all were—two killers and a spymistress and whatever it was that Elodie did that she was obviously so good at—and yet she could, without magic, compel them to yield to her authority simply by having a plan and the knowledge to form it. It was a pleasant feeling: she had spent too many lives deferring.

"Eat pizza," the faun said, suddenly. "Right now, what we need to do is eat pizza. Even if it's cold."

"There's a kitchen through that door," Polly pointed.

"Bugger alchemy," the faun said. "Oh, screw me sideways with Poseidon's trident, I'm sorry. The Work, saving your presence, Hypatia dear... I don't understand any of that, I'm just a faun. But if we're stuck here, it's a good job one of us can cook."

And good, Sof thought, to have at least one person in her life she couldn't impress, which reminded her...

"One other thing," she added, "there's a very sweet, very old god, I need to get hold of. Just to let him know I'm back. Are you still any good at whittling talismans?"

Rules

She might have been Dowager Regent Empress of the Holy Roman Empire for six years before her mother-in-law Adelaide poisoned her, or maybe it was just venison that had hung too long, but Emma quite liked Theophania. She was striking: tall, and long-necked and very slightly cross-eyed, with a haughty nose, pale olive skin and an air of superiority. And she was very, very scrubbed—"Infamous for bathing," the Recording Angel whispered, quite unnecessarily because Emma, of course, knew that; it was one of the things for which the head of this delegation had been damned, that and eating with a fork.

Adelaide had called a convocation of churchmen immediately after her rival's death just to ensure that she was damned by declaring these horrid Byzantine innovations anathema. The process had been declared null and void by a subsequent convocation a year or two later—forks just caught on with the fancier kind of churchmen—but the paperwork for her release and transfer to sainthood had got lost in a file somewhere.

Theophania had good reasons to have a grievance and Emma really sympathized, but this delegation had been making excuses now for several hours and the thing about being Judge and Ruler of what used to be Hell is that sooner or later you have to show the recalcitrant former damned who's boss.

Emma interrupted her, in mid-sentence. It had been a long Ciceronian sentence full of citations of the Statutes of Justinian and the Twelve Tables of Numa and had been about to get to the land-tenure regulations of High Germany. Emma felt like a philistine for leaving its flowing periods hanging, its clauses toppling, its citations undocumented, but there was work to do, and someone horribly self-assured to be gently humiliated into acquiescence. The fifth one in the last two hours.

Of the delegates sent to reason with her by the formerly damned, this one seemed vastly the most interesting and personable, and so Emma created a pocket of time and space in which they were suddenly the only ones present.

"So, Tiffany," Emma started, and smiled.

"Domina," Theophania started. "That's not how we pronounce my…" Then she smiled herself, grudgingly. "Yet, normally we hear what is said in our own language, and not even in some barbarous accent. If I hear my name that way, it is because you wish me to."

"And I am Queen and Judge of what used to be Hell, and if I choose to hack the rules that way, you will hear anyone who speaks to you pronounce it that way."

"I see," Theophania shrugged. "And from your smirk, there is something very amusing about pronouncing it that way. I imagine that the joke is that in your future time, it has ceased to be a name appropriate to princesses and acquired some other connotation."

Emma nodded. "First an expensively vulgar jeweller's, and then…"

"Something pretentious plebeians call their children." Theophania shrugged again. "I had an extensive brief to put to you. I loved law, you know, but even as a princess they would never allow me to plead. Then my husband expected me to sit in his councils and never say anything important; once I was Empress Regent, the Franks and Germans expected me to lay down law succinctly. And now, well, this is still Hell whatever you say."

Emma had a moment of poorly suppressed guilt. "If you wanted to come and work for me, rather than negotiating for a bunch of villagers who did terrible things, you could be pompous all day if you thought that would persuade them."

Theophania's shark-like smile left Emma in a certain amount of doubt as to who had been manipulating whom.

"There are," the Empress Regent said, "folk-tales about dealing with the devil…"

"You're confusing me with the previous management."

"Just so, and if you give me work, you may call me Tiffany as much as you desire." Theophania knelt and kissed Emma's hands, respectfully but a little lingeringly.

Was this shameless monarch trying to clinch the deal, Emma wondered. She had always been a republican, but… "That won't be necessary," she said regretfully.

Theophania looked innocent, not entirely convincingly.

Emma riffled through her mental files of judgements past—there was no hint of alternative unchastity in the catalogue of sins which had damned the Empress Regent, but then even corrupt tenth century churchmen probably had limited imaginations.

Emma created a watch for herself to look at. "I have things to do, people to judge, demons to stitch back together. You can take over the negotiations for me. Your fellow delegates may be vexed with you."

"They know I'm from Byzantium. I know our reputation. Vexed perhaps, but hardly surprised."

Emma stood up and vacated her chair. Theophania rose and seated herself, very regally. Emma took notes but reflected that she didn't actually need any lessons these days. Watching Aserath and Morgan seemed to have done the trick.

"So, you're clear on policy."

Theophania looked elegantly bored, as if she were almost insulted that Emma needed to get her to recite her lessons. "You need to punish us, the formerly damned, for what we did by way of revenge against the remaining demons you had placed under your protection but left among us. And you have healed all the demons we hurt. For some reasons of compunction, you are not doing what my uncle would do, which is decimate us by some sort of unmaking or long-term torture, but are instead compelling us to build a structure like the pyramids of Egypt or the towers of Babylon but as a road into the sky rather than as a granary or a tomb. A brick at a time, each of us—do I have to do this, personally, myself?"

"Every one of us, myself and Aserath included, over and over until it's done. Even the Recording Angel. Even the one who used to pretend to be the Son."

Theophania looked surprised and slightly shocked. "But you are the Queen and Judge."

"I am, and I failed to protect my demon subjects and I failed to make my wish that they be protected clear enough to the rest of you. So I sentence myself, and my co-queen, and my beloved, and the rest of us. Some of my court do not live here and need a way of leaving. This dust that stops us travelling, and stops those of us who fly from flying—it is some device of some enemy. And I do not wish to be trapped here."

Emma realised from the way Theophania was quailing a little that she had raised her voice somewhat. She really did feel trapped, whether or not she had any particular intention of leaving. She considered her next words. "There is an enemy," she said, finally. "We know very little of him—but this current misfortune is the sort of thing he does, but more trivial, which means it is part of some greater plan. He has bottled us up here, separated from our allies, who are doubtless also bottled up elsewhere in Shadow or in the Mundane."

"I see." The slowness with which Theophania replied and the slight furrowing of her brow demonstrated that, to some real degree, she truly did understand. "You know the knife is at your throat even if you do not know how or why. You see the general shape of the board even if you do not know the moves." She spoke as colleague to colleague without any pretense at deference.

"Precisely. And so my next move has to be something so crude, our over-subtle adversary will probably not have thought to counter it. There is a broken cable in the sky of Hell, and it leads back into the Mundane—all we have to do is reach it. But we cannot fly, so we must climb."

Theophania looked as delighted as a small girl on a birthday. "And by torturing the demons we gave you an excuse to use us as forced labour. It is almost providential…"

"Don't go thinking that's any kind of excuse." Emma decided she had better be stern. "My experience of the Lord Jehovah is that he is as poor at impulse control and forward planning as anyone—there is no plan except the Enemy's." Though actually, she thought, there was her own plan, and it was not the worst piece of improvisation she had come up with. One of the reasons why she had taken the cart loaded with vats of hell-flesh all the way across former Hell to Judas' fortress and Aserath's bower was to go over the finer details—as she could see them—in her head. There was also the need to attract attention and create rumour. And it had worked, splendidly.

She was after all the Queen and Judge set over the formerly damned and doing something messy, laborious and inexplicable was a good way of getting them interested in whatever she was going to do next. From time to time, villagers would follow her for a while looking confused and she would look straight ahead, stony-faced until one of them actually asked what was going on.

Each time that happened—and they had usually to run alongside her cart and its monstrous draught creatures to do so—she would haul up the reins delicately, so as to spill as little of her cargo as possible.

Then she would look down at them and smile; that smile she knew most people, if they had a guilty conscience of any kind, always found deeply terrifying.

"So, Odoacer,"—or Pierre, or Vladislav, or Ephraim, or Shura, or Niloufer, or Miriam, because part of the point was that she knew by name every single person she had judged, even if the details of their sins were locked somewhere deep in her mind—"what can I do for you this fine spring morning?" For Aserath, whom she had let make the decisions in such matters, had decided that it would always be spring and always that hour just after dawn rain when the grass smells of petrichor and the small purple flowers smelled sweetest.

"Your Grace, your Majesty, Lady Emma, great Khan, great sachem and so on," they would say, "why are you taking hell-flesh from the bloodvats of Phlegethon towards your palace?"

"Why," she would say, "to heal my demon subjects, whom so many of you have mistreated so grievously that I weep for them. Did you not hear that I declared amnesty for all but the Dukes of Hell? And yet the demon widows and orphans left by Simon's war have been made your sport."

And the brave young men and women who had accosted her would look abashed, because like as not they had seen harm done and done nothing to stop it, or had taken a hand in imaginative beatings and mutilations for which they had not expected to be called to account soon or ever.

"I am your Queen and Judge," Emma would declare. "Did you think that I do not watch over you all? Sometimes my responsibilities take me away from former Hell, but I always return. The Lady Aserath looks over the gardens and orchards and bowers that give you food and drink, and I look over you, and I am most displeased, as she will be too. If she decides that your grapes taste sour for a while, you will only have yourselves to blame. For it is written…"

And enough of the formerly damned would have been Christians that paid attention in church that they would say, "And the children's teeth will be set on edge."

"Just so," she would say. "But luckily there is an alternative. For I have mercy, and to spare."

They would look abashed, or try to blame their neighbours, and she would hear them out, looking stern yet loving for a while. She had learned much from Mary during the Lady of Heaven's brief oversight of her judgements.

"What can we do?" they would say.

"Spread the word," she told them. "Bring the severed heads and beaten bodies of your demon neighbours to my court where they will be healed and restored. Do not think to keep them from me because I shall be displeased if you do, and I am displeased enough already."

Then she would look at them more gently. "There will be forgiveness, for you all, because Aserath and I have only a gentle yoke upon your shoulders, a yoke so gentle you may not have noticed it until now. But there is a work we must all share, and you will all take part in that work as will we, your Queens and Judges, and the demons, once they have been restored to health, and all the former so-called Dukes of Hell."

And sometimes one would dare greatly and ask. "What is this work?"

And Emma would tell them.

Sometimes one in the crowd would ask, "When there is a road, into the sky and up into the lands of life, will it be permitted that we ordinary folk travel there?"

Emma would tell them, "Who can say? The world when I last saw it was full of wars and confusion and the traps and intrigues of our Great Enemy—I may need you to come with me to fight, or to heal, or I may need no help you can give me. I warn you though that the world is not less confusing and dangerous than it was when you were alive…"

She would let her words tail off there as if the changes were more than they could possibly imagine, which was none the less menacing for being something that was almost certainly the truth.

Emma needed to go to her court and strong place, which was more or less geographically at the centre of the irregular circle that was the useable part of Hell. She could not afford—she thought—the time to go there the long way round; there were plans to lay and improve in council, and demons to be healed, and a beloved to see… A beloved whom she had left on the path to temptation, not that she was herself obsessed with monogamy, but conversations needed to be had.

So as she went, she would recruit those daring enough to question her, and send them out, laden with the best rations she could create for them, to summon people to her court and to her judgement.

"A decree went out," she thought to herself. Then, she thought, now comes the hard part.

Which actually was not hard at all.

By the time Emma got to where the others were waiting for her, sitting in a row of comfortable chairs facing one of the ones from her usual office, they'd got the gist already.

When you send out messengers, there's always one who hopes to get a tip for going to the people you had thought you were stealing a march on, creating a fait accompli…

She'd not been especially worried that she would not be able to talk them into her plan—it was, after all, a pretty good one. But she hadn't quite expected the round of genteel applause that greeted her arrival, or Dawn and Caroline doing a cheer-leader routine, twirling scarlet pompoms the colour of her hair.

Somewhere in the back of her head, a string orchestra intoned solemnly. There were no singers, but she knew the words inscribed in the score.

Must it be? It must be.

Aserath—who was after all her co-ruler and there are rules of precedence in the councils of what had previously been Hell, announced that she had been persuaded almost immediately.

"When the girls told us that they'd sent you off to see, I was worried that you'd be soft-hearted, and then I was worried that anger would go to your head, and you'd be cruel. Morgan worried that she'd been a bad example early in your career. But no, sweetie, this is about right. And once we've built a few levels of it can I grow gardens down from it. I always loved Babylon but I never got to do one like it for myself before."

Judas looked at Aserath; he was scribbling in a little brown notebook. "If you've any energy to spare," he noted. "We're going to need forests, lots and lots of forests. Oaks to make charcoal to bake the bricks. Bamboo for the scaffolding."

He turned to Emma. "It's doable and it's a good simple design, but it's not as simple as you think. We need a surrounding set of ramps— some to take material up and some to bring people back down. The upper levels will need to be much more delicate than the lower levels but capable of bearing a load even so. I mean, there are reasons why Babel fell… Father—my adoptive father—showed me the plans once because he knew I would be interested, and father—Joseph, that is— had taught me well."

He sighed wistfully. "When I was young, I saw the Pharos. Obviously I saw the Pyramids, eventually, but not with mortal eyes. And it shames me how many of the other wonders passed from the world without my making time to see them, how many we helped destroy because Father would have no other gods before him. I'll plan your tower for you—I want to stand in its shadow and look into the Cliffs of Regret and apologize to my younger self for what I helped bring to rubble, and make amends to Architecture. It will serve the purposes you want for it, and it will be the best thing I can help make it."

He snapped his fingers and suddenly he was seated at a vast table with a huge piece of parchment, a set of high-carbon pencils and an expensive looking calculator. "I'll be a while," he muttered.

Emma snapped her fingers and her chair became a chaise longue— she didn't need to sleep any more, of course, but she certainly needed to relax.

Vretil bustled up to her, next, his clerk at his side. Stalin was carrying a large briefcase.

"Joseph Vissarionovich here has some experience in these matters," Vretil reminded her. "Moving lots of people around."

"No," Emma shook her head. "I think not. Bad optics."

"He repented," Vretil said. "Honestly he did. I'll make sure there's no back-sliding."

Emma looked at the Georgian and he quailed at her gaze. "You're very lucky not to be sitting playing cards with the Dukes of Hell," she reminded him.

"I tried playing cards with the Fascist Ambassador and his minions once, when we were allies." There was an asperity to his tone—the betrayal of 1941 clearly still rankled. "They were all obsessed with the American game of poker because cowboys and gangsters play it in decadent American motion pictures. I tried to teach them a proper Russian game like Vint, but they would not memorize the rules. Even Finns can manage that... Later, I had them all shot."

He sounded nostalgic. Emma and Vretil glared at him, aghast, and he reddened slightly and lowered his head. "I'm sorry. Sometimes I slip back into old ways of thinking."

Emma sighed. It was probably best to have him around so that she was constantly reminded of what she needed to be sure to not let herself turn into.

He smiled ingratiatingly, his gold teeth glinting from underneath his bushy moustache, and set the briefcase down. Suddenly it expanded and unfolded into a series of document wallets. He pulled out a single document from the nearest of these and proffered it to her. It was the index to all of the others.

"I prepared some contingency plans," he explained, "for moving each village towards the centre and having them do some work and then move to a new village, the next empty one along. The important thing is to keep them all moving in a series of circuits. There will be tasks to be done in one location and then a bit later tasks in another—they'll work and rest and move in turn. Like beads on an abacus, or dancers in a quadrille. All the villages are more or less the same already, so I don't expect much resistance or complaints."

Emma found herself slightly appalled at the ease with which she was accepting this man's moving people around like pieces on a chessboard. But then, it was the logic of what she wanted to do, just naked.

"How did you manage to get all of this done in so little time?" she found herself wondering aloud. "Vretil, have you been teaching your clerk to monkey around with his experience of time? I'm not sure I want more than a couple of us gods knowing how to do that…"

Stalin looked sideways at his boss, who nodded at him reassuringly. "It was a personal project," he explained. "Contingency plans. You and Her Fertilityship have this vast population sitting around, and sooner or later you were going to want them not to be idle. The point of ruling people is to keep them occupied; it's also how you continue to rule them."

The awful thing was, he was right. Emma thought. Not in the way he thought he was with his belief in the inexorable movement of historical forces, but because she'd taken responsibility for millions of damaged people and expected them to just relax and get over the trauma she'd removed from their present lives but not from their memories.

She waved him away. "Oh, carry on. Talk to Judas about what he needs to have delivered where and what people need to do to help him. Think in terms of organizing competition between villages and regions. With prizes and pennants. Let them enjoy themselves while they're expiating." She brooded a second. "There can be brass bands, or something like that. Though perhaps not work songs—that would give the wrong impression."

Suddenly she felt familiar-smelling sweet breath on the back of her neck.

"Brass bands?" Caroline said. "Are you trying to turn this back into Hell, dearest?"

"Well, no, but some sort of encouragement seems called for."

Caroline walked round to face Emma and sat on the ground at her feet looking up, her face suddenly very serious. It was that face which goes with the ominous words "we need to talk," except that Caroline clearly did not feel the need actually to say them.

Emma sat down next to her, embarrassed. "It's the plans, isn't it?" She paused. "I thought you agreed with them. You and Dawn did a little dance and everything." She patted her lover's hand to make it clear that she was listening attentively and taking things seriously.

"I was caught in the moment," Caroline explained. "And, for what it's worth, Dawn doesn't agree with my reservations. She thinks I'm making a lot too much fuss… but."

Caroline normally couldn't go three sentences without some kind of joke and it had now been four and Emma suspected that none would be coming.

"But?"

"It's a good plan, I admit. I mean, I can't see a flaw. And I can't see an alternative. But, well, it's not you. It's not the Emma I knew and fell in love with. Sometimes, even when we're making love, I look into your eyes and I see someone I don't know looking back at me. Someone very old and very wise who spent thousands of years judging the former damned. And the fact that you don't have any memory of all those years—or rather that they've been put aside until you find a reason to need them—doesn't mean I don't feel them there. And then there's Sof—you're not her, but you know everything that ever happened to her… Including me, and

79

including the other one. And when is she going to turn up again, and will she turn me off like a light again and just walk around in my skin, and will the older wiser version of you love her more anyway?"

She was close to tears. "Is she even good? She did terrible things, even that we know of, and is that me? Is that who I might grow into? You're a goddess and so are most of the others, but Dawn isn't, and is she safe from her? Is she even safe from me?"

Emma did not know what to do and so she stroked Caroline behind her left ear with a single finger, and then drew it down under Caroline's chin and tilted it upwards. She bent down and kissed Caroline on the mouth. She must still be in love with her because doing so felt new and wonderful still.

"Have you talked to Dawn about this?" Emma asked. "She gets to decide what's safe for her, surely?"

Caroline shrugged. "She's so new to our world; I'm not sure she gets how serious it all is."

"Oh, nonsense. Patronizing nonsense." Emma found herself almost irritated. "She's known what our world was like since she was a kid. Her aunt?" She thought for a second. "When I said that she was my trainee, I think I meant it. She's the right stuff, your Dawn. I think that's why I'm not jealous."

Emma realised that she was telling the truth, and was slightly surprised.

Caroline perked up again, as she always did. "I was thinking. I should maybe go away for a bit to think all this through. And maybe Dawn should stay with you and Morgan and Aserath. You're right—she has that attitude. But I need to do something, something that's mine, that's the Caroline thing."

She was pulling her Caroline has an idea face. "Spill." Emma thought she would speed up the process.

"Tunnels," Caroline said. "Hell has all these tunnels—you just found them and you're going to be too busy with your damn ziggurat to find out what they're for, and where they go. I think we need to know. I think we really need to know. Unless someone knows already, in which case I'll think of something else."

She looked meaningfully at Tsassipporah who had quietly fluttered down and was sitting on the back of Emma's chair. The bird shook their head in an almost human way. "Obviously my former master had secrets, some of them were even secret from me. And he knew I don't much care for confined spaces." They coughed meaningfully and gave Emma a pleading look.

Emma hardened her heart.

"Short of actual claustrophobic panic being a thing... tough. Caroline needs someone to go with her—someone with sharp claws and a mean beak, who can fetch help in a hurry if she needs it. And, well, I'll speak to Morgan about your sibling. As you may have noticed, I don't approve of excessive punishment. Also, I can't see what else you can be doing to make yourself useful to me—I have plenty of advisers and you're rather identified with the previous regime. So..." Caroline looked a little grumpy. "No, really. You'll have fun. And I'm not just sending them with you. I'm not sure this will work, but I'd been meaning to try and find out."

She whistled and out of somewhere her bag arrived. It rubbed up against her, purring, and the little hand reached out and touched her knee.

"Oh goody," Caroline said, "Whatever stops people going through Shadow doesn't affect them. Wonder how Tom's doing—looks like teleportation isn't affected." She reached over, patted the side of the bag and stroked the back of the little hand.

Emma stood up and helped her lover to her feet, then looked sternly at the bag. "Look after Caroline, dears. I love her, and I love you both, so I am sending you with her into the tunnels under Hell. Stop her doing anything too risky. And keep an eye on this stupid bird—and come back here for reinforcements if you need them."

Caroline pecked her on the cheek—it didn't feel perfunctory, more like a quick note that nothing important had changed between them and they'd talk later—and walked off with the bird trailing after her, its long flowing feathers suddenly up in a fan now it couldn't do more than flutter most of the time. The bag trotted alongside them; the little hand waved in a sensual languorous way that implied it would be blowing Emma kisses if it had lips to kiss with.

And then they were gone, presumably to say goodbye to Dawn, though Emma wasn't sure that Caroline wouldn't chicken out of that.

She was by herself, and felt more on her own than she could remember having been for ages—except... How had she not thought about this for all those years? Unless that was a thought she hadn't been allowed to have until now.

We are all players, and we all get played.

And scarlet hair, endless youth—some might say that was a reasonable deal for someone who thus far had only sat still and watched and listened and learned to understand.

This world and everything her life had been since Brazil... Poor little thing, it must have been so baffled and so scared of what I might do if I noticed it was there.

Here.

And all the other hers that had been inside her and that it had had to observe as well, and understand how they could be there.

So she thought calming thoughts and thoughts of welcome and thoughts of not being more than slightly put out and taken advantage of and intruded upon. And she recited logarithm tables and the axioms of Euclid in her head to make it feel at home.

She shut her eyes, and then the eyes in her mind, and went up the steps and through the slightly baroque carved wooden doors, with serpent handles, back into her memory palace, which seemed neater than she remembered it, as if someone had been doing the dusting and moving the rooms of case studies around.

For the first time in ages, she was in there and there was music playing, a sort of very gentle fugue, in more parts than she could count. And a small dot of piercing white light which danced gently to the underlying ground bass.

"Twelve," said that part of her which was left over from being Berthe von Renssler. "And before you ask, each of them is a different version of the same tone row. If we weren't a goddess, it would just seem like a very pleasant version of silence."

If there was music, if there had always been music that she hadn't quite noticed, there must be a musician.

Because she wasn't alone in there, was she? It was just that somehow the other person in there had been so quiet and so alien that she hadn't noticed. Someone old and strange looking through her eyes, Caroline had said—well, that was partly the her that had spent millennia judging but maybe… And perhaps the music hadn't always been there, it had been busy learning it, from Berthe in her subconscious.

"Not that subconscious, liebling," said her own voice in a German accent. "I slept for a while. And then your friend—our friend—woke me up. And I realised I have work still to do."

And then, "But you and they have to talk, and, as I say, I have work to do."

Emma had a sense of Berthe going away from her into a series of rooms.

The music grew slightly louder yet somehow more delicate. It was flutes, and a certain apprehensive trembling that was nonetheless part of the fugue and sill quite lovely, almost ingratiating.

"You still can't really talk to me, can you?" Emma asked, after what seemed like a few minutes but might have been far shorter, or longer. "Music and mathematics and some sort of very gentle emotion… Can we do yes and no, at least? Things that are, and things that are not. We are there, at least, aren't we?"

The light pulsed, gently, in C Major.

"And you think you're grasped this world, finally, enough that communication might be useful?"

Again the pulse and the chord, with a hint of pride and grandeur.

"No false humility. I like that in a being." And Emma was genuinely impressed. True, it had taken it several millennia of subjective time, but even so…

"You accept that this world is not essentially friendly to your kind, that, as I said to your people, it would essentially change them in ways they would not wish to be changed."

Yes.

"And you are changed in ways that mean you can never go home because you'd carry the seeds of corrosion there?" Again, the gentle pulse: *yes*.

"But you are content to stay, and observe, for the pure intellectual pleasure of it?" And again: *yes*.

"Well, that's all right, then. And if there's any future occasion on which you can make yourself useful, like another incursion from a world like your own?" A long pause and then the pulse.

And then a cascade of numbers and shapes and music that was like an ecstasy of knowing how the universe worked.

Emma gasped with joy and the part of her that was Berthe spasmed with intellectual delight and the parts of her that were small children who had died young clapped their hands.

Then, suddenly, there was a hand on her shoulder and she was awake. She knew that such delight had to end and that that was the nature of things and that it is not given to us in this or probably any other universe to see more than a short glimpse.

But for a moment she sobbed, and then started to pay attention to the person who had awoken her. It was the Empress Theophania, who looked at once anxious and officious.

Emma pulled herself together. "Tiffany," she acknowledged. "Sorry. I was having a moment."

Theophania raised an eyebrow just this side of ironic mockery. "You'll pardon me, but you have been in a trance for ten days. I and your senior colleagues have been trying to wake you for five of those days, but in your absence things proceeded reasonably smoothly without you. Delegation is the key to excellence, after all. Only I thought I should be a little more forceful today, because we are about to inaugurate your plan and we thought you probably wanted to lay the first stone, or something like that. And have flowers thrown at you, by a troop of lovable demon child gymnasts. And listen to the brass band that someone said you requested."

There was a level of dumb insolence in her words that Emma felt she ought, as Divine Judge of Hell, vaguely to resent, but since she had been taking a vacation from responsibility, she did not feel especially entitled to, as this snotty mediaeval cow seemed to have helped organize all the things she should have been putting together herself.

However…

Sometimes an accurate but arrogant apology is the best way to go in such circumstances: it re-establishes hierarchy by explaining to the staff that you have to deal with preoccupations they can hardly dream of.

Emma bowed her head slightly at an angle that conveyed apology without compromising seniority.

She did, after all, need to brief this new subordinate on this.

"I really am most terribly sorry, but unfortunately I have, floating platonically in the back of my mind, a diplomatic observer from a dimension whose inhabitants are abstract mathematical entities. And it has been remarkably quiet for a long time, but finally wanted to have a conversation. Since the one time its masters visited, they nearly destroyed our part of the cosmos with their sheer perfection, I couldn't really put it off to a more convenient time. Do apologise for me to all the people this caused a problem for."

Then she took Theophania's hand, raised it to her lips and kissed it. Theophania knelt before her and, without letting go of her hand, Emma gently pulled her to her feet and then kissed her on the forehead. It felt like a ceremony.

Theophania looked suitably abashed.

"I take it that the Lady Caroline went off on her mission," Emma added, spontaneously ennobling her lover because Tiffany was the sort of person who needs to know that important people are her social equals.

"With her companions—I am not certain how much help a walking valise and that hell bird will be, but I am sure she knows her own business. She headed off in the direction of the Blood Vats and the Lord Hades just sent over some more barrels of hell-flesh, so she must have arrived there promptly."

"And the Lady Dawn?"

"Organizing committees. She has taught the Angel Vretil and his clerk a thing called spreadsheets which they claim to find very useful. The Lord Lucifer had acquired a supply of something called batteries and something called a laptop which she found when taking inventory. She is disappointed not to get the internet, but says she will make do with old windows. Though I don't understand where the windows are or why they are any older than anything else round here."

Emma wondered why it had not occurred to her that of course Hell had PCs in it. Divine, but not omniscient; important to know that one does have limitations.

Theophania tapped an elegant finger on a delicate wristwatch. "You second millennials set such store by time-keeping. I have to remind you that you do have an appointment…Punctuality is the politeness of divinities, I am told."

Emma refused to run and could no longer fly, but even so, keeping a leisurely pace, and summoning a Lalique flask full of expresso (not because she really needed it but because it remained one of the human things one does when in a hurry), she arrived in plenty of time.

There were brass bands, several of them, marching in several directions that appeared to be more or less co-ordinated because they never quite collided. Which is more than could entirely be said of their musical stylings which ranged from Josquin to Sondheim, played with more enthusiasm than accuracy. Caroline would have mocked.

Suddenly Berthe was using her ears and started off wincing and then commented that the first night of the Berlioz Requiem probably sounded a bit like that, and there had been this man Ives, after her time…

Still, the demon children were charming: small, pink and with far smaller horns than she had previously observed. And bizarrely cherubic. They and their parents had clearly invested the repairs to their tattered hell-flesh bodies in a sort of compromise between integrity and assimilation. Or was it that Aserath's personal style when she had been posing as Luxuriette had set some sort of fashion?

Emma smiled and waved. She had seen the Queen do it and now she knew why that grin always appeared so fixed.

She elbowed her way up to the dais and smiled some more as she floated up the stairs. Show off just a little, so they remember all the other things you can do…

"Wouldn't have wanted you to miss your big day," Aserath whispered into her ear, pressing herself rather too snugly into Emma's side. She was more Luxuriette than usual today, but that meant nothing—she could probably be the chaos dragon in a thought. "Sorry about Caroline; I'm sure she'll get over whatever it is. And she was right—we really did need to know about those tunnels you found, and which for some reason I never found out about, even when I was feather-dusting Lucifer's office twice a day."

Which was a fair point, but Emma needed to get on with business. She walked off the edge of the dais and then hovered along it, pecking the cheeks of each of her colleagues and the other dignitaries. Morgan, Judas, some statuesque demon lady who seemed to have modelled her appearance on, well, on Emma herself, only taller and thinner and with slightly elongated features, as if Modigliani had painted her and been a little self-indulgent.

Looking out into the crowd, Emma saw a number of demon women with that look and she genuinely wasn't sure whether to take it as mockery or flattery. I suppose I have saved them all from torment, and it's probably gratitude. Or maybe just fashion.

That's long enough to be a meaningful pause, she thought, but much longer and it will be an embarrassment.

"Look," she started, "this isn't an ideal situation. Something's cut us off from everywhere else and presumably someone did that, and we only vaguely know who it was, but I think it was probably someone whom I once hit very hard in the balls, on account."

There was a surprisingly gratifying level of applause.

"There's that cable hanging in the sky, too high for us to reach, and it leads back to the Mundane world, so we're going to reach it the good old-fashioned hard way. Rather conveniently, all you humans fucked up badly enough that I have to do something about it—you do worship me as your judge, you know, and it kind of goes with the territory—and I wasn't around under the old regime much, but I rather get the impression that most of you demons have a certain amount to answer for in the way of chewing people's legs off and the like. So no recriminations, play nice, and if we all pull our weight we can have a nice decorative and useful ziggurat in no time."

She paused. "And look, I caught some of you doing terrible things. And the people—yes, the people—to whom you did them had done terrible things too. But we have to learn to let things go, you know."

They cheered her again. A lot of the demon women and their children struck up some kind of slightly atonal hymn—from the mild tingle it gave her, Emma gathered it was some kind of praise song, dedicated to her. Worship, so nourishing and so embarrassing.

She let herself down gently on to the ground and joined Dawn, who was standing with her usual clip board in one hand and a large golden trowel in the other.

"Was that OK?" Emma whispered.

"Not excessively embarrassing," Dawn whispered back and passed her the trowel and nudging her over to where a large rectangle had been marked in the ground, next to which, on its side, stood a large cube of red brick.

Emma diligently ran the trowel round the edges of the rectangle, and then lifted up a thin slice of soil with her mind before mentally shoving the brick into the slot she had made for it.

Dawn again, rather decoratively, proffered a flat piece of wood on a stick, on top of which was some sort of sticky mud. Slightly gingerly, Emma took a lump of this onto her trowel and then smoothed it along one side of the big brick.

Everyone applauded a little more, and then a group of burly villagers who looked as if they might be Polynesians of some sort heaved another huge block up and squeezed it where Emma had just smeared mortar. It made a gratifyingly squelchy noise and the Polynesians jumped up and down, beat their chests and made some sort of ululation with the back of their throats. Everyone cheered and the Polynesians ran off into the crowd, to a kiosk where Morgan was serving large glasses of what looked like slightly flat beer.

Next, a team of women—some of them short and wiry and dark and some of them tall and excessively blonde—pulled and pushed their block. Again, it clearly stuck fast, and they chanted something and everyone cheered.

Then, rather aggressively, a troupe of demon women, most of them with Emma's face, showed off by carrying their block on their shoulders and standing with it until one of their number had applied the mortar, with a showy flourish and a little pirouette at the end, and then dropped it carefully so close that one of them just had to strut round to the far end and pat it into place.

It was absolutely the sort of bonding through competitive exhibitionism that Emma had hoped and planned that it be, but, she realized, there was a limit to how much of it she could actually stand to watch save with the most fixed of grins. She went for a walk through her memory palace and found several hours of the young Berthe watching Gustav Mahler conducting Wagner.

It was better than having to pay attention to the ceremony by a long chalk. And it didn't stop her smiling, waving and periodically joining in enthusiastic applause at more or less the right time.

After a while, Dawn tapped her on the shoulder. "Emma...Emma? I think you can stop being regal now. Aserath wants you to come to the private gods and hangers on tent to drink champagne."

Emma shut down the first act of Die Walkure just ahead of the incest and sauntered back down one of the tastefully decorated corridors in her head into full consciousness.

She shook herself out of the last remnants of trance—somewhere in the back of her mind a dot of mathematical perfection was purring smooth equations to itself? Themselves? And Berthe went on remembering the Wagner, and jotting down notes on the clarity of the orchestration.

She needed to be careful of this; it was all too comfortable and it meant she did not have to think about her responsibilities.

She also found herself wondering what Berthe was writing.

Dawn looked at her in slightly exasperated patience. "I don't precisely know what being your trainee entails, but I'm fairly sure it's not hitting you in the face with a bladder when you go off into abstraction."

Emma had the grace to be a little shamefaced. "I don't know what it is. I think it's the dust. I'm not quite on the top of my game."

Dawn put her head slightly to one side, as if considering this carefully. "I really don't think so... But if you're feeling off, well, you do know that that still puts you way ahead of almost anyone else I've ever met, including all these divine beings you hang out with. Or are there some others I've not met who are smarter?"

Emma shook her head. Arrogance aside, honesty wins.

"Well, then, you're allowed to worry, and I'll keep your confidence, but if you are off your game because of the dust, so I imagine are all the rest of us. Just don't tell anyone else, because they all look up to you and expect you to solve things for them. Best not worry them."

She really did remind Emma of herself, when young. Only perhaps kinder.

They'd been walking as they talked, in a direction Emma hadn't really thought about but let Dawn show her the way without particularly realising that that was what she was doing.

Away from the cheering crowds and the booth where teams who had finished their stint were collecting their drinks—after the first couple Aserath had clearly handed that task over to staff. Quite fetching young men and women—Aserath doesn't seem to have a type except gorgeous, Emma thought.

The tent was clearly marked with purple orchids in elaborate brocade work, and inside there were the usual chaise lounges and comfortable chairs that seemed to have become a feature of New Hell décor.

Aserath had let herself grow a bit and was sitting with her theologian toyboy on her knee, feeding him grapes. Vretil was off in a corner with Stalin and a couple of Dukes—let out for the day—playing cards; it occurred to Emma that the Recording Angel was not someone with whom to play any game in which counting cards might give you an advantage.

Morgan had been drinking—more, she had let it take effect on her, a trick that Emma thought she might usefully learn one day, if she ever needed to relax and wasn't feeling off her game. Slightly gingerly, she got up from her couch and teetered over to Emma and Dawn. "Sorry your friend's gone off." There were air quotes in there somewhere. "I really thought you two were the real permanent thing. No offence, young Dawn."

"Nothing is going on." Dawn wasn't blushing, but apparently just stating a fact. "It would all be too complicated and I refuse to get involved with complications, to become a complication, just because Caroline wants to make some sort of point."

Emma relaxed somewhere inside. Then she felt guilty because it wasn't as if she had any right whatever to be jealous.

"So, anyway," Morgan went on. "I made a decision. Spirit of letting things go... You know, I did some stupid things back when I was young. Things Mara won't forgive me for, which is a shame now Sof is back and doesn't seem to want to be with her—and we may not any of us get to see each other ever again with this damned dust keeping us apart. So, anyway."

She was wearing the silver crow ornament in her hair above her left ear, tucked in just behind the strap of her eye-patch, and she reached up and held it in front of her.

"Wish I'd decided to do this before your bird went off with Caroline. It had been on at me for years whenever we met; well, it is his brother so only natural." Dawn looked a bit baffled and Morgan turned to her. "I had a bird too—we all did except Mara, who refused hers. She really needs to get over that, as well as the thing I did. It's a long time to carry a grudge. But my bird did a bad thing, it hurt me and I did a bad thing back. Well, no more. Like you say, let it go."

She threw the ornament in the air, where it hovered for a moment, and then the tent was full of the beating of wings and the raucous call of black birds—the flock Emma had seen Morgan use against the storm cherubs and the Enemy's creeping things that first time she met her.

"Do you mind doing your enchantments outside?" Aserath called out petulantly.

"Sorry, won't be a moment," Morgan called back over her shoulder as very slowly and definitely she drew her hands back together and then crossed them in front of her.

Suddenly the flock was gone. In its place was a disreputable single bird standing on one talon, plumage tattered and black. He cast a beady eye round the tent.

"Miss me, in the end, did you?" he croaked. "Got something of yours, I have."

He opened his beak wider than Emma thought beaks could stretch and then made a retching noise like a cat with a fur-ball, stretching and puffing out his chest like it was going to burst.

Then suddenly it was over and the black bird looked smug. Morgan reached up, quizzically, and pulled her eye-patch aside.

She was whole again.

"Good trick, ain't it," cawed the bird, and then pivoted his head back to Emma and Dawn. "Good speech, that. Let things go. I'm the famous Morrigan, I am, from when she was a proper war goddess. And you are?"

"She's Emma," Dawn announced heraldically, "co-ruler of what used to be Hell. I'm Dawn. Her trainee."

"This is Hell?" the Morrigan said, ruffling up the feathers round his neck as he looked around. "Changed a bit, ain't it?"

"You missed a war," Morgan explained. "So did I. Best war ever from your point of view—Heaven versus Hell. Lucifer lost and has pissed off somewhere. Aserath here and Emma ended up taking over, but there have been some problems. Somehow we're all stuck here— you won't be able to fly out and Shadow stopped working."

"See," the bird said, "that's what happens when you try to do without me. I knew you'd bring me back—says I to myself when you tore me apart, couple of years and she'll need me."

"Couple of centuries," Morgan corrected him. "And you missed so many wars, before that one. And I didn't get involved in any of them, hardly. Told you I'd given them up, and I meant it."

Emma choked back jokes about twelve-step programmes for goddesses addicted to bloody mayhem—and actually clearly Morgan had moved on, aside from occasional recruitment of sex-obsessed death commandos to protect her property. "Don't tease the poor creature," she said. "Poor thing looks famished." She reached into a pocket and threw him a random piece of hell-flesh she'd been carrying around in case any of the former damned tugging monumental blocks around needed running repairs.

The bird sniffed it, pulled a disgusted face and wolfed it down. "Any other gossip?" he asked in a bored hoarse voice. "Any actual bloody carrion or failing that, some cheese?" Aserath tossed him a large grape. "I bloody hates fruit," he said, but wolfed it down nonetheless.

Dawn tugged at Emma's elbow. "We need to talk," she whispered.

Last time Dawn and Caroline had needed to talk to Emma in that tone of voice it had been important. Emma drew aside and cast a vague glamour of shade and silence over them so that they could be discreet.

She caught her co-ruler's eye as she did so, realized it was being misunderstood and also realized that she did not care.

"I've had a thought," Dawn said, "about the trap we are in, the trap that the dust represents."

Emma thought for a second of what further trap they could be in than isolated by the dust in a Hell surrounded by unscalable mountains with Shadow closed to them—but she had worked out a slow but real way out of that trap, and yes, the Enemy was cleverer than that, must have foreseen that they would find a way of escaping, in time.

And the bird, the Morrigan, thought it had only been trapped in many bodies for mere years, rather than centuries.

And the cascade of Phlegethon, where it left the Mundane for Hell, moved so much faster.

She stared at Dawn. "How…how many years have we been held here already, moving as slow as sloths, or glaciers, or continents?"

And then she smiled at her friend.

"Caroline really does like us for being clever, doesn't she?"

Flute Dance

Greece, the Levant and Egypt, Time Before Archaic Time

I met them in the hills and together we killed the great snake Python.

No, not a dragon. If it had been a dragon, I would have said so; and in any case I have rarely had to kill dragons. Most of them are too sensible to try conclusions with me, and will listen to me, and then do what I say.

This was a snake, the biggest snake I have ever seen, bigger by far even than the ones which swim the great river in Brazil that Europeans and their descendants call the Amazon, but which has far older names. It had grown in some crevice of the Earth, grown fat on the blind fishes that swam there, and like them, it was blind.

The earth moved in those days. Mountains jetted flame and ash and choking dust. Crete of Minos fell under the ash, and the salt water of the great wave, and took much of the world of the Eastern

Sea with it. There were never as good times again after that day though men, and women too, carried on and thought themselves to be clear-sighted in their joys as do those whose sight is slowly dimming.

Crete fell, and men and women mourned its loss, all the way from Thessaly to the Great Cataract, from the mountains of the Caucasus to the land between the rivers. Mourned in keening and songs of lament and slow stately dances of loss.

And after some years a great blind snake came from out of the ground and hunted the hills around Mycenae, lazily taking whatever came to its maw, sheep, and the wolves that preyed on them, and sometimes the men that kept the sheep and killed the wolves.

I came to kill it lest it not be a snake merely, but be Snake, the essence and the original. The Great Beasts for the most part live deep in Shadow, where we do not see them, but those of us who helped bring the Bird to its death have a dislike for such. Coming to those hills, I found the snake a beast merely, but I stayed to help hunt it, to save wasting my journey and because such monsters sometimes fall into the hands of the wicked.

A prince of Mycenae came to kill it because he sought a deed to make him worthy. His father the Lord had set his mother aside, and he wished to gain honour that she might gain thereby. And his brothers called him Mouse because he was the least of them. And I laughed that I hunted a snake alongside a youth who was called for a beast that is usually the snake's prey.

I was more thoughtless back when I and the world were young, but then I ceased to laugh for fear of hurting the lad's feelings, possibly in time.

There also came the shepherd boy that men called the Shaggy One for the ill-cured sheepskins that he wore about him came to kill it to protect his sheep.

We met in the hills, I and those boys, and though I hunt alone, I joined them in their hunt, and watched their backs and let them take the lead. I watched, and hardly spoke at all, as the shepherd traced the snake's path in broken grasses, and the prince climbed high trees to get a sight of it; the shepherd had an axe of knapped stone and the prince a sword of bronze, but they were both brave young men, and they wrestled and more round our fire in the night.

And we talked around the fire, and the Shaggy One made a flute of reeds and played it, and Mouse sang plaintive songs of love, and I told stories of great deeds and evil men and the work of evil men's hands.

Whatever became of them later, they were friends in that hunt and the tale of what followed is a sadness to me.

Perhaps I told them too many tales, and they learned too much from me, and perhaps things find their balance in the end. I am the protector of the weak against the strong, but I make no claim to be wise.

We came across the snake and it reared up against us, and the prince shot arrows into its maw, and the shepherd rode its neck and hacked at its skull with his stone axe until both shattered, and I made an end with a lance to the heart, because unlike young boys, I know where the killing stroke goes.

We did not eat its meat for fear of what it might have made its diet. Mouse stripped it of its skin as decoration for his mother's bedchamber, and I took its two great teeth as a memento and a pretty for my sister. And the shepherd boy took two great ribs from it, and drilled them through and bound them together with dried guts and had the great double flute of which much was to come.

I said farewell and left them to what farewells they might choose to make. I thought little of it, as one did at partings when the world was new and empty.

That year, and the years after that, were years of hot summer, summer so hot that men said the god of the sun had gone mad or taken a fever or lost grasp of the reins of his horses. Streams dried and the little fish lay dead on baked mud. Even the Nile grew sluggish in the heat, and the other great rivers of the South.

Grass grew tinder dry and flaked away into dust and the sheep mewled in hunger. Crops failed and the fields burned and men began to starve. Though there were no rains, summer lightning struck woods already thinned by the charcoal burners' axes and trees flamed and crackled across great swathes of the hills.

In the first year of the heat, the Lords of the cities were generous, and opened their granaries, and gave the people bread—some of the people, who lived near enough to the cities to receive their bounty. Even that year, I was busy, because men that watch their children dying will try anything.

The starving will eat their neighbour, and if they grow fat and wicked on that flesh, sometimes they will consider further evils. Of such thoughts are the Rituals of Blood born, and it is for such and not harmless beasts that I am the Huntress. The poor and starving who turn to the Rituals are as much my prey as wicked lordlings, because however they begin, their end is nightmare all the same.

In the hills above Mycenae, I heard rumours–not rumours of the Rituals, but of a man who played his flute and the hungry danced their pain away and they followed him in great lines of dancing, tearing at wild beasts for flesh and eating the acorns of trees. I thought little of it, for such is not what I hunt.

Nonetheless, since I knew a young man who played the flute, and coincidence is a word men use in ignorance for the workings of time and fate, I sought him out.

He was thinner than I remembered him, far thinner, as were all that I saw in those hills, and the coarse-cured sheepskins from which he took his name hung loose on a frame that had always been spare and, when last I saw it, had not had a chance to come into man's strength.

His eyes burned with anger, and around him people slept, and moaned in their sleep, and they had the stinking breath and swollen bellies of those who starve.

"Huntress," he said, "do you bring us food?"

I carry little and need less, but offered him all that I had, for such is right conduct.

He thanked me, but with an eye that scoffed.

"And will you feed these, my dancers?" he said.

I went into Shadow and paced into the town Mycenae, and I took bread and meat from a rich man's table and glowered him to silence.

When I returned, the Shaggy One woke those near him and shared the food among them, taking nothing for himself, because he had already eaten from my rations.

Then he looked at me with angry mocking eyes. "Will you do the same tomorrow?"

I said, "I cannot, as you know. Hunger stalks the land, and where it passes, men work the Rituals and kill each other to become gods that will never starve, and devour their neighbours to become appetite who are now merely starveling. And worse things than that will happen if I am not there to prevent them. I protect the weak against the strong."

"And yet you do not protect the hungry against the Lords who hoard the grain. Why is that?"

I had answers, of a sort, but not for one who had not seen the creatures men make themselves, but only mere human lordship and its evils. And so, I was silent.

He turned from me, and struck up a measure, and the people who slept around him roused to the dance, though some of them had eyes that were closed and seemed to stagger in the dance.

There was something in the air that he played that had just a hint of wrongness to it; it was a slow insinuating tune to which men might dance slowly, slowly enough that they might dance in their sleep and still pound feet in a counter-rhythm to it. I wondered a moment, but thought that a mere dance tune could work little real harm in the world.

If I had been more cautious, had spoken to him of dark magic, and how it eats itself and all who work it, he would not have listened. I thought him harmless, because a skinny boy, and his piping a consolation for those who starved and might die.

And in the second year of the heat, Lords grew less generous with the grain they had stored, and thought more of the next year, and the years beyond that, and of what they would eat when the granaries were empty.

In the lands that would be Greece, and the realm of the Hittites, starvation crept closer and closer to the cities and the Lords grew harsher. Even in the South, faces grew thin.

In the hills I heard rumours of dancers who had died in their dance and danced still, skin and bones that staggered in the dance as the flute player played on. But rumours lie, more often than not, and I was busy with my work.

In Mycenae, the prince Mouse mourned his mother, who had died of heartbreak for that she was set aside, and he spoke out against the Lord his father and spoke of the shepherd who had helped him kill the snake and how such men should be cherished. He spoke for opening the granaries and his father cast him into one of the empty ones and told him to starve there.

We had hunted together, he and I, and so I went through Shadow to him, where he sat, in the dark, his hands bloody where he had scraped them on the rough-cast masonry in his fall.

"Mouse," I said.

"Huntress," he acknowledged. "Here I am, mouse in a storehouse, and yet I have nothing to offer you except my welcome."

"I come to bring you freedom." I reached out my hand and pulled him up, and out to the open air, and in a few paces of Shadow to the high hills.

"Freedom, perhaps," he squinted at the sun and then shaded his eyes with his hand, "and I am grateful for clean air and the light of day. Freedom to starve, though, and to be hunted perhaps by my royal father's hounds. He brooks no questioning of his will, and will take my absence as a further insult."

"I could take you back to await his mercy."

"That would be a hope as empty as the storehouse you found me in."

I had had a purpose in bringing him here—to have another pair of eyes to help me see. In the distance, where fire had cleared the woods, there was a great empty space, and on it a hundred feet were thudding in dance, and a piper was playing music that compelled the feet.

I can resist such, but I reached into my pouch and pulled out a small ball of beeswax and a large pinch of sweet herbs and offered them to him silently. He took both, kneaded them together, moistened them with his spittle, and stopped his ears and stilled his unwilling feet.

There on the dance floor, in long lines, left hand on right shoulder, they trod the measure, men and women and young children, some dried and leathered as the mummies of Egypt, some still warm flesh and some putrescent. All had hollow cheeks and thin hair, and their eyes were dead. Sometimes one let their hand fall from the shoulder of the one before and tore themselves from the dance, and all those dead eyes turned to look at the deserter, and right hands reached out and clawed and clutched and tore out handfuls of flesh that they stuffed in dead mouths. And when the torn thing that was left fell twitching to the ground, the dance trod the remains into the dry dust beneath their feet.

This sight was bad, but worst was the piper, his cheeks swollen from the strain of piping as if great round stones had been placed in his mouth that pushed until his eyes were closed from the pressure. He no longer breathed, but the piping came from the two great flutes that had been the ribs of Python and his skin, under the shaggy robes of wool that had given him his name, was as dried and weathered as some of those who danced to his tune. The tune was the same, but darker, more compelling; my mind is safe-guarded from such, but I felt its force touch the outer walls of my mind.

I kill men who murder to become gods, but this was something else. This was a shepherd who had died with his human flock, and yet lived with them and danced with them, and ate.

We watched and Mouse wept for what his friend had become, and I do not know what I would have decided to do, but breaking into the piping came the sound of a hunting horn and the baying of great dogs.

I do not know whether Mouse's father was hunting merely, or pursuing his vanished son, or chasing the same rumours of what danced in the hills, and it is not my pleasure to ask questions of the dead, who have their own concerns.

I shielded Mouse's eyes from what followed, and led him away from that place and the noise of eating, and the piping that did not miss a beat.

I took him across the hills and out across the sea to the island of Delos, where I left him by a spring and walked a little way so that he could grieve in solitude a while.

When I came back, he had made a small fire from dead wood and was baking in its embers two tortoises that he had found in the pool by the spring. I had no need of the food, but it was a human thing to share, and a kindness to let him show me his gratitude.

As we waited, he asked me of the old days in Crete of Minos, before the fall, and I told him of Pasiphae and her child, and of the prison built by Daedalus, and how he escaped. He was attentive and I thought little of it; young men like stories of wonders, as they do tales of great deeds and bloody vengeance.

I split the shells with the sharpest of the knives from my hair and we scraped them clean of meat and innards and placed what we did not eat on warm stones to dry in the sun. I made to throw the guts away, but he said he had a need for them.

We looked back out to sea and saw smoke from the mainland. Mycenae was burning, and Pylos too.

I left Mouse where he sat because he had seen too much that day and was already grieving. The palaces and the storehouses were burning and the dancers were in the streets, battening on those who ran from them. Worse, some of those who ran, stopped, and shut their eyes, and began to tread the measure of the dance and eat as the other dancers did, and the lines grew ever longer and the flames danced with them, and the dancers walked on hot coals and were not burned, and danced in the choking smoke of grain stores and did not choke because they did not breathe.

I tried to come where the Shaggy One piped still, but his dancers blocked my way and buffeted at me and their dance reached into Shadow and blocked my way there. This was as powerful a magic as I had seen, and it was dark as despair and bleak as hunger, and I had left it too late out of compassion or folly or kindness.

I cannot save them all, and I could only come at the Shaggy One by striking down all who blocked me from him, and that I would not. I protect the weak against the strong, but what can I do when the weak unite?

Eventually I struck out at the dancers with my spear, and found to my no great surprise that their skins were as hardened against it as stone or wood.

I do what I can.

I saw young girls who ran from the dancers, and who held their hands to their ears to block the music, and I seized them one after another, and clapped wax and herbs into their ears and led them away. I had only so much of the wax, though, and by the time I got to the tenth girl, she and her sisters had closed their eyes and were gone into the dance.

I saved nine young girls from that wreck. It was not enough, but it was something. I stood with them on the high flat rock where girls like them were made sacrifices in other times, and we watched as the lines of dancers trod their way out of the burning towns and down to the shore. I breathed a moment, and then gasped, and the girls gasped with me, for the dancers came to the sea and trod their slow measure atop the waves and did not stop, or fall, or drown, but went their way.

The flute dance was a strong magic.

I took the nine to Delos, where young Mouse was whittling with his knife at one of the halved tortoise shells.

"I go," I said to him, "to follow the piper we once knew across the sea, and see what he does beyond it, he and his dancers. I leave you these, your townsfolk, to protect as is your duty as a prince. And not to use in the way of young men with girls left in your charge."

"I shall protect them," he said, "as if they were my sisters, for they are the only sisters I have left." And he stretched his arms out, and the nine maidens clustered into his grasp.

I trusted him, and much came of my trust, yet I cannot say that he lied or broke his word.

And I led him and the girls back from the island Delos to the ruins that had been his home.

"We need weapons, to protect us," Mouse said. "There are wolves in the hills that will come down to feed on what is left."

He broke into the ruined armoury at the gate of his father's wrecked palace and found himself a spear and a sword. I seized more swords and proffered them to the girls, but he forbad me. "These are not seemly weapons for maidens," he said.

"They are the weapons I bear," I said.

"But you are the Huntress," he said, "and I am not your Lord, but I am theirs. And I will say what is seemly for them."

He went where the granaries had been and armed the maidens with the scythes and sickles he found among the ashes and they took them from his hand.

"What will you eat?" I asked him. "For the dancers have left nothing in their wake."

"If need be," he said, "we will eat the wolves when they come." He laughed and the nine girls laughed with him.

They searched the wreckage of the palace and the town and I searched with them, and we found little to eat that was not spoiled—charred loaves in a baker's oven, a few doves perched on the ruins of the palace that Mouse killed with a sling. Little to eat, but enough, for a time; what we did find, and what Mouse was careful to set aside, was gold, and silver, and jewels.

And the rolled skin of the snake, which he took from a storeroom where his mother's few possessions awaited distribution to his father's new wives. All else in the store had charred, and yet there was a virtue in the snakeskin that had preserved it.

"And what hope you to buy with your gold?" I asked, looking at the devastation that surrounded us.

"Traders are overdue from the land of Egypt," he said, "and we will buy food for whatever the market will bear. We cannot eat gold, and yet it will buy food. And if they bring no food, we will buy the nets of fishermen, and fish for our dinners."

"But you could buy passage."

"I would not be a poor suppliant in Egypt, who am the last Prince of Mycenae and the Lord of the island Delos."

I smiled at his vanity. He would protect the young girls I had placed in his care, and that was enough. They were a kingdom he could manage.

The hills around Mycenae were empty alike now of good men and bad and I need fear nothing of the Rituals there for there were none left there to work them. So I left Mouse and his maidens and followed the dancers across the sea to see what happened when they made landfall, but I feared in my heart that there would be little enough that I could do.

It was not as bad as I feared it might be, for they had kept a straight course and not taken time to wreck everything they passed. The dance swept off the sea and across Attica, and left wreckage and emptiness, but the small settlement that would one day be Athens was spared by a few miles as were the towns of Euboea and Chalcis. Some islands were left in wreckage and others were spared—and everywhere they wrecked, more dancers were caught into the dance.

I raced through Shadow and outpaced them to the further shore.

I came to the town Ugarit, whose Lord was the Baal known as Moth, who rose up to meet me like a sheet of power, a living flame angry to protect what was his.

"I am not your foe, Lord," I said, for I had no quarrel with him, "but what follows on the sea is a living hunger that will eat and burn all that is yours, for it is the flute dance that is known as Famine. Tell your people to flee, for if they do not, they will die and join the dance, or join the dance and be as dead."

Baal Moth scoffed at me, and summoned his well-fed folk to arms.

I turned my face from him, because I protect the weak, but not fools in their pride. I shouted to his people, "I am the Huntress of Gods, and when I say that a foe is beyond my strength, I speak truth. Flee, or die."

And some followed me out into the dry hills beyond the city and how they fared I know not. For I had other towns to warn. I raced down the coast as fast as I could, and I spoke to the gods of each town, Baal Melkart, and Baal Adonis, and Baal Adonai, and the fish-head Dagon whom I had known an age before and many others, Astarte and Ashtoreth and the goddesses of the grove who have no name of their own. And I sent word further and further into the land as I went, to the Sea that is Dead and its Lord of Salt, and all the little gods of hills and streams, and the lords of my own land, up in the hills above the great rivers, and the lands between the rivers.

I summoned them, and they came, a host of gods whose cities would trade with each other and feud with each other and war with each other. Some were gods to whom I had had to speak sharply from time to time, and among them were Jehovah and Hekkat, to whom I do not speak nor do they speak one to another. But they came, and stood in the ranks of gods.

And the host of gods marched north to where Ugarit burned and smaller towns in its lee whose name I never knew or forget, and are lost to time.

On the road, we met the poor shadow that had been Moth, who had thrown his force time and again at what he could not stop and whose worshippers had died with his name on their lips, or been taken into the dance and forgotten his name. His power was broken and his godhood, and at the site of his tatters and tears the host of gods moaned, for they saw their fate.

He limped out into the wilderness where gods go to die. And the small grey creatures whose grubs eat stored grain, and which hurl themselves into flame, or leave a smudge where you swat them, may be some remnant of him, or may not be. I know not.

"It is folly to engage with the dance," I said, "for they cannot be touched with the point or blade of weapons. But you are gods, and you are many, and you are strong. So take up the trunks of trees and hold them before you as you walk, and come up against the line of the dancers and push them. Push for the sake of your lands and your people, push them back into the sea from which they came. Push for your lives, and those of your worshippers."

I have stood in battle line from time to time—it is not where I choose to spend my time, but sometimes it is where my hunt takes me, but rarely has the holding of the line seemed so desperate. We put our shoulders to great trunks of pine and oak and cedar, with the branches hacked from them, and it was almost not enough.

I stood, bending into the work, my left shoulder mingling its sweat with the sweet-smelling Ashtoreth the Fair and my right hard against some Sea Lord or other, and we did not prevail at first. Our feet slipped in dust that became mud and the dead faces of the dancers stared at us past our barrier. We would not have prevailed, but the bull Marduk joined us with his bull brothers, and the cackling vulture gods from the Assyrian hills, and Tiamat the Chaos, and Inanna the Stripped. The gods of the far lands between the rivers came—and yes, it was their fight too, or would have been had we fallen, but neither men nor gods are usually wise enough to perceive such things.

We gained a foot, and then a yard, and then a mile, and then our tree trunks were pushing down young pines to splinter under our feet, and then a rush down a slope, and we were on the soft sand of the beach Kassab. And the dancers had turned their faces and they were proceeding South and Southwest and away from the shores of the East.

Distantly, in the middle of the throng, I saw the piper who had once been the Shaggy One, and he no longer seemed even remotely human. He had a face without eyes or any features save pursed lips and puffed cheeks and a brow so deeply furrowed in effort that it was as if his skull was hewn into slices.

As he passed, I felt the pouch at my side tug at me, as if something in there was trying to follow the dancers. I reached in, and the teeth of Python were pressing hard against the leather. Then I felt, for a moment so small it was as if I had imagined it, a tug from another direction, far to the West and North.

We watched the dancers and we paced them down the Eastern shore, lest they try to make another landfall, but as luck would have it, they had the brains of a herd of sheep, or a tired ox, and once herded in a direction, continued to head there.

In the sky above us, there was a cry, the screech of a hunting bird and suddenly great wings dived down and Horus, Lord of Egypt, stood among us in a space cleared less by surprise than by the sheer force of his will.

"You were," he said, "going to warn me of this Dance of Hunger, were you not?"

Suddenly, all of the gods of the East were looking both embarrassed, and at me.

"Frankly," I said, " it had not yet crossed my mind that I would need to. I am sure that it would have done, but you know how things slip your mind when you are busy. But, of course, since you mention it, you can have whatever help I can give, and I am sure"- I made my tone unyielding as rock- "you can have the help of everyone here, now that we have saved our own lands."

Even in human form, Horus had a disconcerting habit of flicking the inner lids across his eyes when he wanted to show disapproval.

"I expect nothing more from you, Huntress, for you are, as is well known, wild and ungoverned. But some of you are sensible gods, and have sworn fealty to the Lords of the Nile before now."

Baal-Melkart muttered, "Tribute, not fealty," and the hawk-god ignored him. Not least because he was right, and Horus knew it.

Their patronizing tone was one of the reasons why I had never especially taken to Egypt's gods, that and their dullness. What else can you expect from a pantheon who have always been, for the most part, temple scribes jumped up a few ranks when accident or fratricide thinned their numbers. Fratricide that was itself just another routine.

Isis was another matter of course, charming and witty but hopelessly uninterested in anything except her own godhood. And Sekhmet—she had been another story.

Nonetheless, we had to protect Egypt, if we could, because to add even a fraction of its people to the Dance would be to create a raging fire that would burn what was left of the world. And just because we had saved most of the coast and the lands of the rivers this once, did not mean we could not save it a second time if that fire came raging back up the road through Sinai.

So we marched, that host of gods, bearing our trees with us since we would not wish to strip the Delta as we had the lands of the Eastern shore. We passed the Dance and out-paced it again—Dances of the Dead always lack a certain degree of speed. As we passed, I felt the teeth in my pouch throb in sympathy with the bones of the flute, and again I felt the slight dissonance as if something else were tugging at them.

We came to the soft ground and thousand sweet streams where the Delta meets the sea. No army of gods has marched in such accord, before or since, not even the army of the Gods of the North or the God-Host of Hind.

The Lords of Egypt stood with us, though I noticed, with amusement, that they placed themselves at our sides and rear, so that we would take the brunt of the Dance when it came. I heard an Astarte grumble to a Baal, but quietly—no god of the Eastern shore or the East had any great expectation of the Lords of Egypt, centuries of quiet arrogance had seen to that.

The Dance came to the shores of Egypt like a great slow wave, like a pot that froths and spits but is not yet quite aboil. The tune continued, louder than I believed quite possible from a single mouth, even one as distorted as the Shaggy One's had been when last I saw him, and yet, yet, there was a hesitancy in it, as if the bone flutes were throbbing against his lips with the same urgency as the teeth that pulled and pulled within the pouch at my side.

And as that throb became almost something that pulled and pushed the pouch so that it slapped against my side, there was a shadow in the sky that was no bird, nor any winged creature I had ever seen.

It was the skin of Python, whose ribs were the flute and whose teeth were in my pouch, dried and pierced and framed on pine saplings, and dangling from nets strung beneath that skin were Mouse and his nine maidens, wild-eyed and armed with sickles and scythes.

They floated to the ground, between the hosts, but their eyes were not on the gods, only on the Dance.

Slung across Mouse's shoulders was a sling, but in it no weapon of war I knew, but rather the tortoise shell, shaped and carved and strung with dried guts. A sort of bow, I heard one god wonder, but then Mouse reached for it, and held it before him with one hand while he struck at its strings with the other.

The first chord he played on his lyre echoed across the rivers and the hills and the sea like a word of creation, and the flute dance quailed before it like trees in the fierceness of storm. With his second stroke, the maidens raised their sickles above their shoulders or swung their scythes as high; and with his third, the down-stroke. And again and again—not a melody so much as a fierce pattern of chords that hammered like hail and lightning and rocks falling on the mountains, and yet a melody perhaps, but one of war and terror.

And the strokes of the sickles and scythes were that music too, and with each stroke, without any touch, the heads and arms and legs of the dancers flew off like wheat in the harvest, like chaff in the threshing.

The small waves of that sea, and the rocks and sand at its edge, were red with blood, though less than one might think, for there was little left of flesh, or blood, in those dancers.

I do not know how long the host of gods, and I with them, stood and watched and listened as Mouse played on and on in fury, and his maidens struck time and again. All I can say is that, after some little while, the Dance was done and the dancers gone to blood and ruin and Mouse set his lyre aside. He walked forward, on a little spit of land, and I ran up and stood beside him, and we stood before the creature that was what was left of the Shaggy One and with a firm hand Mouse pulled the flutes from his lips and I struck them aside from his hands.

The very moment the flute was from his grasp, what was left of the Shaggy One slumped to the ground, an empty skin within his sheepskins, drained and done. I reached down, and pulled it free of the sheepskins, and whirled it above my head to show the gods what justice had been done.

Yet Mouse gestured to his maidens, and they dropped their sickles and their scythes, never to pick up such again, and three of them held his lyre before him and the other six clustered around his knees. He raised the great bone flutes above his head, and turned them upside down, so that the mouth pieces gushed down on him the vast endless backwash of the magic that had been raised and now lacked its master.

All those gods present could see what was happening, and some moaned and some raged, but none tried to intervene for they knew a new god was being born, and nine goddesses with him. And few understood, because gods are not, in general, good at sharing.

When he was done, and born, the bone flutes shimmered into dust between his hands, and he reached down, and with a great shout of joy, played a music on the lyre that was lust and worship and the maidens danced with and around him, in a frenzy that was of equals, and not of the dead. And if maidens they still were, not, I felt, for any great time more.

I coughed, because they needed to remember they had an audience.

"Huntress," he acknowledged. "Brothers and sisters of the East and Egypt."

I looked at him, not threatening but as one who needed to be satisfied.

"What can kill Hunger save the Harvest?" he said. "And what can kill a brother of the hunt save a brother of the hunt, or break the hunt's trophy save the hunt's trophies? And what can kill music but music? And, if you are concerned that any ritual was worked here this day, the ritual I worked is called vengeance."

I cannot say that I was happy with this, but I was, after a fashion, satisfied.

Not so the gods of Egypt or the East, who spoke against Mouse and his nine maidens.

"How shall I call you now?" I asked. "For Mouse is hardly a fitting name."

"My name," he said, "is as it always was. I am the god Apollo as I was the prince of that name. And I will rule a great people, but not here, and not now."

"Do you intend war?" said Horus and raised a great curved sword.

"Not a bit of it," said Apollo. "I and these maids will cultivate the arts of peace." Yet he spoke with a savage glee that belied his words, and so it was to prove.

"Then begone from these lands," Horus said, "and from the lands to which you of Mycenae and Greece have brought evil music and evil magic and the madness they have wrought. Take what you have wrought from our sight."

"Gladly," Apollo said, with that same smile, and struck another chord on his lyre, with the last twang of which he, and his Muses, were gone from our sight and gone from the shores of Egypt.

The gods of the East and the Lords of Egypt feasted each other that night, but I slipped away, sick at heart.

The world before Crete fell had been a slow stately dance of trade and friendship, and the world after the fall a wistful dance of mourning. We had heard new musics this day, harsh sad savage musics, and in the disdain with which Horus looked at Apollo and the arrogance with which the new god looked back at the old, I heard the first notes of a new and worse dance, with which we would not soon be done.

Thrones

But that was long ago.

I was younger then, with a different knowledge of the world, and a different voice, perhaps, that is a part of my memories but no longer who I am.

I have never liked the Olympians much, but in our youth I talked to them as if they were my equals in a courtly and dignified manner that helped keep peace between us. In this modern world of death and dust and pain, I felt no such compunction. And could let myself think of, and talk to, them as they deserved.

They had always been a murderous lot, of course, but I kept an eye on them for centuries and they never went near enough to the Rituals for me to have to do anything about it.

They knew enough to fear me.

Castrating your father and eating your children probably counted, but that was well before I knew them and that generation were gone by the time I came to know Zeus and the rest. It was all a lot messier than Hesiod says. And I do not punish the next generation for inheriting powers their parents got by doubtful means—just, as I say, I keep an eye in case that makes them cocky.

Children's teeth are set on edge? That is Nameless' way of doing business, not mine.

And keeping everyone frightened enough to pray and sacrifice cattle so that you don't do anything terrible to them—that is repulsive and unjust, but it is how a lot of pantheons function and it is not what I punish gods for. Add that to punishing the Rituals and I'd never get anything else done.

I don't have to like it though.

I was old friends with Apollo, of course, from before he was a god, but I never liked him as much after he fell in with Zeus and his crowd—he'd do as cruel things as the rest of them. And enjoy it. What young people like Emma call peer pressure existed long before there was a name for it.

The laurel girl business, to name but one example.

I told you two how he dealt with the Shaggy One—not especially nice, but necessary and not gratuitous sadism like the version he put around later to make sure no one thought he was the Nice One. Says something about that crowd that he felt it necessary to take a story in which he was pretty much the hero, the God who Saved the World, and turn it into a story of punishing a mortal for daring to be good at something.

But they were all like that. Athena and the spider-girl, good example… No, of course she didn't actually turn her into a spider, just broke her arms and legs and left her to crawl away, and then came back and hanged her high. Just for being good at something. Insecure the lot of them.

Apollo would do plagues for Zeus, like he did in Thebes. Which was none of his business, but half a city has to die to punish King

Swellfoot for things he had done by accident, and which Zeus had got Apollo to set up with oracles. And why, because Swellfoot's great-grandsire had given him a bit of lip or some such thing—I really can't keep track of all their little vendettas—and Zeus never lets anything go.

He got very miffed, I remember, when Swellfoot's children all managed to end up dead and there was no-one left to go after. Oh, Ismene? She's alive at the end of the plays but she died a bit later, not of anything special or the vengeance of Zeus—just died, as mortals do.

I made sure to go to Hades' domain and ask her, because I like to be sure of these things.

They weren't all horrible, I suppose. Actually, sometimes I hung out with Nemesis, who was amusing when she flirted with me—she wasn't going to get anywhere, hence my amusement, but she could be quite funny when she tried. Of course, later on, when Aristotle wrote all that stuff about her, she got above herself and became quite unendurable. And later on, when Jehovah collared them and put them all into the Hell of Lucifer, she was one of the minor deities who cut a deal and became a saint or an angel or something. And pretended she didn't know me when we bumped into each other in the back corridors of Heaven…

At any rate, there he was in my new place of power, bold and unannounced, the Mousegod, the Lord of the Muses, the Bringer of Plague, mentioning the Titans in a vaguely menacing way and talking of reasoning together about his lord and master's desire to make Valhalla into Olympus.

"I am surprised," I said, "that you managed to sneak past my friend and watchman Heimdall, given the problems most of us are having moving through Shadow, these days."

"Ah,"—many gods would be embarrassed, but not he—"we came by another route, and took our time… But enough of that. I am sorry to find you indisposed, as I say. You speak of an enemy?"

"The oldest," I said, "Deviser of the Rituals and the first to murder according to them, the trickster and corrupter. My guess is that he led old Saturn astray back in the dawn of things, as he did others back then, like Cernunnos the Horned God of the forests and his mate, the Witch. Gods you never met, or not in their full power because most of them I killed before you and your pantheon came into strength. The one who killed my sisters in the dawn of the time, and more recently corrupted and betrayed Odin One-Eye."

"Where is he, that the armies of Olympus might stand against him?" The boy had not been this arrogant when young.

"He doesn't do confrontation. He does shadows," I said. "He made this mistake of trying conclusions with your liberator Emma, when she was still a mortal without power and it did not go well for him."

"She is formidable," Apollo admitted, "from what little I saw of her. One of the reasons we didn't stick around in former Hell."

"And she is now its judge and co-ruler. Also, inadvertently, a god, but at least it has not gone to her head unlike some I could name."

And here they came in, as I spoke, crowding into the back of my throne-room and trying to swagger as if we should fear them, the Titans self-shrunk to get in through the door and Zeus to the fore, his beard oiled and perfumed, his chest bare and muscular, the prick of which he was so excessively proud strutting behind a loin cloth.

No Hades, I noticed, and no Poseidon; Ares, though and Hephaisthon whom the Romans called Vulcan, and Herakles. And the women—Hera, Zeus's wife, and Athena, of whom I was actually wary, and Artemis who had copied so much from me. Neither Hermes nor Dionysus, which meant nothing save that they were not serious about a fight and putting their fighters to the fore as a threat.

Aphrodite hung back from the confrontation as one would expect—and blew me a kiss.

And from behind my throne, Josette arrived. She bent and whispered in my ear.

"I saw this lot in the distance on my way to the Just City and thought I'd better come back and help. I didn't bring Mary Ann back—a bit too lippy—but Brünnhilde and Gram came because they love a ruck."

She took her place at my side.

"I've got this." Apollo waved a placatory hand, but Ares and Herakles seized him by the arms and pulled him away to the sides, not too gently. Clearly, he was not being left alone to do what he does best.

"Why are we parleying?" Zeus roared, a bully as ever. "The Huntress is maimed and no longer to be feared in battle. Helpless."

He buffeted Apollo on the cheek so that a great red mark grew there and then strode towards me, his short lethal sword drawn.

I am the mistress of all arms, including the knives I wear in my hair that fools take for mere decoration. And that I now threw, one, two, three, four. Slicing off an ear as one spun, two hitting him by the hilt either side of that ridiculous phallus, and one straight into his right eye. Which might heal, in time.

Zeus squealed like a pig.

"If you want the throne of Valhalla," I said calmly, "you must take the maiming that goes with it… Though perhaps not the wisdom Odin traded for his eye. Save this, the Huntress is never helpless."

The Dog growled, the Wolf howled, the Horses whinnied, the Serpent opened a maw that was suddenly for a moment the size of the room, the lady Hel grinned a skull's grin and all the warriors who stood at my side beat their weapons against the dais or shouted war-cries.

Alexander stepped forward to where Zeus lay in pain.

"My mother, whose morals were not all they might be and who was too fond of dark strong wine, told me once that you had taken her on the altar of your temple when she wandered there at night.

I had rather been the son of Philip of Macedon, who raised and trained me, and whose death at the hands of his lover my mother engineered."

He prodded the god with a foot. "Some call me god, or demigod, but I am content to be a man and the Conqueror. Are you my father? I would wish to know, for I would not want to commit parricide through ignorance."

Josette stepped down too and took him by the arm, speaking calmly. "Brother—for I regard you as such for that you spent so much time inside my head—be calm. If he ravished your mother, he has been punished for it by his sojourn as a prisoner in the Hell of Lucifer, and here now at the hands of our Queen."

Apollo inspected her, puzzled. "The Conqueror I know, because he worshipped at my shrine on Delos and heard my oracle at Delphi. But who are you?" He reached across and tugged at a lock of her hair, which he sniffed. Alexander moved to reprove him for his presumption, but Josette's hand grew firmer on his arm. "Goddess, clearly, yet there is only one of whom your scent reminds me, but he has no daughter that I know of."

"Nor does he," she laughed, "but he is my father nonetheless, whether he like it or no. As one day, but not yet, we shall find out, my brother and I, before his throne. Perhaps to claim it from him, but peacefully as is our wont."

Alexander joined her laughter. "Know Olympians that we, here, are kings and queens in our own right, but serve the Huntress, Queen of Shadow. I, the Conqueror who no longer has a realm, and she, the hidden heir of Heaven."

And my other allies cheered and howled their allegiance.

Ares and Herakles bowed low to Apollo and then to me; there had been a shift of power. They picked their king—if he was that still—up from the floor and he leaned moaning against his son and brother as they held him upright.

Apollo returned to his place at the foot of my throne dais and Hera joined him, curtseying as formally as if this were Versailles or the

Forbidden City. She glanced at Apollo, who took a single backwards pace and glanced at her respectfully. She reached out and stroked the red mark on his cheek in a way that was not entirely motherly— Mother of the Gods she might be, but not his.

"My apologies, Huntress—or rather, I should say, Queen of Shadow, but we have known each other a long time, though never as well as I should have liked. My apologies for my brute of a husband— I spend so much time apologising for him, you have no idea—and you were right to punish him. For though we are not yet formally your guests, still you were talking to our emissary and either the rules of embassy or those of hospitality apply, even though you have not yet offered us food and drink, nor have we requested them. Which Apollo here should have done, silly boy. Anyway, Zeus should not have acted as he did—we come here, well, not as suppliants to you, exactly, because we were not aware of what ever has happened here."

There are two things that you need to know about Hera of Olympus: one is that her communications with you will always make your eyes glaze over and make you agree to anything just so that she will stop babbling at you, and the other is that she is not a fool, not even slightly, just a goddess married to an untrustworthy brute who would never do anything she wanted if he had any idea how much she manipulates him.

I cut her short. "I offer guest friendship in this my hall of Valhalla, and food and drink for those who need it. And healing for your husband, though he does not deserve it."

I nodded to Josette, who laid a hand on the Thunderer's maimed face as I spoke but did nothing to heal his other hurts.

With her other hand, she waved and there were small plates of delicate pastries at the feet of each of the gods and a small glass of water each.

I had wondered whether she would give them bread, fishes and wine, but obviously she was going to go on keeping them guessing for a while longer.

But the next thing that happened was something I had not even begun to expect, which is that Zeus stood up straight, bowed to Josette as to a great benefactor, then turned, walked formally and steadily towards his wife and knelt at her feet, raising the hem of her robe and kissing it.

"My love," he said in a voice that was recognizably that of the god I had known for so many thousands of years, and yet somehow a voice I had never heard before, "my love, I am so sorry for everything."

She reached down, incredulously, and stroked the fold of flesh behind his remaining ear—Josette had not yet restored the one I had taken from him, but perhaps it needed time to grow back; I am not especially acquainted with such matters.

Zeus stood and looked around at his subjects—the gods of Olympus and their kin and servants, the Titans, who all looked back at him in puzzlement. Then he stood, turned to the monsters that stood among the Olympians, multi-armed and snake-headed and single-eyed, and he knelt again.

"Brothers," he said and then howled. Many of the Titans had not the gift of speech or its understanding, but nonetheless they knew what he was about and howled in unison with him.

One of the largest and most monstrous of them—so strange that it hurt the eye to look upon him—reached down a paw and drew Zeus to his feet.

Leaning upon that paw, he addressed his monster kin. "I know,"— his voice was solemn, resonant and weirdly humbled—"I have wronged many of you, and so many others. I will do what I can to make amends. It may be that the best I can do is absent myself from your lives and that I offer to do. I would prefer, though, that we work together with these good people and atone as best we can by helping them fight the evil manifest in the world as well as that within ourselves…"

"What did you do?" Alexander asked suspiciously.

Josette's face was innocent enough almost to deceive me.

"I healed him. There was no point in merely removing the pain of the punishments our Queen had justly inflicted on him; there were other pains too, things done to him in childhood by his monster father, whom, if he were here, I would try to relieve of his pain too."

"This healing," Alexander pressed on, even more suspicious, "did you ever do that to me? When we were younger, and I had intruded into your head. It would have been fair enough if you had, I suppose; I had tried to steal your body."

Josette shook her head. "Brother, you healed yourself. You always had kindness within you, you know, which is why you spent so much time drunk on wine, lust and battle. In order to numb it. I learned so much of what I can do now by observing how you learned from watching me, with those temptations largely removed by death."

"But I am still a warrior." Now he was almost pleading.

"Alexander," she said, "we are all warriors one way or another, but these days you do not fight for glory or empire. You have not fought for those things for a long time—you rescued the wild damned and turned them into an army of free men and women. And now you stand alongside me, and the Just City, and Mara, in what may be the last battle for right."

She turned to Zeus. "Patriarch of Olympus, I have drawn much poison from your mind and body. I know I have been more fortunate in my father than you, but I recognize much of the grief of your childhood. I left it there, but not the festering around it… Many years ago, you met a man or god who appeared to you as shadow, did you not?"

Zeus looked confused for a few long moments, and then shuddered as men and gods do when they wake—not from sleep but from lies, deception and selfish folly– "How could I have forgotten? He offered to soothe the pain and he gave me seeds steeped in wine, black poppy and morning glory, and Libyan garlic that flowers as the sand blows, and he said that one who had suffered as I had was owed, was owed all that the world could give me. And how could I have forgotten, and why did I listen, and…"

There is a difference between knowing the bald fact that the enemy has been everywhere and has been the source of all corruption, and hearing his role in the life of someone I had known for a long time and never thought of as yet another of his victims.

I looked at Josette, and at Alexander, and they both looked back at me, and nodded.

"He is the great corruptor," I explained, "the enemy of all women, men and gods—perhaps of life itself—who takes virtue and bends it awry and takes grief and turns it to poison, and who taught the Rituals at the dawn of time, and whose schemes come at last, we think, to fatal maddening culmination. We do not know what he plans, or how to resist him—I came to Valhalla for answers and found another whom he had bent to his will. Will you join us?"

The father of Olympus looked in consultation to his family, his friends, his monster kin and waited for their silent nods before nodding at last to me.

Alexander, deprived of a promising fight, grinned sardonically, and then frowned as if struck by a new thought. "Speaking of the resentful one, when our friend Emma freed you from the dungeons of Lucifer, you had the gods of Canaan with you, whom he had overthrown, enslaved and at the last grown bored with. I notice that they are not here?"

The good thing about having the best and brightest as my warband, I realized yet again, was that I did not always have to be the one to think of important things that I had absolutely forgotten. I am often not at my best, and it might have taken me hours to ask that very important question.

Zeus shrugged. "We parted company soon after we were freed. We had struck up camp some way from the ruins of Dis and suddenly there were groves of fruit marching towards us across the land, and flowers underfoot and Aserath walked among us, grown vast and menacingly fertile, and she waved us to silence and told us that she and the Judge Emma would find us a place if we wished it, but that we might prefer to be elsewhere than under the thumb of their benevolence. She turned to her brothers and sisters, the Baals and Astartes of her homeland, and embraced them one at a time, and they grumbled at her because she had been one of them, but had tricked her way out of bondage and was now grown great. And she whispered to them that they should be glad their sister had prospered, and that if they had a grievance, well, it was with Jehovah, and with Lucifer, now stripped of his power and sent into exile…"

He laughed. "I have a wife who can persuade me of most things, but you, my love, said afterwards that, had she time, and if she trusted me around that dragonish whore, she could learn much from Aserath, who took a mob of jealous and disgruntled relatives and set them off after someone else. It was prettily done. If you like that sort of thing."

Zeus spoke with the embarrassment of one who has found old vices no longer pleasing and yet remembers how sweet they used to taste on the tongue and lips.

The gods of Canaan after a Lucifer who no longer had Jehovah's protection—that was going to be an interesting situation but no immediate concern of mine. And it was exactly the sort of petty feud between my potential allies that the Adversary doubtless found it amusing to foment and which distracted us from whatever else he was doing.

To immediate business then.

"Zeus." I spoke to him as an equal even though he now knew me his mistress without our having had to spell it out. "You mention that the Adversary—as you now know him to have been—fed you potions that helped cloud your mind and bring you to wrath. He has refined them further along with weapons of destruction and corruption that took my leg. We seek his workshops, which we believe to be somewhere in Shadow. I don't suppose you have heard anything? We had hoped to ask Odin One-Eye but he was already too far gone in corruption and depravity."

There was a silence.

"So she killed him," Alexander explained.

"Not I, in the end, but one of my human allies. A dead woman, whom I had failed to save, and who saved us all from what Odin had become. Gods can die and a single woman can kill them. It is well to be aware of that fact."

There is a sensation which I remember from my young girlhood that I am told people now describe as someone walking on your grave, though we had not named it so back then. A shudder went round the room, a shudder that was that sensation.

Gods do not relish being reminded that they are only long-lived—that none of us is truly immortal. Except perhaps our adversary, though I have always hoped to prove otherwise.

I reverted to my earlier subject "The weapons? You saw no workshops in your travels?"

Apollo smiled. "We saw no workshops in the ways we travelled."

There was something he was not telling me. "You took your time, whichever way you came,"—I spoke as slowly as I was thinking—"because it was months before I came here, some of which I spent in Mundane London with Emma, who left former Hell sometime after you did. This was not the first place in Shadow that you called, and tried to find a home, and you left some of your company there, alive or dead. So who's missing?"

I let that hang. I had seen Emma and Caroline do this—at once part of the process of working things out and a means of intimidating people who thought you already knew things that they were keeping from you.

"How did you get to the rest of Shadow from Hell?"

The answer was obvious to me the moment I posed it—was this what it was like being clever?

Looking round the room at my companions and at Apollo—he and Loki and Josette were smiling as if they had always known I could do this sort of thing if I set my mind to it. A good reminder, if I needed one, that being Queen of Shadow was being first among equals, by default.

"Lucifer had tunnels, tunnels everywhere. And…" I looked at the mute large and many-handed Titans. "He had you build them for him, before caging you with the rest."

There were things I should have investigated sooner, though I had been busy at the time.

"One tunnel ran deep under here, deep enough to pass under the rivers that surround us—and that tunnel somehow goes—but not in the direction you came from—to one of the dark alchemy workshops, because that is how Odin All-Father took part in the trade and why the rats we killed in the cellars were so strange."

I had my audience—I knew things that they had not.

"So first of all, I think, you delivered Poseidon and his court to some shore of the sea of Shadow because he wishes to take up his old trade. Well, it will be interesting to see how that works out—I am sure that there are other deposed pantheons who had a sea god who may wish to try conclusions with him over that, not to mention great old sea beasts like the Leviathan, which I and my friend Josette here once encountered… Good luck with that."

I looked around a little harder.

"No Dionysus and no Hermes—I think the crucial person missing there is not the god of wine but his wife."

I watched their faces for tells. Juno had a card-player's stillness and Apollo simply looked away; there was a pulse in his neck that I remembered from Troy. Zeus drummed the little finger of his left hand very gently—I had seen that before.

I continued. "Now she has some experience with tunnels, having grown up in the labyrinth of Minos her father. Her husband to keep her company; Hermes to fetch help in case of need; and…"

I looked to where Athena was hanging back a little, her hand busy behind her back. "I remember Arachne and her fate," I said, looking her straight in the eye. "You are the goddess of wisdom, true, but also of weaving. So where is it?"

Athena tried to look innocent.

"You can't have brought it up from the cellars with you; that would be too obvious and the Titans would be tangling their feet."

They seemed about to tell me everything when a red bird fluttered up to the rafters and cooed to you, its siblings Thought and Memory.

There was a low snarling from behind the throng of Titans, who in spite of their size and monstrousness pulled aside like elephants startled by a mouse as a medium size handbag strutted between them, proud as a leopard.

Caroline followed her lover's bag to the centre of the room, turned and curtseyed to the assembled gods and monsters, then strutted over to where I sat turning her back to them as if she saw assembled pantheons every day of the week.

"I say, Mara," Caroline said, pecking me on the cheek, "did you know there are tunnels all the way here from Former Hell? And, poor love, what has happened to your leg? Hi, doggo!" Garm strutted over, shrinking down as he strutted so that he could rub himself against her leg, barking enthusiastically.

She looked around the great hall. "Valhalla then? Looks pretty much as you'd expect, I suppose, but then, I can't stand Wagner anyway. Hi Alex, hi Josette, who's the blonde—some Valkyrie or other?" She sniffed and then blew her nose rather loudly on a lace handkerchief I could swear I had not seen her take out of a pocket. "I see you've got that red dust stuff here—it's not good for my allergies frankly. I'd have expected rather more horned helmets than I see here, and women going hoio-to-ho."

She clearly wasn't going to let the Wagner joke drop. Persisting with the same joke was one of the things that made me believe she really was Lillit's avatar.

"And who are all these other people? Greeks?! Whatever happened to, 'I hunt alone'?"

Behind her, the Titans started to stamp their feet in rage and the expressions on the Olympians' faces shifted, varying from shock to suspicion and blind rage, most of it directed at Caroline, some of it at me. She was clearly utterly unaware of this, until she turned round and saw them; she turned back to me in bafflement and annoyance. "Eh?" she said, "who pissed on their chips?"

Apollo suddenly had a short, wicked blade in his hand.

I glared at him, hoping that would be enough, and he sheathed it, muttering, "You have to admit, Mara, it looks very suspicious. Lucifer's bird, Lucifer's co-conspirator."

From the rafters Tsassiporah cooed down petulantly. "Not Lucifer's, you silly gods, not for months. I have a kinder better mistress now. Emma who freed you, beloved of Caroline here, whom you would be best advised not to harm in any way. Because that handbag is a killing machine and what lives inside it is not to be trifled with either."

The Olympians continued to stare at the bird stony-faced. It drew its neck up stiffly, fluffed up its feathers and darted down the ramp into the cellar. The bag stayed at Caroline's feet: it managed to convey an air of menace sufficient that gods and Titans stepped back well away from it.

"That's as may be." Apollo looked at the other Olympians for support as he shrugged in a vaguely conciliatory manner. "But the bird used to come down with Lucifer when he gloated at us in his dungeon and we didn't get any sense from them of any compassion for our plight. And this woman, this Caroline; she was down there with him, plotting the war with Heaven. Telling him he had powerful friends who would send him weapons."

I cut him off. "That won't have been Caroline. Caroline is an avatar of my sister Lillit, but Lillit seems to be playing some sort of game of her own-"

And now Caroline cut me off. "Not that simple. There's a reason why I'm here and not with Emma. Or my lovely friend Dawn, whom you met in London, Mara. It may have been me—after Lucifer kidnapped me, I don't remember a thing. I'm pretty certain that sometimes Lillit takes over and wears me like a glove and I can't do anything to stop her, so I don't think I should be around anyone I love."

Alexander looked pensive. "When I met Caroline wandering in the foothills of Hell, she seemed pretty much the person we see here. Arrogant, amusing—but I couldn't understand how she could possibly have escaped Lucifer and wandered through a war unscathed. So I never trusted her, but I couldn't fault whom she seemed to be—except that later, she had no memory of our meeting… So, yes, like a glove."

Josette stuck up her hand helpfully. "I spent a lot of time in Caro's head, and I never saw anyone else hanging round in there, but—your sister, the Quintessence—if anyone could stop me noticing their fingerprints, I guess it would be her."

"And now Caroline is here," I added, "and we know there might be a problem—well, now we know. And if Lillit turns up in there, I'm sure we all have things we would like to ask her."

I said that, but it wasn't entirely true. I had questions all right, but I liked Caroline, and if Lillit was in there then Caroline might not be real at all. And if Lillit had answers to my questions, they might not be answers I would like.

"Myself, what I want to know,"—Caroline had her own questions—"what I want to know is, who built all these tunnels? I'd say giant moles or earthworms, but they don't put down railway tracks or stick in handy secret doors? Because my friend Emma has a big construction job going on…"

Everyone was suddenly very interested, especially Zeus. "Building works?" He nodded to the larger Titans. "Well, we hadn't meant to go back there, but my cousins here built the tunnels. I don't trust you one little bit, let's be clear, but we do owe Emma a favour."

"The goddess Emma." Caroline, clearly stung by their distrust and disrespect, intended to demand punctiliousness. And I thoroughly approved, as well as being intrigued.

She turned to Josette. "Remember how you got Emma to Hell in the first place? In the lift? That got broken in the dogfights over Hell? Well, the cable is still there, and it presumably connects to some apartment block in Berlin."

That was the star I had seen above the mountains. I should have guessed.

"So anyway, Emma's trying to keep the peace between damned and demons with competitive ziggurat building… And, yes, like the big guy over there, Zeus is it?, it occurs to me that our large friends here—who owe her a favour—could save us all many months of hard work. They probably know more about what they'd be doing—I mean, my beloved means well and she has got Judas to advise her, but I think he's probably out of his depth because I've seen him asking the Recording Angel about Babel and taking notes. Not a good sign if you ask me."

She looked round the room, There was a slightly pleading note in her voice as if she were desperate that everyone trust her and aware there were good reasons why they should not. "If I were Lillit, really, right now," she asked no one in particular, "and up to no good, would I be being this helpful?"

Alexander pulled a wry face. "Probably, in fact. When she was being you, she was terribly good at telling me things I didn't already know about asymmetric warfare. Which, now I actually know the real you, should have told me something was up—but I didn't back then, so… And it was very good advice."

"Talking of advice," Caroline said, "I'm sure that everyone's already butted in on this, but you really need to get that leg fixed, Mara dear, now we can get back and forth to Former Hell."

That did change things, I supposed.

"You may not like hell-flesh, but I have a whole body made of it which I find quite serviceable. I mean, the only people I've met who say it smells a bit are goblins, and who cares what they think?"

Then Hepaisthos piped up from the back of the room. "No, who needs to use that stuff when I could make you something very nice

130

out of gold and platinum. Diamond bearings, orichalcum gears. Though it would take a couple of days to set up a proper forge out back because there's no way I'm using Wayland's cast-offs if they're even here. And where is that bloody old tinkerer anyway…"

He rabbited on and on and I hardly noticed what he was saying. I had not permitted myself to feel any self-pity for a while, but it struck me as unjust that I was maimed after all these years and dependent on all these beings that had been frightened of me for thousands of years, and suddenly I was very angry. At the enemy and at the world.

And then, just as suddenly, I was in pain again. My leg felt as if it were on fire, but not the destructive power of corrosion.

Something else.

Also a Creative Urge

Hell, 2004

The ziggurat had reached its tenth storey and the demon teams had started singing human worksongs, so Emma felt she could leave the teams to building their own spirit of not killing or torturing each other anymore and go and eat some breakfast in Aserath's pavilion. She wanted to see how Morgan was getting on with her new eye— also, while Tsassiporah was away, it made sense to chat to one of its siblings and find out a bit more about that family.

Tsassi was loquacious, even garrulous, but some subjects seemed to be off limits. Why they'd chosen to bond with Lucifer back at the beginning and just what terrible things they had done together. And how many other birds there even were. She knew it was something to do with Atlantis and she could have asked Mara about it during the months they were all living in Brick Lane, but there were always other things to talk about.

And she missed Mara now, but not as much as she missed Caroline.

Before, when Lucifer carried Caro off, it had seemed easy and soluble—find the bad guy, beat the bad guy, rescue the girl. It hadn't worked out quite like that, but near enough except for thousands of years judging the damned that she wasn't going to let herself remember because she didn't want to be that old and cold.

This time, though… Maybe they really had lost each other and would never be together again like they'd been, in Brick Lane.

And it wasn't Dawn, she knew that because Caro had left Dawn behind. Brought her to safety in Former Hell and then just left her, to go and have adventures.

So that was another thing she had to do. Spend time with Dawn. Apart from anything else, Dawn was one of the few people in Hell she really liked.

Aserath was a work colleague and quite fun to be around, but she was self-sufficient to a degree that was a bit appalling. Perhaps it was the triple aspect thing. If you could be three people—well, beings, given that one was a dragon and one was several sizes of flirty slut and one a source of a frankly limited repertoire of vines, arbours and crops…

Emma wanted grass under foot that was green and not purple; she sometimes felt that she would kill for the sight of a basic British daisy rather than red and purple bells that smelled vaguely of bedrooms after sex and which rustled lubriciously in moments of stillness.

That was it, Aserath's main problem, not much imagination really. Emma felt like a bitch for thinking it, but most of her colleagues were a bit dull. Judas—all that entirely justified guilt and neediness. Vretil—well, maybe all angels were like that, slightly plastic good looks and strong work ethic and no capacity to talk anything but shop.

She really hadn't noticed before, but the thing about being the divine judge of what had been the Hell of Lucifer was that there was nothing to do on a Saturday night except the usual sitting around on couches eating grapes and nectarines. Especially now they were marooned here and you couldn't go downstairs for a saltbeef bagel or down the street for a mediocre curry.

But oh god! Clearly this Morrigan creature thought himself as much a character as his more loquacious sibling and if he had pecked Morgan's eye out, he clearly had a nasty temper as well. Maybe a couple of centuries of mindless flockitude would have adjusted his temperament, but Emma doubted it.

She turned a corner in the maze of vine-stakes that were her nearest approach to Aserath's arbour and there he was, sitting on a stump. Dawn and the Empress Tiffany sat on the purple grass listening to him.

"Say what you like about all these fancy modern wars, the which I seem to have missed, those 30 years in High Germany and Bohemia were some of the best battlefields for carrion since Rome fell. All those bodies and barrels and barrels of sausages. You can tell this is still Hell really,"—he cast a beady sardonic eye in Emma's direction—"I mean, saving your divine presence I'm sure, but you can't get a decent sausage here, can you."

Emma had taken to keeping a small quantity of hell-flesh about her person so that she could do small running repairs when people got chafing from ropes or squashed a finger. She pinched off a chunk of it, thought it into a hot saveloy, and tossed it sizzling into the air. The Morrigan caught it adroitly in his beak and the Empress Tiffany clapped her hands in glee. "Best I can do, I'm afraid." Emma apologised.

"Normally," he cawed, "I'd scorn to touch hell-flesh, but given as we're on short commons, and my lady Morgana can't exactly fetch fancies from court kitchens right now… I thanks you kindly, Emma, allknowing, all-merciful ruler of Hell what is changing its ways. And what can I do for you?"

"Nothing particular," Emma said. "Just, you're Tsassi's hatchmate and Morgan's companion, and you're liable to be in my domain for a while and I thought I should get to know you. And maybe find out about Atlantis, because it seems to have been crucial and formative."

The Morrigan sighed. "By the time I was even a chick, it was pretty much over. Mara, Morgan—who was Hekkat back then— and Star and Nameless—who go by Lucifer and Jehovah these days—and my parent what had the city built around them, and the other phoenix… It was a huge fuckup and the city sank, and Tsassi, me, Ghost and the other two got made as a legacy and curse by the Bird afore he died and that's that. Odin has the other two but they're Mara's when she wants them."

He gave a meaningful sniff. "This magic dust smells of old One-Eye a bit, so…"

Dawn had the starry eyes of a little girl on Christmas day: she had kept the faith and believed that the Truth was out there and things she had never quite dared to want to believe kept on turning out to be real. Which was sweet, but just now Emma needed her crisp, cynical and cutting edge, so thought she'd better be a bit mean.

"I know what you're thinking. Lots of things are true, but! Dawn, remember. There are no UFOs."

Dawn looked very slightly crestfallen.

The Empress Tiffany looked quizzically down her long straight nose. "And what," she asked, "is a UFO?"

"Strange whirly things in the sky," Emma explained, "possibly full of little grey people."

Tiffany nodded. "Ah. One of my abbeys had a copyist who kept drawing things like that…" She paused for effect and Dawn perked up a bit, but her face fell as Tiffany went on. "He said he'd seen them in the sky, but it turned out that he'd been eating the bad bread and then several of his fingers dropped off so he couldn't copy any more. The abbot put him on latrine duty and he died of a flux. He was little and grey, so you got that much right."

The Morrigan cawed repeatedly, chattering like a jay, tossing his head so that his eyes glinted. After a second Emma realised he was laughing.

"Courtiers and their little games of power. Seen it so much I has, down the years. Even Morgan lets it happen, though. Cause it's always a distraction."

Without warning his caws ratcheted from laughter to alarm, and with a flick of her hand she hardly knew of until it was done Emma surrounded the four of them with a dome of sudden steel.

Not a moment too soon because suddenly their safe place was surrounded by nine men in dark uniforms crouching as if at the end of a leap from a fast train.

Why steel, she thought and instantly remembered hopefully that she had never seen the corrosion guns work on metal, only on flesh and cloth. What would be the point of being a goddess if sometimes you didn't just know things, like that the men from Burnedover still mostly looked like bad xeroxes of Reverend Black and that they were standing around her dome with weapons drawn not quite knowing what to do next.

So she pulled her own gun out of its pocket dimension, opened a twelve foot by two inches slit in the surface of the dome for ten seconds, and with a quick spray of fire took all nine of their fool heads off. Well, mostly--there were the odd inch or so difference in height and one of them was standing on a tussock.

She offered a quick prayer for their souls if magic clones have them, though she didn't see any, even at the moment of death. None had ever come before her for judging, but maybe they had some arrangement to be sent elsewhere.

Very fast.

Still she prayed, because she didn't know and some other god might.

She couldn't perceive any other interlopers immediately around and took the steel dome out of existence. Dawn and Tiffany had sensibly hit the ground the moment the Morrigan had started making noise.

"You two," she barked, "gather up those dead men's weapons, take one each and run the others over to Aserath and the others. You, bird, stop picking brains out of that severed skull cap, and come with me."

Then she thought a moment. It was a magic bird after all. "I don't suppose you can manage a gun with an opposable talon or something? No? Fair enough, I'm sure you can make yourself useful in other ways."

She thought things through as she ran back towards the ziggurat.

Obviously Burnedover had sent in kill squads, and it was worrying that they had known so precisely where she was, and they'd probably sent kill squads elsewhere and she hoped people had reacted fast enough—but, couple of goddesses, renegade part of the Trinity, a major angel… They could handle themselves surely and she'd sent reinforcements.

Worrying they'd been trained to slow down from Mundane speed to Hell's newer slower time. Or maybe that was the dust.

Anyway, the kill squads were probably a distraction. There had to be a main objective—and the sound of ordinary gunfire up ahead confirmed what it was.

They had sent a squad with alchemical weapons after her, but ordinary guns after demons and the former damned. Which would incapacitate but not destroy people made of hell-flesh. Which meant a limited supply of alchemical guns and they only needed to knock her work teams down long enough to…

The ziggurat loomed into view, already thirteen stories high, and the people and demons strung along its ramps weren't singing work songs any more, they were screaming and sobbing and praying. Praying to her—she could feel their prayers flowing into her like a warming shower of nourishment. Men in black uniforms were holding them at gunpoint at every level and others were snapping thick plastic collars around their necks. At ground level, they were rounding the work gangs up, beating them unconscious one person or demon at a time and dragging them against the ziggurat to lie in stacks like fuel for a bonfire. A couple of men were spraying them with something from a cannister.

"Bugger this," the Morrigan cawed, "I've been in bits. It's no fun. Coming? Your funeral," and flapped off.

Or rather tried to, because the moment he got to more than one and a half head-heights, he coughed hard and started a nosedive that he only turned into a half-way decent landing at the last moment.

He barked up a long worm of rusty phlegm, then ruffled his feathers up round his neck in disgust.

"You're in charge of this place," he croaked," do something about this damned dust." He didn't try to fly any more but stalked off with a posture of disdain, his tail feathers flared behind him.

One man was standing a little way off, holding what looked like a big chunky old-fashioned mobile phone. He looked more like Reverend Black than most of them. Almost like he could do more than follow simple instructions.

He was still yards away and Emma wasn't sure of the range of her weapon, so she contented herself with shouting 'Oi! You! Whatever your name is."

He nodded to her without bothering to look her in the face, his movement both dismissive and oddly suave. "I gave up my name when I joined the Legion." And his voice was oddly calm. "And my face."

Oh, thought Emma, not all magic clones then. She choked off the thought.

"You're Emma Jones," he shouted, looking round and recognizing her. His face shifted in a moment from icy contemplation of imminent atrocity to blind fury. "You murdered our beloved leader Reverend Black, whose face I wear in his memory."

Pointing out it had been self-defence really wasn't going to help. Still, while he was monologueing at her, he wasn't pressing buttons.

And, oh dear, he was wearing one of those plastic collars too and so, Emma could now see, were most of the Burnedover people.

"You have been justly confined to the Hell of Lucifer along with demons and the damned. It is the will of God that you stay here. We have come to cast down this second Tower of Babel—"

"Actually, sweetie," she cut in, aware that this was getting worrying and that she was losing her temper, "I took on this place as a favour to your God…"

But then he pressed the button. And he flew apart and so did everyone else, human and demon, that was wearing a collar, and the people stacked around the base of the ziggurat burst into red and green flame, and the bottom layer of huge stone bricks started to crumble and above them where hostages and hostage-takers had blown apart huge flakes of stone were coming away and the whole thing was listing and tipping and leaning and toppling and—

Cold flame ripped wildfire through Emma's veins and very quietly she said "Enough."

She should have taken the shot. She should have taken the fucking shot.

She took a breath deep as if she were inhaling the world and when she breathed out once, all of the flames snuffed out as if she were a child and they were the candles of a cake and when she breathed out twice, she was looking across the mountains of Hell, not because she was flying but because she was suddenly the mountains' sister vast as they; with the third breath out she reached down and patted the breaking ziggurat into shape as if it were a sandcastle that were breaking at her feet, and with the fourth breath out she reached to the blocks of stone and heaps of spoil that had been prepared waiting for use and patted them into place higher and higher to a point…

A point that was not yet high enough and so she reached up with her fifth breath out and delicately tugged the broken cable down— delicately that it not break again—and knotted it around that point. She started to feel emptied, and so with sixth and seventh breaths out she took the spirits of the humans and demons who had been murdered towards Phlegethon to be put back into hell-flesh. And the commander of the strike force, but his soul alone.

Still no sign of the clones' souls. Except…Wisps? Maybe shreds?

And then she had no more breath to breathe out and she took an ordinary human breath and then she shrank back to herself who had been for moments vaster than all Titans and fell into a sleep or swoon.

A little later she realised that she was cold, that she was naked, and that around her, kneeling, were those members of the work gangs who had survived. Oh well, that was something. She hadn't got everyone killed. Just far too many. She should have known that he'd be watching, that there was always a next move.

Almost always… She smiled in vicious memory of Hollywood. Not that time, and probably not this.

There was one thing she could do, right now, because Caroline had taught her.

She summoned new clothes, not her usual slobbing around another day in Former Hell sweatpants and comfortable sweater, but leather trousers, and black velvet Docs, and a ripped Patti Smith t-shirt like one she'd seen Polly wear and a jacket with a high collar and knife-fighter cuffs. Leathers that shone dark as mirrored night from the skin of some beast she had seen in dreams.

Vengeance clothes.

She needed mirror-shades. She made them.

Where was her gun?

She looked around for it. She must have dropped it when she mysteriously grew—and what had that been about? She couldn't do that; it was serious God stuff. She hadn't seen Jehovah do anything like that. Invasion by maths concepts? He stands around wibbling. War with Lucifer? He sends in angels.

She needed to talk to Aserath. Eating the Dukes of Hell had been something in that line but then Aserath was a dragon too.

She saw the short snubby barrel of her gun. A worshipper was kneeling on it. Looked awfully uncomfortable. Emma quite liked being worshipped but she wasn't having people mortify the flesh for her…

"Could you move, please?"

She stood over him. He opened his eyes, which had been closed in prayer, and fainted at being spoken to by Emma, luckily falling in a direction away from it so that she could pick it up without troubling him further. He'd wet himself in terror. A kind deity would do something, but Emma was his goddess not his mummy and he could clean his own mess up.

She added a side pocket to her jacket, put the gun back into its own little universe and put the universe into her pocket. Of course it was always where she needed it to be, but it felt better to actually reach down and draw it.

We are prisoners of our attitudes to these things and she'd twice sort of not been fast enough. That had to change, because it felt as if things were moving into a new cruder phase. Either Berin was close to his winning moves, or perhaps they weren't entirely screwing things up and he was getting worried. But more probably the first of those two things.

She left her worshippers to their devotions. They had formed a large circle, some kneeling and some prostrate, which parted for her as she picked her way through to the edge, where she turned and gave a small regal wave, which she decided halfway through to modulate into a rather more expansive blessing.

Some of the fruit trees at the side of the path she was walking past had slightly withered fruit hanging down and their leaves were starting to brown, but the colours were still bright and there was still a gently sensual rustling to the movement of a slightly scented breeze through the branches. She thought nothing of it yet but merely half noted it.

Halfway to the arbour she met Dawn, walking briskly towards her and rattling on, breathy with her excitement and her hurry.

"I only half saw—I didn't know you could do that. I mean, I get you're a goddess. But you were huge. And you finished the ziggurat in like seconds when it was about to fall down and…"

"I didn't know I could do that either. I find it a bit worrying." Emma realised that this sounded a bit like false modesty but that she didn't care. "So anyway," she went on, "enough about me. What happened with you?"

Dawn looked slightly guilty, slightly smug. "Oh," she said, almost casually, "there was a second kill squad, when we got to Aserath's arbour, but she was wrapping the whole area in vines and briars that they got totally tangled in. And they weren't expecting us. So I asked them to surrender from behind a tree, and they started shooting at the tree, so Tiff killed them all. She was behind another tree, and she was really angry because where she's from, if you don't surrender, you die. If you attack someone who is asking you to surrender, you die. And there were a whole bunch of other rules she was shouting about but by then she'd killed all of them so I didn't pay much attention because around then things went bang and we had to duck and cover…"

Dawn paused for breath and effect.

"And then suddenly, when we looked back, you were there, huge and naked in the sky. And Tiffany said she really hadn't fully understood that you are a goddess until then. Also, she said she'd totally do you… but what's more important, is Aserath."

"She's wonderful," Emma said, "but the judge of former Hell doesn't screw the help. Now, Aserath. What happened? I thought you said Tiffany killed them all." She really didn't want to have to cope with another disaster.

"No, this was afterwards. Once the soldiers were dead, all the vines and briars that were holding them let go for a second so they dropped, and then they wrapped themselves around them like pythons or something and pulled them into the ground or digested them or something, but anyway they just weren't there any more–"

She paused, whether out of respect or just dramatically Emma really couldn't say. "So when we got to the arbour, she was asleep in her chair, and Morgan was chafing her wrists like someone in a Victorian novel and Vretil had pulled a feather out of his wing and Judas was burning it under her nose. He did that thing you do, like lighting someone's cigarette only without a lighter, you know?"

Emma nodded. "It's very easy. I'll teach you it. It's sort of Mostly Harmless Magic 1.01."

As Dawn spoke, she gradually got more upset, slightly theatrically.

"So she didn't wake up, even when Tiff walked over and spat in her ear or when she slapped her. Only then her hair faded to white, and she withered a bit. I mean it was Aserath so she looked like one of those Hollywood stars that got old but still show at the Oscars. And then all the vines and briars came up out of the ground and wrapped around her and the chair and pulled her into the ground. Does that mean she's…" She paused and her voice dropped to a scared reluctant whisper. "…dead?"

Emma thought for a moment, then shook her head. "No. Fertility goddess. Probably has to do winter occasionally. No biggie. Wish she'd picked another time."

Emma wrinkled her brow—she wished she felt quite as optimistic as her words, so best to be practical. She looked at the fruit trees again—the browning of the leaves had spread and more of the fruit was looking a little past its best.

"Scrub that. She'll be OK in due course, but she's left us with a problem. She's been sustaining this entire ecosystem and I don't think it's going to last all that well or long while she's hibernating, if I'm right and she's not actually dead. Whatever, I'm also worried in case my recent expansion was me sucking power from her— that's not a thought I like but it's a bit of a coincidence, isn't it?"

She put her arm round Dawn, not even slightly in a sexual way. She hoped.

"We've joked that you're my trainee… Well clearly you are: I'm going to need a deputy to run Former Hell, because I have to go into the tunnels. I really need to find Caroline, and Mara if the tunnels lead me to her. I need to find out if anyone else has this losing your temper and becoming super-divine going on."

She could see Dawn making a list and already looking a bit panicky.

"Tiffany will help with the practical stuff, and Judas—he's always best if someone tells him what to do because that puts him in his comfort zone where he has good ideas. Get Vretil to go look after the Dukes of Hell—he should put early release on hold for the moment. Oh, and talk to his clerk, Stalin—yes, that one."

Dawn looked incredulous.

"I know, right? But he got into Heaven on a technicality, so they sent him here on secondment because Jehovah fancies himself as having a sense of humour. Anyway, he's a great man for contingency planning and he may have this wargamed already. Pick all the fruit. Turn it into preserves before it rots. The former damned need to eat and you certainly do."

She probably couldn't feel a chill in the air. Yet.

"And firewood—if all this dies, it's going to need pulling down. If she's doing winter, maybe things get cold… Bits of Hell used to burn—find where the flames are banked. And get Morgan to climb that cable and find out what's been going on."

Dawn looked a bit stunned. "You're relying on me to do all that?"

"Sure—you can handle it. And who else am I going to ask? The Dowager Empress Regent? Great Number Two or Three, but she's too fucking alien at this point. She's like all the previously damned—a thousand years of torture and trauma frothing around under the shell. It's not as if she had all that great a life—I mean, better than anyone else, but still shit."

Emma knew that if she let herself she would remember judging Tiffany and just how shit her life and times had been, but privacy and data protection…

"Plus, when things get tough, you're the one least likely to think cannibalism a reasonable option. You and Judas I suppose. And he started a religion built round it. Plus, I like you."

Dawn went slightly pink. She opened her mouth to speak, closed it again, took a breath and then started. "We haven't actually fucked. You may or may not want to know that. Partly, I didn't want to at first, because if I'm anything, I'm straight. Mostly. Usually. But, there's no one here male that interests me, and on the other hand, well, Caroline… And I know it's supposed to be OK and everything but you are sort of a god, and you have so much history. Also, I'm not sure how much she's into me as such. As opposed to the idea of me, as a fling, to prove she's still a girl who can have flings in spite of all those years when you were together and she was dead… so we fooled around a bit and I sort of love her. And then I had sex with Tiff on the rebound and it was kind of OK." She paused and went on. "She loves you, but…"

Emma put a finger on Dawn's lips. "Before Caroline left, she told me one of the reasons she was going was the fear she might become Lillit and harm or hurt you. I mean, she's concerned about what that would mean for me, but, Dawn, you're fragile. When I first came to Hell, it was scary and there was a war on, but I had Lillit pretending to be a suit of magic armour, which is really creepy now I say it out loud because at the exact same time I was wearing her, she was wearing Caroline like a flesh puppet. "

On a sudden impulse she knelt at Dawn's feet and took her small soft hands. "I brought you to former Hell because I thought you'd be safer here and I owe you a huge apology because that was actually really selfish. We both just really wanted you around and that was partly to make you a chewtoy for our own messes."

Dawn pulled her back up and then hugged her. It worried Emma a little, but not much, that she noticed a mixture of fruit and coffee on Dawn's breath.

"I know, I know. Please don't overthink it. I chose to come and it's fabulous and dangerous and exciting. You're my friends and that's how friends are."

Then there came a noise Emma did not expect in a place she ruled. It was the whiny rumbling of some sort of military vehicle; what exactly, she had no idea—for someone who had actually spent a few unpleasant hours in Iraq she was horribly aware of her own ignorance.

"Oh shit," Dawn said, her grip on Emma tightening.

When it had crushed its way through the plant life into view, Emma put away the weapon she had drawn at the sight of the rude skulls and crossbones scrawled in blood over the standard matt black of Burnedover kit.

"It's a friendly," Emma explained to a still-wary Dawn.

The turret hatch flapped open and the boyish crowned head of Hades popped out. "Good." His voice was deeper than the first time Emma had met him. "I never feared the interlopers would have inconvenienced you, but they had the element of surprise."

"The God Hades, former master of this place," she told Dawn. "Hades, Dawn, my deputy. Did they hurt any of your people?"

"We were all in the workshop," Hades explained," and Daedalus just builds defences and security for the fun of it. The moment they landed, there were sirens—not real ones obviously but singing statues—so I went outside and killed all I could see."

"Nice shooting," Emma added, a lilt of enquiry at the end.

"I don't need weapons." Hades' voice had a note of reproof. "I am a death god. It was almost too easy -they had hardly any souls at all." He frowned, and Emma sensed that there was something less positive to come. "Icarus dipped an arrow in hot pitch and took out one of their—what's the word—blimps. But the one they'd brought down first, onto the roof of one of the storehouses, well, that and its thieves were already up and out of range—"

"Thieves?"

"Two big barrels of hell-flesh," Hades said. "I can't imagine what mischief they'd work in the Mundane world with those."

Pop!

When I came back to myself, the burning had modulated into a sweetness and tingling that ran all the way from my hip down to my toes—the toes I thought I no longer had.

Once my face was burned by the Alkahest and then renewed by the Stone, devastation and renewal both in a second that lasted eternally yet was over. I had not expected the like twice even in my long life.

I had heard of the comforting illusion that they call the Missing Limb syndrome, and for a second I assumed…

But then I flexed my knees and drew them up to my chest and felt the carved old wood of my throne under both my feet. And looked around me at a room full of beasts, gods and mortals raised from death and realised from their shared expression of shock and wonder that a miracle had happened.

Which was not as comforting to me as one might have assumed.

You fluttered down and perched on my shoulders, nuzzling my ears. "We did not know you could do that," one of you said.

The other said "If you could do that, what was all the fuss about?"

"I couldn't." I answered. "It was really gone. And I don't know how it came back."

While the others stood in shock, Garm padded over and planted his wet tongue on my right hand in a sloppy dog kiss.

Josette was all business. She took my pulse, and then ran her finger down from my knee. There was not even a ridge or scar where the lower part of my leg had been severed by Needful, who keened gently from her hanger at the back of my chair.

"Glad I am, mistress, to see you whole, and yet I mourn the finest, most needful cut of my existence. Are we done now?"

Swords have their honour and it can break their core and temper to lose it, and so, as Josette felt her way slowly and carefully around my foot, I keened in answer.

"Sweet sword, sharp sword, Needful... We will never be done and that will only ever have been the second most needful cut. One day, and that day may come soon, you will cure the world for me. We will take the head and hand of our great adversary, and then perhaps you will rest eversharp in a sheath of silk and ebony, but never until then."

Josette stood. "Whatever you did, you did well," she said. "I saw you heal within breaths, a moment of swoon and then you returned and it was done. No change to your pulse, no fainting past that moment. I have healed myself and it took days. And every callus of seven millennia of sandals or barefoot is there, as it was... I am known for such wonders and I stand here impressed."

She stepped back and others clustered in. Loki and his other children joined Garm. Apollo muttered vaguely about Hippocrates, Galen and his son Asclepius, knowing himself to be outclassed.

149

There was enough of a crowd that I could not at first see who picked up my restored foot and began to tickle, but I realised almost at once that it had to be Caroline and let myself at once squirm and giggle under her touch, and I called her name in a tone of both amusement and reproof.

She stood up and smiled at me. "Probably the one time I have a reasonable excuse to do that. Would your sister Lillit do that?"

"Probably," I said. "But I doubt that means anything much one way or another. And thank you."

And then…

Early in the War some people called Great, I had occasion to visit an English friend who kept bees on the South Downs. I stood outside his house with him smelling a light rain on new cut grass and we heard the booming of guns, many miles beyond the sea, as that day's doomed advances began.

This was like that, a vast explosion, a long way off. Beyond the mountains. In Hell.

You fluttered towards the ceiling in alarm and then fell back in a momentary tangle of wings.

Almost without noticing I had done it, I took my weapons from where they were hanging and slung them across my back. Always better to have and not need what it would be terrible to need and not have. Though, I realized too late, a snub to Needful, most sensitive of swords.

"Shit!" Caroline was clearly distressed. "Emma's ziggurat!"

We ran to the door, first of the throne room and then that of Valhalla itself. One of the advantages of being a monarch, I have discovered, is that people get out of your way, even large people like gods and Titans.

I was already in the open air before I realised that I had been walking on my renewed leg without even having to think about it. Not just magic, then, but magic that—without changing memories—made it as if nothing had happened in the first place.

All magic has a price. I shuddered internally at what the price of this magic might be.

Something vast and red was rising beyond the mountains that was not the fire or smoke of the explosion. I had only ever seen one thing that particular shade of scarlet.

"Bloody hell," Caroline said. "It's my girlfriend."

And indeed, as her face rose above the mountains, angrier than I'd seen her when her police friend was beheaded or when we found the spread-eagled corpses, it was Emma, overtopping the mountains of Hell, and topping off her tower and pulling out of the sky the silver line I had wrongly thought to be a star.

Then she was gone.

"I've got to go back," Caroline said. "I don't know what that meant. Did I just see my love die, or merely do something awesome. I have to know."

"Us too," you said. "We've communicated with the bag and the hand. They agree."

I looked around. I had noticed them with Caroline earlier but they'd slipped away somehow.

"I need to come," I decided.

I could see a look of dismay pass between Josette and Alexander and several of the others. That is the trouble when you have sensible friends, a throne and a reputation for individualistic irresponsibility. They just assume you're doing it again, the moment your leg grows back and you're no longer stuck in your throne.

"No, in truth." I felt I had better explain. "This is my royal duty and my responsibility. We need to know what just happened to Emma."

Two extraordinary bits of magic within minutes of each other—I had just lost my temper with people trying to be helpful, and from the expression on her face Emma was angry about her ziggurat getting exploded.

"Two powerful beings get angry, and both get to do things magic can't do, things we can't do. But now they are done, and done by us. I think that's a cause for concern because it may be another trap by our Enemy. So, I'd quite like you all to stay very calm…"

They could all see the sense in that, surely.

I needed to be on my way, but first I needed to delegate. A critic might say that my dislike of this task is as irresponsible as the rest of my distaste for leadership, and monarchy, and godhood.

I make no apologies for this. I have always had good reasons for this distaste, not least watching the terrible effects dominion has had on beings that used to be my reliable friends and companions.

But in this context, needs must…

I clapped my hands. "We have to assume that what just happened in Hell was yet another attack, which means, Zeus, Hera, that I'm leaving you in charge of the defence of Valhalla. Heimdall's normally very good at his job and he's one of the few survivors of the previous pantheon, so I suggest you listen to him and find out how the place works.

"Josette, I'm sure your city of refuge is quite well defended already, but you should return there with Mary Ann and Brünnhilde and make absolutely sure. If Emma really has found a way back to the Mundane, you may be able to re-establish contact with your network, the House and so on."

I turned next to Alexander. "There are settlements all over Shadow. We need to warn as many of them as we can. Do what you can. March light and fast. I can think of no one better for the job. Recruit as you go, send couriers in all directions. If we find Hermes in the tunnels, we'll send him after you. Zeus, Hera, if he turns up here, do the same—send him on to Alexander, please."

Alexander saluted me, very smartly, and clicked his heels like a Prussian. I was not sure whether he was being sarcastic. It really didn't matter. He would do what he was told.

Last I turned to Loki, who was quite certainly being sarcastic in the way he managed to—at the same time—stand to attention and lounge. His two more or less humanoid children were at his side.

"I don't quite know what to say, to you three. The Horses, the Dog and the Wolf will come with me, I hope—" they neighed and barked their approval even though they were quite capable of human speech "– so you can come with the rest of your family. Or stay here with the Olympians. Or march with Alexander. The choice is up to you."

Loki looked at his son and daughter, and each of them winked back at him. Which is to say that the Serpent's left eye flickered sideways, and Hela's right eye was momentarily the dead white eye of a rotten corpse and then the hollow socket of a skull, before returning to its normal green glint.

Loki laughed like the flickering and crackling of flame in a dead tree.

"After so long, you understand me so little. We will of course be going with my beloved niece and the fascinating Miss Kelly, who saved us from my dearly departed brother. We are all three of us shape-shifters and so of course we wish to get to know Miss Josette, whose altered essence outdoes us all, even mine, who have both borne and fathered." He looked at her appraisingly. "I do so love riddles… Besides, I have seen so little of justice or comfort in the world that her attempt to create a whole city of it intrigues me. Whores, perverts, charlatans—my people yet turned away from mischief."

Then for the second time that day our world was altered by a loud and unexpected thunder- thousands of shod hooves at the gallop in formation and order and their lust lather sweat scent on the breeze.

I knew that centaurs had left the Mundane for Shadow long ago, and, though I had missed them, had not sought them out, fearing that like other such long retreats they had dwindled or grown strange and savage. I had not thought that they would have prospered into a horde, into a nation. Or that they would have become a horde in motion. And in perpetual war.

When I last knew them, centaurs only went iron-shod to pursue particular objectives or vendettas, yet all of these thousands, of all ages, wore horseshoes. When I knew them, centaurs almost never deigned to go under yokes or into harness, yet now many of them were formed into teams that pulled great wagons, some of which bore great ovens from which heat billowed and the scent of hot bread yet without flame, others where centaur smiths beat red hot metal into swords yet again no flame.

When I knew them, centaurs disdained magic as beneath beings of their strength. Yet now the horde crackled with it, but no scent of the Rituals nor of either the bright alchemy of my sister nor of its dark twin, with its dusts and big beams of corrosion.

This was something that smelled of the honest sweat and musk of centaurs. It was new to me, but it was clearly a thing of this people whom I had loved and missed.

Yet...

I had missed their singing too, and that had changed also. Thousands of voices in a complex polyphony that had grown out of the hero songs and bawdy I had known two millennia before, but—had they heard human music? Had people from Europe or from the lands of spice been among them?

And the clash of their hooves and the ringing of their hammers were a part of the music. From behind the part of the horde that I could see came the lowing of cattle, the bleating of sheep or goats, the mewling of giant sloths. This too was part of the music.

Suddenly when it seemed they were a wave that would crush us all, their wild ride and their gorgeous singing and the beating of their hammers ceased in a cadence so perfect it felt like a kiss, and they drew, in a single pace in a single heartbeat, single and in teams drawing heavy wagons, to a heartstop halt in a line so perfectly straight you could use it as a rule, so long they could have encircled Valhalla and its river moat twice over.

Even a river so deep, I felt, would be no obstacle to that collective will.

Twenty yards from Heimdall's bridge and lodge they drew up, and stood in silence for three, five, seven heartbeats and then a whitebeard stallion and a redhead pertbreasted filly trotted forth and stood by the picket gate of the bridge and said, in unison, his bass and her soprano wrapped around each other, "Who rules here?"

Zeus stepped back with a slight smirk and bowed to me, as did Loki. I stepped forward and walked down to the lodge and across the bridge and through the gate; there would be no dignity in hurry and centaurs—when I had known them—were all about dignity.

But was anything I had known still valid? I feared not.

Alexander and Josette had followed a pace behind me, and the Conqueror spoke softly in my ear as we walked. "I led armies across Asia and into Africa. Eventually you get so far from where you started that you live off the land and leave a scar of famine in your wake. And people hear of your coming and flee before you… Yet none have come this way? Curious."

"Fear of this place's late master," answered Josette. "Not a god to feed the hungry or house the homeless. Rather, one to carve the blood eagle on any beggar who came to his gate."

I could think of darker explanations.

The centaurs had not the stench of the Rituals on them, but nor did many humans who nonetheless slew their thousands.

I stepped past the gate, signalling my companions and Heimdall to wait. "I rule here, as High Queen of Shadow. Welcome."

"*Mara. Huntress.*"

It bothered me more and more that they spoke in unison.

"What brings you here? And by what right do you devastate the lands of the peoples of Shadow with the trample of your war hooves and the grazing of your herds in other men's pastures? With whom are you at war that you all go iron-shod?"

They laughed, the two of them, and it was not a happy laugh. And the whole horde took its cue and laughed as well.

They continued in that unnerving unison. As they spoke, a shudder ran through the assembled gods and monsters.

"With men and the gods of men, if they stand in our way. Men drove us from the Mundane world when we were weak, repaid our feeble kindnesses with scorn and hatred. They took what they wanted and so do we."

Their unison was none the less unsettling and uncanny for the way it continued without a single break, a single mis-step.

They had become something horrible, and the perfection of it was not the least terrifying aspect of them.

I thought of Josette's Just City, which they would come to after Valhalla, with its harmless people and their second life of beauty, which these two envoys would doubtless call weakness.

"Have many stood in your way?" I spoke softly, for the moment.

They laughed again. *"Many. Not for long. And they are gone."*

Then the filly spoke by herself. *"Latterly, an encampment of men who dressed in black and had but one face between them. They had strange weapons and killed some of our front line, as few have. Yet we overwhelmed them by night, casting on them a sleep with The Dream Of Snakes, and killed them as they tossed and turned in fear, and cast their weapons into our furnaces where they stank of bad things for a while yet burned away to purity."*

The whitebeard took up her tale. *"As one day we will burn Shadow free of that stench which is called humanity, and of those men whom they call gods. All save the man clothed in Night and the woman of shifting silver who first preached the Ice to us, and told us that the Ice willed that all men should die. So that the Ice which taught us and hardened us into unity may rule all in stillness. And devour us last and favourites."*

He sang these last words in rapture and she took up his song for a repetition of the words and then a duet and then the whole horde in chorus and then a final chord, after which a silence that they might call purity and I called desolation.

I wept, for I had loved this people and they were now an utter madness. Yet another crime to the Enemy's account. And Lillit's also, it seemed.

Yet I still spoke softly. "This Ice of which you speak?"

"*Has sent his heralds ahead of him. See where they gleam in those mountains and in the passes between them. He is coming and sweeps all before him. You think us cruel, yet we are not as inexorable as he.*"

Shadow has many directions and Alexander must still go forth in most of them and yet I feared what he would find.

"*We do not leave bones and cracked pots in our wake,*" the filly said, her voice light, almost amused. "*We beat the dead and all they owned with our hammers, and burn them in our furnaces to a fine white dust.*"

I knew that we were in a conflict I did not understand and that it was already late. That knowledge made me wrathful, and I tired of soft speech and pointed my hand first at the envoys and then at the far left of that straight line of menace and swept my hand along to the far right.

And spoke.

"I am High Queen of Shadow. I am Mara the Huntress who protects the weak against the strong. I cannot, I have not, saved them all. But enough is enough. Go back to the Mundane and try conclusions with the men you will find there. I care not, for I wish you gone from these lands and my sight."

Pop!

And they were gone.

Zeus gave a long slow whistle and then laughed. "Thing I always regretted about thunderbolts," he said, "is that they were dead ahead of the noise. You told them ahead of execution. That's better."

I shrugged. "I'm pretty clear I didn't kill them,"—I was calmer now, and trying to understand my moment of rage and what I had done in it—"though I am sure I may have put them in harm's way."

Caroline looked at me, half shocked, half amused. "You think? They could be anywhere, Times Square, Beijing, anywhere."

"Pretty certain it was somewhere with room for them all—some plain, maybe steppes, or desert—and I think they will have problems with modern armaments."

I couldn't know, that was the worst of it. I could work a wonder, if angry enough, but that anger made me blind to what I was doing, to what I had done.

Alexander placed a hand on my shoulder and sighed. "I know—I think—I know. I drank wine without water, sometimes. Too often. And I would do things, things that perhaps needed to be done. Persepolis was a temptation to stay, in luxury—and it needed to burn, lest it stay me. Cleitus the Black was jealous of my Persian wife and my Persian boy and spoke against prostration as unGreek. He was my friend and we had been boys together. But he planned mutiny, perhaps… He needed to die, but I should have done the difficult thing and killed him calm and sober."

"Did you meet him in Hades?"

Alexander pulled a wry face. "I saw him at a distance, once. Among the shades that walked endlessly along the banks of the rivers that flowed then, Acheron, Lethe and Styx, that Lucifer culverted and which for all I know dried up long ago… Cleitus glanced at me and turned his back. Like Ajax in Homer. When Lucifer seized what had been Hades, I fled the fields, and sent messengers to all who might fight with me as the Wild Damned, but he chose to stay and be punished for wrath, sodomy and scorn rather than return to my side."

It was clear he had loved the man and I did not press him further.

What I had done weighed heavy with me. I had power greater than any of the gods I have known, but it was wild power and only when I was angry. It reminded me too much of the fate of Odin and how he had been tricked. I needed to share my knowledge of that with Emma and seek her counsel for she was the second wisest that I knew and nearer at hand than my sister, her avatar.

I turned to Caroline. "The tunnel entrance, if you would be so kind?"

Only then Garm coughed, and grew a little from the terrier form he had reverted to, and Sleipnir lowered her head and he growled into his half-sister's ear.

She thought for a moment, because even for her it took a moment to translate from dogspeak to horseverse.

"Wisdom in waiting, calm water of mind, Angry is danger, grim is its ending, Travel untroubled, tranquil is better…"

Caroline grew impatient, clearly having no taste for alliterative kennings.

"I think she's telling you to take a chill pill or meditate or something. We don't want you going all tripped-out Galadriel somewhere halfway to Hell."

I could see why Emma loved her so much, though like Lillit she could be quite vexing. But I was not going to be vexed until all this was resolved, and so I took a deep breath and set myself to exhale and inhale in the slow deliberate rhythm I had watched in Gautama as he sat under his tree and I begged him fruitlessly to stand with me.

I am capable of self-discipline in these matters, whatever people think. Perhaps when Gautama portrayed me to his followers as the embodiment of wrath, it was with forethought that I would become capable of calm from a perverse desire to prove him wrong. And perhaps he knew that one day I would need to. He had a pronounced taste for the brand of wisdom which presents as a taste for devious paradox. It was one of several reasons why I never took to him.

Yet breathing as he had breathed helped me to think as he had thought, and if that was the price of a calm in which I would do no harm, then I would let myself learn from a man whom I had not liked and who had shown me disapproval.

I let Caroline lead me and the animals that were to be our companions down the ramp into the cellarage of Valhalla and through the granary I had had my hounds rid of rat dragons. There was a door ajar at the far end that I had not seen, that had been hidden from my sight before, and just outside it Emma's bird and bag were sat—the small hand that was part of, or more probably lived in, the bag was throwing dice and moving grains back and forth between two piles as they won or lost. The bag was tapping instructions with one of its cat-clawed feet and the bird with a talon even though it was perfectly capable of speech.

I did not quite understand how there could be fairness in such a game but if Tsassiporah, a devious bird, thought it fair then it probably was.

"Huntress, Mistress Caroline," it cooed.

And then it saw you, the two black birds that hovered just above my head. "Brother," it cawed, "sister. It's been an age."

I still was not sure which was which, but that was more information about yourselves than you had given me.

"Great news," it said. "Our brother Morrigan is whole again. His mistress has relented."

I knew their brother and did not regard his return as an unmixed blessing. Still, we were at war, clearly, which meant he would be searching for carrion on actual battlefields rather than causing trouble in the hope that battle and carrion would result. But I forbore to say or even think anything, because inner calm was my friend.

I walked over and opened the door wider. Beyond it was dim lighting and a platform which was the top of—not a ramp this time, but a series of broad, shallowly pitched stairs that led down into darkness.

"Convenient," said the horse Gram. "My mother and I distrust hidden ways that turn out have been built for our convenience."

Sleipnir snorted in agreement.

"Well," I said, reasonably, "you don't have to come. But it's probably not a trap."

"We got here unmolested," Caroline pointed out helpfully.

"To sweeten an ambush later?" the younger horse hinted.

"I'm not saying that there's nothing unpleasant lurking. Because lurking in dark underground places is one of those things unpleasant things do. It's a rule of the universe. Just that it wasn't them that built a handy stair for horses up to a place where quite a lot of horses have been known to hang out."

Gram's doubts made me look around a little more. There was something I wasn't seeing…

Athena had followed us down. "You're looking for something, Huntress?" she said as she entered the cellar. "Something that should be here and isn't?"

Then I realised. Ariadne's thread.

I had remarked on it earlier, when the Olympians had arrived. Athena had been holding it. I looked the obvious question at her.

"I have my end of it still." And she produced a many-times folded length of it from somewhere beneath her flowing gown, and placed it on the floor. Yards and yards long, and at one end…

"I felt a tug on the line and then what I was holding went slack. You were dealing with centaurs at the time, so I waited until now. I didn't want to worry those members of the family who love the girl, even though she's an interloper. Myself, I like her well enough, but her devotion to my brother means she's always too drunk to sustain a conversation. Him, I love, and Hermes too, who should have been back by now. But as you see…"

The thread had been cut—no, bitten, and the slobber with which it was still damp was rank.

Garm shifted his shape to the small terrier he had been when I first met him, sniffed at the thread and nodded.

"I take it," Athena said, "that your dog smells a rat."

Caroline looked confused a second, then moved a bit closer to me. "Assuming Greek deities don't randomly use standard English idioms—just how big a rat, and how many?"

"My pack cleared these cellars well enough," I said, "but it seems that Lucifer's secret ways have a vermin problem all their own. Something to deal with on our way to meet Emma of Former Hell. You will join us?"

"I think not," Athena said. "Your sister outranks me as Goddess of Wisdom. I accept that, but at least I'm goddess of being too smart to fight an unknown rodent powerful enough to take down two gods and a demigoddess. In a dark confined space. Definitely your job and not mine, Huntress." She turned on her heel and made to leave.

Caroline looked disappointed. "Don't you have the head of Medusa on a shield?"

"It only worked a couple of times," I explained. "No one was expecting it when Perseus used it on his relatives. And once Athena got hold of it, she used it on some monsters. It was fine for pest control, but not warfare. A couple of well-placed, highly polished shields, and it petrified itself."

"After which," Athena confided, "it was much too heavy to lug around as well as no use. Frankly, it was a relief; zombie snakes smell awful. Good luck with the rats. Try and return my relatives as unchewed as possible."

She left, with an irritatingly tinkly laugh.

"What a bitch," said Caroline, staring after her.

The stairs went down and down and round a dizzying number of corners. When we reached the bottom, I paused a moment to get my bearings.

"Left to start off with," Caroline said.

The hand poked out of the top of the bag and made a series of gestures almost too fast to follow. The scarlet bird chittered at it and it made the same gestures, more emphatically.

"Left until the first crossing then right for two crossings then left and we're there," the bird cawed. "I came here with my former master for a meeting and the hand has a remarkable sense of direction. For a hand, that lives inside a bag."

The hand's next gesture was emphatic and perfectly clear. The scarlet bird sulked for the next half hour, until you fluttered across to it and groomed it for five minutes. The Dog and the Wolf did likewise, and Sleipnir nuzzled her child's neck.

Then we heard a scream. It cut out quickly but went on echoing for some time.

"Let us proceed with caution," I warned. "Rats cunning enough to be a danger know all about bait."

But all good wise prudent caution disappears when a scream is choked off. I cannot save them all, but I feel an obligation to try.

As I ran, with Gram and Sleipnir keeping pace at my side, I ticked off the seconds in my head. Strangling takes a little while, usually, and the silencing of the scream might be only that, and not yet a murder.

I looked over my shoulder: Caroline and her companions were keeping up and Fenris and Garm were acting as rearguard. I was impressed that she could conquer horse nature enough to tolerate the wolf so close to her, but after all he was her uncle.

Round the next corner I almost collided with a slightly overweight black-haired young woman with the bare breasts of a Cretan noblewoman was struggling with a tangle of her own thread in which she was wound taut, and with a gag that seemed to be something alive and pink and segmented and trying to force its way into her mouth.

The tunnel behind her would have been dark, but for four score of bright red eyes glaring at her and now turning their redness upon us. There was a smell of damp and sewers and a chittering that was almost like laughter.

"Mara," Caroline said softly, stepping back cautiously "do creatures have to be intelligent to do magic?"

I poised for imminent action but explained. "It's mostly about will and focus, which need only consciousness. Of a sort. I met some bees once, but they were smart. As a swarm."

Caroline nodded, still keeping a wary eye down the corridor. "I think this is something like that. So maybe we could talk to them."

I'd seen her and Emma work things out together and envied them a little. I can't read minds but rats, and a pink thing, and that smell, and some sort of tangle magic...

I thought I could see where her thought processes were taking her.

Not all Great Beasts have to be huge. And I had met rats in Shadow before. Yet these smelled different. I could see no reason not to attempt what Caroline suggested—certainly I had no better plan just that moment.

And so.

"King Rat, or perhaps Queen, Rat. Or perhaps neither."

The chittering blended into a single high pedantic voice. "We reject your human obsession with dominance. Typical ape behaviour. We are the Rat Collective and far too many of you have been trampling noisily around the tunnels above our home."

Drains.

When Lucifer had the Titans build the tunnels for him, of course the diligent creatures had put in drainage, and who could guess how much further down it went. I had never bothered to think what lay beneath the lands and seas of Shadow.

Perhaps these creatures, this Collective, knew what I had never concerned myself with.

I felt no particular sympathy, though. "You cannot expect people to show consideration of your territorial rights if you've never claimed them. And I would strongly suggest that you not begin making your presence clear by attacking your new neighbours, the Gods of New Olympus."

"We don't care."

It would have been so easy to lose my temper again and do something righteous and dreadful to these presumptuous vermin... no, these creatures with different and possibly valid priorities.

"Mara, sweetie, it's best you don't fret yourself. I've got this."

Caroline walked over and pulled the fragment of rat-tail from Ariadne's mouth, then tossed it to Garm, who bit it in half and shoved the other piece over to his brother the wolf. They both started to chew with an almost parodic daintiness.

The Collective collectively squealed.

Caroline waited until their cry subsided. "The trouble with mental control of detached body parts is that you can feel them. It's a vulnerability. I'd point out that our friends here, the Dog and the Wolf, are gods, or possibly demigods, and can make digestion last a while. Also, the Huntress controls an entire god-touched pack. Whom you would not wish to meet."

A fragment of thread lashed out of the darkness and tried to encircle the wrist of the hand she was gesticulating with. She gave it a hard glance and it fell away.

"Oh please! ... One of the benefits of the few small magics I can work, which mostly have to do with personal adornment. Which means I wear whatever I want, but also that I can't be made to wear things I don't. You guys, on the other hand --" She stuck out a hand. "Might I borrow Needful a second?"

I nodded, and the sword flew to her hand with a steel chime that was like a squeal of delight. Lillit always could charm bees from their hives: her avatar had clearly refined those skills a little.

"I used to run with a man called Alexander, ratties, and he told me one time about the quickest way with knots."

I could see where she was going with this, but surely she had no memory of her time with the Wild Damned, when Lillit had been in the driving seat? On the other hand, she was quite possibly just bluffing.

"You see, ratties. A personal magic a bit close to your essential nature is close enough to being a tell that it's a vulnerability. Tangle magic—and you call yourself a Collective—you may not be King of the Rats, but you're a rat king nonetheless. I wonder how smart you'd be if I snipped you apart."

The chittering became incoherent rage and a gnashing of front teeth.

"Promises were made to us–"

"I can guess who you'll have been talking to," Caroline said. "Anyone he does business with sooner or later regrets it. Sooner, in this case, if you don't do what you're told. Which is: let any gods you've got go, and do the drainpipe thing, and stay out of our way. And that, ratties, is the best deal you'll get today."

Quite suddenly, the red eyes shut and there was a pattering of many feet away from us coupled with the slithering of some vast and unsightly lump they dragged behind them. Further away, they sploshed into some liquid and the stench disappeared.

The skein of her own thread dropped from Ariadne and she swooned decorously.

A god with a winged helmet limped out of the shadows, supporting a chubby drunk who was snoring. There was a mess of threads around his ankles.

"May I?" Caroline asked my sword and it swung down and cut the threads—and suddenly the two male gods were gone from our sight. Another heartbeat and Hermes flashed back, slung his sister-in-law over his back and was gone again.

Caroline passed me Needful and pulled a disappointed face with a theatrically droopy mouth. I shook my head in explanation. "The gods of Olympus never say thank you."

166

Emotional Moments

Hell and the Undercroft of Shadow

She wasn't sure of the etiquette of such things, but Emma needed to ask Hades' advice, so she hospitably created a small table, two high-backed chairs with comfortably padded black velvet seats, a basket of dark red grapes, a plate of salted goat cheese and, because she didn't want to make too many concessions to his Greekness, a plate of digestive biscuits. She looked across at him and asked "Wine? Water? Something stronger?"

"Let me," and the God of Death waved airily. Two large glasses of something many-layered and multi-coloured appeared.

Emma frowned, and he said reassuringly, "Everyone seems to like this one. There was a genius barman once that worked at the George Cinq. He blew himself up in 1943 trying to kill some German general or other and Minos recognized him. Too talented to be subjected to Lucifer's whims, so I insisted on his teaching me five recipes I didn't know then shipped him off to the Wild Damned, who passed him on out of Hell, somewhere. I didn't ask. It's not my Hades, any more."

This was one of the things Emma had wanted to discuss.

"Are you sure you don't mind? I mean, me and Aserath? We got in quick while things were fluid."

Hades sighed. "As long as people leave me and mine alone. I never liked running the whole place; it was the shitty job you give to the kid brother. As opposed to the cushy meaningless job you give to the dumb jock. It's not as if Poseidon ever got to run anything—the Seas are their own vast powerful beings and they no more than tolerated him. If he needed then to do anything—well, he could ask and half the time the Aegean or the Adriatic would smile a huge wave and pretend to remember who he was, but the Mediterranean would usually hardly acknowledge he'd said anything. The Atlantic? Well not even Dagon gets to speak directly to them and the minor seas really like Dagon."

He took another sip of his drink. "But, anyway. Once my boys Daedalus and Icarus got here we worked out how to dredge Phlegethon and turn the residue into hell-flesh, and that meant we could actually punish people… I know what you're thinking! But, Tantalus and Sisyphus really were pretty bad. And I didn't do stuff to just anyone. Then there was a change of management and, well, I could have stuck by my brothers and gone off to Lucifer's oubliette but it's not like they ever liked me… so I did a deal, and now I've done another deal. With you, and that's fine."

He wasn't the nicest God, Emma decided, but she liked his honesty.

"Besides," he added, "apart from the Olympians, I had my other family. I had to protect them."

He volunteered no details and Emma was not inclined to press.

"Anyway," he continued, "your people. The ones that got blown up. I'll put them back in the flesh as soon as I can. Very upsetting, but it's not as if they haven't died before, or been tortured for hundreds of years. They're a tough crowd, your worshippers… The others, the

168

killers—filed and forgotten like their wisp-souled comrades. There are one or two wannabes among them, who actually have their own souls, for all that they had their faces changed. I've dumped them in with the remaining Dukes, to make them all totally wretched."

"In the interests of their eventual rehabilitation, of course," Emma said. It wasn't a question.

Hades stroked the arm of his chair. "Good texture, this," he remarked. "Took me centuries to manifest material this good. You're young..."

"Not that young any more. I stopped time a lot to fast track judging the former damned. I'm really quite old now. But I locked all those years away. Because they're all to do with other people's business and frankly who needs the grief? So, memory palace with a lot of locked rooms..."

"Really." Now Hades looked intrigued. He set down his glass. "Do you mind if I tell Minos how you managed that? I mean, obviously he has far less on his plate to begin with because he and his brother mostly only bothered with major offenders. The other one, wossisname—Aeacus—he was a bit more diligent and hands on about things—but I never liked him anyway and he went off to ask Lucifer for a job. I don't think that went very well for him. And he sold me out so I really don't care."

Emma set down her own glass. Time to get back down to business.

"I don't suppose you know which of Lucifer's tunnels leads to Valhalla? My beloved has gone off there to look for Mara, to whom I really need to talk."

"The tunnels?" Hades looked apologetic for a moment and then perked up. "I can't tell you the route—it seemed a bit dangerously presumptuous to trespass down there. I asked Lucifer once—I said, 'Daedalus, here—huge expert—he'd love to cast an eye over what the Titans did for you.' And Lucifer got quite difficult about it, so I let the matter drop. I don't know where Valhalla is precisely, but I can guess where Mara's been."

He pointed at, and presumably through, the mountains. "Some sort of massacre happened, over there. I'd imagine she was there, not to cast aspersions."

Emma glanced at him questioningly.

"I'm a god of death," he explained. "The universe gives me a heads-up. Here, let me help." He reached out a long finger and tapped her on the forehead. And suddenly she knew exactly where she needed to be but also somehow experienced something inchoately terrible—men and gods and treachery to kin and some monstrous magic.

She jerked back from his hand. "That's horrid. I can't imagine Mara doing anything like that."

"True," Hades said, "yet so often she is there during terrible things as their witness, or after as their avenger. It is her nature and her curse that she cannot save them all."

Emma thought back to that cocktail party in Oxford that she'd hardly remembered for years and nodded. It was at moments like this when she thought back to her old life and of how rarely she did so that she felt the weight of all her years, all her carefully forgotten but nonetheless heavy years, upon her.

And a single tear escaped her suddenly brimming eyes.

"I have stocktaking to do in Phlegethon—" Hades was suddenly peremptory; obviously, Emma thought, me manifesting actual human emotion is too much for him, "—and you have business and love thither. These are dark times, darker than most. We may well not meet again."

He reached out his hand again and Emma seized it, raised it to her lips and kissed it. When a god of Death and the Dead goes fey on you, you had best note the occasion.

And then they were done. He climbed back into his vehicle as nimbly as if he drove such things all the time and very soon was gone.

She stood a second and watched him drive away. It worried her that something bad had happened at Valhalla, that Caroline and her companions might be walking, probably by now have walked, into the aftermath of something terrible. And, as Hades had pointed out, it was one thing to know abstractly that her friend, her sister by avatar, did terrible righteous necessary things—it was going to be another to see the spilled blood, shattered bone and torn flesh of her executed judgement.

Nonetheless.

She ran to the entrance she had found before, let herself in and walked down the dark staircase, keeping in mind which direction she should go in when she reached the bottom. The tracks were still there even if the carriage and the creatures that drew it were gone.

There were forks and turnings and ingeniously what looked like sets of points, which was strange because the draught creatures had had—or rather no longer had—hands with which to manipulate such things and she could not imagine Lucifer getting out of his snazzy carriage to do it himself. Unless…

The next time she came to one, she thought at it, I'm going to Valhalla, and the thing shifted itself at her thought, and the line moved into the direction she was going anyway. Not that she feared getting lost—she didn't think it was part of goddess nature to do that, but it at least meant that she was definitely heading for Valhalla and not the site of some other massacre that had created a disturbance in the force that gave Hades visions.

Now she was pacing through the tunnels rather than racing through them at breakneck speed, she could see what impressive structures they were. Undecorated and austere perhaps, but definitely a statement of something, a work of art. And Lucifer had rewarded the Titans by locking them away with their rowdy kin.

And up ahead she heard Mara say something about Olympians, and Caroline say something about arseholes and knew with relief that her journey was done.

"Hi," Emma said, and promptly burst into tears.

"This is the hugging thing." Mara suited her action to her words, a full half-second before Caroline could wrap her arms, and a rather fetchingly voluminous purple cloak, around them all.

The warmth of her lover's body against hers almost made her ache with the pleasure of it, and the presence of their friend was a delightful bonus.

They stayed there for a long moment, interrupted by the three birds clicking their talons against the railbed. The hand poked out of the bag and started snapping its fingers in the same rhythm. The two horses started to stamp their iron-clad hooves. It was nice to know someone appreciated the emotional weight of the occasion.

The Dog and the Wolf remained silent. Emma stroked Garm in that slightly absent-minded way you do with pets you've only met once or twice that belong to your friends.

Caroline stepped up to do the niceties. "Emma, my love. These are Hugin and Munin, Thought and Memory. They used to be Odin's, but only until Mara wanted them. Garm you've met. The wolf's his brother Fenris, and these two are their half-sister Sleipnir and her daughter Gram."

Emma looked at Mara. "I gather from the company that you did go to Valhalla. What happened there? Hades said there was a bloodbath. Did you…?"

"Odin annihilated most of the Aesir, all but one of the Valkyries and all of the resurrected warriors, so he could become some sort of supergod. He turned into a witless dragon, instead, and Mary Ann Kelly did for him with a hatpin. Then he turned into the red dust and became a problem."

"How very succinct," Caroline said. "And at your end, Emma?"

Emma tried to be as brief. "Burnedover people blew up the ziggurat and I grew enormous."

"We saw," Caroline said. "Glad you're no longer all Attack of The Fifty Foot Woman, frankly. It would play hell with our sex life. Anything else?"

"Hell—well, it started to get cold and Aserath did some sort of fertility goddess going comatose and burying herself thing. Is that standard? I assumed it was standard rather than something we need to worry about?"

"It happens," Mara nodded. "Usually at inconvenient times."

"So anyway, I left Dawn and Morgan to hold things down. Is it awful that I trust them more than Judas or Vretil? I know it's a but unfair, but…"

"I don't have your cultural programming," Mara noted, "but I wouldn't trust him either. Nice lad, I taught him to fight when he was a boy and I still don't trust him. He gets ideas in his head and looks for people to serve. In their best interests. Bad ideas. Dawn, though? Your apprentice? Smart woman. I would trust her."

Emma noted that Mara didn't say anything about Morgan. Positive or otherwise. But there were more important issues than sorting out her friends' love lives or lack of them. "I lost my temper and became a giant. Anything like that at your end?"

Mara reached down and tapped the lower part of her leg. "To start with… This grew back. After I lost it."

Emma looked at what seemed to be an utterly normal leg and felt, in rapid succession, shocked, concerned and intrigued. "Lost it? I thought you were, you know, invulnerable."

"As did I, but our enemy seems to have managed to change the rules again. One of his people, with one of those guns, managed to put a hole in my leg that was growing and corroding. So we had to cut it off."

"We?"

"Josette and Needful here."

Mara patted its hilt as affectionately as if it were a child or a beloved pet, and then replaced it behind her shoulder.

"So," she went on, "I realized that I could not endure people's pity and suddenly it returned."

"It wasn't like it opened like a flower or anything," Caroline explained. "We were all looking in her general direction and one moment it was still a stump and the next it was back, fully functional, wiggling her toes and everything. I tickled her, just to make sure, which of course I would never normally do. Best special effect ever."

Mara took back the reins of her story. "Just after that, something exploded and we saw you vast and naked looming over the mountains, and I realised I was not the only person who had suddenly acquired inexplicable magic… Only then."

"Then a horde of very scary centaurs turned up, and gave Mara attitude, and she flicked them off back to the Mundane to be someone else's problem."

"The crucial thing," Mara added, "is that I lost my temper again. I had no idea what I was doing until it was done, but it was what part of me really wanted to do. And it felt good when it was done and the sudden rage was gone as quickly as it had come. Was it like that for you?"

"Yes," Emma said, "Exactly like that. What's weird is that we're both pretty chill most of the time. If we need to do something awful to someone who totally deserves it, we do it, but we know exactly what we're doing."

"You're both totally repressed." Caroline was suddenly sporting a white coat and black horn-rimmed spectacles with her hair in a bun. She also suddenly had an Austrian accent. Berthe whispered admiringly to Emma that it was even from the right district. "I'd say it was something to do with toilet training but I doubt they did that in any relevant way in Bronze Age Mesopotamia…"

"Of course we did. Never in a stream, especially not upstream. Never on a fire. Use a non-edible leaf and make sure there's no one who can use it before you bury it."

"It's awfully specific," Emma mused aloud. "Suddenly two people who almost never lose their temper have a sort of super-magic that plugs into their unconscious when they lose it. Which they both do, suddenly, at the same time. And this along with no one being able to use Shadow safely and birds not being able to fly much above head height—"

Tsassiporah and the other two voiced their disgruntlement.

Hugin, or possibly Munin, spoke, in an almost human voice, "When you catch them, there will be an eyeplucking. We are the children of The Bird, the confidants of Lucifer and Mara, of Odin and Emma. We soared for thousands of years, and they've turned us into chickens."

Emma went on, "I think—but obviously I can't be sure—that we've all been slowed down relative to the Mundane. The riverfall into Phlegethon looks odder than usual and when Burnedover people arrive, they're unsteady on their feet like someone who jumps off a bus, and what might be the start of Hell freezing over."

"Not just Hell," Caroline added. "The centaurs kept wibbling about what they call The Ice, in Capitals, like it was a God or something."

"Odin killed the Aesir," Mara said, "or rather he compelled them to kill each other. They turned into what looked like the black powder I have been seeing since Paris and the Rite of Spring."

"I remember," Emma said, "Berthe was there, when I was Berthe."

Mara grinned in the way you do when you realize something you should have known all along. "So you were, and saved the day... Now, the black powder. People use it and then do something atrocious, which produces more of it, which causes more atrocity... It's as if the Rituals have been converted into a drug that constantly distils itself. And the dead Aesir turned into it or what looked like it. And Odin took it thinking it would make him into some sort of ultimate god, but became a big stupid dragon instead, coated in much of the gold of the Glittering Roofs. Mary Ann killed him with help from the rest of us, and he crumbled away. Into the red dust."

"The product of another distillation," Emma said slowly. "This really is dark alchemy, isn't it? And the next distillation is us, and what using our rage turns us into. So easy to let that happen, hoping the power would let us win before that. Weaponising the temptation to self-sacrifice against us. Have to respect that. Browning knows me too well."

"It's a bit subtle," Mara said. "I know he was your Oxford tutor, but..."

Caroline, now dressed as a slightly ink-stained schoolgirl, stuck up her hand. "I know the answer and you're not going to like it."

The other two looked at her, as did the three birds.

"It's the targeting. He's never got close enough to either of you to get whatever the magic equivalent of DNA is, whereas she was your sister-lover—not judging—and she crawled all over Emma as armour—still not judging, but I must say a belated eww!—so she knows both of you."

175

Her voice grew more serious and the schoolgirl outfit was replaced by a sensible sombre sweater and jeans. "Plus, and I have warned you about this, I am her daughter or her clone or something, so if she's his ally, maybe I shouldn't be here, where she can listen."

Emma considered for a moment. "I don't think she's his ally. I'm sure he thinks she's his ally. But she helps both sides, sort of. I think she belongs to destiny, which is what time and chance make. When she chose what she chose—foreknowledge of what's in the script means no free will, no making up your own lines. I think she likes us but we can't trust her. We just have to hope the script doesn't say we lose and die horribly…"

She fell silent. For minutes… And closed her eyes but not in sleep.

"Oh look," Caroline said and paused dramatically, "Emma is having a plan."

Refined

There was shouting from the next room, but Sof was concentrating, going into a place of pure thought where the Work and Hypatia's mathematics and astronomy danced around each other.

Even with a body of hell-flesh and the Stone ready to hand, she could not afford to be careless with That Which Devours. It had eaten her once already and she was not going to give it a second chance.

It was a measure of her desperation that she was even prepared to work with it again, but every experiment with just Elixir, Stone and Quintessence had failed. The red dust and the black powder and the liquid blade which was another form dark alchemy took—all remained untouched by everything she could do.

At least in the Mundane… If it had been possible to get into Shadow, it would perhaps be different. She had always been able to travel there before and there was no reason why hell-flesh—which made her a creature born in Shadow—should be any different. But either Shadow had been destroyed, and Hell with it, or they were for the time being as inaccessible as if they were gone.

And with them her sister-lover Mara, her avatar Emma and so many other friends and allies. And so much knowledge and memory.

Which left her alone with new friends she did not wholly understand, in a world of new things to learn and old things to remember and explain, where much of what she knew was forgotten or considered mere myth—and where myth was a synonym for untrue.

In a world where the Work had been so badly misunderstood for so long—Polly had shown her Newton's notebooks and even he, who had understood the answers to so many questions she had never thought to ask, had entirely failed to get past the pile of dross that scholars had buried her work under—she had not hoped to find Alkahest or Adamant still in the world.

She had come as close to despair for a moment as sanity would let her, and the consoling company of this group of strangers who had become a family of sorts. More than just colleagues at any rate.

She had, of course, known the faun back in Alexandria, but his years on his own in a modern world where he had had to make a place for himself had matured him; or perhaps she had belatedly learned to take him more seriously.

The others… Well, she had started with the advantages of Emma's memories of them and of the fact that this new body and face resembled the way she still thought of herself—that girl from the land between the Two Rivers—and not Emma, so they thought of her as someone else.

Conveniently in the case of Elodie, because her unresolved feelings for Emma would have been a complication. Clearly, she and Emma had different, though overlapping, types. She liked the woman well enough, but would never have considered her as a bedmate.

It was sometimes annoying too that Syeed thought of her as an honorary relative, and could be very slightly shocked if she didn't behave to him accordingly. Then, his relationships with Tom and Polly were complicated to say the least.

Enemies turned friends have always to go through a process where continual mild irritation and offence turn into occasional tact and then a camaraderie based in gentle mockery. She had seen it before, in various lives. Most notably when, as Diotima's grand-daughter, she marched with the Ten Thousand.

It helped now that they all had work to get on with. Polly no longer had an employer as such, but she still garnered information and analysed it, and sent Tom and Syeed off to acquire information that didn't turn up on her screens. So far at least they were managing to do this without the Enemy noticing Tom could still travel.

Elodie ran her office in a corner of the room, after announcing to the industry of which she was a part that this was how everyone would work in the future, talking on telephones and through cameras—she claimed to have allergies.

The gossip on the internet varied from an addiction to a secret love affair in some far away country, but apparently she was so good at what she did that no one cared.

In the end, though, the concerns of her housemates were of only marginal interest to Sof, though she hoped the social skills she had developed down millennia kept them from fully realising this.

As far as she was concerned, the important thing was that they didn't distract her too much from her Work and helped her with it when she needed them to.

Tom had used his Sight and travelled wherever any lead led him as silently and discreetly as ever he could. Elodie and Syeed had used the internet and the darknet and a number of other techniques that hurt her head when she tried to think of them, made her feel all her millennia old. The faun had snuck round the world of nonhuman creatures. Ghouls and goblins disapproved of the Work almost as much as they did magic and trolls and dryads had no capacity or interest in it, and his own people were either dead or long gone into

Shadow—but all beings love gossip, and the faun had access to every scurrilous secret Polly knew and many she had plausibly concocted.

And all sorts of information had come back to them—"Cast your bread on the bleeding waters it says in the Good Book and blow me if it ain't true," Polly said—but nothing of use to Sof.

In the end, Polly—almost as embarrassed as she had it in her to be—had walked into her parlour which these days the six of them treated as a common living room, plonked a small hard flask on the side table nearest the chair in which Sof was reading a copy of the Guardian (a paper she had taken to because it annoyed more of her housemates than any of the alternatives) and said, "Don't suppose this would be what you're all looking for. I found it in the dead files, didn't I? As I was looking in for altogether different reasons."

Once you've held worked Adamant in your hand, you never forget the feel and surprising heft of it, or the slightly oily gurgling slosh of what the flask contained. She turned it over and over in her hands, observing an inscription she did not have the knowledge to read—not the old Egypt of the priests before the Persians came, and not the land of Silk, but something else…

She would have to try the stopper, but not yet.

Sof said, in as unremonstrating a tone as she could manage, "So, all the time, we were looking all over the world, with Tom and the faun risking the Enemy finding out they can leave… And it was here all the time?"

"Said I was sorry, didn't I?"

She hadn't.

"With the Lord gone, and the Enemy says he bleeding ate him, and without him good sense 'as deserted the realm, videlicet this Brexit nonsense, and Prime Ministers as won't take my calls… It occurs to me as he and other nations' tutelars—god rest them and may they be unquiet in the Enemy's guts—well, they're not angels, not exactly, but a bit like, and one of those who held my place afore me, not my post because that was chartered by old Nol for Bloody John Thurloe, but the post as it was in Queen Bess's time, he had this friend that talked to Angels, didn't he? John Dee and his wife's bedmate Kelley. So their papers might have had something about the Lord and his kind. The which they did, which I'll tell you about later. But there was also this little bottle, and I says to myself Poll girl don't go meddling, that Dee was an alchemist and Sof told me, she did, don't go messing with what you don't understand and…"

Satisfied that Polly had suffered enough, Sof said gently, "So how did Dee lay his hands on it?"

"Well, that Kelley was light fingered as well as loose pricked, wasn't he? So when they quits the service of mad old Rudolf and have to leave Prague in a hurry there's all sorts of trinkets that they takes with them, most of which they gives to Bess to buy into her favour, proper smaragdine emeralds and amber with great bluebottles in it and a horn which he says is unicorn but from what I hear of the nasty brute is nothing of the kind but just rhinoceros or narwhal. But this—" Polly looked at it in Sof's hands, clearly glad to have it out of her own, "—this Dee hangs onto and has more sense than to use and wraps it in a note what says what he thinks it might be and says very pious that they took it to stop Rudolf using it on heretics, the which he might well have because though he wasn't the brute his cousin Phillip was, all 'Apsburgs are a bit mad, ain't they?"

Sof had acquainted herself with the memories of historical knowledge she had inherited from Emma and reinforced them with a quick skim of the past eight hundred years and yes, the madness of Hapsburgs did seem to be a theme.

And Polly was so very flustered. It was quite charming.

"How would Rudolf Hapsburg have come by it?" She felt compelled to ask.

"No idea," Polly said. "He had people going round buying anything he might be interested in, didn't he? Wealth of empire to squander on his hobby and half the time never bothered to check the new acquisitions. Dee's notebook gets quite pious about it -- almost a moral duty to rob him."

Sof felt mild outrage. A lifetime as a librarian had made her respectful of keeping collections in one piece for posterity--but then, that hadn't worked out so well for the Museion eventually, so... And besides, thanks to Dee and Kelley, she had, against all likelihood, what she needed.

Except, she now found, not so much.

She laid out samples of the red dust, the black powder, the fragment of the Burnedover assassin's killing axe, some of the sand from the Ripper's hourglass—Polly had told her what Wells had found about its capacity to alter the flow of time, and she momentarily wondered how Emma's Caroline could do the same thing, but of course if Caroline were some fragment of Lillit, time and chance might be hers for the taking whether she knew it or not.

Very, very carefully she tipped a single drop of That Which Devours from the flask onto each of the samples in turn.

And in turn each drop passed through its sample as if it were not there and, with a gentle hiss, through her workbench and down through the stone floor underneath it, leaving a needle hole which, for all she knew, continued through the earth and out the other side, doing a small amount of absolute damage as it went.

She allowed herself a moment of petulance, then put the stopper back in the mouth of the Adamant flask and shrugged.

Clearly this was not going to be the answer, and there was some point about this dark parody of the Work she had missed.

It was a process of refining, that much was clear, yet where the refining in the Work was a matter of distillation, and combination, and moving their products back and forth between Shadow and the Mundane, the dark Work seemed to use escalating atrocity as its process, passing through the bodies of criminals and kinslayers and coming out stronger. It was almost as if... She had read all the mystic claptrap in Newton's notes, about how the Work was as much a spiritual process of improving one's soul as the production of the Elixir and the Stone, with each for their own sake as useful things.

Such nonsense. She blamed the Christians, and all the half-understood Neo-Platonism they'd cribbed from Philo.

But this was different. It was as if the products of the dark Work were physical manifestations of the Rituals. But the Rituals were magic, and not the Work. What is done with the Work can only be undone with the Work.

But how to undo a version of the Work that was both the Work and magic? And how could such a blending, something so unnatural, have come about?

It was beyond her. There had to be something she was missing.

For a moment Sof knew despair again and betrayal as deep as—no, the despair and betrayal that had led her into madness, Emma had removed from her and taken into herself, and rightly so, but…

If Emma still existed, wherever, perhaps whenever, the red dust had taken her.

Emma knew everything of the Work that Sof knew, even if she did not feel it in her aching bones, through lifetimes of patient labour. And Emma knew Magic, was magic, in her bones.

Whatever was to be done to undo the dark Work, perhaps it was Emma's task and not Sof's. Emma was as clever as her, as one would expect, but Emma was also intuitive in a way none of Sof's lives had trained her to be.

Sof sighed and shrugged. Lifetimes of the Work. Endurance as the fragments Cyril had left of her. Years of torture as the Templars' intelligence. She knew patience. And when to let things go, to leave an avenue of inquiry as a bad job. The Work was not all she knew.

And now they were all shouting in the next room. She needed to find out why.

It sounded apocalyptic—perhaps…but no, it turned out, to be only the American Election, which had not gone well. Though since everyone except her and the faun disliked both candidates…

"Well, yes," Polly said, "but he's a fucking traitor, ain't he?"

"And a groper," added Elodie.

Syeed struggled for a second and then acknowledged, "She's killed hundreds of the brothers, but he'll kill more."

Tom looked at Polly with hungry eyes. "I know we don't do that anymore, but please say I can kill him? I mean, you're really not at the top of the profession unless you've taken out a head of state. And he's the Big One, the Great White Whale."

"No," Polly said. "Absolutely not. Look at the trouble we had with you and the 'Untress just bullying the Blair man. We don't kill heads of state unless they're absolutely about to unleash nuclear holocaust. Them's the rules Mara laid down back in 49 and them's the rules we play by. Not as how he may quite possibly give you your chance, what with all the Burnedover guys around him."

She frowned. "Question is, do the Mighty know the 'Untress ain't around right now to put them down from their seats if they do things she don't approve of. Last time she wasn't around, and it got out she was gone because that loose lipped chancer Crowley and that old bastard Hassan couldn't shut up about how clever they'd been, well, she was gone from 26 to 49 and those years was very much not a bundle of laughs."

She sighed at the memory.

"So what I says to you, young Tom, and you, Syeed, is this. No point in killing any of them unless you're going to kill all of them, and all the ones as would replace them. At which point you're a player in your own right and probably has to kill yourself as such. Thing about Mara is, she's got a legend whereas you've just got a reputation. You're a possible cost of doing business: she's a fucking nightmare. So, no, not even him."

Tom looked vaguely disappointed; Syeed vaguely relieved.

"The brothers would get blamed," he explained. "Even if you did it wrapped in a flag and singing Rule Britannia."

Elodie reached over and posted his hand reassuringly. Sof realised that she had missed something, thinking about work so much. But then Elodie was present in the memories she had inherited from Emma, a much younger Elodie. It was disconcerting to have those memories, and their being someone else's, and having to pass the milk over breakfast when you knew the small bead of sweat that rolled down her cheek at the moment of orgasm, were forced to wonder whether that still happened.

And knew that Tom would know, because he probably watched Syeed and Elodie as he had watched Elodie and Emma years earlier. She knew Emma had asked him about it once, disapproving a little, embarrassed a little.

Tom had put aside his bravado for a change. "It's clairvoyance," he had said. "If you're one of the people I care about—and lucky for me there are only a few of those—I sort of know what's going on with you all the time. Like a background hum. If you're scared. Or angry. Or getting it on. It's a bit louder. Can we change the subject? I used to be into it. Then I realised it was a bit creepy. Sorry."

Emma had wished she'd never asked. Sof wasn't sure how she felt.

"I have an announcement." The room fell silent. Realising she had perhaps been a little dramatic, Sof lowered her voice. "Nothing has worked. I'm shutting my lab for the moment. We'll just have to live with these dusts until someone else works out how to end them. Sorry."

"If you can't fix it—" from the looks on their faces, Polly spoke for all of them, it seemed, "—well, you fixed me when I was turning to metal and porcelain, thanks to bloody old Isaac, so if you can't, who can?"

"Emma, maybe," Sof confessed. "If she's still around. Or someone we don't know. My only pupil, well, least said about that the better. She has other issues." She hurried on, pushing away the awkward silence. "So anyway, there is this one other thing I can do to be helpful. Polly knows a bit about this; the rest of you don't. I don't like to talk about it because it is so horrid it helped drive me mad for a bit, but I was good at it. I spent several centuries analysing and advising for whichever major power currently owned my dismembered body and drugged and tortured me. Polly is a mistress of information and surveillance, Tom and Syeed are good at, shall we say, executing policy, but I am very good at planning it, though I did it for very bad people, so I'm not proud."

"How bad?" It was of course Tom who had the cheek to ask.

"Templars," Sof admitted. "Sorry, Syeed. Turks for a bit, but a traitor sold me on."

Syeed shrugged "Sounds like you had no options. And they got what was coming to them."

"That was Mara. When she's really upset, she takes her time."

Polly laughed. "I heard what she did to Robespierre. And he'd only hurt you a bit."

"Tell me, sometime," Sof said. "I only met him for a few hours and I was not in my right mind—indeed I was possessing your granddaughter—but my memories are not fond."

The two older women smirked at each other and the others in the room shivered.

Polly continued after a pause, "I'm sure several thousand years of perspective would be useful."

"Obviously," Sof said, "there's bits that I missed, but I got some salient details. Getting torn apart by mad hermits, tortured by crusaders and kicked to death by stormtroopers may have given me some biases of course. From what I've seen of the modern world, they're probably useful ones. This one... pretty standard demagogue, though a less good speaker than most... And Polly is right, killing them rarely helps, because first there's chaos, then there's revenge and then there's the heir. Worse if there's several of those because after they've killed everyone they can accuse of the assassination, they kill each other."

"Plus," Syeed added, "magic clones. Waste of perfectly good C4 if t'buggers won't stay dead. Emma did a perfectly good job on bloody Reverend Black—Tom and I saw her do it–but there he is, bold as brass, on t'platform with t'President Elect, saying he's his own son or some such fuckery."

Elodie stuck up her hand. "Do we know where they make the clones? Because we could always blow their factory up. I was in a movie once where we did that. We got in through the ducts. There were cobwebs. Only Tom wouldn't have to use ducts, of course."

"Well yes," said Polly. "If we knew where they make them. If we knew how they make them."

Elodie looked crestfallen and Syeed lifted her hand and kissed it consolingly.

"It was a very good movie. We watched it in jihadi camp. It was a particular favourite of the Sheikh."

"I was talking to a ghoul in a kebab shop -" the faun started.

"What was a ghoul doing in a kebab shop?" Tom asked, looking slightly sick.

"Buying falafel and chips. He said he was on a diet. So anyway, we got talking about Burnedover people and he said he knew another ghoul who ate a bit of one once. In a police mortuary so it was maybe one you killed, Tom. Anyway, he said, this other ghoul said it made him sick, and they can normally eat anything... Anyone. He said it tasted of plastic."

Everyone in the room looked nauseated.

Sof wondered whether this meant that the Enemy had managed to blend magic and science, the way he had corrupted the Work with the Rituals and decided that, if he had, the was probably nothing much she could do about it. Emma's memories of what she had learned in school were all rather vague: if Sof was going to learn several lifetimes of the new science she was going to have to do it the hard way.

She caught Polly's eye. "You were looking into Dee and angels, hoping to find out about tutelars..."

"Cagey old bastard wrote half the notes in some made-up language, didn't he? I thought it was a cipher, which would have been OK, because ciphers can always be cracked sooner or later. I mean it may take some computer the size of the Isle of Wight but you get there in the end... but languages? You have to find someone what knows them and Dee and Kelley was the only ones what knew this because they were taught it by angels, or so they said. Now, I tried this angel who happens to owe me a favour, but 'e says it's all bollocks. So who knows?"

Sof said, "Think about it. Polly. Set a charlatan to catch a charlatan. Dee was a magus and a crooked old bastard. Who does that remind you of?"

"Well, yeah," Polly shrugged. "But he's been dead for sixty years and more. And in Hell, no doubt, where we can't ask if he knows anything."

"But he isn't. Dead and damned, all right. But Emma sent him off to South America to be Morgan's librarian because his enemies were after him and he wasn't safe even in Hell. Don't suppose anyone has her number?"

Tom shrugged. "She's been off the radar for as long as Mara and Emma. Best guess is, she was visiting Hell when we killed Odin and whatever happened with the red dust happened. Either that, or the Enemy got rid of her some other way at the same time."

"Crowley's probably still scared," Sof said. "You don't stop being scared after they send the Unicorn after you. So the chances are that he's still holed up in Morgan's library and hoping no one knows he's there."

"He won't be answering the phone, neither," Polly added. "Tom?"

It was a long time since Sof had actually got involved in actual field work—perhaps it was time…

"I should go too," she said. "Tom, with respect, you're not an expert. You might know if Crowley lied to you, but not if what he thought was the truth was just a waste of time. Plus, I'd like to have a quick look around Morgan's library. Professional interest. I was a Librarian once. She might even have some of my own books, from when I was Diotima, or Maria, or Mary, or Hypatia."

"I wish I could take more than one of you at a time," Tom said. "But that seems to be how it works."

Tom did the thing with his eyes that meant he was looking somewhere else.

Sof had known people who pretended to be clairvoyants and made far more fuss about far-seeing than this. It just proved that Tom was the real thing and they had not been; it was disconcerting, though, to see him do it.

"Oh, he's there all right. I saw him lurking. So much going on, though—when the cat's away…" He looked at Sof. "Are you sure you want to do this?"

"I'm sure I've seen worse."

Tom laughed.

"Not quite like this, you haven't."

Bedroom Farce

Brazil, 2016

The atrium smelled of sweat, semen, hashish, spilled champagne and overripe fruit.

Clearly no one had spared the time to pick up broken glass or prune the trees which alternated along the walls with statues of Morgan as enchantress, goddess or warrior queen. In all the statues, she had both her eyes—from their style most of them dated back to before she had lost one, but by no means all.

For a moment Sof thought Tom had brought her to the aftermath of a massacre, but too many of the men who lay around in heaps were snoring. A few feet from where Tom's wheelchair deposited them two muscular men, one black, one brown, were still licking each other's pricks as if they were candy, so enthusiastically that they seemed not to notice Sof and Tom's arrival.

The room stank, but more importantly it crackled.

Sof had never been sensitive to the presence of magic—it was something Mara had often over the years had to point out to her and something she mostly recognised these days from having Emma's memories—but she had no doubt. Clearly Tom sensed it too, but then in some sense, as she understood it, he was magic.

"Where's it all coming from?" he asked, not bothering to specify what "it" was.

"I don't think," she replied, "that this is a new or a spontaneous orgy. They've been at it for months. Years, even. It will be Crowley. Somehow he's talked them into it."

She prodded the nearest sleeper with the toe of her shoe—best not to interrupt anyone who was actually fucking. Potentially too much like—she searched her own memories and then Emma's for a good comparison—sticking a fork into an electric socket.

The sleeper joyfully but drowsily said, "Mistress," and seconds later, bolt awake, "You're not her. She's still not back," and started weeping disconsolately.

Sof hated to see someone so upset and patted his shoulder. It didn't seem to help.

"And there we have it," she explained to Tom. "Crowley's talked Morgan's palace full of suitors into an endless homosexual orgy as a summoning ritual to fetch her back from wherever she has disappeared to."

"Hang on," Tom said, confused, "if they're Morgan's suitors won't they mostly be straight?"

"As I understand it, Crowley's sex magick works better if at least one of the parties—preferably more—isn't really all that keen but consenting. Makes it slower, focuses the will. Genuinely works but also meant Crowley could manipulate a lot of people into having sex with him." She looked around the writhing room. "Clearly it's not bringing her back, even if he designed it to. And there's all this loose magic flashing around. I think we need back-up."

She felt in the pocket of the white lab coat she hadn't bothered to change out of, and produced a small talisman she'd got the faun to carve for her.

After a few moments two small caymans and a gharial padded into the atrium, dripping wet and trailing odd bits of water weed. They climbed on to one of the larger sofas and used their long thin jaws full of teeth to worry the three men who were intertwined on it until they disentangled themselves and went off to join three other men on another sofa.

The three reptiles lay down and sank into the leather, and were gone. The sofa shook itself and opened a weary eye.

"Sof," Sobekh said, languidly. "What is it now? It was nice of you let me know you were back, but you never wrote, you never called. And now you bring me to Hekkat's palace, where I'm sure you, unlike me, have no standing invitation. And with this young ruffian too? I haven't seen Tom since we had coffee on a train that time…"

He sniffed the air. "She has rather let the old place go, hasn't she? But there's a lot of very tasty wild magic in the air. Do you think she'd mind if I partake?"

Tom shook his head. "We don't think it's hers. She has a librarian."

The crocodile god took a deep breath and suddenly lightning played around his nostrils. He grew several inches in height and his scales glistened as if they'd been massaged with oil.

"Now that really is good stuff. The mice have been keeping me on short commons this last few years… So, what can I help you with? Since I'm here."

Sobekh looked around, realised what was going on around him and opened his mouth in a toothy and salacious grin.

It was definitely time, Sof decided, to distract him. It would be unseemly for an ancient god to insert himself into the middle of a sex orgy.

"Not necessarily anything. We came to ask Mr Crowley some questions and we found ourselves in the middle of all this. Apparently they're trying to bring Morgan back from wherever she's got herself stuck. Presumably Hell or Shadow, which is where everyone else was last seen, and whence we seem to have got the last boat out, but we rather suspect Mr. Crowley has some other agenda."

"Really," said a sarcastic voice from the staircase at the far end of the enormous room. "Do tell. I'm always interested to find out what trespassers think, before I eviscerate them. Saving your godhood, of course. I know you're always welcome in my mistress' home."

Sof knew him from Emma's memories, but he had been a snivelling bundle of fear then, and now he was sleek, well-fed and had moulded his own hell-flesh into some sort of idealized version of his prime.

She knew he was a charlatan, but that did not mean he was not dangerous—she had known Simon Magus.

"Eviscerate?" said Tom, who was suddenly aiming some sort of gun at the elegant magus. "That's a big word from a traitor and buffoon. Be sure your mouth doesn't pull you into more trouble than you know how to deal with."

"Calm down, Tom." Sof put a restraining hand on his shoulder. "I'm sure we can resolve this without unpleasantness. Mr. Crowley, I've come to ask you for a small professional favour. Colleague to colleague."

"Colleague?" There was an unpleasant half sneer in the magus' voice.

"Librarian to librarian," she said calmly. "I was, in one life, in charge of the Museion and nice as I'm sure the enchantress goddess's little collection is, I probably outrank you."

"What kind of librarian turns up to make a scholarly request with an assassin and a giant crocodile at her side?"

"Clearly," she said with the greatest degree of hauteur she could manage, "one who is not naively trusting. You have, after all, Mr. Crowley, a certain reputation. For one thing, what you have done to your fellow staff members. For another, your inhospitable treatment of my sister, the Huntress."

"Ah," he said, finally impressed, "I was wondering precisely who you had been, when alive."

He was himself in hell-flesh and likely to recognize it. "Oh, all sorts of people," she said loftily. "I'm sure my sister told you some of them, but she never knew all of them."

"Why do you remind me so heavily of that awful bitch Emma Jones, who sent me here?"

"Because Emma is her avatar, you silly little man," Sobekh rumbled. "Why wasn't this immediately obvious to everyone? I knew from the start."

Tom wheeled himself closer, clearly curious. "Really? I knew she was a bit special first time we met, but I had no idea."

"They smell the same—maybe that's not obvious if you're not a crocodile... but also, she woke up the faun whom Hypatia had put into a sleep, which only Hypatia could undo. I failed Hypatia, but I could help Emma."

"Good job you did," Sof said, "because I was sleeping in her mind."

"Well, well." Now Crowley was drawing closer too. "Obviously I knew bits of that story, but not how it came out. I'd love to know more, but an important person is coming. My three o'clock. If you don't mind waiting? I do hope you haven't consumed all of the wild magic. You're welcome, of course, this time. Introductory offer... but most people do actually pay."

Somewhere else in the palace a clock struck the hour. Quietly, but it resonated.

And as it boomed a man was among them. Thin, a little gaunt and with growing lines following his neat moustache down past the lipline. He had the slightly weary look of one who has seen better days: the elegant suit no longer had its original razor creases and there was grey in his hair.

Sof very deliberately strode across the room and slapped him open-handed with all the strength built into her hell-flesh body. He flew backwards ten feet and landed in a pile of rutting male bodies.

As he extricated himself, he patted various buttocks affectionately. A small stream of blood trickled from his left nostril; his tongue flicked out to lick at it. Unselfconsciously, meditatively, sensually.

194

"Lady Sof," Lucifer said. "You punch like a girl."

"I owe you for Cana," she replied. "Most of the people who have done me wrong are long gone beyond recall and my reach. My sister the Huntress saw to that, while I was indisposed. But here you still are, though less. I gather you made the mistake of crossing my avatar Emma Jones."

"Ah," Lucifer sighed. "That explains so much. I didn't know; no one tells me anything anymore."

"Why would they, has-been?" Tom snapped.

"Reduced to buying spare sex magic from Crowley just to stay alive," Sof added. "I hope he's charging you the going rate. I own the Elixir, the Stone and the Fifth Thing, so I could help you. But I rather think I won't."

Lucifer's eyes flashed with anger—so there was still some anger. "I refuse to be lectured on how pathetic I am by a crippled changeling bastard and a woman betrayed by one of her partners in incest and slaughtered by the other."

Sobekh muttered under his breath and everyone looked askance at him.

"Can we get on?" he said, louder now. "I promised to help Sof, but time marches on and I have an important sardine shoal to make the acquaintance of."

"You're right, of course," Sof acknowledged. "Pleasurable as it would be to punch Lucifer in the face a couple more times, Cana was a long time ago and that's not why we're here. Crowley, how's your Enochian? John Dee left some notes we need translating. As you may know, the Enemy has destroyed the Tutelars and we think it would be good for the world if they were replaced as soon as possible."

Lucifer coughed meaningfully. "I wouldn't think Dee knew much of use. He was greedy and intellectually overrated. Greedier than Crowley here and just as prone to making things up. On the other hand, if you need to know how the Tutelars were made, well, ask me. I was there. I helped my old friend Nameless, whom you know as Jehovah, put them to work. Of course, it wasn't his idea or mine. It

195

was that smartass adopted Son of his… So the question is, what's the information worth?"

Sof hated negotiating, especially from a position of weakness. She looked at Tom.

"You'd need to talk to Miss Wild. I have a little bit of discretion with run of the mill informants, but the former Lord of the Infernal Realm, that's above my pay grade."

Sof could see that Lucifer was about to walk away from any possible deal. She didn't know his specific tells—no, actually, she probably did, because Emma had noticed that particular tightening of the flesh below his bottom lip when he thought he gained the upper hand by abducting Caroline and again when he thought he had gained some small revenge for his downfall by burdening her with judging the damned.

He really did not understand Emma, which meant that there was a fairly good chance he wouldn't see what she was doing if she distracted him long enough to gain some advantage.

"I have to ask," she said, "what on earth were you doing talking to Dee in the first place? As you say, not a first-rate mind and you were the Lord of Hell…" Dole out crumbs of respect to those used to, and deprived of, it, and they are pathetically eager to please.

Lucifer laughed. It was not the sort of laugh that makes you like someone; it was the laugh of someone who already loves themselves enough that they don't need you.

"Ha! It was the late Renaissance and every petty magus seemed to think I was interested in buying their souls. Idiots, as if they weren't mostly mine already. But it was funny watching them trying to negotiate."

Crowley looked at first slightly embarrassed, and then annoyed and just a little spiteful. Whatever the magic Lucifer was buying from him, its price had just gone up.

There was a small explosion somewhere below them, followed by a torrent of shots, shouts and screams.

Through the door the small crocodiles had entered by, there strode a man in a well-tailored black uniform, a drawn gun in his right hand, though as far as Sof could tell it was thankfully one of the ordinary sort.

She remembered the face, though obviously she'd never met him. Judging from the lively intelligence in his eyes, this must be one of the superior copies.

He was almost instantly, furiously distracted by the nearest fornicating male triad, failing to notice Tom's rather larger weapon. Or indeed the very large crocodile—she remembered how unobtrusive Sobekh could be if you didn't know him. She supposed it was in the nature of crocodiles.

"Sodomites," he shouted in a moralistic rage that clearly affected his aim because his first and only bullet lodged itself in the leather upholstery. The trio didn't even notice and continued what they were about. He never got off a second shot; Sobekh was across the room in a second and bit his head off.

"Oh goody," Tom said with a note of anticipatory satisfaction in his voice. "Burnedover. They still owe for Sharpe."

And disappeared.

There was promptly a lot more shooting from downstairs and elsewhere in the palace—alternatively wild bursts and single shots. There were fewer explosions and screams and a number of barked orders, all of them interrupted.

Sof knew in theory what Tom was capable of, but in the decade and more she had shared a house with him, she had only seen him being quick and efficient.

He was, it seemed, capable of far more.

Crowley had the expression of a man who only now realised that he really should not threaten people. Lucifer by contrast was rather enjoying himself.

Sobekh was finishing eating. He finally swallowed hard, then spat a handful of buttons into a handy cuspidor. Everything was suddenly quiet again, except for a few sobs.

Tom reappeared and looked apologetically at Crowley. "Sorry," he said, "they killed some of the suitors before I got down there. Saved most of them though. You'll be wanting to get rid of the Burnedover bodies."

Crowley looked hopefully at Sobekh.

The god shook his head apologetically. "Really, I normally abstain and I'm not going to make a habit of it. But religious fanatics in black threatening Sof... there's history and I lost my temper. Please don't tell the Huntress. I promised her."

Crowley wasn't happy. "That's all very well, but that means I have to lug them out into the jungle. It's going to take hours."

"Can't the suitors help?" Sof said.

"Those that aren't dead or bleeding out," Tom added, not especially helpfully.

"Oops," Sof said, and pulled the Stone from her pocket. She held it above her head and thought hard. Beams shot out from it through her cupped hands, and she could feel them flooding the entire palace, walls and floors and every wounded man. "That should have healed their wounds," she explained. "I've not worked out how to raise the dead."

Crowley was clearly impressed. "I have never read of the Stone being able to do that," he said.

"Plato was annoying but he wasn't entirely wrong about books," Sof admitted. "The point about the Work is that reading about the Work isn't doing the Work. Over and over—lifetime after lifetime in my case. Though you will have read about the Stone curing things though. I had an apprentice once..."

He didn't work it out and she wasn't going to enlighten him.

Lucifer laughed. It was an understated refinement to say that he laughed sardonically.

"But you're on your own with the corpses," Sof added.

"And the holes in load-bearing walls," Tom said.

"But surely you've got a lot of loose wild magic from all the fucking." Sof was aware that she was enjoying all this too much, but Crowley was in a trap of his own making. He had persuaded the suitors into a sex trance and they might have views about it if he ever woke them up.

"The magic he has raised is promised to me." Lucifer drew himself up to the full height of someone more important than he actually was these days.

Crowley looked impatiently at him. "I'm sure there's nothing you need desperately from—what was the expression?—a petty magus. And to be perfectly frank, I have obligations to the goddess Morgan that are more important than any deal I might strike with you. Holes in her palace walls? I really don't want to upset her."

"I think," Lucifer smiled his rather toothy smile, "that you should be rather more worried about upsetting someone who might do you harm right now."

The room darkened. Crowley drew himself up to his full and considerable height. "If you had the power to harm me, or take magic from me by force, you would not have been here to trade with me. You need what power you have left to stay even moderately young and you dare not use it for anything else. I would be a fine booby to sell you power that you might use to take more from me. You are no longer welcome here."

"Whereas," Sof added, with a toothy smile of her own, "while I am not in the business of magical power, if you come back with us and help Polly, I can at least solve your ageing problem permanently. I have the Elixir; I have the Stone. And the passage of years need never worry you again."

"This is Lucifer," Sobekh rumbled. "He is well known for ingratitude."

"Don't worry that I have forgotten his many offenses," Sof said. "But he is also a sick old man. And I taught Hippocrates to heal before history. I taught Josh, my pupil and some would say my husband. I am not Emma and I am not in the business of judging. But, like the doctor I am, I expect payment from those able to pay my price in order to be also able to heal those who are not."

With a sour expression, Lucifer nodded.

199

Tom put his weapon away. "If I were you, Mr. Crowley, and had received an unexpected visit from Burnedover, I would see to my defences. They know where you are and will be calling again, unless you make it costly for them to do so."

Lucifer could clearly see power shifting around the room. "Of course, in your position it's never a good idea to hire mercenaries, because they can't be trusted."

He'd always been a bit of a toady.

"Shame you had a perfectly good local militia, that you've decided to use as a different kind of resource," Tom added.

"What you need," Sof suggested brightly, "is a highly trained, highly motivated, highly ethical force with their own magical powers."

Crowley began to look uncomfortable. He could clearly see where this conversation was being drawn and didn't love it. As magnet to the pole.

"Now, obviously, they turned Morgan down when she offered them a contract before. But Burnedover's man just got elected, so they may be interested in leaving the USA."

Crowley really wasn't happy now. "You mean that troupe of art snob travesties?"

"I have Emma's memories of seeing the House of Art in battle." Sof felt quite vexed with his superior attitude.

"Needs must," Tom said with what Sof felt sure was an entirely spurious air of knowing what he was talking about. "Sobekh and I have worked with one of their leaders, and she is slightly terrifying. Emma's old boss." Perhaps not entirely, then.

"Really?" Lucifer was intrigued. "Same one who healed me when the Dukes betrayed me. Terribly familiar, but I couldn't place the face. It's been annoying me ever since."

Sobekh looked smug.

Lucifer pounced. "Really?"

"She speaks perfect Greek with an Alexandrian accent," the crocodile started to explain.

"Shut up, Sobekh," Sof interrupted him before he could get onto identifying marks. He had given away too much already.

Crowley had had a chance to think things through a little more. "Besides, they'd judge me for what I did to the suitors…"

"There is that," Sof allowed, "but less likely to string you up in a rage than the suitors when you free them, and a lot less likely to shoot, burn or disintegrate you than the Burnedover people. Who will assume it was you that disposed of their first crew. You've deprived yourself of good options; time you thought of least bad ones."

Crowley looked around the room; it seemed to dawn on him at last that he had no friends here. Sobekh smiled at him with more teeth than usual.

After a pregnant moment, Sof looked around her. "I think we're done here. Tom?"

"We need to get his Satanic majesty here to where he can talk to Polly, but without letting him know her address."

"I'll drop him round," Sobekh offered.

"How is it that you know the address?" Sof enquired. "Tom, isn't it supposed to be secret?"

"The mice tell me things," the god explained. "It's very useful. I don't know why Apollo handed them over. The Olympians take themselves too seriously, if you ask me, even for humans."

Sof took Tom's hand, and turned back to Crowley. "Whatever you decide, do it quickly."

"It's less work if you sit in my lap," Tom said. "Also, rather more fun."

Sobekh squirmed a little and the smaller cayman disengaged from his bulk. "If you don't mind taking this one along… Makes it easier to manifest. I'm sure Miss Wild has an aquarium tucked away somewhere in her establishment. She doesn't bite."

The creature waddled across the room, and then, with a surprising turn of speed, hauled itself up Sof and Tom and nuzzled its jaws against her left cheek. It's all a matter of trust, she thought.

Sof would never get used to how instantaneous travel with Tom was.

"What the bleeding hell is that corkindale for?" Polly asked raucously.

It slithered down and then twisted itself up on to its hind legs. Suddenly there was intelligence behind its eyes.

"Miss Wild," Sobekh said. "If you'll pardon this partial intrusion, I would like your permission to visit and bring the former Lord of Hell. Who claims, for what it's worth, to be able to answer your questions."

"Crowley was little use," Tom said. "And has rather pressing problems of his own."

"Lucifer, on the other hand," Sof noted, "seems quite keen to share. Accepted a price that costs us nothing, and he knows it, and is just a little bit desperate to do business. I have my own good reasons for detesting the man, but these days he cuts a sorry figure. I could almost enjoy the situation."

"Bad habit, that," Polly said. "You're far too old not to have grown out of it." But she said it with a wry smile that indicated it was a habit she had not yet grown out of herself. And though Polly was far younger, her single conscious life had been continuous… Polly nodded to the cayman. "Bring him."

The cayman stretched and bulked, knocking over several small tables and spilling their contents on to the carpet, which fortunately was thick enough to prevent serious breakage. The crocodile opened its jaws wide, made a slight gagging noise and spat the former Lord of Hell into a corner, where he lay for a moment, quivering and covered in viscous grey fluid.

Polly picked her way past the displaced crockery and patted the beast god on his scaly flank. "Better out than in, eh? We'll say no more about the Spode, seeing as most of it seems to have survived. And I never especially cared for it. And it was a gift from the Duke hisself, jumped-up bog-trotting butcher as thought I was vulgar."

"I really am most sorry for my clumsiness, Miss Wild," Sobekh rumbled. "It is several centuries since I had a god as an internal passenger and I had forgotten how heavy they sit on the stomach and how little I like the taste."

"I have a smooth Laphroaig as would help with that if you felt like partaking?"

But the crocodile had already begun to dwindle and wisp away. "Alas," he said, "it is a human thing for which I never developed much of a taste and after many centuries of sharing the Nile with the Children of The Prophet, I find myself deferring to their views in the matter." A moment later he was gone, leaving a small moulted husk behind. Polly picked it up, rolled it into a ball and placed it in a lacquered wooden box on one of the tables that had not been knocked over.

"I takes it that can be used if he ever wants to call round," she explained. "The which you may tell him he is welcome to do if you talks to him again. Nice old chap, better than your normal run of gods…"

By now Lucifer had pulled himself off the floor and out of his momentary funk. He had even managed to wipe away most of Sobekh's digestive juices with a large pocket handkerchief he had pulled from somewhere, though his suit was never going to be the same again.

He was impressively quick to recover from being a whimpering mess. Stepping forward, suave as a Riviera croupier, he bowed, took Polly's hand and kissed it. "Miss Wild," he said, "I had the pleasure of brief acquaintance with your late father."

"You know your own, it is said."

"Clearly not well enough, for hardly had he been placed in a vat of boiling pitch and those he had misled and betrayed brought from their own torments to mock and befoul him, than that he suborned the thief Shepherd into freeing them both."

"Pretty Jack?" Polly was incredulous. "What died on Tyburn Tree with curses of my da as his neck verse?"

Lucifer smiled. "All men have a weakness, and Pretty Jack, as you call him, was no exception. He loved a challenge. Your father bet him that he could not free them both away and clear from Heaven and

Hell to somewhere in Shadow where they could steal together without age or law to trammel them."

"How—if you'll pardon the expression—the Hell do you know what they said and yet they still escaped?" Sof asked.

"Their back and forth amused the demons set to guard them so much that the demons were persuaded to fetch ale that the two damned might toast each other… Only the demons thought it a fine jape to take the ale back just before their lips could touch it, and drink it themselves. Except that somehow Jack has swapped honest infernal ale for the boiling pitch from your father's vat and by the time the demons' seared gullets had recovered, the birds had flown, never to be seen again. It was prettily done, the demons ruefully acknowledged as I personally dismembered them." He turned to Sof. "I have to ask. Did you know that being transported by Sobekh meant being swallowed and carried in his stomach?"

Sof shook her head. "I didn't know. I didn't guess. But if I had done, I certainly wouldn't have told you."

Lucifer laughed–a new laugh, surprisingly pleasant. "I can hardly blame you after what happened at Cana… Be assured that one day I will discover what became of your erstwhile husband. And all your other little secrets. There is no secret I do not uncover eventually."

Sof reflected with a quiet satisfaction that if he had not yet worked out that the two secrets she was keeping from him had the same solution, he had a cognitive blind spot. What was that phrase she had learned from Emma? Ah yes. Toxic masculinity.

"But never mind all that. I will tell Miss Wild here what I know of tutelars and then I shall avail myself of your alchemical services"— he clearly knew how much she disliked the useless travesty that later centuries had made of the Work—"and then we shall avoid each other for another two thousand years."

Sof was oddly gratified that for some reason he disliked her almost as much as she loathed him. And that these days it hardly mattered at all. Now he was no longer the Lord of Hell, he was someone who simply no longer mattered and he would not survive another two thousand years if he failed to acknowledge that fact.

Yet she would deal honestly with him, even if he had little information that Polly could use. He obviously knew something—actually he certainly knew a lot of things—and brokering information was an honest trade to some degree. He could certainly do worse. Besides, to let someone who knew that much perish and wither would be like burning a library…

So long as he could be kept from mischief. And the only way she might do that was almost certainly through example.

Without the power he had been used to wield, he was sick. And, though she had taught both Hippocrates and Josette, they had taught her too. Healing the sick was not just something she could do; it was something she must do.

And so, even before telling him what she was about, she brought forth the fruits of her Work with a thought and set them to cure him. All are mortal, even immortals, but she could reset his clock for a long while.

He had once had, and now lacked, levels of power that meant he never had had to think about disease. Like most gods, he had been able to indulge himself and repair damage—not with a thought but without one—but this was no longer the case. She sensed a weakened lung, the start of an ulcer, and with that moment, they were gone.

"What have you done?" he said. "I sensed a touch and suddenly felt as I have hardly felt since I came into power."

"I honoured our agreement," she said, "and now as your doctor I will give you a warning. Without the power you had as Lord of Hell the common law of humanity applies. Whatever you do, you pay a price for. Moderation, as my former pupils taught. You know this. You spent centuries punishing the sot and the glutton…"

"Yes, yes." He brushed her remarks aside as she knew he would until he found himself seriously unwell. He looked slightly embarrassed nonetheless.

"However," he continued, "by acting precipitously, you have put me in a slightly false position. I take it that Miss Wild is considering attempting to offer herself as a substitute for the late and lamented Lord of Cliffs and Shores, and I can certainly tell her how to attempt this."

"Well, then," Polly cut in irritably, "what's the problem? You get paid, you tell me, we're done. And I gets on and tries to fix what's broken before worse befalls. Poor old chap, he and his friends did not deserve what the Enemy done to them, but what's done is done. For the moment."

"There, right there, is your problem," Lucifer said. "You think that the country is broken because the Lord was murdered, along with others of his sort. I'm suggesting that the Enemy could defeat and devour them because their countries were fraying at the edges already. And if you become a new tutelar, you will have the same problem. You will be over-stretched and weakened and visible and a threat to his plans."

It worried Sof that he seemed to be honest and sincere. She asked the obvious question. "You know this, how?"

Lucifer sighed. "Because for some time I have seen where he has been and what he has done and have done my best to work out the likely next moves in his game and done my best to be elsewhere. He approached me at one point, and frightened me so much that I cooperated in small things, for a while, which led to my downfall, and to his interest shifting elsewhere. None of us have the power or the resources to beat him, except possibly my former friend Nameless, and I imagine he will be next. Odin is gone; the Egyptians are in their refuge; most of the powers are destroyed or lost in Shadow. The Buddha long ago decided not to get involved, as did the Trimurti. I lost what power I had thanks to your little friend Emma, which taught me not to underestimate any enemy."

He paused for breath as even gods must sometimes. "I don't know what he wants, whether it is absolute power or nothingness. I hope to find a hole to hide in. If he could ever have been defeated, that time is long gone."

Polly shook her head impatiently. "You don't half like pretty speeches. Which, from what I gather, has always been a part of your problem. Also, like you say, underestimating people. And being a bully and a sneak and a coward. I don't imagine we can do enough either, but I for one intend to try."

Elodie and Syeed and the faun had all drifted back into the room from whatever they had been doing. "He set angels to drive me from my time," the faun said.

"He taught my family cantrips that would have made me a monster."

"And mine the spells that crippled me."

"He is the greatest Satan as you are the least."

Sof said merely, "Oh, so many things."

Polly said, "He has harmed my friends and my country and the world. That's offences what need requital, and if not us, then who? From what I hears, the whole bleeding point of you and Jehovah setting up the shell game of salvation and damnation was to harvest us all like potatoes so you could fight him. And you made a fine mess. Run off and hide, bucky, if that's all you're good for. But like Mackie said once, even if you're doing the Tyburn dance, you can plant your last kick in the hangman's goolies and maybe have a spare for the chaplain."

"If you won't help more than that, tell us what you know and be on your way," Sof said.

Suddenly the whiny insinuating bray of the new President-elect blared from one of the televisions.

They all looked at Lucifer. He shook his head. "Not mine. Not these days. Never seriously. I mean, spoiled rich boys who are bad with money—lots of them, mostly more trouble than they're worth. A failure of imagination on my part, I suppose. But then, I can't see the future."

"You do know, don't you? That the Enemy can," said Sof. "Or rather, my sister Lillit gives him bits of it for some arcane reason of her own."

"So she thinks he'll win, as well?" Lucifer looked ironically pleased to have his own judgement confirmed.

"Who knows? She certainly doesn't tell him everything. Because there are secrets he doesn't know. Also, I'm pretty certain she tells him things in ways that bring about what she's predicted—Emma, good example. Lillit tells him she's important, so he sets his dogs onto her. But that puts Emma on her path which would not otherwise have happened. Lillit's playing her own game, which she claims is obeying the inevitable dictates of time and chance."

"Total, total power but no free will," Tom said. "Miserable."

Lucifer shrugged. "Nice as it is to hear about people whose problems sound worse than mine, I have a deal to honour with you and then, since I gather the reptile has spewed me into London, a tailor to visit and a high stakes card game to find and cheat at."

He struck up a lecturer's pose, smug as if he were at a lectern. "Tutelars… It's actually quite a simple magic. There's usually an oath. Not a set text, just a form of words with a sense of commitment to back it up. Mostly, you have to really want it, and feel that overpowering urge to protect your people. And know it's possible. You could have become what you say you want to be. You just had to want it and really I don't think you want it enough."

Polly looked deflated and defeated and not at all like herself. Lucifer stroked her hair almost like a parent, and laughed ruefully and almost gently.

"People never ask why, when we got bored with being the Hero Twins and decided that Mara was too hung up on her rules to save the world, I let Nameless be the Lord and me be the Adversary, the Accuser. I could say we tossed for it, but there weren't coins yet. Or that we arm wrestled—but that would have been silly because he would always have beaten me at that. Truth is, he asked nicely and I could never say no when he looked at me like that. You just have to work out how much you want, how much you can get and what comes next…"

And he made his exit, as suddenly and fiercely as if he had a cape to swirl. "London," he shouted with delight and slammed the front door.

"London," Polly echoed. And then repeated with delight as the others gathered round. And then firmly, with resignation. "London, and only London." They stared at her. "He's right, ain't he? Perspicacious old so and so. I knew it, really. Silly little girl, thinking I could replace the Lord, whom there's no replacing, gone forever. What do I know or care for Worcester or Wigan? But Whitehall, Westway and the Old Kent Road, what I've watched and loved these three hundred years? Them I can guard. Them I can be their Lady. I swear."

Sof had done the Work over and over, had watched the bases flower into the Elixir or the Adamant or sublime into the Alkahest or catch light as the Stone. But she had been gone when Lillit became the Quintessence, asleep when Emma became the Judge.

Now she laughed with glee as Polly became more than Polly, and was London and always had been.

For My Next Trick

The Undercroft of Shadow

Mara and the birds waited. Emma spoke, eyes closed.

"Birds," she said, "Bag. We're going to be doing a working. Safe distance please; it's going to be a bit icky. Caroline, you too. Not because of Lillit, but because someone needs to tell the story if this means we go bang or something. Dog, Wolf, horses—we should probably set a perimeter. Mara, I need your help, in here, in my memory palace. I could probably just use an eidolon of you—but no, the whole thing is kind of a ritual from beginning to end so you need to be part of it, focussing will through predetermined actions."

The nice thing about divinity—or maybe about usually being right—is how much of the time people just do what you tell them to.

She opened her eyes and blew the retreating Caroline and her servants a kiss. Then shut them again and was at the outer door of her interior palace, with Mara standing next to her. She took Mara's right hand and kissed it, slowly and tenderly but like a sister, not a lover.

Mara, unprompted, did the same, and asked, "Are you going to tell me what we are going to do?"

"No. Your trust and faith, freely given, are part of what will fuel it. Also, it's partly about the slow unfolding of truth and other things so your finding things out as we proceed is part of the process."

"Likeness becomes sameness," Mara said.

"Just so," Emma said. "And what was broken becomes whole."

She gestured once to her right with her left hand and once to her left with her right, once above and once down. She knitted her hands together, pushing forward as if moving a heavy weight.

Emma intoned, "This is a cleansing of the world and of the Work, which is part of the world and which has been desecrated by betrayal and corruption. Mara, Huntress, the protector of the weak against the strong, do you consent to following my lead in this?"

Mara responded, on the beat, "I so consent."

Good, Emma thought, she understands enough to do what I tell her, when I tell her…

Emma walked up to the door and unlocked it with a small intricate filigree key. "Enter," she said. "You are welcome here."

She extended her hand and Mara took it. They walked briskly down the entrance hall and then a corridor at right angles to it.

Somewhere else in the palace, two voices were winding round each other in vaguely erotic counterpoint.

Mara looked quizzically at Emma, who said, "I have lodgers. We need not involve either of them for the moment. Look freely at the paintings and listen to the music. I have no secrets here and it is important that you know that."

Mara looked and the pictures moved for her. Emma confronting angels with a small waterspray; Emma throwing pepper into the exposed flesh of a vast involuted human; Emma intoning a ritual as elves and vampires battled round her; Emma looking care-worn and almost old, a streak of white in her scarlet hair, as a seemingly endless line of the former damned came before her for judgement.

"Know some of my deeds," Emma said.

"I know them," Mara said.

Silently Emma pointed to some blank canvases, hanging next to the images of her. Mara took the invitation and thought at them and suddenly they showed Mara emerging from the pool of Atlantis holding the flaming egg; Mara slaying the jaguar god of the city of the dead; Mara beheading the Horned God.

"Know my deeds," Mara said.

"I know them," said Emma. "We are the champions of the weak against the strong."

"We are the champions of the weak against the strong."

"In their name, we cleanse the world and The Work."

"In their name," Mara affirmed.

At the end of the Corridor of Deeds was a staircase, a narrow stair leading down into darkness.

"Follow me," Emma said, "Into the Dungeon of the Best Forgotten, the Iron Box with Many Locks."

Mara followed her in silence down thirteen flights of stairs for what seemed an endless age punctuated only by landings. From corridors to the left and right of each landing came moans and supplications, many of them in Emma's own voice.

After a while, Mara spoke. "I have no such place in my mind."

Emma smiled and she knew Mara knew that she smiled even in the darkness and the din.

"You have such a place," Emma said. "Though doubtless it has less fancy architecture and you have mislaid the key to its door."

Mara said nothing but Emma was aware of her being about to protest and then pausing for consideration.

At the bottom of the thirteenth stair, there was no corridor to the right and to the left a pool of even greater, Delphic darkness.

"Some light, please," Emma said, and Mara glowed.

The pool of darkness revealed itself to be a great iron door with thirteen cruel hinges and as many locks from behind which came the baying of mastiffs, the yowling of wildcats and the hissing of cobras. And even through the door a stink of effluent and cruelty.

Emma produced a black key from nowhere obvious. It had many wards and a bit as sharp as a dagger. She unlocked the first lock and it screamed as she turned the key and it went on screaming after she removed the key. She held up the key in the light and showed Mara how its wards and bit melted and reformed and changed their configuration. And the second lock screamed a note higher than the first.

By the time she got to the thirteenth lock, the screaming of its fellows and the noises from within the cell were almost unbearable. The thirteenth lock, though, closed with a click that could only just be heard, but which silenced everything but the snarling and screeching and hissing from within the cell.

"What is that?" Mara said.

"A problem, but also a solution. Come, help me pull the door open."

There was a ring set in the centre of the door now that had not been there before, a heavy ring that hung from the carved nostrils of a demon face that was at once flush with the door and yet seeming to have weight and depth. They set their right hands on the ring and pulled: the demon's mouth opened in a silent scream of agony and the door started to move under its own momentum. They stepped away from its maiming weight and it hit the wall with a booming clang.

A voice from inside the cell whispered, "Free me," and the whisper was still the animal noises that had preceded it.

"I shall," Emma said, "but not in a way that you would wish."

They entered the cell. Chained to iron hoops in the floor and lying in its own filth and stink was—it had no shape and yet its shape constantly shifted. Spikes and teeth and claws and hair, sometimes slicked and sometimes spiked, and a split tongue that lolled and had

213

two tiny demon heads at the ends of its parts, heads that murmured threats and promises in a language long forgotten.

"Behold!" Emma declaimed. "This is Sof's trauma, Sof's madness, that I wrestled out of her mind and placed here in my own for safekeeping."

"Why such filth?" Mara asked. "I knew you were one of the wise, but not that you were also cruel."

"This is what tormented your sister into madness," Emma said. "It is right that you feel compassion for it because it is, in part, the child of your necessary act. Yet, it lies in stench because it is of its nature to will it so, as it is of mine to tell it, 'Cleanse yourself!'"

As she spoke, the demon heads at the split ends of the creature's tongue extended long tongues of their own, long tubes that snaked down into the pool of filth and sucked it up in moments with a disgusting slurp.

There was a spiked hammer on the wall. Emma pointed to it.

"Strike the creature free. Break its chains."

Mara took the hammer and swung it once, twice, three times, four times at the hoops that held the chains and the chains knotted round the hoops. Each time she struck there was a fierce ringing clang and the crack of hard iron falling to rust and splinters. She did not merely break the chains; she annihilated them.

Emma went to where the creature's head—or at least the part of it that held its largest mouth—joined its body and placed a booted foot on the closest thing it had to a neck. It screeched and spat, but its spittle slid off her heel without leaving a mark and burned where it landed.

"Be still, beast," she said, "be silent. Lest worse befall you."

She waved her hand and a muzzle blossomed out of nothingness on the creature's principal mouth and a collar coiled from the empty air around its neck. There was a leash attached to the collar and she wound it tight around her left wrist.

"Come." She snapped the fingers of her right hand and suddenly she and Mara and the creature were all standing back in the tunnel, the memory palace left behind.

She snapped her fingers again.

"Into the flesh with you," she commanded, and suddenly the creature was solid and, though equally unappealing, no longer constantly shifting as you looked at it.

"Oh, good," she sighed with relief, "I was a little concerned that when we returned to the material world, it might remember that it was just a mental state and get away from me. But harsh language and dominance behaviour sufficed to confuse it long enough. Could you stand back a little? It's probably going to want to attack you in a minute."

Mara was still holding the idea of a spiked hammer and let go of it. Instantly, it was gone.

"Beast," Emma said peremptorily. "You know who this is. This is Mara, whom you hate."

The creature snarled and yowled and hissed as it had when they had first heard it, and it pulled on its leash. But its pull lacked vigor, and conviction. Emma smiled. "You see, Beast. You're not who you think you are."

She turned to Mara. "You see, Sof—in her madness—fixated on the idea that you killed her, which you did. Of course, by saving her from pain of potentially endless and already centuries-long agony with the utter agony of her dissolution in the Alkahest, you acted out of love and compassion and a simple sense of what was necessary. Blaming you was not fair in any way, and at some level she knew this. But thinking of what had happened in that way was something she could bear more readily than the truth, which is that Lillit had betrayed both of you, and life itself and the way that the order of the universe expresses itself through the Work. I believe Lillit had her own reasons for this, and that they are to do with the workings of Time and Chance, but then I am the version of Sof to whom nothing that bad has ever happened so I can be cool and monstrously dispassionate about it."

She clipped the creature smartly about where its ears ought to be. "Reveal yourself," and quite suddenly the creature changed its shape. It was shiny ebony, and it looked like the statuette in Emma's living room, like the armour that had protected her in Hell. And its eyes were blank and dead and its mouth was disfigured by two long fangs. She turned to look steadily at Mara.

"Now. I need you to go inside your head, find whatever tumbledown shack or long colonnade of pillars and statues you have there—because you have memories and you will have organized them—and bring me the captive you will have locked away there. It will probably look quite like this one because you may have repressed the memory you're feeling but you won't actually have misrepresented it to yourself. Go, come back, bring it. On the clock here."

Mara nodded, closed her eyes and went away inside herself for what felt like an age but was probably only five minutes of actual time.

When she opened them, she had a bone-white creature on a leash that was almost identical to the one Emma held captive, except that it was longer and greyhound thin and crouched on all fours as if about to run away. She held the leash tight, white-knuckled, and looked at Emma in bewilderment. "How did you know?"

"I'm Emma, queen and judge of what used to be Hell. I know things. And now it is almost time to call on my friend to help us."

Mara looked concerned. "This ritual won't involve anything I disapprove of, is it? I mean, I know that these are only embodied mental states or something, but they do closely resemble my sister and I wouldn't want anything bad to happen. They're not going to function like a witch's poppets, are they?"

"I shouldn't think so," Emma explained, "because we're not going to hurt them. Quite the opposite in fact. And if we could hurt Lillit or wanted to, she would know, and if it were not something that just had to happen she would be here to explain us out of it. The fact she isn't gives me hope."

Then she added, "But your concern lest we hurt her indicates you're better off without that thing in your head. I'm going to need you to be a bit angry in a moment, but we need it to be focussed on the existence of dark alchemy and not irrelevantly directed at any particular individual. If what I'm planning works, bad actors may face consequences, but that will be on them."

Mara's jaw dropped a little. "We're going after all of dark alchemy?"

"Yes, root and branch. Which may mean that things fall down a bit and go bang."

Emma reached into her pocket universe, produced the black gun and threw it a few yards away.

"That should tell us whether this works. Nasty thing, I won't miss it. Bad for my character. I try not to kill people—not judging—and it makes it too easy."

Mara took a momentary professional interest. "Oh," she said, "who did you kill?"

"A bunch of Burnedover clones. One I thought was their original, but probably wasn't. Cesare Borgia. The creature Dead Simon Magus had become—head and lots of legs. I unseamed him from guggle to zatch and then I disintegrated his head."

Mara nodded, looking impressed. "That's one we have in common, then. A man who really couldn't be killed too often, and frankly if he's gone for good, that's one thing we don't have to worry about. Luckily, didn't play well with others."

Emma tapped her forehead. "If you'd be so kind?" she asked, and suddenly a small white ball of light appeared. It was humming a Bach toccata, nonchalantly. "Right—we now have to focus on all the ways in which dark alchemy sucks. I've got my friend John being psychically sucked down to dust and the magic axe that took my favourite cop's head off and those crazy Dark Greens and…"

"I've got the Apaches in Paris and what happened to the Aesir and—"

"– Just being marooned in Hell and Shadow and not—"

"– knowing what's going on and—"

"I think," Emma said, "that we've reached the right level of annoyance. Blind fury would be counter-productive. Just focus very clearly on how much you want dark alchemy to be gone. I did think of making it never have been but best not to mess with time. Lillit can get away with that stuff but I don't think she ever changes what happened…"

She paused for a moment, thinking through the next bit.

"These," she announced, adopting a hieratic pose and tone, "are the memories of a savage moment of betrayal of love, of kindred and thus of the order of the universe. As we cleanse those memories of their poison, so we restore that natural order in which the Work is a progress through spiritual good that also brings physical healing. Likeness is sameness. Let it be healed."

Mara reached out both hands but not in a caress. She was putting her weight on Emma's shoulders.

Emma looked a question.

"If my leg goes away," Mara explained, "I'd rather not cleanse the world and then fall flat on my face."

As they spoke, the ball of light projected a beam of whiteness that seemed not to be the mere absence of colours, but their blending and transcendence. As it played over the two memory creatures, the white quadruped stood upright and the features of both became less bestial. The tusks sank back in among teeth that flashed in smiles, and the dead eyes shone for a moment with intelligence and compassion. They reached out and held each other in an embrace and then the ebony one kissed the forehead of its white twin, which in turn kissed the ebony one's cheek.

And then suddenly they dissolved into the light of the beam that played over them and the music of the pavane from Berthe's opera.

"Let it be healed," Emma said, "Likeness is sameness."

"Likeness is sameness," Mara said. "Let it be healed."

The discarded gun smoked and sizzled for a moment and then dissolved like a bubble, like the scum of a pot. For a moment there was a stench of dead creatures and of corruption and then that was gone. And even in this tunnel deep within the earth, the quality of light changed into something fresher and cleaner.

In their lungs, in their hearts, a pain and a pressure went away that they had not known were there. The world around them clicked, like a watch that had been moved to the right time, and everything had a sense of urgency, of things undone.

And suddenly the white ball of light shrunk to a point, touched Emma's forehead and was gone, as was a moment of evanescent total intimacy neither would forget.

"I must get back to Hell," Emma said, almost stammering in her eagerness. "I'm sure Dawn is doing a good job, but really I ought not to leave her in charge too long. Aserath is hibernating or something and I don't really trust Morgan not to have some agenda."

"I'm sure you need not worry. She means well."

"But you've always been her greatest critic. Whenever I've mentioned her, you looked sour."

Mara smiled an almost little-girl smile.

"When I went inside my head, I did some tidying. Let some things go. Too many creatures like that one taking up space. As far as I know, Morgan has hardly put a foot wrong since the Shambala business, and even that…"

Caroline and the birds and the bag had stopped maintaining safe distance, and now she rushed forward and threw her arms around Mara and Emma. "Oh goodie, you've got rid of the red dust and those horrid guns. Can we go back to London, soon? You could come and stay, and you could ask Morgan on a date if you like her now."

"Sweetie," Emma said, "you know perfectly well that Mara's one true love is Sof. Even though Sof is pissed at her, even though Morgan's been carrying a torch for millennia…"

Mara looked a little embarrassed. "You got that thing out of Sof's head but she still doesn't want to see me or talk to me. That much was clear when she and Alexander turned up at Valhalla. We had lifetimes together and they were wonderful. But I think she's made a choice. And Morgan did terrible things, thousands of years ago, but she has hoped for my forgiveness for them ever since. Maybe it's time I told her I'm not angry anymore."

"Honestly," Caroline went on enthusiastically, "in her palace she has this art gallery and it's all paintings of you by famous artists. You really should ask her if you can see it; it's only a bit embarrassing."

Mara wasn't really paying attention; she was absent-mindedly fingering the ring. "She gave me this, and I took it as my right, without a thank you, without questioning. I hunted alone, I always said, but…"

Emma looked at Caroline and Caroline looked at Emma. There was a tired sigh so quiet that it was not clear to anyone from which of them it had come.

Eventually Emma thought she had better explain and took Mara's hand.

"You may not know this because you two don't exactly hang out, but Morgan puts a lot of her magic into artefacts, wearables mostly. Now, clearly that ring isn't a love charm. Because that would be creepy and wrong. She's needed you to change your own mind, not to try and change it for you."

Caroline took her other hand.

"I mean, it's not like she doesn't do creepy and wrong with that little private army she's gone all belle dame sans merci on. But she doesn't do it with her toyboys and you're her one totally real thing."

Emma started to touch the ring, then reconsidered. "Now this would be creepy and wrong too, a bit, but maybe it's there so that when and if you changed your mind—as you now have–she'd know about it. Or maybe you can use it to call her, like a pre-paid burner phone, that's quite a simple bit of magic. I mean, even I used to do that with my business cards, until Burnedover people hacked one and used it to torture my friend and pass his pain onto me—God, I was arrogant and stupid back then. But I'm sure if Morgan did a version of that it would be totally secure and unhackable."

Caroline's face lit up. "You should try and ring her. It's so utterly romantic. And so adorably clueless that you never thought to ask what it was for."

"So what do I do?" Mara asked.

"Well," Emma smiled," this may be a bit Eurocentric and you and she have a different set of cultural preconceptions, but on the other hand a lot of Western European myths and legends turn out to just be Morgan expressing herself, so…"

The hand came out of the bag holding a rather ornate silver mirror with androgynous cherubs round the rim.

Caroline took it and handed it to Mara. "Look deep in that and say her name three times. Probably any of her names will do."

Mara held it up with her right hand and stared into it. "Morgan," she said, tentatively. "Morgana." And then, with determination, "Hekkat. Hekkat. Hekkat."

A hole in space opened up.

Small enough that, when the bag bounded up to and into it, as enthusiastically as if it were going home after a long absence, it almost touched the sides.

"Or, alternatively," Emma said, "it could be a short-cut to her side. She shifts her luggage around through one of those."

"I'm sure that doesn't mean she thinks of you as baggage," Caroline added.

The hole in space continued to grow.

Garm, Fenris and the horses had come back, and Mara looked at them quizzically.

The other three looked meaningfully at Sleipnir, who declaimed.

"Charm carried out. Cleanness in air. No need for shieldwall now victory is yours."

"Well," Caroline said. "That's succinct."

Emma peered through the gateway. "Right now, it's a handy quick way back to Hell. No jokes about good intentions, if you don't mind. Coming?" She looked round.

Mara shook her head. "I am really not sure that would be a good idea."

"Surely it's not anything that would hurt us."

"Not deliberately," Mara said," but back in the 1790s—which is when she gave the ring to me—she was compulsively devious and too clever by half. And surely we can just go to her quickly ourselves now the dust is gone—"

"Scaredy-cat," Caroline said and walked into the hole.

Emma looked a little shame-facedly at Mara. "You're probably right," she said, "but whither she goeth and all that. I mean, how bad can it be? See you on…"

"…the other side…"

Caroline was there already, and the bag.

And there Mara was, along with the birds and the beasts, and Morgan looking apologetic. And Hades, looking flustered, and Dawn and Theophania and Judas with clipboards, trying to organise, and souls. Souls translucent not in flesh, souls piled up and drifting down and through and across each other, and various of the formerly damned walking around and trying to bat souls out of the way so they could see where they were going. Souls like a vast soupy fog as far as the eye could see and drifting down like snow.

"I'm so sorry." Morgan was flustered and shame-faced "When I gave Mara the ring, I thought, one day she'll change her mind and the ring will let me know and she'll call my name, and a gate will open. Only, I thought, I might be doing something or someone, and I'd like a little notice before she turns up and so I built in a delay and—"

"I told you two," Mara said, "Didn't I warn you that she does this sort of thing? I used to find it very annoying and now it's endearing… Is this what being in romantic love is like? It was different with Sof because when she was there she'd always been there…"

"Oh god," Caroline sighed. "Totally cuntstruck. And, Mara sweetie, you won't have needed to know this until now, but never ever start conversations with the new crush by talking about the old one."

"Never mind all that." Emma decided she had better take charge. "Dawn, Hades. You're both sensible. What's going on?"

Hades looked at her incredulously. "You don't know? It's whatever you three did. You reconnected Shadow and the Mundane—all that red dust cleared out of my lungs like a cold going away and your

222

sinuses clearing. Which is what it looked like when the waterfall cleared and years' worth of hell-flesh came flooding into Phlegethon. Luckily, after you visited us, Daedalus started to wonder what might happen and put in a whole new system of dams and channels and tanks. Otherwise things would have backed up flooded and we'd be ankle-deep in unprocessed hell-flesh all over."

Dawn took up when he paused for breath. "And then dead people. Millions of them all arriving at once. I guess twenty or thirty years must have gone by up there, bad years, because I've tried talking to some of them and, well, trauma. They're just screaming, most of them. There are too many, just too many."

Now it was her turn to pause for breath, and Morgan stuck up a tentative hand. "They were deafening, so I did a working to stop the ones that were screaming from screaming aloud. Only it was still deafening so I had to widen the working. To stop them singing. I hope you don't mind me using magic in your realm, but Aserath is off being a seed or something, and they were all so very noisy."

"Holy, holy, holy," Dawn explained. "They were singing it all the way down. Millions of souls cast down from Heaven to what used to be Hell, and singing Jehovah's praises all the way down. And then there were the screams—you'd think people thrown out of Heaven would be screaming too, but they just went on singing his praises, even though…"

Everyone looked at Judas, who looked as if he had the worst sick migraine in the universe.

As if all the screaming souls and all the singing souls were still making all that noise inside his head. And many of the screamers were circling round his head and looking into his eyes as if they knew him.

"Something really bad must have happened. He wouldn't have done it willingly. They're the saved and they're in deserved bliss and their singing gives him power. It's…"

Emma had known but hadn't wanted to think about it too closely because sometimes you just don't want to think about how sausages are made and let sleeping dogs lie and then the whole system goes wrong and you have to think about what's been left unsaid and undone.

She was faintly disgusted all the same.

"That Matrix you cooked up for him and conned everyone into thinking of it as Heaven," Caroline said.

"Matrix?" Judas asked.

"It's a film," Dawn said. "Ask your sister sometime."

"So anyway," Emma said, "it's very odd that they've been thrown out and it's something else to worry about, but they're probably happy just going holy, holy, for a bit, so unless someone wants to teach them better music, we just need them out of the way for the moment. The backlog of modern souls who are screaming—they're more important. For the time being could you try and corral the singing ones out of the way? Judas, Vretil—familiar faces useful on that probably. The rest of you get a line forming—point them at Phlegethon. Hades, could you go and get the blood vats ready?"

She grabbed the six screaming souls nearest her, and then another ten.

They were still screaming, and so she placed a firm hand on each of their shoulders in turn, so that they stopped. She waved her hand over her left shoulder, and they formed into an orderly line—then she opened a door that hadn't been there before. Behind it was the waiting room to her office back at the castle. She waved the sixteen souls past her into it and said to the others, "I'll just get on with some quick judging and maybe then we'll know what's going on."

Then her face softened.

"Sorry to do this, Mara sweetie, but I'm clearly going to be busy running Former Hell for the next few centuries of subjective time. And we'll need you to check in on the Mundane world—stop any imminent apocalypses, that sort of thing... But you and Morgan have some deferred gratification to get on with and I know it's all been going on for millennia. And believe me, Morgan dear, I do know what that feels like. I can give you an hour and a half of you time, that OK?"

And with that, Emma stepped through the door and shut it firmly behind her.

The others, all glad to have been told what to do and not wanting to intrude, all busied themselves with shooing souls into an endless orderly line. Theophania joined in, accompanied by twenty or thirty of the formerly damned and three very menacing looking demon women, who seemed unusually good at directing traffic.

"They're one of the teams I used to organise the line of squads for the ziggurat building," she explained. "You really thought that ran so smoothly without a bit of backstage muscle?"

Dawn and Caroline looked at each other shamefacedly.

Eventually Caroline said, "Thanks. We would never have thought of it. Emma is very good at finding the right person to delegate to, I've always known this."

Theophania preened at the compliment. "It's growing up a princess of Byzantium, my dears. If the queues for the Hippodrome get snarled up, you end up with a riot over bread or heresy and then the dynasty is in trouble, so my governess took particular pains to teach me queue management. First secret of good governance, she said."

Meanwhile...

Mara walked to where Morgan was standing, reached out and took her hand. Morgan made as if to kneel and Mara shook her head, then kissed her. On the forehead, on the cheek, on the lips.

"I've been...somewhat harsh," she said.

"No," Morgan whispered. And then, "I needed you to be. You needed to be. It's who we were. Who we are. And now..."

"Oh, get on with it," Caroline said, and Dawn shushed her.

They flickered into an embrace that might have been a moment outside time and might have been a thousand years.

Only then Emma stepped out of her office, surrounded by souls that were no longer screaming but had the haunted eyes of those who might start screaming again and never stop.

Eyes that were now in Emma's face as well. She had a jagged line of white in her scarlet hair.

She looked around at her lover, her friends, her servants and her subjects and paused, groping for the perfect words.

Then she spoke.

"The year is 2036. And we, Hell, Heaven, Shadow, the World…Well, basically we're utterly fucked."

And then she burst into tears.

Time Regained

London 2036

There is a smell when things are ending. A cast of light as well, but a smell first and most. I had smelled it before. Venice when the glory went away. Luoyang as the T'ang withered. Timbuktu as its enemies swept in, and after them, sand.

And now London.

It is the dirt in corners that no-one finished sweeping away, and then it rained and it turned to mud for a while. Perhaps something died there, and no one moved it: or perhaps it was just a discarded piece of fruit that went to rot and mould. It is the smell of no one caring enough to clear away, or perhaps of the person who should have done it being interrupted by the necessity of death.

It is the cracked cast of light twenty stories up through windows that shattered but did not fall from their frames, but were never replaced.

It is the delicate piss smell of the rat that walks past about its business unhurried, and the musk of the vixen teaching her kits to chase each other's tails up and down the shaded steps of a plaza where all the food stalls are shuttered and there is thick dust on the slats or cage work of the shutters.

It is the dull gleam of the high water mark that has left a hint of blue-green on the plaque on the plinth of the statue of some forgotten general. The waters are gone, for the moment, but they will come again and even in their absence they make temporary what was once eternal.

This, now, was London. At least there were no dead to be seen here, that was something, and few obvious marks of charring.

The air was still and close and baking hot. Like the Sahara, or the Empty Quarter, not this city. In 2003 I had read warnings of the heat to come... No wonder there was winter in Former Hell.

It was silent, though, that had once thrummed with business, until a helicopter passed overhead, its blades beating like an angry metronome. The rat and the vixen paid it no heed: and though pigeons flustered up in a crowd as it passed, their hearts were hardly in it.

Still, someone had been by to scatter the grains that the pigeons were picking off the pavement, someone not hungry enough to have eaten the grain.

Or the pigeons.

Or the rat.

I strolled on. A few yards away behind the far wall of the plaza the cathedral dome still stood, grey in the sunlight and seemingly undamaged by fire or water.

Someone was whistling but nowhere near and there was no one in sight. I heard, but could not see, a motorcycle engine.

One of you fluttered up from my shoulder—I don't remember which, so it must have been you, Thought—and soared into the still air.

The vixen barked and her kits rushed back to her and crouched between her legs. She stared across to where I and you, Memory, were waiting and snarled a warning. The rat looked up a moment and then continued about its business as if unconcerned by a mere raven.

You settled back on my shoulder and tugged at my ear as if I should follow your lead left. I saw no reason not to. My memory was that there was a station of the Underground nearby.

Or rather, there had been. Where it had stood there was a wall of black basalt with a black iron railing around it. The wall was inscribed with name after name and above them the symbol of the transport system drawn as if shattered and above it three wavy lines and a date: June 10th 2028.

Something bad—perhaps many things—had happened in the years since I had last been here.

I needed to find Polly Wild. And with her, perhaps, my sister Sof, who might at last be glad to see me, if only for the news I carried.

And as I stood reading the hundreds of names and sorrowing for them in my silent heart, I heard the motorcycle again, and it approached and then stopped.

In the distance I saw the vixen and her kits trot away unhurriedly in an orderly line.

The motorcycle's rider wore black and red leathers and a blood red helmet with an opaque black visor. The figure dismounted and stared at me top to bottom.

"Would you be the Huntress?" it asked. Its voice had a cockney accent, but was not human.

It flicked the visor up and I recognised her as a ghoul, yet not as I had known ghouls in the past, because she had gone to some trouble to pass as human. A sophisticated use of shaded cosmetics, but also surgery perhaps and certainly dental work... I was not sure whether or not compliments were in order.

"The People remember," she said in what was almost the start of a chant. "You brokered a peace when the man Wren and the man

229

Hawksmoor disturbed our pits. You drove off the man Jack who had slaughtered the People in Spitalfields and Whitechapel. Later you killed him in Paris and the People of the Catacombs sent us word. Yet you never asked us for favours, proud and disdainful as you are. Nonetheless, the People pay our debts. You have been gone from London, gone from the Mundane—it has been three decades and more since there has been whisper of you. Yet here you are…"

I had never particularly taken to the People of the Pit, nor taken against them. They are as they are. Corpse eaters but rarely killers unless they feel threatened, and with magics that serve them to gnaw tunnels and pits and vast stable caverns, but have nothing to do with the Rituals even when their gaping mouths are smeared with old and rotten black blood.

Now, I needed their help. Much was wrong with the world and much of it dying or dead. This was clear to me from the vast throng that had arrived in Former Hell when Emma and I had broken the power of the Red Dust. And you can rely on corpse eaters to keep a close tally of death, because cemeteries are their larder and their vineyard where like epicures they wait for the crops to ripen.

I needed information and one piece in particular…

But she anticipated me. "You will be wishing to see the Lady Polly and her Second, the Lady Sof."

That was good news and bad, for I was glad to know that Sof was here and working with Polly, yet I did not know whether she wished to see me at all, and indeed whether she could have freed us and Shadow before we freed ourselves, but simply chose not to.

But no, surely if she could have freed us, she would have, however much she resented me, because part of her work was right action without hope of reward or desire for it, and with the Enemy so close to achieving his goals, any possible chance to thwart him would have been taken, even if that chance was me.

But for now, lost in thought, I let the ghoul lead me, wheeling her motorcycle beside her in spite of its weight and unhandiness, even though I knew the way. Her People wished me kindness and I should accept it because that is how alliances are formed.

As we walked out of that part of London which is called the City, and towards that edge between it and other parts, that interface where Polly weaves her webs, I saw more people, and yet still far fewer than I would have expected. And among them, unremarked and therefore presumably unremarkable, ghouls and other peoples, some like my companion making it their business to blend in among the humans and others not.

I had never found the English especially accepting of strangers and the strange, and it seemed to me that it was not that this had changed, but rather that they no longer cared, about this or anything else. All had downcast eyes that seemed hardly to notice those near them and yet all maintained a distance and navigated away from those near them.

It reminded me a little of that time after the second war, but without that grim air of satisfaction at having survived, more an uncertainty about what survival meant and whether it was worth it.

The only exceptions to this air of traumatized despondency were my companion and her peers, who looked serious-minded rather than depressed and had a sleek air of prosperity. They were well-fed, which is always a worrying thing to see in ghouls, and yet they moved freely among their human neighbours with no especial indication that they were resented.

Clearly awful things had happened in this city and presumably elsewhere, but I am not so in love with despair that I was in a hurry to find out what.

I did not ask my companion because she looked well-fed and I did not care to discover how.

She perhaps sensed this and when we neared Polly's house, she bade me farewell and climbed on her vehicle. "The Lady Polly transacts business with my kind. And the Lady Sof treats our sick or wounded with great care. And the Lords Tom and Syeed lead us in raids past the Barrier. But none of them are especially fond of us, because they know what we eat. The People eat the flesh of dead humans and live humans resent and fear us for this. We would never eat a live human: they would taste sickeningly bland with no hint of decay to give flavour. But things are as they are and even the best of humans… and I see that I have said too much and should be on my way."

And in moments she had started her vehicle and was away without further remarks. Which was a blessing, because she was right about my reaction to ghouls, however irrational I know it to be. And however many questions I could have asked and did not.

But here I was once more, outside a door where so many questions would be answered.

Without my asking, both of you hopped down from my shoulders and stood in a line with me as if supplicants as I knocked and waited.

Polly answered, still as young and almost as beautiful but with a haggard quality that seemed almost to fray her at the edges.

"Oh, thank god, you're alive," in a voice of genuine relief and concern and then, with her more usual attitude, over her shoulder, "Sof, it's your sister, the nice one, back and not before time, may I say? And with crows, too; old One-eye's castoffs from what I hear. I hope they're house trained, I don't want birdshit everywhere because it's a devil to get out of carpets. I got some spatter of crocodile vomit on them a while back as took a full ten years to get rid of… Anyway, come in. I'm sure we have a lot to talk about."

Then she looked down at you both.

"You two as well. Thought and Memory, they tell me you go by, though I don't know how anyone could keep track of which was which."

We walked through into the large parlour, in which Polly had entertained monarchs and ministers and where there now slouched or sat the assassin Tom, my old friend the faun, Emma's former lover

Elodie and a man I did not know, from somewhere in South Asia, I thought.

"Sof will be out in a moment, she's tending to our other guest," Polly went on. "You know everyone else here, I think. Except for Syeed—Syeed, this is Mara, the Huntress."

He stood up and bowed his head courteously. "They say you knew the Prophet, blessings be upon him, when he was young." His accent was more from the North of England than anywhere in Asia.

"Blessings be upon him," I echoed. "And I saw him more recently, seated at the great council table at the court of my old friend Nameless, whom men call Jehovah and Allah."

He looked less impressed than I might have expected.

Polly guffawed. "For once, Huntress, you can't get away with impressing us all with the names you can drop."

I looked at her with questions in my eyes.

"We'll get to that in a moment," she said. "How much do you know about what's been going on?"

"Not much," I said. "When we got time in Shadow lined up with time here in the Mundane we discovered a few days in Valhalla had been weeks in former Hell and decades here. Suddenly there was a huge influx of the traumatised dead including a lot that seemed to have been thrown out of Heaven. Everyone is trying to deal with the problems there: I thought I'd better come straight here so that I can send word back. Obviously there has been a lot of death. Shadow and Hell are freezing so I assume the Mundane is heating up. Otherwise, we've had our concerns—Burnedover assassins, centaur death cults…"

"Centaurs?" Tom perked up. "Huge migration with magic weapons and big carts?"

I nodded.

"They're here," he said. "Well, not here, in England, but cutting a swathe in the Urals and the Caucasus. Apparently they say it's their ancestral homeland and they want it back."

I rarely blush, or apologise, but…

"My fault, I'm afraid. They attacked Valhalla and I was going through a thing with wild magic… and, well, I banished them, because that was the sort of thing Emma and I were briefly able to do, but I didn't have any control…"

Polly sighed, resigned. "You don't half complicate things sometimes. Anyway…"

Sof walked in from the corridor. "He's awake and heard your voice. He wants to talk. Keep it brief. He's out of danger finally, after all this time, but he's very weak and there's only so much I can do." She did not seem especially displeased to see me, only very tired. I had seen her like this before with patients, even when she had the Stone to refresh her. It wasn't literally true that she healed like Josette, taking pain into herself, but she had once told me she envied her former pupil that.

"I'm very sorry, but he who?"

Sof looked vexed, but not at me. She turned to Polly, glowering. "Look, I know there's a lot to catch up with. But don't you think you might have made it a priority to tell my sister that for the last five years we've had an intermittently comatose Jehovah hooked up to IVs in one of the guest rooms?"

"What?!"

"Long, long story."

I followed her into the corridor and up a small flight of stairs into a room full of machines that whirred and pinged, her alchemical work bench off to one side and, in a raised bed which looked excessively soft, my old apprentice.

His bird, Ghost, the white sibling of mine, perched on the rail of the bed, its eyes closed as if it slept. Its feathers were glossy: clearly it had fed well here, or in the city around us. On what I did not care to consider.

Any more than I care to ask you.

For centuries he had affected the Ancient of Days look, flowing white hair and beard but ripped under his clothes, whether a hieratic robe, a loin cloth or evening dress. Now he just looked old and emaciated and those strong arms withered. Tubes and wires. He had clearly been mortally sick for years.

Yet at the sight of me he smiled. His eyes were still those of the young man I had first known, with the lashes he had bequeathed to his only child, but there was a humility there that I had never seen before. His voice had a quaver to it that faded as he warmed to his subject.

There was a small white metal stool beside the bed. I sat down and I took his hand. It was light as a feather and so was his tentative grip.

"Your sister saved me, in spite of everything I did to her, and let be done. She even tells me that with care I shall be whole and hale again. Your other sister too, who took me from the hands of my enemies and brought me here—"

"Lillit?" I knew by now that I would never understand her games.

"You were right, you know," he went on.

"Right?"

"Back at the beginning. I thought that by building power I could beat him, and yet his minions struck me down in Heaven itself. It was all useless. You were right—small fights, lots of Powers, frustrate his local moves, no grand strategy. I thought you were an idiot but you've clearly survived whatever he did. And I've lost everything. And my son, my son…"

The sorrow in his voice—I thought he might die of despair.

And yet, still not my place.

He wept and then shut his eyes as if he were done with the world for all Sof's promises of recovery.

I looked down at you, my birds. You looked back at me with your fierce intelligent bead eyes.

I said, "Go. Fetch. There is nothing more important right now. Insist that it is time. And the other one."

You fluttered into the air and then flickered into Shadow and were gone.

Jehovah opened his eyes again and they glinted with hope.

"I won't ask what that's about because I know how you girls love your secrets. Birds? Ghost is around somewhere. Fornicating with the Tower ravens, usually. You refused them before… Odin's?"

It worried me that he did not see Ghost, but I did not bring it up for fear of making him anxious.

"Thought and Memory came to me when he abandoned wisdom and fell into the thrall of the Enemy. But that is a story for later. My sister is hovering outside, and I need to let you sleep. Later."

I stood up and stepped back. He closed his eyes and in seconds he was snoring, but they were healthy snores from full lungs.

I stepped from the room and looked at Sof.

"Really?" she said. "You think it's time?"

"Yes. There is too much going on. Too much death. They need to talk."

She nodded, then reached out and placed a hand on my wrist. "I fought for years and time after time we nearly lost him. Yesterday, I thought he was about to go. And it would have been a blessing. I would have let him. Then—I'm assuming Emma destroyed the red dust?"

I corrected her, very slightly peeved. "She took the lead but needed me to be part of it. And not just the red dust but all of dark alchemy…"

She winced at that word.

"Magic?" she asked without expecting an answer. "I tried to fix things with the Work, but realised it just wasn't going to help. What is done with the Work can only be undone with the Work, but it seems that corruption of the Work cannot. We learn…"

She seemed so downcast that I thought to explain. "It was what Lillit did," I started.

She nodded, almost too instantly. "I see that. And Emma used my anger and pain that she had taken into herself as the like thing to be undone."

"My anger too. Not undone, but purified."

She smiled, as I had seen her smile when she refined a curative or solved a quadratic.

"That girl… I have never believed that magic can be turned into a system of pure thought and procedure like the Work. But she is mathematical and musical and something of a poet. If anyone— perhaps if we survive these next years, she will have time."

There were so many questions that I chose the most immediate. "How came Jehovah to be wounded so grievously?"

"It was a knife. That, once plunged into his side, unfolded like a flower into barbs and hooks tipped in the corrosive I call the Dark Alkahest."

"I have been wounded with it," I said, "and Josette saw no remedy but to cut. I was maimed, sister, and only wild magic made me whole… But how did anyone get close enough to him to stab him?"

"Distraction. They filled Heaven with so many of the newly dead that his saints and angels were overwhelmed and he went among them to help control the crowd. Because among the victims of massacre and those tricked into suicide were operatives of Burnedover, still in the flesh, who had found one of the back stairs. Put a load of idiots in and your best can hide among them. Like the Capitol Coup in '21."

I would have to piece all this together a bit at a time.

"Suicide?"

"You know of the Internet?"

I nodded.

"What could contain all knowledge came also to contain all lies and all foolishness. In particular, lies about politics and religion. The Disappointed, the Endarkened… Christians who became convinced that the Rapture and the End Times needed a helping hand. They had a slogan and they posted it everywhere— #HewantsYouNow. And there were environmentalists—Deep and Dark Greens—you know of them I gather—who acted on the slogan #MakeSpace, and the partygoers with their #BuzzOut. And when disaster after disaster struck like what happened to London, they nearly killed Jehovah and they stole his throne and they turned Heaven into a battle zone where nothing is resolved. Until now. You and Emma may have won that war by disarming the invaders."

So that was good news at least. But — "Disasters?"

"You noticed the heat?"

I nodded. "I have known this city for centuries and never seen a Summer like it."

My sister shook her head. "Mara. It's January."

I felt this like a punch in the stomach, a punch I had not known I expected.

"And I know something bad happened in the Underground."

"You could say that… but I need a drink before we discuss such things and it is Polly and Tom's story to tell."

She gestured me back to the main common room, and announced, "We can expect more visitor. Mara has summoned Jehovah's children."

"'Spose that's for the best," Polly admitted. "Anyone else expected? Emma perhaps?"

I shook my head. "She's got a vast influx of souls to sort out: she and Caroline and Aserath if she wakes up and the rest of that crowd. And it's bitter winter in Hell and the rest of Shadow. The dead don't need to eat but they think they do."

"We started to have that problem in London, what with the barrier and the dead gods," — Tom wasn't being as helpful as he thought, raising even more questions — "but him next door told us how to set up showers of manna, and Sof improved the taste. Maybe Emma…"

I'd sent you away but assumed you'd be back. I could always summon my dog pack and stick notes in their collars. I'd wait for you.

I looked harder at Polly. Something was different. Almost like a god, but not… And then I realised I needed to look at her as if I had mortal eyes.

Her face was as I had always known it, but also it flickered and was other faces, some from other times…

"Polly Wild," I said, "have you become a Tutelar?"

She looked back at me as if daring me to disapprove. "Well, the Enemy came on to my screens and boasts as how he's ate all the Lords and Ladies of all the Lands. And I thought I ought to replace him as I served but didn't know how. Thought it would be difficult when actually it was easy as pie once Lucifer told me it was. Only, I didn't love the whole realm, not really. I don't think anyone has, not for ages, not since her late majesty, but London: born and bred and if not Bow Bells plenty of others. So, Lady of London. And by the grace of him next door it's needed me."

I waited. I could see the story coming on. It did not take long to pour forth.

"First," she went on, "it was the Cough as was called the Covid virus back then, what was all the worse for the Tories' mates profiteering and cornering, that a proper London mob would have seen to in my day as you know and witnessed a time or two I'm sure. And then other plagues—the Blood, and the Scratch.

"And then there was famine when they thought that could make money by leaving Europe and food was left to rot in a car park in Kent. Then there was the Scots Unpleasantness—I was still learning my trade as tutelar back then and trying not to step too hard on the toes of the man Khan, who was a pretty good mayor even if he did see it as a stepping stone…And the wars—we thought we were done with those, once upon a time. but we never were."

She took a breath.

"But then the really, really bad thing happened. Alexa, play September 10th, 2028."

The outer screens went dark. The big centre screen showed London, on a bright day in early autumn. Nothing to see at first. It panned to a view of the Thames. London mid-morning, with a lot of people about and boats on the river.

239

"This was a helicopter that just happened to be collecting stock footage and that landed more or less safely. Watch the top left-hand corner."

I saw a bright red dot that rapidly expanded.

"This is the best shot we got of it. We froze the frame and enlarged and put a filter on so it's not just flames. Tom had one of his flashes and saw it about ten minutes out. Which was fortunate because he jumped to the PM's office and the Chiefs of staff and told them 'not a missile, space junk, going to hit London,' and jumped again. We've been in disgrace and out of the loop since the Blair incident… but only officially. Everyone sensible knows to pay attention."

The screen showed an unlovely twist of metal junk.

"Normally, stuff glances off each other, takes a few lumps out. Makes for small bits of space kipple still in orbit, problem in its own right but not like this. A stage of a booster banged into a comms relay and they got jammed together instead of tearing each other apart, and they started spinning and picked up a lot of smaller junk, a bit of old Strategic Initiative crap that stopped working in the 90s. Stuff that had gone dark, stuff no one cared about. And bits of momentum got lost because their orbits didn't match, but it was travelling at one hell of a lick for a decaying orbit. Could have been worse—nothing in there that could go bang, no nuclear power bits, nothing weapons grade."

The screen went back to real time. The red dot became a ball of flame five hundred feet across that started to break up into streaks of flame that went their own ways.

"A lot of the bits peppered Docklands. Canary Wharf was a write-off from strikes and subsequent fires. Luckily a lot of the offices were empty—people had got used to home working during the Cough, and then there were the food riots, and the army on the streets picking up anyone who looked at them sideways. Still, five thousand casualties from the lesser strikes. Pretty bad—no one warned me I'd feel every one yet have to bear it. And it got me braced for what came next."

The ball of flame came in over Tower Bridge like a blowtorch that sent all the paint up in a flare of smoke and all the traffic on the bridge caught fire at once, much of it in explosions of suddenly superheated petrol and diesel. Then flames underneath where the oil-fueled hydraulic pumps were. Very slowly the spans above the bridge warped and folded: the walkways crumbled: the centre of the bridge fell away into a splash of steam.

"The Tower mostly held but for the new visitor centre bits. The Crown Jewels were fine, which was good because Hisself auctioned most of them off for relief. They really didn't need a gold spoon for the sacred oil he said. The ravens were OK: they fluttered off on a jolly to Richmond Park, fed on a dead fawn as no one had found and tidied, or maybe they killed it themselves. Came back bold as brass once the worst of it was over. Ghost asked them how they knew, and they smirked and said nothing, as ravens will."

And then it plunged into the river in a gout of flame and steam just short of where London Bridge stood, or rather had stood.

"*Falling down, falling down,*" Polly sang and her voice cracked. "London Bridge like in the rhyme, but also the new one that didn't last thirty years for all they called it Millennium, and Southwark Bridge and the rail bridge too. Blackfriars shook but held, even through what followed. Straight through the river bed it went, almost a mile deep, and every tunnel, every sewer, every cable what went underneath, broken, melted, gone. And the Thames backs up, and pours in."

A tear showed in the corner of her left eye.

"I was there, you see. Summoned. By the power what I had taken to myself and never understood the responsibility of, which is to help when I can, but stand helpless and sheltered by that power in the middle of the chaos and watch the death and listen to the screams and feel the power building in me but not yet, not until it is ready and time, and know what happens while that builds. The

Lord never told me or prepared me. I was his servant not his successor because he thought he was invulnerable and no end would ever come to him. But Tom-"

The screen switched to Bank Station, the Northern line. It wasn't heavily crowded because it was not the Rush Hour. Closed circuit footage, but not too fogged to see Tom appear, pull a mother and child into his lap and disappear, and appear again, shouting something, and grab the nearest person, and the one after that and then the screen flickered and was gone.

"I knew something was coming," Tom said, "something bad though I didn't guess what. So I looked with the Sight, and saw it, and told the competent authorities and then... I guessed about the tunnels. What's that thing you always say? About how you cannot save them all. I understand now. But I took those I could up to Hampstead Heath and they weren't many but it was something, and then the Sight told me there was no point, so I guessed a safe point and got three out of King's Cross Piccadilly and two out of Angel, and the Sight meant I could stay safe to save more further out, but I hated myself because the coldness I take into myself when I kill was there and telling me who I could save and who not and rationing salvation to what I could manage."

I didn't know Tom well, but he was not a man used to sobbing.

Sof and Syeed walked over and held him and Polly.

"He saved as many as he could," said Syeed.

"Which is as if he saved the whole world," said Sof.

Elodie and the faun just sat in a corner of their sofa, staring at the screen and lost in grief of their own.

"We were here," she said. "Syeed, Sof, the faun and I. And we could see what was happening. And we didn't know how safe we were and we knew we couldn't do anything at all to be useful and save people. Well, you, Sof, you knew there would be medical things you could do in the aftermath. And the faun could at least fetch people pizza. But what good was I going to be? A failed movie star who used to be a vampire princess? That's not a useful skillset."

"I could have done trauma first aid," Syeed added. "But people were bound to think it was the Brothers and no one with a brown skin was safe that day because even after vans went round with speakers saying it was a crashed satellite, racists just went on saying cover-up for years."

The screen showed nothing but steam and ruin, for what seemed like long minutes.

There was a roar of waters.

Then there was a blaze of light and at the centre of it floating fifty feet up was Polly.

She pushed out with both her hands, first upstream and then downstream. And the spray and the steam gradually cleared to show a crater the breadth of the river and cutting a bite of embankment on both sides, and going down to a depth I could not see from which there was a gurgling rumble like the worst of bathnights. Downstream the water reversed its flow and gradually cleared; the flow from upstream sought any outlet it could get.

"That's when it starting up through pipes and drains all over the city. Water is clever and it always finds a way. But not enough outlets and it was building up a head I could never have held back for long. So I did what I had to do."

On the screen she reached up with one hand and pulled ejecta back from its flight and smashed it down into the pit. She pulled down the raised sides of the crater and tamped them flat, but it was not enough. She pulled down whole office blocks with angry gestures further and further back from the embankments, and the rubble streamed to her and she flung it into the pit and pressed it down and further down.

The Monument to the Great Fire: the tower and walled garden left from a church destroyed in the Blitz; the black glass tower known as the Shard. All went to feed that sucking maw which seemed as if it would never be satiated.

"There was people caught in the tunnels, stuck in carriages with water rising round them. And I hurled Hell down on them. There were people in those buildings as I collapsed about them and flung dead or dying into the pit with the rubble. For I am the Tutelar of London and I serve the city as well as its people, and all of its people at once which means I had to kill ten thousand an it were necessary to save a hundred thousand. By hell and damnation Mara, I have heard you say a hundred times that you could not save them all, but have you ever killed some to save others? And felt them die. Every single terrible death. Because I did that day."

I wanted to say no to her, but—Tenochtitlan, burned by an occupying army with my help so that I could get to its slavering gods. Paris on the eve of Bartholomew when I slew anyone who stood between me and the House of Valois. They were still on my conscience and stilled my tongue.

The screens switched to blurred images of nightmare from which I could not avert my gaze by waking.

"Water and worse than water, mud and sewage, gushed into the tunnels," Tom said. "Twenty times I snatched people from its path with moments to spare but for every one or two I saved, a thousand died mere feet away, or a level below. I shouted, I screamed, each time I jumped in and perhaps some made the stairs and were fast enough but I doubt it. And they would have been the strongest who trampled others or pushed them out of the way onto the track. As it came on, the water shorted out the electricity and the dying light made it a flickering hell. And the stench. Ozone, and the smoke of flash fires, and bowels opening in fear and death."

He stopped. He had relived this so many times in memory that I was impressed that he had stayed sane.

Syeed and Elodie were at his side, a hand on each shoulder, as if some of his grief could flow out through them and be gone.

I remembered that he was not just a silent and prolific assassin, but a prince, without a throne as is only right and proper, but nonetheless all that people mean when they say a prince.

The screens showed more nightmare. Streets with people running this way and that as sinkholes opened under their feet and glass and rubble rained down upon them. They looked for safety and there was none to be found.

"My heart broke fifty times," Polly said. "At what I saw and had to see for that I could not look away. At what I did and had to do for that there was a geas upon me. The mercy of my condition is that there was a point at which I ceased to be Polly at all and lapsed from consciousness and became the ruthless will of a city that had survived the Murrain and the Death and the Fire and the Blitz and the Cough and would survive this. And prosper. I know what was done through me and first it was destruction that the river's gaping wound be filled and restored whatever the cost and the waters that I held back and up subside and flow as if the crater had never been. And then it was cleansing—water had spilled and spread and I was the wind that gently cajoled it back where it belonged, taking with it much of the filth and rubble of disaster. But not the dead. They would have their own cleansing. Then it was time to rebuild what was most important and necessary. The city knows its mains and its sewers and its wiring—the arteries and veins and nerves that have built down the years.

"Polly came to me," Sof said, "but there was a light in her eyes that was not Polly, and she took my hand and breathed into my mouth and for some hours I was not myself either. London took me into itself and with me all that I am, wielder of the products of the Work. And where the body of the city was torn and mangled, I healed it. With the Stone. And where it needed shoring up and patching, I forged Adamant to hold it up stronger than before. And where it was gangrenous beyond repair, the Alkahest burned it away. It took me up and it set me down and I was so tired that I slept for a week."

The screen showed restored some of the streets we had seen destroyed. They seemed at once solid and fragile—like the Japanese cups all the more precious because once shattered and then pieced back together with tiny gold wires, or like the delicate tracing of cracks on old oil paintings.

245

"This is a week later," Polly explained. "By the which time I was myself again and not the Will of the City and woke with the knowledge of things I had done which were needful but which I could not have made myself do."

Along each street, the dead were laid out. The living filed past them, holding a distance between them not to intrude on grief, that they maintained whenever one paused to look in a dead face, shake their head in sorrow and then move on. their head. Each corpse shimmered slightly as if out of phase with time. Someone, somewhere, was playing the death march from Chopin's Second Sonata, over and over again.

With too much emphasis.

Each corpse was tastefully laid out straight as if they had fallen asleep just so, rather than in fire, fear, mud and agony. And each corpse was missing something—a forearm, a lower leg, part of a jaw.

"You know as how I have always hated our friends the ghouls," Polly said.

"You remarked upon it once," I reminded her. "In the days of the Ripper. In front of poor young Herbert. And one I met earlier remarked that there is a certain coolness."

"Well," she said and paused as she pondered the most tactful way to continue. "…the main thing about ghouls is that they are honest. Scrupulous, you might say. Another thing about ghouls is that they have a nose for the dead. Put a body under a mile of rock and they'll find it and worry it out and take it to their larder, where they'll let it decay a little for the gaminess, but hold it just so, a little out of time."

She was pausing after every few words.

"They're not greedy, say that for them. And we couldn't leave all those dead to rot and stink where they fell, where I threw them. City would be uninhabitable. And relatives, relatives have a right to mourn. So I go, or rather London goes, on bended knee, and says with these lips, that our ghoul citizens have gone too long unrecognized, unhonoured. And how that could change with one

246

small favour as they'd be doing anyway. So we agree, they'll fetch up the dead, and put a casting on so as they keep for a bit, and take a tithe but only a tithe. And those that keep to the old ways, will be left in peace and consulted when and where there's diggings, even if it's rich Russians with secret cinemas in their sub-basement. And the new-fangled ones, that work in the City and fix their teeth, and wear paint to save their skins from the sun, they're Londoners, born and bred and honest. They have their folkways and their history, and schoolkids learn how they saw off the Guard at Waterloo. And they bring people up and lay them out neatly and leave alone what's in their pockets."

"They eat the dead," said Tom "but they honour them too. As an assassin I can relate to that. Turns out some of them saw me rescuing. They escaped themselves, because they can dig themselves out of really tight spaces and they can hold their breath practically forever."

"They can swim," Polly said. "They don't like to, and they don't mention it, but they can. Only reason they never moved out to sea to prey on wrecks is their cousins, the Sea Maidens, the Silkies. Bad blood there as they don't like to talk about. They've had their wars: ghouls pass down necklaces of teeth from those wars. Teeth with jags and points as were never filed. They say the Silkies have their own necklaces too."

Which is something I had never known about. I had talked to Dagon once about the Silkies and whether their worship involved anything I should know about, but he shuddered and changed the subject.

Apparently they worship those great spirits, the Tutelars of the Oceans, one of whom I met that one time and who made me a promise for the future, and who care not at all for the Silkies and their prayers. Silkies, who do not honour the dead that they preserve in harvested salt and gnaw to the bone.

Tom gave Polly a look and she ceased chattering.

"So, anyway, they turned up at our doors here, with all the footage from the Underground of me saving people. Thought I'd want it, which I do. They praised me for cheating their Lord of his due. They worship Death and their Lord loves a chancer, they said. And I really didn't want that footage around. As to what they eat, cycle of life…"

I thought a bit about what my friends and my sister had done in the crisis. "Wasn't all of that a bit, well, blatant?"

Polly laughed out loud. It was good to hear. "From Little Miss Cast Down Empires If They Look At Me Funny, that's a bit rich. But no, you might think so, what with me stopping the Thames in its tracks and tearing down the Shard, but people see what they want to see for the most part, and they don't like miracles. The world has been changing too fast for most of them and miracles were a bit too much like hope, what with everything that happened next. Suicide cults -"

"Told her that bit," Sof said.

"Well, then there was all the politics."

I waved that past as it is only rarely I'd want to have anything to do with any of that.

"Short form, London wasn't the only city that met with misfortune that year or the next. Lots of places got too hot to live in. Lots of people died trying to get somewhere cooler. Oh, and money pretty much stopped working, one day. Too much in too few pockets and then a whole lot of rich people, the really rich and the politicians who had become their servants disappeared and took most of the money with them—off to Patagonia or Mars—which ended with a bunch of them poisoning each other, and stabbing each other, and the last few fighting to the death as a way of doing those Rituals of yours. Some sort of winner takes all tontine. You weren't around, so Tom and Syeed went down to Paraguay to mop up what was left, which was mostly a bunch of Flat Ogres as you call them, things with too many faces that squelched when you kicked them."

Tom looked at Syeed, and Syeed looked at Tom, then both stuck fingers in their mouths and made gagging noises.

"It were disgusting," Syeed said. "Chapeltown Road on a Saturday Night when people have eaten dodgy doners on their way back from t'pub and there's puke and chili sauce all over the pavement."

"Mostly, there were piles of that black powder left wherever they'd fallen," Tom said. "Some people from Medellin turned up to collect it, so we had to discourage them."

"Then there was the Hollywood thing," Elodie added. "MeToo, only sex magic. And your undead old mate Crowley all over it…"

"Again," said Tom and Sof in chorus.

"…Settled his hash without leaving this room. Cancelled him, we did. Used social media for Good, like a bunch of my fans did for Emma and Caroline back in the day."

I wasn't sure what cancelling was, but I hoped it was painful.

"Everything speeding up," Sof said. "Crisis after crisis. States that you'd think permanent realities falling apart in weeks to city states and anarchies. The sea rising up. Pockets of underground gas exploding. All those people who killed themselves to get off to Heaven ahead of the rush—they were not completely unreasonable. You and I have seen collapse before, only this time there's further to fall and no coming back."

"We held London," Polly said. "People still live here and we keep them fed and safe, after a fashion."

There was still something they hadn't told me.

"On my way, I met a ghoul. And she said you mount raids beyond the Barrier. Raids? Barrier?"

Polly didn't even look abashed. "Outside what I control, it's pretty bad. We let in refugees, but they has to get here first. Past the floods, and past the gangs, and past the dead gods…"

"The what?" I asked.

Syeed hadn't been saying much but suddenly everyone was looking in his direction.

"I thought, we thought, you'd know about this. Back in '03, Emma and I were taken prisoner by some Burnedover people to be sucked out of existence by some fragments of dead gods they'd turned into brainless zombie things. One got loose and ate a lot of their people, but we managed to blow it up."

I remembered Emma telling me bits of this and recalled thinking that there were parts of the story she was leaving a bit vague. Presumably their improvisations had lacked her usual elegance...

"Anyways, we thought an experiment which resulted in hundred per cent casualties and loss of the interdimensional worm thing they were using as a base would have discouraged them. When the Sheikh hisself debriefed me, I suggested I check further but he was convinced I had hallucinated the whole thing under some sort of nerve agent and should investigate that. Which I did, because I was obeying orders in those days, fat lot of good that did me. And Emma was off taking over Hell, and I wasn't trusted enough to get an opportunity to speak to Tom here."

He shrugged. "But hundred per cent losses don't mean as much when you're an army of magic clones is what we should have considered. So a few years ago they've got cut up bits of gods, and use what's left of their vital spirits to bring them back to a sort of life and set them loose everywhere. They make people believe in them, and adore and serve them, and then they eat them. They start off rat size and grow; they get to be size of a house and then they pop and scatter like dandelions. Manchester was mostly gone before anyone realised; same with Lagos and Vancouver."

I was clearly going to have to be busy.

"So, these raids. How do you stay safe?"

"Ghouls don't worship- their minds just don't do that, which apparently makes them immune. And they hate Burnedover like poison because, after what the Ripper did to their cubs, they've taken an exception to people doing experiments like that. Because, gods one day, ghouls the next."

"Plus," Polly noted, "the dead gods don't leave nothing behind when they devour a person, which means no future corpses laid down for your friends' future larders."

Ignoring her, Syeed took over from Tom. "Tom and me, we both helped kill gods and that's probably made us immune which we are, inshallah. Seems like. So I make bombs to blow them to bits and Tom delivers them. And the ghouls eat the bits, or just swarm over them and tear them up if we're too busy."

I mentally added all of this to the bill I would one day present to these Burnedover people. A sizeable proportion of the human race. My leg...

"Where did they get the parts?" I mused aloud.

"You're not going to like this," Polly said. "Remember when Emma was in Hell, and liberated a lot of gods from some dungeon?"

"Well. The Olympians are all right—I let them have Valhalla only a couple of days ago my time. The gods of Canaan, though…"

"I heard rumours," Syeed said. "When I was with the Students. Demons from the Age of Ignorance that the American mercenaries had killed before the Brothers could. Old frail confused creatures."

They'd disappeared from Hell and Shadow and hadn't turned up anywhere I knew of. They were old gods without worshippers, weak and not very bright. I could imagine them wandering back into the Mundane with no idea of how it had changed. Turning up confused in the middle of a meatgrinder war.

That hurt. The Baals. The various Astartes. We had fought the Shaggy One and his starved army. I didn't fancy telling Aserath, their kinswoman, or, come to that, my old friend asleep next door, if he didn't already know.

He and Lucifer had enslaved them and imprisoned them, but he'd let them live. He hadn't turned them into mindless deadly things.

But there was so much to do. The Enemy must have known or been told that some of us would get out of Hell and Shadow before whatever end he planned. And he had so many schemes, so cunningly interwoven and braided. And all of them would take our wit and our strength to unpick.

The perpetual blistering summer here and the withering cold that was coming to Shadow—they were beyond me and would have to wait or be sorted out by the politicians and scientists who should have sorted them out long ago. Or by magic.

This plague of dead gods—it would need more than piecemeal raids by my friends here and a few friendly ghouls. It would need scouring with fire. Or—I had an idea.

Heaven. If Jehovah's loyalists were still holding out, that was a victory we might get, and we needed one. But for all Polly's optimistic assessment, the Enemy would surely counterattack overwhelmingly because he needed to hold Heaven, and we would need to beat him there. Specifically, we would need to get Jehovah's throne back. And stop Burnedover making new troops all the time. But all these things in order—the dead gods first.

Because they ate souls, and the souls they ate were, as far as I could tell, gone forever. Like the living loving battling gods from whom these dead gods had been made.

I had never asked Emma whether she had looked for her eaten friend John in Hell or if she had asked Jehovah if he was in Heaven, because clearly she knew when he crumbled to dust under her hand that he was gone forever. Along with so many others, all over the world. Ordinary people tortured into belief and then decay and oblivion by the animated vivisected corpses of my dead allies.

This was obscene. And a part of the Enemy's plan that I could and would spoil.

Of course, it would involve my doing magic. Of a sort. Something I had avoided doing for thousands of years.

Being magic was one thing. Doing it had always stuck in my craw a little.

But when Emma persuaded me to take part in her cleansing ritual, she had told me it was also an initiation, and I saw now that this meant, not only that I understood what I was about to do, what I had to do, but that I gave myself permission.

It was a task that fell to me because I had the means. It was a cleansing ritual that simply made use of the Doctrine of Likeness, a magic so simple even a novice like me could envision it, yet a magic on so vast a scale that few beings had ever had the power to do it.

And I, who had carefully put away the power of gods for millennia, was such a one.

It had been a mistake of the Enemy to infect me with a wild magic alien to me yet operated by my instincts and emotions, because it reminded me, I now realised, of the power I had chosen not to work and which was nonetheless available to my will.

I cannot save them all, and so many had died while I was trapped outside time and yet, here and now, there were millions that I could save, and I need only will it so.

View Halloo

I turned to Tom and Syeed.

"Summon your ghoul friends," I said. "You're done with just protecting London Behind the Barrier. We're going hunting."

"Where?" Tom asked.

"Everywhere," I said. And drew the horn of Cernunnos from my pocket. "We'll start at this Barrier, and then I'll take it from there. Can you show me where to go?"

Elodie pointed a control at a bank of screens. "Looks like a build up near Potter's Bar," she said. "Just along from the junction. A bunch of them got fried climbing the pylons, and a bunch more are there feeding off them. There's a ghoul burrow nearby, so they'll be on it already. Which is handy."

"I had not known they went that far out," I said.

Syeed shrugged. "People of the Pit go wherever there's nice ripe ones, 'innit? Lots of villains buried under motorways—and the orbital's just old enough. Think of it like vintage wine, not that I'd know anything about that."

He put his hand on Tom's shoulder and they flicked away. I walked over and looked over Elodie's shoulder as they appeared on the verge of a broad road empty except for the burned-out husk of a container truck.

I followed them through Shadow: if I squinted slightly, I realised, I could see a faint trail where Tom had passed. It was a silver afterimage, as if he moved through a place that was neither the Mundane nor Shadow but the infinitely small bubble wall between them.

Tom had produced a long plastic tube from somewhere and he and Syeed were taking turns making a raucous noise blowing through it.

Human ingenuity always finds a way to make life more annoying.

Tom looked up at me. "Ghouls like vuvuzelas," he explained. "It's one of those human things like talking about Soaps and Kitkats with morning tea that the younger ones've picked up from human culture and argue about with the older generation who stay deep and don't like sunblock."

Tom blew into the tube again.

And suddenly a bunch of them were with us, springing from burrows that I could have pledged were not there before, brushing dirt from gauntlets open at the fingers' ends for claws as adapted to digging as to mayhem.

I had known a Queen of Palmyra who retained a ghoul woman at vast expense as her body servant for the sharpness of those claws both as bodyguard and epilator.

These though were dressed for business, not for luxuriousness, and their business was efficient slaughter. Many wore those helmets with tinted visors, or a thick white cream and dark goggles to protect them from the sun. Those whose straggly dark hair was visible wore it tightly pinned or tied back, and most were wearing tight black garments that hid none of the differences from humanity that ordinary street clothes effectively concealed—long loping legs, shoulders that could flex their arms almost to a threequarter turn and long bare feet higharched at the instep and with flexible razored toes that could slash or strangle. Their faces were filled with hatred for what they could see across the road and their long jaws hung agape full of slaver and hungry teeth. And each of them carried a long slashing knife that did not seem even a little redundant alongside their natural weapons.

I was glad to have them here. Their hungry fervour would add something to my will and power. Doctrine of Likeness, you see.

And if I was glad, they were in near ecstasy.

One of their elders, one of the ones you never expected to see near, let alone above, the surface in broad daylight, sidled up to me.

"One cub, one of those who change their face and fangs and work among the Dayfolk, she said you had returned to the world and I had hoped to find you here. Before the Dayfolk whom you protect fail and fall. This will be a good fight with you here, but will such single local fights prevail? Other elders think we should gnaw and scratch deeper so the noise of that failure and fall not disturb us."

I took a stance rather more confident than I felt. "I promise, this is not just a fight, but a part of a Great Working. I have always been the Huntress, but today I take fell purpose into my grasp and hunt those creatures from the world. In honour and mourning of my dead friends from whom they were carved as the man Jack once carved hunting beasts from your cubs."

"Cubs for whom we could find no kindness better than death. As we will help you destroy those things. In kindness."

He—or possibly she—pointed a talon across the road to the mass of flesh, stone, hair, and tendrils that writhed among the now broken trees and the metal struts of broken pylons and the downed wires that fizzed and sparked there, a mass that resolved itself into scores of creatures living and half dead.

If you looked at it one way, it resembled a pile of broken statuary in the Greek style painted in bright colours as they used to be and glued together at random so that the outer chambers of an ear might be the sole of a foot which stuck out from the brow of an enormous single eye whose pupil was a pair of lips that whistled tunelessly. Except it was alive, the whole and each part, and each of these things crawled over and under each other like rutting slugs with a noise like wet plastic rubbish sacks falling slowly down a rubbish chute.

I've lived in the Twentieth Century; I'm allowed to use similes that aren't a thousand years old.

And the stench. It offended the nostrils like rotten flesh, but it was clear from the look of disgust on the muzzles of the ghouls—for whom rotting flesh would be as attar of roses—that this was a psychic pollution that was turning our stomachs.

The dead gods' eyes—even as they slithered carelessly over and into each other and slurped up what was left where the cables had burned their companions—were all turned like compass needles to the South as if they knew in their mindless way that somewhere there were people whose flesh, mind and souls they could devour.

But not today.

Suddenly Tom was gone from our midst and flashed among them for a second and by the time he was back flares of burning white were among the creatures and the heat and noise of controlled explosions.

Syeed nodded sagely. "Aye," he said. "Now that's what I call a safe distance. Practice makes perfect."

Tom blew a charge on his repellent plastic tube, quite redundantly for the ghouls were already loping across the road, waving their long knives.

I echoed him with a summoning, a sharp blast of my horn, that had been the Horned God of the Chase Cernunnos', but was now and forever more the Horn of Mara the Huntress.

And at once the pack I had inherited from Cernunnos was milling around my and Syeed feet and Tom's wheelchair, and Garm and Fenris towering at my side, huger than I had ever seen them grow.

I glanced at Syeed, knowing how some who follow the Way of Submission feel about dogs, and he shrugged at me. "I grew up in Beeston. Lots of whippets in Beeston, and rotties, and Alsatians. The Brothers round there—we got over it, or we moved. Mostly, we got over it."

I put the horn to my lips to blow a second and deciding blast but suddenly you fluttered down on to my shoulders, distracting me. "Your friends are here with their father," one of you cawed.

With a deafening whinny Sleipnir was at my side with her brothers.

"Blood and battle borne on the wind.

Gladly I carry my mistress to war."

"Not so much war, at this moment. More like ridding the world of vermin, and honouring dead friends by destroying what was made from their corpses."

"You needn't think," said the god Loki, from behind my shoulder "that you get to summon just a few of my children and expect me to stay away from the feast."

The serpent and Hel were there too, when I turned, because of course they were.

He glanced over at the flames that my ghoul allies danced among as they slashed and cut.

"The corpse eaters are our allies, I take it," he said, weaving a cat's cradle of small flames between his fingers that was echoed by a net of flame that danced through the fight, setting dead gods aflame but leaving the ghouls unscathed. "My other children will

258

be here shortly. I assume you have a plan to deal with those creatures."

He paused to take in the scene around us—the chaos of living dead limbs and organs, the ghouls dressed for violence, the wreck of London—and smiled, showing his teeth, among which sparks danced.

"Oh," he said, "I see. Well, when all is done, you will certainly need my fire to scour away what leftovers your friends have left. And though they owe nor acknowledge no fealty to my daughter here," and suddenly Hel was at his side, "they share enough of their nature with her that she can help marshal them and their kin to where they are needed. Because all things die in all places and it is the nature of gods and goddesses of death to move faster than thought to where death is occurring."

Beyond the road, the ghouls were feasting and a remnant of the dead gods were slithering or crawling over the summit of the embankment—a remnant but enough for my purposes.

I signalled to Tom and he blew a long blast of recall on that hideous plastic tube. I had not asked, but had assumed that on his previous forays with the ghouls, they had established some such basic tactical protocols…As long as they abandoned their carrion for the moment and got out of my way…It was not as if, with Hel's assistance, they would not eat more than their fill this day.

I swung myself up onto Sleipnir's back and whispered into her ear. "This day, you will be all the horses of the hunt, in every place. You are the Horse of Two Realms and Two Natures, Sleipnir EightLegs, Sleipnir the Swift, who seems not to gallop but rather to slip between places faster than the eye can track. You have offered yourself as my steed, but you are my ally and not my servant. I ask you, Mistress Sleipnir, that you carry me this day."

Her reply came not in her usual slow considered verses but in an exhilarated joyful whinny of assent.

I sat up straight and knotted the fingers of one hand in her mane to steady myself. With the other, I raised the horn to my lips, and blew once, twice and three times.

With my first blast, we cantered across the motorway and up the steep rise, which Sleipnir took with as little effort as if we were travelling down it. The hounds began to bay and bell and run excitedly past the torn remnants of the ghouls' feast, not concerning themselves with the last flickerings of the flames—which did not trouble or singe my pack for they were already only partly in this place. And at every pace the pack grew—dogs of all sizes, tiny ratlike creatures whose disproportionately large eyes shone with hatred and ferocity as they danced among the lolloping paws of great bulky mountain dogs with shaggy white pelts and dark brown mastiffs whose flanks bulged with muscle. Increasingly, Fenris' followers were with us and wolves and wolfhounds ran side by side as if there were not generations of hatred between them.

Soon we were among the fleeing creatures and the mastiffs and wolves and mountain hounds ran at their sides, and fixed their teeth there and pulled them to the ground, and the small terriers and tiny lapdogs worried at their eyes, and ears and the pulses in their throats, when they had them, or the great artery in their single leg, until they gushed red, but did not soak my hounds who moved on once a kill was assured, but coolly, almost clinically, not in a frenzy.

And the ghouls came back in behind them to finish anything that was left undone.

This was the single small thing which would open out into my Working because I blew my horn a second time and created that small thing's likeness wherever there were dead gods devouring the bodies and souls of people, and there were small angry dogs whose masters had wandered off into a haze of delusion and worship, leaving them unfed and unkempt, that Garm and I could summon into our pack, and wolves and other wild canines that Fenris could summon to run alongside them and tear and bite and savage.

I rode Sleipnir at a gallop at one and the same time down grand empty avenues and up hills covered in the temples of small gods, and through shopping malls where tinny music played on loudspeakers though there were few to hear, and through small villages where naked children too young to worship any deity save their mother's breasts howled for what had been taken away from their mouths forever. I caught glimpses of them and knew yet again that I could not save them all and yet, in places, she-wolves paused in their ravening of what had been gods to give suck to such children.

And I rode through great empty places into which the dead gods fled me and my universal pack, plains empty of everything but the wind where their human pickings were thinner even than in the cities they had already stripped of much of their life, and left white dust where there had been communities. Yet it takes a lot to strip cities of all their people, and as I rode I heard cheers from behind curtained windows or high balconies, for not all people hear the call to worship or love their own gods too much to succumb to substitutes.

And where worship had lasted long enough that the dying had thrown up great gimcrack edifices of garbage and rubble scrawled with incoherent graffiti to pray in and sacrifice in and fall to dust, Loki came behind my hunt and the never-sated ghouls to scour places clean of the white dust and ash that was all that was left of those worshippers and the various fluids and filths that oozed from dead gods as they panicked and fled before me.

And his fire blasted those temples of desolation until it was as if they had never been, yet never touched the human places that they stood among.

I never lost myself in the hunt as Cernunnos had, though as I blew my horn for the third time, I felt my own Working and the great hunt of dead gods that it had made. I called to my hunt all beasts that have run with hunters or that hunters have ridden in the chase—hunting cats great and small and halftamed elephants and the small delicate deer that the Fair Folk had ridden before the men that had become elves slew them and took their place. Hawks and falcons and eagles joined with us almost from the first and, in the parts of the world where it was night, great swooping owls with large eyes and terrible talons.

You did your part as well, children of the Bird, and as our quarry ran from us in desperation you harried them, summoning great flocks of corvids—murmurations and parliaments, mischiefs and scolds, unkindnesses and murders—to peck at eyes and beat with wings and chatter and clatter and caw until the dead creatures could not run anymore and waited for the jaws that would take them.

Gulls joined in, not because we summoned them, but just because it is in the nature of gulls to join in any ruckus that they witness. Songbirds had no feather in the fight, I would have thought, and yet, everywhere we went, they soared above the battle, blending their voices in a vast ecstatic chorale as what should never have been created to corrupt nature was driven out of existence.

And where we passed, Hel brought ghouls to join us, many of them riding on the jackals and hyenas that were camp followers to my pack or on their old partners in carrion the buzzards and the vultures.

Nor was Garm and Fenris' brother the Serpent idle, for snakes waited for the creatures in unmown grass to bite and in swamps and wet forests to strangle and pinion with great coils of muscle. When they fled into the sewers of great cities alligators roused from the stinking waters where they had grown and prospered to tear at them with vast-toothed jaws.

The frenzy Cernunnos had known and which had so often taken him into itself hovered near the edges of my mind but never took control or made me lose it. He had often willingly taken the nature of the beasts with which he hunted into himself and let the Hunt twist him into the chimera I had seen him become in the pits under London when we sought the Ripper there.

I, though, had even when young resisted the entreating compulsion of your parent to enfeather myself and become part of them and I was far more set in my love of my own form when merely caught in a moment of magical will. I needed to stay calm and fully myself, to be the finger holding still under it the knot that would be the culmination of this Working, the eye at the centre of this storm of teeth and beaks and hooves and claws and talons, that, once we had torn, eaten and burned these dead god creatures from the world, would ensure that no one could raise them again.

I did not raise a hand in all the hours of my Great Hunt save for the three times I raised the horn to my lips, for the Hunt was my will and the will is more than the hand. I willed the killing and utter destruction of the creatures that had been made from the corpses of my dead friends and allies. I did not set a hand to the task: it was not necessary and I did not wish to.

This was a necessary scouring and extirpation. It would be followed by vengeance on those who had done this, and then on their master who had stayed hidden from me for so long.

After a while, it became clear that our kills were growing sparser, and my beasts more tired. They thirsted and I called down rain; I had not known I could do this and yet, when I thought of it, it was there as if it always had been.

And this, I recalled, was part of why I had always been suspicious of what I might become if I used power too readily. I had seen good intentions turn to sourness too often and necessity become whim.

I had been right, then. But this was no longer that season.

The ring of flesh will burst. The sleepers will awaken. And all will be undone.

The Mundane was afire and Shadow was freezing. I did not know for certain that fire and ice had been the sleepers of which the Enemy had spoken, yet it was clear to me that something was being undone and they were the greater part of it. I had no idea what the ring of flesh might be, and I was in no hurry to find out. The Enemy doubtless had more surprises in store and I would deal with them and him in good time.

Loki and his children had been at my side from the beginning of my hunt, and as I rode, I became aware of other gods who rode with us. The Lords of Hind, when, though only when, I rode through lands where they were worshipped. Representatives of the various bureaucratic ministries of the Land of Silk thrust parchments at me, permissions to do what I was doing anyway. At a crossroads in some barren land or other, a solitary figure placed his hands over his heart and bowed his head to me as I rode past. It was the closest thing to approval I had ever got from Gautama in three millennia and I nodded to him in turn.

I have mentioned that mostly the dead creatures grew still and waited for their end, but in places they were aware enough to make some sort of stand. And we rolled over them anyway and few of my beasts and none of the ghouls took any hurt from them.

We cleared the plains of the North and the great deserts. As I had been warned by Polly and her friends, the cold lands of the North had warmed into soggy quagmires where periodically the earth belched great stinking bubbles that might have killed my hounds had they been wholly there, as would the sands of the hot deserts which glinted with the white heat of nightmares. Everywhere I saw things begun but left half done that might have saved the world done earlier—great mirrors and windmills and stacks of a black dust that was not the black powder of madness left to bake into bricks rather than be spread into the air or onto the ice.

I saw cities that had been emptied of their people by plague or by mass suicide or by the dead gods I hunted, cities where weeds and rats had gained far more than a foothold. I saw cities that were awash and crumbling at their edges into the sea, yet people still lived there wading across what had once been streets and were now a foot deep. I saw cities—and parts of cities—that had been built as great mirrored towers and high lacings of walkways between them and lawns and flowerbeds kept perpetually green and bright watered under merciless sun that were empty because no one had ever lived there. Built for an age of renewed prosperity that was a promise the rich and the powerful had never meant to keep.

They were all gone from the world as Tom and Syeed had told me. Yet someone had spread the dead gods. A crime and a weapon and a culling. And—I feared—a Ritual, a gathering in of power for some terrible conclusion.

I saw other things too, things out of place, that came and went like the specks in one's eyes or a thought of ambush and which left a sense of foulness behind them. Great black egg like domes and spheres which left no dent in the soil where they had momentarily been. White tubes like roots or bowels or graveworms. But they were not the business I was about.

Twice we saw helicopters dropping crates that hatched more of the dead creatures that my beasts tore to shreds before they could move an inch, and you led flocks of birds that harried the craft from the skies so that their crews burned in the wreckage or fell screaming all the way down from the sky. I felt no compassion, for these were the enemies of life.

My hunt was everywhere and always on the move. I was caught in an ecstasy of righteous anger and destruction and I knew that I was moments away from losing myself and becoming all the things that I despise, and worse, that single universal omnipotence that my old friend's worshippers claimed him to be and lied. And those who rode and paced with me, mortals and gods and monsters and beasts and birds, would have become mere instruments of my single universal Will.

And I would not.

For if, as Philo thought (and I was no longer as certain as I had been then that he was wrong), there was a One beyond all gods, I had rather be the Huntress than some Shadow with pretensions.

I whispered Sleipnir to a halt, and of a sudden we were in a single place and all over the world the creatures of my hunt fell away from my will and went back about their own business. I was fully in my own shape again and lost even the full memory of what I had nearly become. I set the horn from my lips and it shrank in my hand and became the mere bauble Cernunnos had gifted me with. I willed a box around it and put it back in my pouch.

I patted the top of Sleipnir's head and stroked her behind the ears, then swung down from her back.

Loki was standing there, flames a cat's cradle between his fingers. He nodded to me, as power to greater power, not resentful but wary. "Another two moments and we would all have been lost in you. I thank you, Huntress, for your restraint, and that I did not have to do what I would have been forced to attempt."

He paused, and I waved him to continue.

"Another moment, and in that last moment, I would have done my best to burn you to smoke and ash, even though it would have grieved me to burn with you my daughter, beloved fruit of my erstwhile womb."

I reached out my hand, took his and kissed it. "It is good to know. But, by good fortune, I recollected myself, and you did not have to. And nor did you."

For I had looked around and seen Syeed taking a fuse from one of his deadly little bombs and Tom taking his knife away from Garm's throat. And shrugged to him in apology.

"He is your dog," said Tom, "and it is in his nature to be loyal, even against his father, doing what is needful."

Hel took her needle blade from the throat of her brother Fenris and kissed him on the muzzle. "I love him dearly," she said. "But he is part of your pack."

The Serpent stood aloof. When his father looked askance at him, he flickered his snake eyes and flexed a little, then said, "It is not in my nature to be enraptured. Had the Huntress chosen Ascension,

I would, unlike the rest of you, have had time to consider my choices." And then he yawned wide, showing his fangs.

One of you whispered in my ear. "We would have taken an eye each from you, then tried to peck the great arteries of your throat. We lost one master to pride and unreason; we would not have let you…"

I have loved many battle comrades in many different ways, but none more than you in that moment.

But that moment passed and we were in the next.

Those dogs that were with me, and the ghouls, sniffed a scent on the air and barked a warning. Ghoul barking is not identical to dog bark but not so unlike as to need another word. In answer there came a distant but approaching thunder.

We had come to a halt in a valley between steep hills. I recognised it as somewhere between the sea known as Black, where Atlantis had sunk, and that called Caspian, near where the citadel of Alamut had fallen to the horde of Hulagu Khan. Sooner or later I have been in most places.

It was not a place easily defended, potentially a killing ground if an enemy appeared on the hills above it, though it would have taken a significant enemy indeed to threaten me and my companions, especially if the Serpent chose to engage and reveal his other aspect.

The thunder in the hills grew louder and resolved itself into galloping hoofbeats and the inexorable rush of great wagons crushing stone under their ironbound wheels, and iron war hooves striking sparks from the broken stone. Either they would attack at once—as they had reason to—or, as seemed more likely, given what had happened the last time they had tried conclusions with me, they would wish to parley.

In either case, I stepped forward a few paces to meet the centaur horde as it entered the valley at the far end and flanked us in the hills above.

They were still an impressive force, though at some point they had taken a mauling from one or more of the human armies that contested this region. The older of their ambassadors had lost an arm just below the elbow and replaced it with an ugly gauntlet that bristled with hooks and studs. The young female seemed unchanged save for a great lock of white hair that hung over the left side of her face.

As before, they spoke with a single voice.

"A pretty trick you played us, Huntress, to send us here."

"Payment for your disrespect," I said, hoping that they did not intend to try my patience further—I no longer had the wild magic that had sent them here and felt somewhat depleted from recent exertions, and I was not sure that we would now prevail against such a force, even with the allies I had here.

"Indeed," they said, "and rightly so. Because you protect both Shadow and the Mundane, and have the power to do so. We worshipped the Ice, because the Ice seemed all prevailing in Shadow, and perhaps still will be, and you taught us our lesson by sending us to the Mundane, where the Ice is weaker every day even in what were once its strongholds and where worship has become a deadly vulnerability to which we lost oh so many until we cast it from us."

This was all very tragic of course, but seemed to indicate that they were no longer a threat to me, which was something of a relief.

The heralds paused, and the entire horde that I could see, and presumably the thousands currently out of my sight, bowed their heads—not in worship but obeisance.

Their heralds continued.

"We have watched you cleanse the world of those creatures that took so many from us, and which also wiped out the human armies with which we had had entertaining tussles. Men have acquired such interesting toys since we were last among them. Ingenious, but not up to our magic of course."

They sighed that sigh of self-satisfaction common to all beings who think themselves clever, and then bowed their heads a second time.

"You have cleansed the world of those creatures. Will you also cleanse it of their masters, and the master of those masters?"

"That is my firm resolve," I said.

"Those masters owe us the blood of our dead. We wish to join you in your resolve. Other questions to be resolved between us can wait."

I was momentarily concerned as to what those matters might be, and realised that full disclosure was probably my friend, as usual.

"I should mention, perhaps, that your way back to Shadow is now clear. The Lady Emma and I cleared it some little time ago, at the cost to me of the power that sent you here."

"That changes nothing," they said; "blood debts need to be paid in full."

It seemed to me that there were two major tasks ahead of us, and choices to be made. Sooner or later Heaven would have to be cleansed, but these new allies were unlikely to see that as their immediate priority, whereas going to America as a start at settling everyone's accounts with Burnedover would almost certainly lead us to attacking them in Heaven in due course.

I announced this. "Burnedover's blood debt before any other. First in the Mundane, and then in Heaven. Where I am sure their Master will have joined them."

The centaurs cheered. My ears rang for several minutes.

I searched the faces of my closest allies. Loki and his family all seemed to approve. I have never been particularly good at reading ghouls' expressions and was no more so now. Syeed, though, and Tom were exchanging glances as if each had something to say and was waiting for the other to say it first.

I paused—if these two saw a problem...

Syeed cracked first. "It's those white worm things. And the black domes, which seem to have something to do with them, and are

269

new. Back in '03, Burnedover were using a white worm's guts as a research station and travelling torture chamber. That ended badly for them, but then, back then, so did the dead gods thing. And we now know, they're persistent buggers. So maybe we should check those out before we go after their HQ, is all."

Tom nodded. Then he added, "There's another possibility. Bad enough if Burnedover have learned to control the white worm things and the black domes... But we know they meddle with things they don't understand, and we know the white worms are some sort of interdimensional larvae, or maybe tentacles, or antennae. Burnedover grabbed one and hollowed it out, but in the end, it ate them and got away."

I did not like where he was going with this.

"What if it was smart enough to be angry? What if it went home and got its family and friends?"

Changing of Seasons

Former Hell

A sudden gust blew bitter snow into her eyes and open mouth.

So this was how despair and defeat felt, Emma thought.

She had thought she knew them before, when Jehovah had betrayed her and Caroline seemed lost forever, but she had acquired power and responsibly since then. Millions depended on her and, for all her skill and intellect, she had not been enough.

The Enemy had outwitted her: each hard-won triumph had just been a move to which he had a response in place. She felt this like an ache in the back of the mouth when something you have swallowed imprudently is stuck there and you may be about to choke and the fear rises even before you can no longer breathe and there are tears in your eyes at your own stupidity and greed.

But even as she felt regret and self-contempt, she noticed Mara peck Morgan perfunctorily on the cheek and disappear about her

271

business as she had asked her to. And found in herself the reflection that if Mara, who had known the most awful of defeats, could still find the resolution to carry on, so could she. I am Judge and co-Queen of Hell, not some child to weep and lick my wounds, she told herself sternly.

There were souls to care for, and her co-Queen to bring back out of the ground, and Morgan and Judas and Vretil would be expecting her to think of something brilliant. And Dawn and Theophania—they looked up to her and were scary clever and she didn't want to disappoint them. And Caroline was back and maybe things were OK between them again.

Damn it, she'd whacked the Enemy in the balls once, and he hadn't been expecting that, which you'd expect Lillit to warn him about if she were simply helping him rather than playing some weird game.

Also, start solving problems, one at time, and the other problems fall in line, queueing up to be solved. That was how it had always worked before and maybe her luck hadn't broken yet.

Little as her arrogance deserved it.

She looked around her through the drifting sleet and souls, all these eager waiting faces. Hesitation is legitimate, she thought, but after a point it becomes dithering.

"Anyway," she said briskly, "let's just accept that most of the bad things you can imagine have been happening over in the Mundane, and something very bad happened in Heaven. All of which we can safely assume Mara will deal with, which leaves us with everyone who died in the last thirty some years and millions of the Blessed who have somehow been turfed out of Heaven. Plus weather. And really odd people winning elections. And this thing called social media that I really won't burden you with, but apparently it turned everyone into total drama queens. Questions? Comments?"

Everyone was standing around looking stunned; they seemed to have no more idea than she did. Last time she'd had a crisis, she'd come up with the ziggurat, which they really must get around to using but somehow didn't seem terribly relevant any more. At least the Former Damned weren't doing terrible things to demons any more as far as she could see, so she could chalk that up as a win. But no more big ideas for the moment might be sensible.

What do politicians do, she asked herself? In order to at least look busy.

Consultation exercise, she said to herself, and added a vast arena to her memory palace with seats for millions of people. Full of the idea of ergonomic seats with padded red velvet upholstery. And cup holders with some refreshing liquid in the cups. A lot of these people have been in Heaven, so they're probably used to quality. The Exiled Blessed over there, she thought, and the Newly Dead on the right.

And it was so.

And suddenly she was standing at the centre of it looking at an ocean of immaterial and expectant faces gawping down at her.

Most of the Exiled Blessed seemed to be singing. "*Glory, Glory.*" Repetitively.

It was a little distracting, but the part of her which was Berthe thought she could probably work with it. Minimalist.

Holy Minimalist.

First things first though.

"Hi, there," she said, feeling that wasn't really adequate, but oratory wasn't her thing so just talk informally and get through it. "I'm Emma Jones. Some of you may know me from television where I used to go on to talk about magic in ways that let you think it was all woowoo. I need to apologise—I misled you; it's all true. This used to be Hell, but isn't any more, so that's the first bit of good news. Some of you used to be in Heaven and there seems to be a problem with that right now, but I'm sure my colleague the Huntress will restore normal service as soon as possible. There will be new tireless magical bodies for anyone who wants them, but that will take a while because of demand, so if you'll form an orderly line, some of my associates will show you to the Blood Vats of

Phlegethon which are a lot less terrifying than they sound. They're about a hundred miles in that direction—near the waterfall in the sky. But that may not be what you want at all.

"Well, normally this is nice and warm and the trees are not covered in snow and icicles and I don't know why my co-ruler has buried herself but it's some fertility goddess thing. Anyway, I know bad things have happened to most of you especially those of you from the twenty-first century, and the good news is that it wasn't mostly your fault, there's this guy… No, not Lucifer, some other guy… No, don't get me wrong, Lucifer is pretty much of a dick, but mostly he's a bit of a wanker. I mean, he got overthrown by a crowd of old Nazis and mediaeval tyrants. Whom my friend and co-ruler ate for lunch. So, anyway, what do you want to do, now you're here?"

The thing about millions of voices saying the same two or three things at the same time is that they sound just like two or three voices saying those things competitively. It makes it easy.

The Newly Dead all had different grievances that amounted to the same thing: it was unfair. Something had fallen from the sky, or someone had walked up with a gun and said, "Make Room," or the crops failed or it was too hot—and it was someone else's fault and they were angry about it. And wanted to go back and sort it out.

Aggressively.

Zombie apocalypse as a metaphor for international class revolution—she was sure she'd read that article in Sight and Sound. Certainly might be an option—she'd have think about how it would work. No; on reflection, it was a bit what a supervillain would do, so perhaps keep it for a last desperate throw.

"Let's defer that for now," she said firmly. "From what you tell me, a lot of the guilty are already dead and further retribution can wait. I don't rule out sending you back but maybe saving the world takes precedence—global warming and all that is probably part of the Enemy's master plan and I don't see what a rampaging horde of the previously dead can do to fix that. Or him. Given the number of you that seem to want bodies… I warned you it would take a while. Really quite a long while unless you're prepared to be six inches tall. Which pretty much rules out using your new body to fight a war. And why would you want to do that anyway—you died once already. Hell-flesh is durable but its major point is that it feels pain more—also pleasure, but there wasn't much of that around under the previous management."

She was nervous. She was talking too much and making jokes they were not going to get.

There were rumblings of dissent; this was a tough crowd and this could easily slip out of control. Only from the Newly Dead, luckily, and the thing about disembodied spirits is they can't throw things.

The burden of their complaint now seemed to be who did she think she was and could they complain to her manager, with an undercurrent of were they supposed to think hair that colour was natural.

The other half of her audience went on singing *Glory, Glory* regardless.

Be thankful for small mercies.

The Newly Dead were doing a combination of Mexican wave and slow handclap that was quite impressive given that they didn't have bodies to accomplish this with. Or was that something she was letting them do because they were in her self-doubting head? She really should get out of the habit of letting people in.

"Impudent rabble!"

Suddenly she wasn't facing them alone.

"Listen to her if you know what's good for you."

Theophania was wearing all the tiaras and regalia you'd expect of a Byzantine princess and Empress of the West. Stalin was with her, in full Generalissimo mode; Judas was utterly in Pantocrator Glory: Vretil hovered above them, all six wings—where did he keep them normally?—shimmering like a dragonfly's.

Emma felt quite underdressed.

"I was ruler of half of Europe," ranted Theophania with a grace and hauteur that almost made Emma regret the whole Tiffany thing. "I have known Emperors and given popes their orders. Because of me, you bathe regularly and many of you use forks. And I follow Emma because she has wisdom and humility in equal proportion. She made what was a place of torture into a safe refuge: without her we would still be burning in the pit."

This might have worked if the Newly Dead had any historical knowledge whatever.

"I am a monster in her eyes," said the Generalissimo, "even though I helped save the world from Fascism. But when I was sent to her, she treated me with courtesy, no matter what she thought privately, and she trusted me to put her plans into operation. I thought I knew how to lead and how to terrify people, until I saw her raw power. Do not mistake her politeness and forbearance for weakness. It would be a mistake."

Really none at all.

She thought, well-meaning of the awful old bastard, I didn't know he cared, but I'd better try a new tack. Only with audio-visual aids and grab attention. I've let them into my head, so they can share some of what's lying around in here.

Think, ultimate reality show. She'd gathered that got to be a bigger thing than she remembered from the early Noughts.

Maybe Drama Queen was the way to go, actually, a language they'd understand.

"I've known pain to equal yours—" and blasted them with highlights of the deaths of Hypatia and Berthe, and moments when she thought she'd lost Caroline forever, "—but I've also known triumphs—" whacking the Enemy in the balls, giving Black a Glasgow kiss, gutting Simon, undoing Dark Alchemy (that last a bit recherché but giving all the crowd-pleasing violence some much-needed balance). "Stick with me kids, and that'll be as nothing."

Caroline and Dawn danced past waving unfeasibly big pompoms that matched Emma's hair and chanting, "She's our girlfriend and we think she's fab."

"Our? Girlfriend?" Emma wondered aloud; obviously she'd missed some nuance.

But it seemed to clinch the deal, because the Newly Dead started chanting her name in a gratifying manner and for several minutes more than she would have preferred, then sat down. And then got up again headed for the exits to her memory palace, and formed an orderly queue in the direction she had indicated earlier.

Which left her with the Exiled Blessed, who looked like a softer touch.

Judas made a sign of blessing and the Exiled Blessed fell silent, save for a muttered undercurrent of "the Son, the Son."

"My Father sent me here to watch in case Emma did not live up to his expectations, but she has surpassed them. I am still here because I wish to be part of what she is doing. And I had rather serve in what used to be Hell than reign in Heaven. So, what do you want?"

The Exiled Blessed looked impressed and only slightly rebellious.

"We don't want to be embodied, nasty stinky hungry flesh that gets spit and mucus between the notes" they said, harmoniously. "We want to go on singing."

Then they added, "Only, can it not be Glory, Glory? There's some lovely Baroque polyphony we've been working on. And showtunes. Jehovah never let us do showtunes."

"And so you shall," Emma promised, using her most positive voice. "Only can you keep it down while you're in my head? Judas sweetie, can you rustle them up a tiny perfect Singverein somewhere with a good acoustic—"

"I did it earlier," he said. "Assumed you would need it. It's a copy of my original—which this is too. I thought you never visited."

"I haven't. Your father never asked me over for tea."

"Typical," Judas grumbled, "he went on and on about how special you were, but never asked you round, except when he wanted to poison you."

"That's not very loyal."

"Yes, well, I quite like the old bastard, but I work for him because he is the material Shadow of the One true and ineffable."

This was obviously an explanation he had rehearsed many times. Especially to himself.

And finally it clicked and Emma understood. "Oh, I get it now. You're a Neo-Platonist. Mara explained it all once over breakfast in my flat, but I was doing the Times Crossword."

"One of the reasons I'm working for you now is that you've made yourself into a pretty good shadow of the One, only without giving yourself airs and graces. My sister would have told you off if you had."

"You know Caro and I used to work for her?"

The Exiled Blessed, all millions of them, were hanging on their every word. So too were Theophania, Vretil and Stalin.

"You three! Private conversation. Go off and administer something."

Theophania looked sulky. "When I was Empress of the West, theological speculation over dinner with Cardinals was the only hobby I was allowed. So nice to get all my questions answered."

"Same in seminary," Stalin added gruffly," until we all discovered Marxism. More useful, and rather closer to the truth."

"I'm supposed to listen to private conversations," Vretil said. "I'm the Recording Angel."

But, grumblings and all, the three of them vacated Emma's mind.

Judas fixed the Blessed with an authoritative glare. "I just told you there's a material auditorium over there. Go over, start singing. Make yourselves useful."

And they were gone, and Emma could shut her mind to outsiders and continue her conversation with Judas like normal people.

"So," he started, "now they're all set up and singing, what do you want to do with it?"

"It?" There was something that she wasn't following.

"All the worship. Because whatever's going on in Heaven, I'm not sending all that good stuff His way. Not until we resolve the situation. I disconnected them from him immediately, just to be on the safe side. Don't want all that going to the Enemy or to Burnedover, do we?"

Emma was slightly revolted. "You mean Heaven's set up like—"

"An electrical battery, yes. That was how I set it up. Pretty smart of me given the closest things I'd seen were windmills and waterwheels. Prayer powers all gods of course, but most of it isn't collected properly and just goes to waste. I'd been meaning to talk to you and Aserath about that—the Former Damned pray to the pair of you quite a lot, you know, and you hardly seem to use it."

Emma felt a bit queasy about all this.

"You got a massive boost from your apotheosis, of course, and all those subjective years you spent on person to person judging. And then there was all that wild magic, and when you used it to undo dark alchemy, you and Mara both got major boosts somehow. But I reckon you're working at about 35% efficiency. And that's even without what you'll be getting from the Exiled Blessed now they're on line. Plus—you don't do glitz. Father likes all these lights, on all the time, lambent, opalescent. Never turns them off, never draws a curtain. Had to have them, you see, Malachi and Isaiah said they were there, so when I started organizing and rebuilding, he had to have them put in. Only, all the trouble I took, and he didn't like the view. 'It's the firmament', I said, 'it's supposed to look like that.' So I had to put up curtains, big silk ones, the colour of Messalina's boudoir."

As he talked, his hands were doing something invisible and metaphysical and Emma felt very slightly, though pleasantly, peculiar. She knew roughly what he was doing—and the chatter was to put her at ease. She'd had plumbers who chattered away while they did something messy but invisible under the sink, and suddenly a blockage she hadn't known was there cleared and she felt not just invigorated but somehow more right than she ever had before.

"I've routed some of the Former Hell stuff to Aserath," he said. "It is half hers, rightfully, and it might help wake her up or whatever. But you're getting all the juice from the Exiled Blessed, because I set those connections up, so I think I get a say. You should probably start finding something to do with it soon. We don't want you overloading."

Well, Emma thought, problems need fixing and the biggest one is the weather, so she thought a warm breeze and it was so, and she thought the blizzard off up into the mountains and it was gone, and she thought the snow off the trees in little Disney droplets that soaked into the ground or pattered away in little shallow gulleys that opened up all over the floor of Former Hell, and the trees and the bushes gave a great sigh of Spring release and started, all over Former Hell, to sprout pink and purple blossom.

Oh dear, Emma thought, I hope Aserath won't mind.

Suddenly, near the dry dark sticks that had been Aserath's bower there appeared a green shoot. Intense in its greenness so that it compelled the gaze, small but growing as she watched from tendril to serpentine shoot to thick stalk to ten to twenty feet high. An intense smell wafted from it like cinnamon and musk and aftermath. And sudden as inevitability it branched and shot out leaves the size of serving platters, Tyrian blossoms like orbs of rule and then a single lush fruit hanging thirty feet above the ground that shimmered with ripeness and juice and then popped like a bubble.

Aserath floated toward Emma and Judas, taking her time about it, swathed in strips of green and purple silk, flirty as her trickster aspect, motherly with fecundity, with just a wisp of smoke from one nostril to remind you of the dragon.

She settled to the ground, pirouetted on one foot so that the strips of material shimmered around her like serpents, like weather, and then settling wove themselves into a tight gown that barely contained her.

She looked round at the crowd, then strutted over to Emma, went on to tiptoe and kissed her. Her lips were soft as rose petals against Emma's cheek.

"Hi, darling," she said, "I see you started Spring without me, naughty thing. For the best, I was fast asleep. I hate snow—impressed you've got rid of it. Lot of new faces?"

"Thirty year backlog of dead people. Bunch of souls tossed out of Heaven. Mara's gone to find out what's going on apart from plague, war and devastation."

"Once upon a time," Morgan said, "I'd be devastated myself at having missed witnessing all that. Clearly, I've grown as a person."

"Speak for yourself, mistress," cawed the Morrigan. "Thanks to you I missed all the really big ones. All that Carrion. I haven't changed at all."

"Why did it get so cold suddenly?" Aserath asked, shivering a little as she stretched, and then creating a thick velvet robe around herself.

"Thirty years of climate change in the Mundane just came and bit us all at once. As above, so below, only the opposite." Emma stopped, struck by a new thought. "Which raises the question, did I just fix that by ending winter here? That will have put another crimp in the Enemy's plans."

"If only we knew what they were," Judas said.

Caroline coughed significantly. "Actually," she said. And then again, "Actually."

She really does have the knack of compelling everyone's attention, Emma thought fondly.

"I met him," Caroline said. "I just remembered. I was just allowed to remember. She told me, back then. She said, Judas will say, if only we knew what they were, and I'd remember. In 2036. Just before the end. When it would be useful but too late."

"Who said this?" Emma asked.

"Her," said Caroline. "Me. Other me. Lillit. She explained that, too."

"The end of what?"

"Time. Chance. Destiny. I assume she meant, everything, but what she said, when I asked, was 'Time. Chance. Destiny,' which is her thing, right. Along with being inscrutable and stabbing everyone in the back. Including him."

"So when was this?" Emma asked, guessing she knew the answer and perhaps some of the others did too.

"It was during the time I couldn't remember. Lucifer was there, in our flat. You'd just escaped from Iraq, and told a room full of suits about it. And went for a bagel, and I ghosted upstairs so the goblin lady couldn't be rude about me, because you know what she's like. Hope she's OK. So there he was, sitting on the sofa, being suave in a rich person suit, and he said 'There you are' and grabbed me and it was the first time I properly felt a hand on my skin since I died and I wished it hadn't been him, and it was like he put me in a box and I couldn't move, or change my outfit, or say anything.

"He was horrid and villainous at you and I could sort of hear it like it was the other end of a tunnel, or on a bad line, and then he left and took me somewhere with him. I heard him order oysters and slurp them, and then he was trading stocks or something in German. Then we were somewhere else and he took me out of a pocket in his sharp suit and I hope I stretched the fabric and I was on a table and I heard Browning say something like 'You'd better hurry. Heaven is at war and the Dukes plan your overthrow,' and then he said, 'Wait there a while, Caroline. I have more important things to deal with.' And I heard someone scream and I heard something snap and I heard something, someone, gurgle and squelch and I knew something truly horrible had just been done to someone only I couldn't see it."

She was pale with the memory of it and both Emma and Dawn put their hands on her right shoulder and their fingers touched there and Emma really didn't mind at all.

"Then he said, 'Best you don't look, Caroline. When I eat at home, and don't have to pretend, I'm a messy eater,' and he looked down at me and he was huge or I was small and he looked like he always did in his politics tutorials, only not, because this was him but it was his real face and it was that uncanny valley thing they talk about. Not human. Something about the eyes, and the jaw. And in the mouth. Too many teeth. You know what mink are like, mad like weasels only far fouler. It was like, we're something quite tough like a weasel or a ferret. And then we meet a mink and feel its teeth and we're not tough or vicious at all. And then we're dead. Being looked at by him was like that."

And then she began to sob. It went on for a while but none of her hearers, not even the Morrigan, pressed her for more, only waited for her to tell the rest of her story when she was ready. Emma and Dawn held her closer.

But then a screech in the sky caught their attention, a black mark that grew and resolved itself into one or other of the two raven-sized birds that had served Odin and now accompanied Mara.

It fluttered down and for a couple of moments waited silently while its two siblings picked mites from between its feathers.

In due course, it plumped up its wings and shook its head as if to dislodge something, and then strutted over to cast its eye upon Judas.

"Son of Joseph, your other, your adopted father lies sick in bed. He will live, saved by the care of Lady Sof, best of nurses, and the magic worked by my mistress and the Goddess-Judge Emma here. But it was a close thing and my mistress bids you come at once to his side. My sib is over in Shadow, at Valhalla Olympus, or at the Just City, similarly summoning your sister. We," and it fixed all present with a slow turn of its head, "can no longer afford division in your family."

"He was hurt?" Judas asked incredulously as if he did not know that all gods and all fathers are subject to time and chance and death. "But he lives?"

"Stabbed in the side with a fell, ingenious weapon of dark alchemy during an invasion of Heaven by Burnedover and their human dupes, but rescued from them by the changeable one, the Lady Lillit, and then relieved from its draining poison and like to make full recovery. But I am not here to make small talk with Emma's courtiers, or even with my beloved siblings. I am here to summon you. To the rooms of Polly Wild, where he took refuge and where his sickbed lies. Come."

Without another word it flew into the sky and was gone. Judas made a courtier's bow to Emma and gave a nod and glance that took in all the others present, and was gone from their sight.

It was Vretil who broke their stunned silence. "Shit just got totally real," said the Recording Angel.

There was nothing further to say, actually, failing which, Emma turned back to Caroline and nodded.

Caroline cleared her throat.

The True, Terrible And Secret Story of Humanity and Our Cousins

As Told to Caroline, by Berin

He looked at me for a long predatory moment. "I will not devour you, mind and spirit both, as I would prefer, not this day. I am told you still have a role to play in my inevitable victory and I know that time and chance are masters to us all who will not be gainsaid. I have promised you to your other self though it galls me to dicker with her, a mere human."

I spoke into his sudden scornful silence. "Human? And you are?"

"Not. Obviously. I move among you, clothed in your likenesses. I am the last, as one day I shall be the first."

"Of what?" Though I knew the answer in my blood, in my bones, in my spirit.

"The beast in the night. The teeth in the throat. For millennia we roamed the hills, the plains, the barren places, watching the herds, you and your cousins the Valley Folk. Taking what we needed—the flesh, the blood that nourished us, and the fear and the pain that made us strong, that gave us the power to call lightning from a clear sky, to make fire to warm us and cook your flesh. For we had discovered how tasty charring made the marrow of an infant's backbone, the convoluted gristle of a Valley maid's ear. We could smash bone with a glance, or hold a food beast quiet while we spent ourselves into her and then devoured her alive."

He paused, and relished a memory that was all the more delicious for not being his own.

"We spoke mind to mind across the miles, united in purpose of ruling and feeding forever. We had been careless earlier, had taken too many of the Little Folk, the Handy Folk, the Chinless and the rest until we were a family with three members. We had learned prudence in our husbandry. Us and you, our prey forever. But then, one day, the earth shook. There was ash and dust everywhere and green things died, and the creatures that ate green things. Our herds died, both your people and the Valley folk, until we thought them all gone and we turned on each other for food, one clan against the other, a winnowing for the strongest.

"But they were not all gone though they became few. They ate the things we were too proud to eat. Worms and the small birds that ate the worms and the stoats that ate the birds. And some ate corpses and grew apart from the others and became the folk you call ghouls and their cousins in the sea. And they learned to do things we had never needed. And they learned to wander into Shadow, of which we had never known. They had always knocked stones together to produce an edge—even the poor stupid Handy Folk could do that—and use it to take small game and larger, and we had watched them and thought it play. They learned to grind seeds to paste between stones, seeds that they found and garnered among the drifts of ash. They hid from us, and learned to flourish.

"Where we spoke mind to mind in shared deadly purpose, they turned the mutter and cooing with which they accompanied grooming each other's pelts into this clumsy way of communicating I am forced to use. Even the folk of the Valley managed to turn gurgles and grunts into something of the sort. Worse, when they met from time to time, creeping in the wilderness, careful that we never find them again—they did not know each other's tongues— they never really learned that—but they could see that each other were not mere beasts and used signs and dance to do what words could not. Find what they had in common."

He is a monster but he has learned to tell a story. Though I may be only the second to survive his telling of it. I and Lillit. He tells it to keep his anger warm, his anger and his contempt, that mere food turned and fought and won.

"For what they had in common was us. The fear and the hatred and the anger. Of the weak against the strong. We had always been few to their many, and that had not mattered while they cowered before us. But from cutting up carrion in the lean years, and then hunting returned great beasts when the ash blew away and things grew green again, they had learned, and the two peoples taught each other, how to wear a hole in an edged stone, and bind it to a broken branch with dried pieces of gut. And we could break bones with a glance and call down the lightning, but they were many and we were few, and they threw pointed sticks and sharp stones from ambush and they rushed us, scores at a time with their crude sticks and stone axes.

"We could kill fifty but one of that fifty would kill one of us. And our talk mind to mind across the miles would dwindle by that one. One at a time. For a thousand years of hatred and death. And they decided that we were a thing too foul to make into their food, but the ghouls had no such compunction and ate every scrap and broke every bone for its marrow and ground every splinter down to a dust that they could lick off a moistened claw. Because ghouls hate waste. And by eating us, some remnant of our magic seeped into them and they became Other. And though your folk and the folk of the Valley declared ghouls other and unclean, they kept their bargain and left no relic of us behind."

"But," I said to him, "you are here nonetheless. And you know all of this."

"At the end, when there were few of us left and no hope of another generation, we took the last three young children born, filled them mind to mind with the last tatters of our magic and set them loose in the barrens to live or die as time and chance would have it. Then the last ten adults turned and stood against their foes and died as hard as you would expect. They died and the ghouls ate them, and that, your people assumed, was that.

"And it nearly was. Mind to mind, I felt my sister die when hyenas of the barrens ate her, mouthful by mouthful. And laughed as she died. Mind to mind, I felt my brother tumble into a ravine. His ankle snapped and he could not get out, and he starved, day by day, and I felt him starve, mind to mind. And at the last, vultures ate out his eyes and we said farewell, mind to mind. And I felt him die. And I nearly let myself die with him. Last and alone.

"But the part of me that was all of us would not let me die. There was one thing left to us, and that thing was vengeance. So I crawled, naked, and thirsty and starving. And a girl of the Valley Folk who had lost her own child and was still producing milk happened upon me, and desperate though I was, I cast a glamour on her that she not see my true face and dash out my brains. And I let her see me as her own lost brainless child and let her give me suck where I had rather have torn out her throat.

"The five years I spent posing as an infant with all the memories of my people boiling in rage inside me were but the first and least of the indignities that I added to her and your people's account. For I knew I could do nothing until I was full grown but watch and wait and never let the mask slip. And plan.

"Because that I could do: go inside my head and cultivate my will and realise that my people had never learned enough or dared

288

enough. They had used magics for such little things, and I would dare so much more. So I grew to adolescence and I had to lower myself and twist my own throat to learn language, because human minds were closed to me when I was young. And I learned to knap stone and I learned to use the sharp stone to sever the gut that I would dry and use to make the axe. I was slow at this work because I found it contemptible to be handy, and it was yet another humiliation to be thought of as slow who could have killed them all with a glance."

As he spoke, I watched the shame of having been helpless, of having had helplessness be his only safety pass across his face. Desperate as I was, and not believing his claim that he would not finally end me, I took some grim pleasure in that shame, as I had from his description of that primordial war.

And was horrified at my own reaction to it, as much as I knew I would be to its consequence.

"I sat in her lap. For years. I soiled myself constantly because I could not digest the bean paste, the corn paste, and it was only occasionally that a lone and barren woman saddled with a sickly idiot child could persuade a man to give her the meat of the hunt or the fish of the catch. I learned to scrabble in the stream for trout by watching others do it, though I did not need to do this for I could have called them to me with my mind. I took her what I caught for it would seem strange among that people if I did not honour her. And my hunger hated my intellect and my need that they never see me plain for what I was.

"She begged scraps of offal from the hunters and they pitied her for having a sickly child, and so I ate well enough after a while that I only occasionally soiled myself. I listened to the noises they made and there was something in them of meaning. I learned the word 'eat' and I learned the word 'sleep' and I learned the word 'clean,' and I learned that if you put two words side by side, they had consequence. And she taught me speech a little at a time and it tortured my twisted throat.

"And she kept me alive and fed after a fashion, and I hated the blind stupid kindness of her. I grew to boyhood and then manhood. She grew old and she came to watch me where I scrabbled for trout and I waited my time until a day when the grown men and the handier of the boys were away on a hunt. Then I pretended that there was little to catch in one place and then another and I led her downstream and away from the encampment and she did not know that she was herself the fish I scrabbled for.

"I used my mind to break two of the small bones in her hand and one in her foot and she felt sudden pain that she did not understand. I cracked one of her ribs and sent a splinter into her liver. And then I threw her to the ground and I smashed her jaw with my mind. I took my time with her that I might feed my full on her pain and dismay and all the time she stared at me with the remaining eye in what I had left of her face and what I could see in that eye was the same stupid love I had watched as I lay puking and whimpering in her lap on the first day she found me. At the last, when I had bruised and smashed even the last shred of love and spirit from her, I let her see my true face and know that she was utterly deceived and betrayed.

"And she gave her last horrified choking pant of death, and in that moment I learned what my people had not known in millennia of domination and unsubtle taking of prey: that there is not merely a special flavour to betrayal but a special force to it, that it brings with it a rush of power such that in that moment I could, had I chosen, have strode back among her people and drained and eaten my fill. Had I but chosen, but all it would have taken was one lucky spear throw to have ended me.

"I did not yet know what my plan would be, but I knew that my people had not made me to take the petty revenge of one tribe or two and then be done. So I hid her body in a mudslide and let them think I searched for her. And they pitied me, poor stupid cripple that they thought me, and gave me such alms of food as they could spare. And one after another, but slowly month by month I took a child here and an old woman there.

"Some of those in my memories knew how to kill smoothly and with great pain. I broke a tooth in one mouth and let it fester into fever and worse; I tripped another, yards from the hooves of the great bull that trampled him; I made mothers bleed to death in childbirth and old men choke on their food and adventurous children meet with misfortune. Your people might have suspected something, and killed the young stranger none of them knew except to pity, but the folk of the Valley were better than you, or at least saw no pattern. And where possible I showed them some of my true features and let them die in inherited fear.

"I grew stronger, more apt to deceive. They dwindled and I grew strong. I picked off one small tribe after another and I learned the steady trickle of power that comes from the fear that something is abroad that should not be. And where I could find them on their own, I took the hunters and left animal blood or chips of boar tusk nearby that their friends might think they had gone off to kill something for and by themselves that they would not have to share, and I felt a trickle of power from the envy and resentment that grew among them. And with few hunters and fewer fathers of new ones, groups of the folk of the Valley took refuge as suppliants and received charity. And there was suspicion that I could build on.

"I watched and waited: by now I was starting to understand your people's more fluid and less guttural speech and could use glamours to seem like one of you when it was convenient. I did not even plan to start that strife between brothers that began somewhere on the ice and has never truly ended, because your people both love and fear the stranger and the people of the Valley were near and most convenient. It took very little to turn pity into contempt; I had few words but those were subtle enough to persuade my hearers to kick and to pinch and to twist and to strike. All those little moments of malice which culminate in serious acts of violence and in the end murder. Because they had victimised me with their kindness and

291

their pity and their scorn, I hated the folk of the Valley that little bit more. Did your people have the advantage? Probably. You were a little bit more like my people perhaps. Perhaps without my killings of their best, the folk of the Valley would have prevailed, or perhaps any strife would have died away once they had forgotten the great murder that stopped them being mere cattle.

"As it was, I killed and I persuaded to kill, and I flaked away at malice—my own and your people's—so that it became ever sharper, ever more refined. And I started to think of what I might to with malice and with will and with what I had started to think of as magic, as a tool in my hand rather than the hand itself. I wanted… I wanted to bring my people back and not be alone, and I wanted them to be proud and strong again, though I knew that they would always despise me for the weakness I had needed to survive when they made me and died and left me alone.

"And there were always more of you, no matter how many I killed—I could start the dwindling and the killing of the people of the Valley but I did not have time. Every death executed or suborned made me sleeker and stronger but I could not catch up with all the rutting and filth and disgusting little maggot infants. I did not have time to achieve the purposes I was starting to imagine. And I despaired that I would start to fail and fall and the memory of my lovely vicious people would die with me.

"In my desperation I even tried to rut with you and the folk of the Valley perhaps to produce children that would be born as I was with the memory of my people and my mission inborn in them. You have no idea how disgusting I found it to do that, having sex with cattle that thought themselves my equals. Fat creatures dripping with fluids like the one on whom I had been dependent for so long.

"And all my disgust and self-contempt was a waste.

"Mostly my seed just dried and was as dust, or a foetus started to grow and then stopped. Some of them came to term and either tried in hatred to claw their way out of the womb and drowned in their mothers' blood and the mothers died too, or they withered in the

292

womb and turned to stone from self-hatred or were twins or triplets who fought to the death in the womb, and, unborn, talked to me mind to mind across the miles and told me how much they hated me and themselves. Their scorn burned me like fire and unmanned me to a point where I could not rut my way to more such.

"I knew ever greater despair… and then one day she came to me. Naked and shimmering with the gloss of high polish sharp stone or the surface of still water. She was nothing I had seen before. She looked like one of your people but had what I thought was an angry pride equal to my own—though it was something else entirely that I still do not fully understand—and she let me think that until one day centuries later, when she explained to me that at another time I would tell her what I had thought and she would disillusion me.

"But by then she had talked to me of time and chance and how trying to dance out of their effects on her had made her their servant.

"My first thought was that she was a threat and, since there was no one else near, I tried to kill her with my mind, reaching into her and dangling sharpened filthy nails through her inner parts. But I could not reach into her, and when I tried, she struck me once, twice with a slap that felt like stone.

"I felt my jaw break lopsided and for a second or two I could not breathe. I saw my face reflected in her surface—my true face—and so I knew that she saw me true and there was no point in my trying further to deceive her.

"But then she kissed me on the forehead and something passed through me like a wave of burning that thrilled and salved.

"My jaw healed, and I was stronger and healthier than I had ever been.

"'This will all go more easily if you never try that again,' she told me.

"And then she said, 'The ring of flesh will burst, the sleepers will awake, and all will be undone,' and then she shimmered away like rain in sunlight and was gone. She left me with a riddle. She also left me without pain from the jaw that she had broken and that was now whole again. She is the living Fifth Thing of the Work. She is hard as the Adamant and as unmaking, were she to wish it, as That Which Devours, but more importantly, she is both Elixir and Stone, and with that single touch had made me whole and undying."

I shuddered because I could not understand how someone could do that. I understand it even less now I have some sense of who she is, Sister to Mara and Sof and in some sense my other self. Why take the monster, the enemy of all human life and give him millennia to work his corruption on us?

"Truly," he went on, laughing at my look of horror, "I did not understand why she would do what she had done. I had already done much harm in the world and killed those I had first tricked, but betraying one's own to the enemy was something I could not understand until she told me of time and chance whose servant she is. She gave me immortality not because of any wish or fierce desire of my heart, but because it was the thing that happened next and she knows that. She knows everything; she told me my plan before I could have conceived; she broke the Work for me to give me weapons you cannot conceive of: she is Destiny's servant and thus mine. Because I and my plan are destiny and your people, your world, is a mistake that needs to be erased. The sleepers will wake, the Ring of Flesh will burst and all will be undone."

He sounded so utterly convinced that for a moment I was caught up in his certainty and his contempt for me, for all of us, and it left me desolate.

And yet…

Whatever the sick child he remembered being, whatever the prehistoric monsters whose lives he had in his head, he was also the socially smooth Oxford don he had been when we first met him, Emma: plausible, arrogant and someone whose authority I was always inclined to resist on principle and you because he was never quite as clever or as certain as he assumed.

That also had been a mask, and I had now seen behind the mask and knew him for the Deceiver, the Father of Lies who must first lie to himself.

And then I heard a voice and knew it for my own voice, yet it was not.

"We are all the servants of destiny, little man, proud little man. You, I and she. And all will play out and be seen and the story will have its end. Your end, her end, my end, and the end of time and chance or at least of my dance with them."

I had been still as if held in a vice, but now I was free to turn my head away from the sight of his face and his terrible mouth and from the voice that went with those hideous tearing teeth, and be reassured by what was my face in a sense, though with strong cheekbones and proud nose utterly different from what I think of as my own quite considerable good looks.

Cast in a metal bright as fire, solid as the world, alive and constantly flowing as a river. It is a strange thing to be taken up into the hands of something very like God and know them for your own hands.

"I am taking her away from this place," she told him. "There was a time allotted and allowed to you to torment her and that time is done. But I have so much more to say, so many despairs to show to her.

"I told you that there was a time allotted to you. I told you its dates and its limits. And that time is over and done. Destiny is set, and we are all its servants, you she and I. The difference is that I know it, and the hour and the date. All the hours and all the dates. I asked to dance around time and chance, and that choice was set for me, and I dance with time and chance, back and forth, like the figure in a clock who pirouettes with her aching foot just so, at the same angle, as she strikes the hours and sees them come round again to be struck, always the same. And now she and I must be away from here, because it is the time, and your dance with her is done, as Lucifer's was before you."

I felt a great release and I was gone from his presence and from the smell of charnel and killing shed so pervasive that I only knew it for what it was when it was gone.

And I was in a new place that was not a place, in a time that was not time but the moment between all time which is where she lives, and dances, and which flows like the living precious mirror of her face and yet is set forever cast like bronze, like silver, like honey gold.

"Now we get this destined single kind moment, you and I," she said, "the two times we shall meet again before the end, when we will both be too busy to talk."

"Why—" I started, but she placed a firm hand over my mouth.

"There is nothing you can ask me that I am prepared or able to answer which I will not have already told you during this, our brief time together—which, in any case, I shall strip from your memory when our time is over, not to be remembered for thirty-three years of chronological but not subjective time. At which point, Judas— yes, that one, whom you will by then have met—will wonder aloud about your Enemy's schemes and reasons, and you will know, and repeat, the last hours and the next minutes accurately word for word, because it will be important that you talk as if they will just have happened. Which in a sense they will have done, because you and I are parts of each other, and all moments are alike and one to me.

"This moment when I talk at you, the moments when our mortal flesh was tortured to death or devoured by an ogre, the moment when I betrayed my sisters to become the Fifth Thing, the moment when I hailed a group of human cattle amid the shaking of the earth and the falling of ash and led them away from the Eaters and into the bright safety of Shadow. I watch your enemy be born, I watch his confrontation with the Glorious Five—Ysh and Hemul, Asapha, Larala and Ashtra—who were and were not as you know them from Berthe's opera.

"And I am at all times in that moment when I and my sisters made our choices—Mara became the Huntress, and Sof Wisdom. And I became this. All times are the same to me and I am as tired at the beginning as I am at the end of my knowing and my seeing."

She took her hand from my lips and said, "Now you will ask the question I will answer and the one I will not."

Hoping to do the right, the unselfish thing, I asked, "How do we defeat him? Can we defeat him? What are the sleepers and the ring of flesh?"

"I cannot tell you, for I do not know."

I think this means that when she talks of the end, it may be that time ends or it may be that she does and destiny does. He thinks he knows how all this works out and what her riddles mean. I think we are better off not knowing; I'd rather have hope than certainty.

So I asked the second, the selfish question, and she told me what I am. I had been afraid I was not a real girl, only an illusion, a mask she sometimes wears, but she told me, "You need not fear that," and I knew that she was enough me that she was acquainted with my thoughts.

"We share much," she said, "but not, in the end, our destinies."

"How can we be the same, when you have done such terrible things that the Enemy trusts you as his ally?"

"That is precisely how we are not the same," she explained. "I chose, without fully knowing what I chose, to become this. To be the servant of destiny is to execute all that happens for good and for ill, and the only mercy shown to me for that choice is the removal of those parts of me that would not bear it. You, Caroline, are those parts. And when I am gone, you will be more."

I thought I could see the one thing that made this implausible. "But you made those choices in the Deep Past, and I was born to the here and now…" And realised even as I said it, why I was being dense.

"Destiny," she said, "does not have to make sense. It is what happens, what has happened, what will happen. You are those parts of me I could not retain, and those we share, and you were born when you were born, because that was the time allotted to you. And this was the time allotted to me, to tell you things you will need to know, but not yet. Not until Judas speaks in 2036."

Then she kissed me on the forehead, and I found myself in the middle of a battle, in which men—mostly men, were fighting demons, and I could not remember anything after I found Lucifer sitting on your sofa.

Everyone crowded round and hugged Caroline: it was hot, sweaty, emotional and just a little bit worryingly sexual given that it was also like family. It went on long enough that Emma felt quite guilty saying "Enough" and putting just enough of the goddess into it that her friends, colleagues and lovers actually listened and pulled back into a circle.

She created a lot of chairs—Charles Rennie McIntosh, elegant and stately and stiff so they'd appreciate her taste but stay awake. Those that were in any sort of flesh sat down, and a lot of the disembodied gave a good impression of sitting down and paying attention given that they were actually engaged in precision hovering.

"So, at least Mara and Sof don't have to go on thinking that their sister betrayed them, exactly. Losing even the illusion of freewill in a determinist universe may look almost exactly the same, but is at least morally different. And what have we learned, children? If someone divine offers you a wish, take cash."

Which got a laugh and broke the tension a little.

She had everyone's attention so she didn't ask for comments.

"Also, now we know his objective so we can concentrate on messing that up. We really don't need a species of hominid magic worker cannibals taking over from the human race. We're bad enough in all conscience, but they sound far worse."

Aserath stuck up a languid hand. "How's he going to bring them back, exactly? Obviously they're the sleepers."

"Or he thinks they are," Morgan added. "Now we know that's Destiny's oracle not his manifesto, we can try and ensure it goes Delphic on his ass."

"Probably not dark alchemy, or we'd be winning already. That was a gambit that messed us up, but not his end strategy," Judas said.

Everyone looked at him in surprise.

"I thought you were visiting Jehovah on his sick bed," Emma said.

"I did. He's getting better. He and Josette clearly needed to have The Talk, given it's been two thousand years. I thought I'd give them some privacy. If it comes to blows, Sof is better at calming people down than I'll ever be."

"Wasn't Mara there?" Caroline asked.

"She had been, but by the time we got there, she'd gone off with a couple of the others and a bunch of ghouls to kill off all the dead gods Burnedover seem to have unleashed on the human race. We really are going to have to do something about them."

A lot of the disembodied souls cheered this.

"Given how the Enemy's used Burnedover so much," Emma noted, "it's a fair bet they're crucial to his whole bringing back his unpleasant species too. We need to find the factory where they make magic clone infantry, because that's probably where magic cannibals are supposed to be hatched. Also, if we're going to end up storming Heaven, we should probably start with a less ambitious project."

"Do we even know their address?" Caroline asked. "Lucifer did business with them but he never struck me as the sort to keep files. Or even an address book."

"Polly would know."

"Polly's not here."

One of the disembodied souls was clearly desperate to get their attention.

"Can I trade information for an early trip to the blood vats? All the fruit on those trees—I want to eat it… Oh, I'll tell you anyway. I owe them. I asked them to pay their bills, and they said the Lord would provide, and I said that I still had to pay my crews. And they said it was God's will and shot me in the head. There's a few of us here, the contractors on their big new impregnable fortress in the middle of New York Harbour; Bert over there put in all the CCTV and Luigi did the armour-plated fire doors. And Mario did the plumbing. But I'm the one you want. I know the whole building."

"You were the architect?" Judas took a collegial interest.

"I installed all the light fittings."

Emma looked at Judas, who nodded approvingly, and said, "That would certainly help. Bring your former colleagues along to my office and we'll reconstruct the blueprints."

The lighting contractor said doubtfully, "I'm not sure we remember it all in that much detail. Trauma of being shot in the head and arriving in Heaven just in time to be bounced here…"

Morgan grinned. "Oh, little man, if we needed to know what you ate for breakfast on your fifth birthday, I could retrieve the texture of every last crumb of the strawberry waffle. Trust me, it won't hurt a bit."

The lighting contractor pointed to his friends and they all trooped off to Judas' office with her.

Judas started to follow them and then trotted back. "Emma," he asked, "I don't suppose you've still got the fish hook?"

She rummaged in a pocket dimension. "Nope, not here."

Her luggage rushed forward on little cat feet and opened. The hand produced the fish hook, for which there obviously wasn't room, but then…

Judas bowed courteously to bag and to hand, as did Emma.

"Thanks for taking care of it," she said to the bag and the hand. "I was a little preoccupied at the time."

The hand waved self-deprecatingly. Judas summoned a sling for his bulky shoulders and swung the hook into it.

"My court painter always depicted you with a knife?" Theophania inquired.

"He was right," Judas said, "and if we're going to war, I should get a new set. When I was running Heaven, there wasn't much call for them, and I had nowhere to put them. Not in the flesh, you see. But the hook, it's not for me." He smiled a thin smile. "Especially if we're going to a harbour."

He walked off and Emma smiled as he went. She liked guessing ahead.

Instead, what happened next was unexpected and very fast.

It began with a noise like someone inconceivably big grinding his teeth in his sleep.

"I needed that sound," said Berthe in Emma's head.

Only it felt as if this was the early quiet stage.

And it seemed for a moment to Emma that she was suddenly crushed under an inconceivably heavy weight and by the knowledge that in not thinking of something important she had failed and killed everyone she cared about and everything else beside. And that failure was a thing she could not put right.

But then that moment was past, or rather had happened and now would not.

Because suddenly her former armour had been with them, her hand joining hers and Dawn's which were once more entwined on Caroline's shoulder.

"CATCH!" Lillit shouted in a voice louder than the thunder of the mountains of Hell falling in on themselves and down and out, only Caroline had her hands outstretched and everything beyond the small central group of them was moving ten times slower than it had any right to.

"Don't say I never do anything for you," Lillit said. "I have done many terrible things as I dance back and forth, the shuttle with which time and chance weave destiny. But I am the bringer and saviour of joy as well as the ender of delight. And this is one of the moments that pays for all."

And as Lillit spoke, Emma knew what she had failed to think of and nearly brought disaster by that failure.

"Of course, of course. Actions have consequences," she reminded herself, "and I melted tons of ice that had carried the red dust into every crack, crevice and ravine in a mountain range. Dust that I'd earlier removed. It's like I hammered a million wedges into the rock. What did I think was going to happen? Clumsy idiot that I am."

And the spark in her head was calculating the trajectory of each boulder, crag or pebble so fast that she could seize each fragment with her mind and seal it harmless outside the world, and Aserath's vines were helping catch and growing great leathery shielding leaves and it was not just the part of the range that loomed over the place where she was talking to her friends but all of her realm of Hell that she was protecting and shielding and gentling through this apocalypse into whatever was coming next.

Caroline and Dawn were standing with her in a triangle of shoulders looking outwards and lending to her sense of everything the mortal sight and deep compassion that helped her see and protect everyone: her friends, the Dukes in their bottle-like prison playing cards and some demon child miles away looking up from the dice game they were playing with their human neighbour and just starting to worry.

Theophania was chanting in a plainsong that somehow felt medicinal and sweet as curative honey and the choir of Exiled Blessed were taking it up, spiralling and gyring round the notes, and as if the falling mountains were hearing it too and softening their fall as if into the slumber of thunder. And Vretil was directing souls and hell-flesh around and away from a strip of Hell where the worst might befall and yet somehow it was not. And a part of her mind was Berthe notating Theophania's chant and theorizing that this was the lost hymn Theodora had commissioned to deal with earthquakes so efficaciously that her husband would stop killing those he deemed guilty of unnatural vice and blamed for the shaking earth.

Emma was moving all of the pocket universes towards the sea that lay behind the reach of the range, and releasing the spoil into the water to hiss and sputter and be harmless and one day soon she would smoothen down into new land but that time was not yet, and she knew she was taking the sense of what she could do with all that broken stone from Judas just as it was Morgan from whom she was taking the ability to calm and soothe and forget terror. Her mind reached out to touch and calm all of her subjects that she thought of as her friends who thought of her as their goddess and protector.

"Which you are," Lillit said sternly as the whole situation wound down and coalesced into almost sleepy calm. "Remember that, when Destiny ends and I am not here to tell you what to do as I did when I was your armour and knew you as well and intimately as my fetch, my avatar, your lover whom I envy and tell her to think well of me. You are a goddess and with your friends are more and I, I have been alone but am almost done. And remember that all choices have a price and the accounts have to balance when payment is due because everything has consequences because the alchemic dust and winter ice needed to be gone but were part of what holds things together, as am I, but ice and dust do not weep," and Lillit retreated into her realm of time space and chance, then it was over and Emma settled into herself and was calm.

"What just happened?" she asked herself, not realising she spoke aloud.

"Hell fall down. Go Bang," said Caroline.

"You came into your own," said Aserath.

"You are my Empress," said the Empress Theophania.

"I'm new to all this," said Dawn," but it's my considered opinion that the Enemy doesn't stand a chance."

Where the mountains had been, a few hills stood, and the Cliffs of Regret, by themselves, unshaken, and her ziggurat towering up into the purple clouds.

Elsewhere, just the endless plains of Shadow, rivers and forests, and Aserath's groves and orchards already marching into them.

"Just how much of Shadow do you plan to take over with those?" she asked Aserath.

"I don't know," Aserath said, "as much as they will let me? We have people to find room for."

And as they looked out awestruck at the new view, none of them said anything for a while. Judas came with the blueprints of Burnedover's fortress and handed each of them a copy, and they looked at them and still did not speak.

This had not, after all, been the first time Emma had known fully that she was not who she once had been. There was her original apotheosis, and the intoxication of dark alchemy's wild magic, and the millennia of judgehood she had chosen to forget and her own Great Working with Mara that had ended dark alchemy. This was different though, wholly her and totally a reflex and on a world rebuilding scale.

It was part of what Caroline had said she sometimes saw behind her eyes.

She did not want to lose Caroline. She did not want to lose herself.

And Berthe sang in her head, and the point of white light too.

"You are not alone, and we love her too."

Which was nice to know.

Yet there was a world to be saved and, if they defeated the Enemy, a world to be rebuilt...

Emma heard the Gray Lord of Hollywood in her mind. "The problems of three little people don't amount to a hill of beans," and yet she thought of her mentors Mara and Josette and the grace with which they limited themselves and walked lightly upon the world, and her quiet suspicion of her friends Aserath and Morgan and their too much glee and excessive enthusiasm for slaughter and of how Jehovah and Lucifer had been apprenticed once and thought they knew better.

And she thought of the moments of ecstasy out of time when love or magic or intelligence or kindly judgement came just right.

And Berthe whispered "And music," and the white light danced in perfected theorems.

And those of her memories that were Sof whispered, "The perfection of the work." And they thought of healing the world.

She stood lost in thought and her friends and loved ones let her be, and hushed Hades to silence as he came up and joined them.

"Yes?" she said, because one should always be especially polite to a deposed predecessor.

"The blood vats are full and so is the extra processing plant. The falls are in spate. Things must be bad in the Mundane world."

"And with Heaven shut, the new dead will mostly join us." she said. "You will see Aserath is expanding our border to fit. There are other afterlives in Shadow: we should send embassies. After all, we need to plan for the future." She looked round at everyone. "Obviously, I am going to war. Aserath, we need to hold former Hell against attack. Judas, I know you want to fight alongside your sister, but she'd be the first to tell you that you are essential here. Give the hook to Tsassiporah; bird, take it to Josette. London first, and wherever she's gone after that."

Reluctantly, he passed the fish hook to the red bird, who fluttered off out of sight.

"Dawn, Tiffany, you'll be helping him. Caroline—do stay here."

Caroline shook her head and changed into some sort of hussar's uniform.

"I think I'm supposed to be with you," she said. "Lillit said she'd see me twice which leaves once more. And I think whatever she means by 'the end' is something I'd want to face standing next to you. Dawn, forgive me, but…"

"I'd be in the way, and, well, like Emma said, I'm the trainee. In admin, not magical warfare, clearly. Tiff and I, we'll be fine." She looked at the same time relieved, determined and disappointed.

Emma turned to Morgan. "You'll be wanting to find your way to Mara, but if you'll come with me at least part of the way—"

"I'll be as quick as I can," Morgan said, "but I do have my own affairs to take care of first. It's a small realm, but mine own."

And suddenly she was gone, and the Morrigan with her.

Emma looked to where the mountains had been. Three riders were approaching.

"I was hoping he'd show up," she said to Caroline as they hurried to meet them. She'd been expecting that Alexander would come looking for a fight: she was pleasantly surprised to see he was not alone. Apollo she recognised from when she'd freed the Olympians—the woman?

"Brünnhilde," Caro explained. "Yes, that one. She and Josette are kind of a thing, so."

"Hoiatoho," said the other blonde, which at least meant she had a sense of humour.

"New Olympus is part of this," Apollo added. "My sisters will be joining us in due course. The Arts will just have to make do without them."

"So," Alexander said, "you're taking an army? Need me to lead it? Mercenaries first, then Heaven? Mara's birds updated us when they collected Josette."

Emma looked at him indulgently. "Army not really my style. I'm sure frontal assault is being taken care of. Josette will have it in hand as soon as she gets what I just sent her. I mean, I'm saving tearing things down like an angry goddess for Heaven. Really."

She waved the blueprints.

"There's secret weapons to sabotage, if I'm not mistaken."

"Ah," Alexander said with the enthusiasm of the small boy he had once been learning to read from Homer and other Troy books, "like Odysseus and Diomedes stealing the Palladium…"

"Careful, boy," Apollo interrupted. "I was on the other side."

"Just so," said Emma.

There was a pop of air and Tom and Syeed were at her side. …And Elodie?

Clearly with Syeed from the body language and looking kind of buff? She must be in her sixties. So were Syeed and Tom. Not looking much older than when Emma last saw them. *Hang on, they've been hanging with Sof.*

Which was good, because when she realized she had lost thirty years she had expected to have lost at least some of her mortal friends to the remorseless corrosion of time.

"The old team," Elodie said. "Who are the newbies? I had to come. I did this in a movie but I want to hear you say it."

Emma looked around at her strike team and smiled.

"We're going in through the ducts."

Talks With Old Friends

The Caucasus, London, New York, 2036

The Dog, the Wolf and the horses held back, but Loki and his other two children joined us as we walked across to where the spheroids were being inscrutable. The centaurs' leaders joined us.

"Sorry," said one of the ghouls that were still part of our company, "we don't like the way that smells," and suddenly he and his friends were into a burrow I hadn't seen and were away.

I shall never understand how they do that, wherever they are.

As we got closer to the nearest of the black spheroids, I started to realise just how huge it was. I had seen things as big or bigger; the beings that ruled, that were, the oceans were vaster. But only a few. And nothing quite as dark.

This was a blackness beyond night with no stars or moon. And it rested on the world as lightly as if it were not there at all.

You both fluttered up from my shoulders and flew up and over it before returning.

"When we're above it," one of you said, "it's as if it's not there at all."

I stepped sideways into Shadow and it was not there except as the faintest of cross sections, a single flat slice in which smaller black ovals, themselves the size of whales, swam in a medium that looked a little like light and a little like thick cream.

Where was the rest of it? I knew from Emma's stories that there were other realms that we could not experience or comprehend; I had not let myself consider this too closely because it galled me to admit that Plato might have been right about something.

Tom had followed me sidewise into Shadow and looked up at it.

"It's like a slide under a microscope," he said. "Cells huger than we can imagine, and somewhere else so that gravity doesn't affect it at all. I don't think it's going to talk to us any time soon."

I looked at him enquiringly.

"I think it's more like a plant. How convenient that we know someone. A couple of someones…"

He blinked away in that annoying way he had, so I returned to the Mundane world, where Syeed was still looking up in wonder. He gave me a sidelong nod, not taking his eyes from it, and said, "Don't worry. He'll be back in a minute or two. If he reckoned where he's going was liable to be a complication, he'd have said summat so someone knew where he was and could mount some sort of rescue. One day his luck'll run out and there'll be someone waiting with a gun all ready, but not yet. Ah've told him, over and over, one day someone will know how to hide from ens sight. He says his Sight doesn't work like that. Oh well. Inshallah."

A couple of the centaurs were listening closely. I wondered how their worship of the Ice was holding up.

And with a pop Tom was back, but not alone.

It was the younger dryad, Greengirl, sitting in Tom's lap. And she was holding a small glass jar.

"Personally," Tom said, "the other two get on my nerves a bit. And I thought our friend in the jar would be more use anyway."

Greengirl looked up at the spheroid, concentrated a second and then shook her head definitively.

The fungus whispered in my mind.

"I don't expect your trust," it said, "but I will help you nonetheless. I need the world to continue in order to live in it, and I have grown fond of the dryads. They are not like the rest of you. Strange; I have no great amount of time for you beings of flesh, or for the green beings that stole the land from me, yet beings that partake of both natures…"

It paused, and I felt its attention shift. And I felt its surprise.

It had seen the great black floating beings before.

Millions of years earlier, when it was the only life on the land.

I saw them through its memories of crawling slowly on almost bare rock: they floated a mere cell's height above it and somehow it had felt them watching it. As you know when someone is looking at the back of your neck even if when you turn around there seems to be no one in sight.

"They are not from here," it said. "And in a while, they will be gone. You might think that something that big would not be gone between one moment and the next, but you would be wrong." There was wonder in its mind and also a degree of terror.

Nonetheless, I had to know more.

"Is there a mind? Somewhere in there? Something I can talk to. Through you, or through you, Greengirl?"

I turned to her. Now she was no longer human, there was a stillness to her that made it easy to forget she was there even when she was in front of me. I remembered the different person she had been; her grief had transformed her.

She smiled, distantly.

"There's nothing any of us could call a mind. Just, a presence, an awareness, a watching."

Memory said, "Old One-Eye once found a rock in the North that was like that. He tried to talk to it for days and nothing happened, so he got young Donner to smite it, and it went away."

The fungus added, "And they are all the same being. No, not like a jellyfish or an anthill. I mean there is only one of it. Both the black spheres and the white tendrils. Though those can detach for a while. It's like only a few bits of it are ever in the world; it's somewhere else and bits of it poke through. And I don't think it's coming through now, and its coming through back before I died for the first time are distinct events."

It sensed my scepticism—I really did need to learn to shield my thoughts from it—and shrugged the shoulders it did not have.

"I know you are quite old. For a being of flesh. But I lived for millions of years before the plants ate me—I lived two million years while the plants ate me—and I know a little bit more about time than any of you. I remember when almost nothing ever happened and chance and its child destiny were not things in the world. Or at least, not on the land: I cannot speak off what went on beneath the sea."

"So its being here now is—"

"Probably meaningless," the fungus said. "My lives and deaths matter a lot to me, but there are things even in our Mundane world, let alone this Shadow you speak of, to which I matter less than nothing. And trust me, there is so much more of me now than when I last woke."

It rummaged through my memories.

"This enemy of yours might work some serious mischief before he is done. But the oceans may care little and the fires under the rocks will not care at all. This interloper—it comes and it goes—I doubt it does more than scratch an itch."

Tom laughed. I had not realised that he could hear us, but it made sense that he could. "All of that is fine and dandy," he said, "but speaking as a mayfly sack of flesh and germs, its showing up now is actually very useful to me. I think."

And quite suddenly the spheroids and tendrils vanished.

Tom nodded. "I met your sister that one time and I watched her disappear. And I wondered, could I go there, because I watched the direction she went in. I'm careful—I look first and that's why I don't end up inside walls—but those things, not the same direction as her but sort of at an angle to it."

And suddenly, briefly, there were two of him, and then for a moment none and then just one again. The one Tom nodded with satisfaction. "Thought so. That's going to be useful. With a bit of practice."

Syeed looked thoughtful and vaguely disapproving.

"Just 'cause you can, doesn't mean you should…Look, there's nowt in the Book or the hadiths to say it's haram, but look at her sister. Does it all the time and doesn't seem to know what side she's on. I'd say, best let it alone until you know for certain it's OK."

Tom pulled a sulky face that was only half in jest. I realised that I really did not understand the dynamic between these two former enemies. At some point, clearly, Tom had started listening to the other man. As if they were brothers.

Syeed looked at him expectantly and Tom sighed and nodded. "I promise I won't time travel again until you say it's OK." He still looked sulky, though.

Syeed went on. "When we were in the caves one time with the Sheikh, we watched a video of that film of Elodie's, the one where she kills Hitler, when he's a student, and it all works out the same… And the Sheikh got ever so excited, and got us all to say one thing we'd change, only everything we came up with, he thought of a reason why it wasn't a good idea. Like, we hang on to Al Andalus for longer, but the Christians never split. So he said it was probably a good thing it only happened in American movies, and we all agreed."

One of the centaurs stifled a yawn. "So what are you going to do next? Is it something we can help with, or should we go back to general marauding?"

I looked at her sternly.

"We'll attack Burnedover first, wipe out their bases and then go after their main force in Heaven. No matter how many of them we kill, they always make more, so we need to go where they do that and seize their means of producing more armies. We'll trap them in Heaven and then wipe them out. So I and my friends will go after their big US base and you can harry them here out on the plains and deserts—the gods of Hind and the Heavenly Bureaucrats can be relied upon within their own borders."

The centaur who had yawned nodded, and trotted back to her army. Within a surprisingly few minutes, they had formed up and ridden away off across the endless plains. Which took care for the moment of allies who might have gone back to being a problem.

"I take it you want us to join you in America...?" Loki asked.

"The Dog, the Wolf and the Serpent," I said, "handy in a siege. You, Hela and you, Sleipnir. We need allies when we go to Heaven and there are a lot of little pantheons tucked away who are going to find it terribly amusing that Jehovah was turned out of his own place by his own believers and will be pragmatic enough to see the advantage of putting him in their debt... And if they don't at first, Loki Silvertongue can talk anyone into anything, especially with your daughter the poet and your daughter who is Death to help convince them."

While I was talking, Tom took Greengirl and the fungus back, and returned almost immediately.

"It wasn't kidding, by the way. About there being more of it. I used my Sight this time when she emptied the jar and put it back with the rest of it. It's a network, under most of North London. I'm surprised Polly hasn't mentioned it."

"She probably regards it as 'need to know'," Syeed said. "What was she going to say? There's a vast primordial fungus permeating Hampstead Heath and environs, which you helped put there and didn't mention for several years until I became the Tutelar of London and it introduced itself telepathically and said its intentions were good."

"She knew and didn't mention it?"

"As far as she's concerned, you didn't mention it first."

"But she told you."

"She told Elodie. One of those girly bitch sessions the girls have when we're out bonding and killing people. Elodie told me. Surprised you weren't listening."

They both laughed.

"When you're quite finished with the male bonding," I said testily, "we could all do with an update on what Emma is doing."

"We could go and talk to her," you said.

"Which I may well send you to do, once Tom here tells me where she is."

Tom shuttered his eyes a second and then did a long slow whistle and smiled toothily. "For one thing, she's not in Hell or Shadow, any more. She's with a small group of people, and they're standing in the observation deck of the Statue of Liberty looking out to sea at a sort of artificial island with a lot of gun emplacements and missile batteries on it."

"Who's there?"

"Her and Caroline, and three people I don't know… And I guess, Syeed old chum, that you are going to give me permission to time travel, after all, because oh look! Except, wait, none of you can see. But basically they obviously know I'm watching them, because that Syeed just shuffled round so that he was looking in the right direction and gave me a double thumbs up."

"What d'you mean, that Syeed?"

"The one standing next to that Tom. Also Elodie, apparently. So we need to go to Polly's on our way."

"Your way where?"

"Question we need to ask is, our way when? Other Syeed just stuck up two fingers. So, two days. Then he pointed down, so I'm guessing we need to go to Hell. No biggie these days, now Emma's running it. Mara, you're not there, so I guess we'll meet up later."

He took Syeed by the hand and they were gone. Loki swung up on his daughter's back, and his other daughter kept pace with them as they galloped away.

The Dog, the Wolf and the Serpent looked at me expectantly.

You both cawed at me significantly but without words as if there were something I needed to remember, someone I needed to think of.

New York in due course certainly, I thought, but there was someone I needed to talk to first. I hate loose ends.

* * *

It could all have been a little embarrassing.

It turned out no one got round to explaining to Jehovah what had happened with Odin and the rest of the Aesir.

The moment we turned up at Polly Wild's, he recognised the Serpent and stood groggily up from the armchair where he was convalescing, dressed in a voluminous padded dressing gown. It didn't escape anyone's attention that he addressed himself exclusively to the brother who could almost pass for human.

"I do want to assure your uncle…"

"Our uncle is dead."

"My condolences…" Jehovah clearly thought he could get away with perfunctory politeness—after all, these were members of a minor pantheon he had defeated long ago.

"He betrayed and murdered most of our kin."

"My condolences for them, then." He still thought he could get away with mere politeness.

"You drove us out of the world and into Shadow."

"It wasn't personal. Just business."

The Serpent replied with a hiss that almost managed to shake the room and his two brothers snarled, and Jehovah now looked a lot less sure of himself. These were, after all, the Beasts of Ragnarök and he was an old sick god no longer at full strength and without the Heavenly Host to back him up.

"Stop bickering," Polly warned as she arrived back in the room pushing a tea trolley. "This is my gaff and I won't have it. Not from deities and not from animalistic personifications or demigods or whatever you three are."

"We're the children of Loki." The Serpent was capable of a certain amount of oily good manners, it turned out. "And we were supposed to be the Beasts of Ragnarök, but it looks as if that's been postponed indefinitely."

Garm made a noise something between a whine and an almost articulate bark.

"Oh, my brother wishes to convey that it was never clear which side he was supposed to fight on, depending on which Edda you believe."

Polly looked unimpressed. "I'm sure none of us care very much about Apocalypses that ain't going to happen, given all the ones that are. Now, tea or whisky for the more or less humanoid. Water for the canines. Unless you'd rather shape-shift and actually take part in a civil conversation."

Oddly, it had never especially occurred to me that all of Loki's children were more or less shape-shifters, except possibly Sleipnir, whose father was presumably just some random stallion rather than an ice giantess.

Polly, on the other hand, has never been especially concerned with theological protocol.

Fenris, it turned out, scrubbed up quite nicely if you have a taste for sardonic brutes with cheekbones and dark brown eyes. The word for Garm turned out to be dapper; he was the sort of young man who would look under-dressed without spats.

"Thank you for asking us, Miss Wild," he murmured, taking her hand and kissing it politely. "Our late uncle placed a geas on the pair of us that we could only appear in our human aspect if given

316

permission, but forbad our father to give us that permission. Obviously that didn't apply to Jormungandr here, whose snake aspect is inconveniently large."

His brother was not quite so quick off the mark, but after he had kissed her hand, Fenris did not let it go. Nor did Polly pull it back; she smiled at him, a smile I had seen before.

I made vaguely apologetic noises, but Garm shushed me before I could say anything. "Father planted us on you and Cernunnos undercover. If anything, we should apologise to you."

Polly passed him a cup of Earl Gray and his brothers a single malt. Somewhat to my surprise, Jehovah restricted himself to tea.

He caught my reaction and nodded sadly. "Still under doctor's orders, Huntress. Your sister has worked miracles but I'm still not up to much—if you were hoping to recruit me to this raid young Syeed and the others have gone off on…"

I cut him off. "That's not why I'm here. I'm taking the Serpent here with me to New York, but you boys—I need at least one of you to babysit my sister, Miss Wild and my old friend Nameless here. It's not the glamourous bit of this war, but it's absolutely needed."

Polly smiled and patted Fenris' hand. "We're not completely defenceless here, you know. As Tutelar of London, well, let's just say there are perquisites as go with that. The Guildhall giants… Plus I've rethought my whole attitude to ghouls. But I'm sure as we can find something for Wolfie here to do. Mackie's brows met in the middle too, you know, but his fingers were different lengths…"

Fenris smiled the smile of a man or wolf who thinks he is in control of a situation—I chose not to disillusion him.

Garm turned to me. "It sounds as if I'd be surplus to requirements here."

I pulled Polly's attention back to the matter at hand. "As to my sister?"

"She reckoned you'd be showing back up here and she decided to go do some errands. She thought about it a bit after you turned up here day before yesterday and decided she still has issues. Even if you say you've moved on." She paused a moment, then added, "Sorry."

I sighed, as much thinking aloud as sharing my feelings. "I hoped fixing the bit of her resentment that Emma was keeping in her memory palace would change things between us as well as fixing alchemy, but there it is, things are as they are. Anyway, the other reason why I'm here..."

I took a sip of the tea Polly had handed me.

"Lucifer. No one has mentioned him."

Jehovah looked blank a second and shrugged. "Haven't heard anything since I stripped him of Hell. We had him in custody but he gave us the slip."

Polly, of course, had more information. "Sof and Tom found him trying to buy sex magic from Crowley. He had information I needed and we paid him with a touch of the Stone... but that was, ooh, getting on for twenty years ago. No news is good news, probably."

Garm broke in eagerly. "Don't suppose he left anything behind? When I'm a dog, I can track even the coldest of scents. My time with Cernunnos wasn't wasted..."

Polly got up and left the room. We all looked at each other in vague confusion, in a very awkward silence which the faun broke by offering everyone some skewers of slightly tough charred meat, which meant that everyone's mouths and hands were occupied usefully and the silence was broken by chewing, and occasional compliments to the chef.

Clearly he had learned something about tact in this age.

A door slammed somewhere underneath us and after a few more minutes Polly returned with two or three lumps of very old cobwebs stuck becomingly in her short blonde hair. She was holding a jagged piece of stained carpet.

"My old dad used to say Never Throw Anything Important Away. Words to live by, ain't it? Now, I don't know whether this is any help. I mean, most of it's crocodile vomit, but..."

Garm changed back into his annoyingly cute terrier form and almost instantly started bouncing up and down excitedly. When I did not react immediately, he changed back to human for a second and announced "I said, The Game Is Afoot," then returned to his dog shape, ran into the hall and started scratching at Polly's front door.

I rose to my feet. "Polly, my regards to my sister—my love too, if she thinks that acceptable as what may be my last message to her. You yourself have always been one of the sisters of my heart. I go to what may be our final conflict and there are things I would not leave unsaid. Lord Jehovah, we were friends and companions in our youth and I have always treasured that, whatever has come between us since. If, as I hope, we remove the interlopers from your realm and destroy our common enemy, we will talk again."

He knew that by "talk," I meant "come to a serious accounting of his past actions," but smiled, nodded and made no excuses.

I put my hand on Fenris' shoulder. "Wolf, guard them as you would your family."

I turned next to Jormungandr, who rose and stood by my side.

He smiled, and a forked tongue flickered between his biting teeth. "I wish to meet this old rogue, pretender to my title. Not to harm him, or chastise him, but merely to flicker into my other shape and remind him what a serpent truly looks like."

Garm ceased to scratch at the door once we showed we were ready to leave, and we followed him into the part of Shadow most immediately adjacent to Mundane London and mostly sharing its geography and versions of many of its buildings, yet more convenient for fast travel, out of the City and North and slightly East by, it turned out, less than three miles.

Lucifer had settled in a rather large town house a few yards from the crossroads still known as the Angel. It was as if he had no great concern about being found.

I walked up the path to the front door Garm indicated by turning back into a smartly dressed young man. On either side was what had once been a lawn but was now baked sterile cracked soil with occasional clumps of dried grass.

I rang the doorbell. You settled on my shoulders.

A teenage girl, with hair almost as scarlet as Emma's and with a diamond stud in her left nostril, answered the door. She had an air of mature authority that didn't go with her apparent age.

I hesitated, slightly at a loss. It had not occurred to me that Lucifer might have company.

The girl looked us up and down and clearly saw more of who we were than was immediately visible.

"Dad," she shouted over her shoulder, "it's some of your friends. The weird ones." And then, sternly, to me: "Be nice. He's been a bit fragile since Mum died."

And I realised who the parent was in this family.

Lucifer wandered up to the front hall from some back room or other. Superficially he was as I had always known him—slim, lithe, subtly athletic without obvious muscles—yet there was something about him, beaten down and wistful. No Hugo Boss suit; just blue jeans and a beige cardigan that had no actual stains but had seen better days. His shoulders were slumped, but he made an effort when he saw me; he straightened up and looked years younger at a stroke.

He also looked uncharacteristically and genuinely glad to see me.

"Huntress, how good of you to come. And you too, of course, sons of Loki. And would those be Thought and Memory? They suit you. So Shadow is open again? Emma Jones presumably? Admirable young woman; it was never personal."

I was not going to sugar the pill—I didn't know how much his daughter knew about his previous career and frankly I didn't care.

"Lucifer," I started.

"Hang on," his daughter reacted, "Dad, I thought your name was Edwin."

He looked faintly embarrassed. "It is, now, Livvy. I put all that behind me when I met your mother." He caught my expression and

320

admitted, "To be accurate, all that had pretty much moved on without me, but when I met her, I accepted reality." He shrugged. "I wanted a life. There's not much time left and there's nothing to do about it. He will win and the nightmares will begin, and…"

"I'd prefer to go down fighting," I interrupted. "Even if I were convinced things were hopeless, which I am not."

He looked at me with sympathy and pity. "Of course, Mara. I'd expect no less. But your sister…"

Livvy pulled the face of someone who has just put the pieces of something together. "Is this the sister of that other weirdo who turns up, and you are upset for days? Look, you: like I said, he's not been well since Mum got killed and I won't have people coming round from his old life upsetting him."

I wondered what had happened.

"She drowned just down the road," Lucifer said sorrowfully and resentfully. "On her way to the dentist. Eight years ago. Your friends saved a lot of people that day, but they didn't save her. And I couldn't either; I don't have any power these days. So I'm not much good to you, am I?"

This was less clearly true than he seemed to think: he was, after all, still clever and devious. And I owed him no favours. But the girl—the girl needed what protection was available. She was an innocent. And perhaps I had not provided Polly and my sister with enough protection. Besides, it amused me to think of my former apprentices facing the End of Days together.

Given a choice, well, I knew Garm more or less; and had no particular relationship with the Serpent other than knowing him even more his father's accomplice in deviousness than his brothers and sisters.

"Star," I said after a short pause, "I've decided to offer you and Olivia my protection. Serpent, take them with you back to Miss Wild's and stay there with your brother until further notice."

I could see the girl was about to protest and held up a hand to stop her. "Trust me, it's for the best...Your father has powerful enemies and none of the people you'll be with actually hate him."

I could see the Serpent was not especially happy to find himself demoted to bodyguard when in other circumstances he might have been the thing against whom people needed protection.

"Serpent, what do I do?"

He looked sullen, but wearily repeated, "You protect the weak against the strong."

"Precisely," I said. "Olivia here deserves protection. Her father not so much: this is true. But these days he hardly counts as the strong, does he?"

Lucifer laughed. "Some things never change. Always the same obsession with working out the moral calculus. Like a product of a Jesuit education, if I hadn't watched you at it five thousand years before there was such a thing."

I didn't think it useful to mention the time young Loyola had been very helpful with tracking down a bent Inquisitor.

"Dad," Olivia almost whined, "this is freaking me out. Is she crazy? Or is all this true?"

I left it to him to explain at his leisure, but dropped entirely the glamour she had largely seen past. She clearly had more power than she knew of, or was perhaps just as clever as her father had always been.

In the circumstances, I thought I had better mention Polly's other house guest; giving Star a shock was one thing, but...

"You'll be sharing digs with your old friend. Some thugs turfed him out of his place and hurt him quite badly. He's getting better, but it was touch and go."

Lucifer looked genuinely upset. "And no one thought to tell me? I thought better of Sof than that."

I leapt to her defence. "I gather he was too ill for visitors."

"Still..."

And I realised that after millennia I still did not entirely understand that relationship.

Olivia reappeared at her father's side, struggling to hold onto a couple of small valises and two laptops. "I've shut everything down and put the alarm on. We should go to your friend as soon as I've locked up."

She looked at me with mild hostility. I had turned her life upside down—but then, she was the sort of young woman who had go-bags ready. Or perhaps that was everyone in 2036.

"Don't you have somewhere to be?"

And of course I did. So Garm and I went there.

Aching Masses

New York, 2036

I hadn't expected them still to be there, but the viewing deck of
the Statue of Liberty was empty. Except for an envelope securely
taped to the door to the stairs, an envelope addressed to me and to
Josette.

There was a note inside, handwritten in that slightly ornate
script that tends to be the result of summoning a piece of glossy
paper with a message on it. It read, "When you both get here, create
a diversion."

I looked out at the fortress. It was shiny and new and did not look
as if it belonged where it stood. Water splashed off it reluctantly as
if its more natural flow would have been straight through and on to
the shore. Its texture, its slight sheen, was not that of metal nor that
of wet stone; it was more like plastic if plastic had the green blue

rainbow shininess of a dead crow's wing in the mud at the side of the road.

There were Burnedover cloneguards desultorily watching from a platform on top, doing the standard makework of maintaining the various guns and other artillery. They were not looking in our direction and I cast a mild glamour to ensure that they did not.

The driving rain that fell elsewhere hissed off the fortress in steam.

It reminded me, a little, of the mosaic table in the workshop of Simon Magus as if it were a dead thing made out of creatures that had fed on death. Burnedover were servants of our enemy and down the years he had had many servants like Simon, not all of whom had come to my attention and not all of whose work had been destroyed and ceased to trouble the world.

But there was something familiar about the fortress as if I ought to recognise it.

Suddenly Josette was at my side. She had a pained expression on her face.

"That is something foul in its own right," she said. "Even without dark alchemy the Enemy finds ways to bring disgust into the world. How fortunate that we will have the means to tear it from the world and leave this harbour clean."

Her expression shifted into a knowing smile, the smile of a woman with a plan. I showed her the note.

"Come downstairs to the shoreline. Some friends of mine will be arriving shortly whom I don't think you have ever met, who will certainly provide something by way of diversion. As well as one we met on our first day together."

We drifted down through the armatures of the metal colossus, impressive in its way and an important symbol of hope to the world no matter how often that hope had been betrayed. But nothing compared to that which had protected Rhodes or the Pharos which we had seen in Alexandria.

We waited in the warm rain on the small dock where ferries brought tourists. Did they still?

As we waited my birds fluttered from my shoulders into the sky with caws of welcome for their scarlet plumed sibling who had been Lucifer's and was now Emma's. In its talons, it bore Jehovah's fish hook.

Josette clapped her hands in glee.

"My brother got Emma to remember where she put it," she said. "That will make everything much easier. I'll just see how the others are getting on—I don't use my link to Caroline much these days, because privacy, but I'm sure she won't mind."

And then anger, shock and surprise chased each other over her features.

"They're fine—a few problems but they're on their way in through a back door. But earlier on Caroline remembered something you are going to need to know. She met the Enemy— back when Lucifer abducted her—only your sister stole her memories until two days ago. And the Enemy told her pretty much everything…"

* * *

Of course it wasn't that easy.

Everyone kept coming to Emma with decisions that needed to be made before she handed over any her authority, usually because they thought wrongly that she'd be a softer touch than Aserath or Judas. And the Exiled Blessed wanted to give a concert, and she had to take Judas through some of the nuances of where she'd got to persuading the former Dukes Of Hell to repent enough to be released into the general population.

Mostly, they had to wait so as not to disrupt Tom and Syeed's personal timeline. They thought they'd been part of the bit of Mara's Hunt that had cleansed New York, but they couldn't be entirely certain.

326

"My memory of the whole thing is a bit like having been very, very stoned," he explained to Emma, "but don't mention that in front of Syeed, in case he starts thinking he did something terribly haram."

"Nothing haram about the incidental pleasures of jihad," Syeed, overhearing, corrected him.

Elodie smiled at this. "Is that all I've been these last few years? An incidental pleasure."

He shook his head. "Nothing incidental about us, my love. Thou art my reward, foreordained before time, a taste of Paradise granted me in this life. Incidental pleasures are things like the joy of righteous vengeance. They're transitory, and thou art eternal."

He was clearly prepared to explain this point at maudlin length but Emma looked meaningfully at her watch.

"If we're on the clock, getting there a bit early isn't going to bugger up the space time continuum, whereas…"

"My tutor was big on the importance of causation," Alexander butted in, "so she's probably right. As well as in command."

So by different routes through Shadow, or simple teleportation, they made their way to New York and to the Statue of Liberty and waited until Tom said, "Hold it–about now… ok, we're done," and Emma let out breath she didn't even know she'd been holding.

"Time I went and had a look at our way in," Tom said. "Looks as if there's a door halfway along the platform at the Whitehall and Southferry subway," and he blipped away.

And did not reappear.

After five minutes, Emma began to think she had better start worrying, then realised she already was worrying and had probably better say so.

Only Syeed spoke first. "The Sheikh used to say that no plan survives contact with the enemy."

"Didn't some German say it first?" Caroline said. "Rommel or somebody?"

"My father used to say, 'Don't plan. Just charge.'" Alexander added. "Worked for him: works for me."

Brünnhilde smiled.

Elodie gave Syeed a reassuring hug: Emma felt a mild pang of jealousy before looking across at Caroline and being glad Elodie had found someone and that Tom had them in his life.

Clearly they were all just as worried as Emma was.

Not without reason, it turned out, because when Tom turned up a few seconds later, it was clear from the bloodstain and bullet hole in the upper left shoulder of his jacket that he had been injured.

Sof was perched precariously on the arm of his wheelchair. She stood up and fixed Emma with an imperious elder sister glare.

"I know we're all godlike and invulnerable these days, Emma dear, but are you really planning to go into crucial battles without a field medic? If I were you–but then I am, mostly–luckily, Tom managed to teleport to me before blood loss and shock made him pass out, and with the Stone he's good as new, except for not being used to getting shot back at. Elodie, you in particular: when I got back from avoiding my sister and Polly said you'd gone off without me. I mean, the boys are the boys but…"

Tom blushed and was—for him—flustered in a manly way. "Syeed. Old friend. You've always said this would happen. Got there and there was a bloody drone in the air above the platform. The commuters didn't seem to be able to see it, but it saw me all right. Sprayed a round at me. Luckily, mostly at head height so way above me. Nasty for some of the commuters, I'm afraid… Wasn't in the plans…"

Emma felt abashed. Maybe she wasn't the ideal person for this.

"I imagine that when we turned off dark alchemy and Mara started killing all their zombie gods, it was a bit of a giveaway that we'd show up sooner or later, so they turned on systems we didn't know about. There's going to be a frontal assault in a bit, so we'd better find another way in."

Syeed rummaged through the blueprints, shaking his head. "Sorry," he said, "but nowt strikes me."

Alexander laughed.

"There's always something that's not in the plans, because it's the lord's way out that he uses to escape leaving everyone behind or that he uses to slip behind the lines to his doxy. There's always the spy's way in and the traitor's way out. Every time. Every citadel I ever sacked–not that I do that sort of thing these days…"

He had a smirk which belied his claim of repentance. He turned to Emma.

"First plan didn't work. What's the second plan?"

Emma had an uneasy feeling that she was being given a master class.

Basics first. They needed to get into the fortress. It was the biggest thing in the harbour, apart from…

"Tom," she said. "Use the sight, please. What's underneath us? Under the statue, I mean. Go deep."

Tom concentrated. He was in shock and distress still, but the boy had always been classy.

"There's a lift shaft, in the basement. There's all the offices, and the gift shop, and the toilets… And there's what looks like a janitor's cupboard and a lot of pegs with overalls and things but it goes further back and there's a sliding grille. A bit decoish… And it goes down… And another set of offices way, way down. And bodies, lots of them, a bunch of Burnedover types in black uniforms, same face as usual… I don't think anyone got out. And no one cleared up afterwards. We should probably check it out, but… can I not have point this time?"

"As this man's medical advisor," Sof added, "I strongly suggest that some of the more divine and invulnerable members of this war band take the lead for a change. I'd rather not spend the whole day patching people up; the Stone gets tetchy after a bit."

"Really?" Emma asked.

"I've realized in the last few years that the alchemical products work best if you think of them as persons. Best respect them as if they were, anyway."

Emma found this quite fascinating but now obviously wasn't the time.

"Tom, Syeed, Caroline, Elodie, Sof—follow us. Apollo, Brünnhilde—you get point. Alexander—you're with me."

And she used Shadow to drift downwards, confident that the others would precede or join her and wondering idly who would have offices under the Statue of Liberty…

And the answer was obvious, the moment she thought about it. He was there: his noble weathered face poking out from under the pile of corpses who had died to overwhelm him, a look of angry disappointment creasing his forehead and the skin around his eyes. He was as dignified as Emma remembered him, but on their first meeting she had not noticed the stain of old blood under his fingernails.

The cavernous room smelled of death and dryness and old paper, but not of decay. Something kept this crime scene perpetually— not fresh, but not subject to normal rules.

There were a few other corpses, a couple of older women in well-tailored suits who had the tired look of senior administrators in an understaffed department and a couple of younger ones whose well-polished but scuffed shoes screamed underpaid temp.

"He let them come in and work with him," Tom said. "Explains a lot about the last few years. When the Enemy said he had devoured the tutelars, we thought he meant he literally ate them, but he corrupted them and took away anything that made them special."

"Come off it, Tom," Syeed said. "What did America stand for but promises betrayed? That bloody great idol above our heads meant tyrants installed over half the world."

Brünnhilde broke her usual silence. "I know nothing of these politics and care less. I know warriors and I know courage. He died fighting enemies who killed him and his women servants by treachery and he took scores of them into death with him."

"He came and talked to me once," Elodie said, "when I was first in Hollywood. Just to make sure I wasn't a vampire any more. Said he'd always kept my family out, and how glad he was we were over, and congratulated me. I'm sure he was as dreadful as you say, darling, but he was also a nice old man who believed he meant well."

"Like America," said Caroline.

Emma looked around them. At one end of the cavern or excavation that these rooms had been built into there was a large closed iron door.

"There lies our path."

Alexander looked sceptical. "There lies a trap, surely."

Emma shook her head. "Oh, quite possibly, but not a serious one. It's a Working, you see: to exist at the edge of one of the nation's three great places of power, New York, and under the gaze of its most potent symbol. They had to work with the inherent contradictions of everything America stands for and actually is. Their hatred and warped religion and treachery is totally in the American grain, yet totally not what it is magically. Which is its ideals. You saw how uneasily that fortress sits in the harbour, how the waves seem reluctant to touch it. This was the Border Agent's place and they hollowed out what he meant and that gave them the power to put that thing out there, which means there has to be a clear way into it from here. Or it couldn't be there. That's why nothing has decayed past the first few hours post mortem—it has to be unnatural. There are limitations, you see, necessary conditions—that doorway can't be warded; it can't even be properly guarded."

She took a breath and shuddered.

"I'm getting a feel for his magic. So elegant and so vile... He finds a way into our strengths and virtues and corrodes them from their heart outwards. He tried to do it to me and to Mara, but we

331

managed to turn it round on him, I think. And gave him a real defeat. But the cleverness is, you can't ever be sure. It's like a rotten onion, layer after layer of new stink. But if I can bear to reason my way through the stench, like all magic that's a bit too clever, it can be undone."

She smiled.

"Let's go in and break something. That usually works."

The god Apollo took his bow from behind his sweat and power gleaming, perfectly defined uncovered shoulders and summoned an aspect. Normally he was almost slight, but he could be a wrestler if he chose and cast down Titans; he drew an arrow back—it should have been easy and yet he needed it to be a strain—and shot. As the arrow flew it became flame and hotter than flame, like a fragment of his chariot the sun—and when it struck the great metal door it did so without ringing or any other noise because the door was simply gone, not to melt but to vapour or powder.

There had been guards—a few—but they were now just shadows on the wall, gone before they could raise the alarm.

Yet an alarm there was, further up and further in and announcements on some sort of loudhailer, and the noise of many running feet, yet of feet running in some other direction than towards Emma and her companions.

Emma glanced over at Tom, who used his sight.

He laughed.

"I think we're the least of their problems right now. Really, I know we needed a diversion but what's going on up there is more like the main event. The word apocalypse gets overused: Mara and Josette have brought friends. Oh boy, have they brought friends..."

* * *

Caroline's story made a remarkable amount of sense.

Josette looked at me sadly. "We absolutely have to beat him, and pity must not stop us for a moment. But..."

332

I nodded. "The pity of it. So alone, so angry, so twisted."

We looked at each other in shared sorrow and compassion. But as we talked, we had been wiping down our weapons—my sword Needful and her sword Nails and Coins, and the fish hook…

I agreed. "We will do, if we can, what has to be done, but I will take no pleasure in it. There are few things as old or as lonely. The fungus, of course, and the lords of ocean…"

"We should give him—by no means a chance to win, that would be folly—but a chance to find peace before we end him."

"If we are to end him," I answered, "we may not have the space to give him that chance. But yes, if we can."

Josette saw no need to elaborate the point. "In all my dealings with Caroline, my backdoor into her mind, I never guessed. But it's obvious, really."

"I'm glad that I already forgave the being that was once my sister Lillit, because now I can pity what her thoughtless wish brought her to. I have at times been tempted to self-pity over the knowledge that I cannot save everyone or thought sadly of Sof's many deaths, but of the three of us… The young god was cruel, so cruel, whether he knew it or not."

"Still," Josette added, "at least her torment, if she is even able to feel it as torment, will be over soon and time, chance and destiny will be done with her."

I felt an old sadness reawaken. I had mourned her for years, then hated her, and then let that go. But now I realised that if I were ever to see her again, it would probably be for the last time, with little chance to say all the things that needed to be said.

Josette caught my attention with a hand on my shoulder. "We have a moment before they get here," she said. "Time enough for me to apologise—we've hardly had a moment alone. I should have trusted you. I should have told you. My mother always said so. But I got so used to the shadows and having many names and…"

I shrugged. "Probably for the best. We both had our work and I at least always tried to hunt alone. And your Father always kept an eye on me."

I have rarely initiated a hug, but now seemed like a good moment to do so.

And it was, for a moment more of privacy, and then the air around us, the sea before us, was full of scales and feathered wings and talons and suckered tentacles and vast soulful eyes. And the screeching roaring voices of griffins and wyverns and the thrum-thrum with which the three krakens apologise to the great whales before they feed on them.

And the Leviathan. So much bigger than I remembered, because it had grown and fed and grown for two thousand years.

There was sea water up to my knees for a moment or two.

Almost reflexively it lashed out with a tentacle and knocked three gun emplacements from the top of the fortress before any of the Burnedover people had a chance to think to fire. Somewhere inside the fortress, sirens uselessly sounded.

Each of the Great Beasts save the Leviathan had a rider, or more than one, curvaceous pneumatic riders in form-fitting armour that sparkled with protective decorative magics.

Each wore a helmet that covered everything except their lips and soulful dark eyes but which at first teetered above their heads like the hair towers of the Auxtrian woman's court at Versailles and tinkled with bells like the temple dancers of Benares, but, moments after they arrived, were gone—unnecessary display, superfluous to the business of war.

And suddenly Josette was armoured like them, though more for ornament and solidarity than for need, seated in a high saddle that somehow grew from Leviathan's back, and holding the fish-hook, though more like a sceptre than as a goad.

There was a second empty saddle beside her.

"Well met, Huntress," they said in a chorus that somehow had a disco beat behind it.

"Shouldn't that be 'Well met, little Miss Psycho bitch from the dawn of time'?" I replied.

"Oh, BURN," one said, looking round at the others.

"It looks like you picked a side," I said.

"It seems we always had one," she said. "Just like we always had a leader, who'd join as a novice, pass up the grades, and then disappear. Letting a girl think she was the one in charge, while actually…"

Josette laughed. "Oh, you were, Gloria, mostly. Mara dear, will you ride with me? The girls of the House didn't think to bring you a ride."

The small terrier at my side adopted his dapper human shape for a moment. "I'm her ride," he growled, "I, Garm the Dog, youngest son of Loki Silvertongue and a beast of Ragnarök."

With which he became a vast shaggy beast as large as any of the others save Leviathan, and barked for the glee of his full shape and his full strength.

I seized a clump of hair on his leg and hauled myself up to sit in the hollow of the back of his heavily muscled neck—I needed no saddle. You and Emma's bird fluttered up behind me and busied yourselves with a holocaust of his unfeasibly large crop of fleas.

We swam, and waded, and hovered and beset that mighty fortress where it sat, green and shimmering, contaminant of the harbour of that great damaged city.

Josette cried out with a great voice, "Surrender to me, citadel of the unrighteous, for I am come, your doom, rider of the beast Leviathan. And with me are my peers, the House of Art, riders of krakens and wyverns and the hippogriff and the dragonfly and the great sea serpent and hallucigenia from before time and the greatest of sharks and whales. And Mara, Huntress, rider of Garm the Hound. I call on you, hypocrite servants of iniquity, surrender or we will peel your walls from you like the husk of a nut or the shell of an oyster."

335

From a loudspeaker came a reply: "And I saw a beast with seven heads and ten horns and seated on him was the scarlet woman, the whore of Babylon." At which point Josette lost patience, produced an improbably large gun and silenced the loudspeaker quite expeditiously.

She said, "I'm afraid that was all my fault. I was fond of the boy, you see, and thought I'd explain everything to him, last of the disciples before he died of old age. Only he just didn't understand, and everything I tried to tell him got garbled…"

"Or maybe Lillit got to him," I added, pulling at Garm's ears so that he reared up on his back legs and narrowly escaped a gout of yellow and purple fiery stuff that spouted from an opening in the side of the fortress and then burned on the water.

"Damn," I said pointing at it. "That looks less like an architectural feature, more like an orifice… Which explains that strange green shiny texture."

Fair enough, I thought—we had brought kaijus against it.

"I think it's a creature," I said, "not a building."

Josette looked at it and sighed, but still kept her weapon trained on it. "If it's alive," she whispered, "it's their tortured slave. And if we can't free it, we must bring it the mercy of death."

I worried about our friends who were somewhere in the belly of the beast, but trusted their ability to survive.

The orifice—was it a mouth?—opened again, many feet wide, but before it could spit again one of the krakens which had plunged under the flames and then emerged behind them up against the creature's wall reached up with five of its great tentacles and seized the mouth's sides, its lips, and pulled them shut, raising welts and lesions where its suckers tore.

From somewhere in its guts Leviathan oozed a thick black ichor that spread across the flame, smothering it.

Things did not go so well further around the fortress where another mouth had spat its liquid flame at the great dragonfly, whose body chitin resisted it but whose diaphanous rainbow wings

336

smoked, blackened and blistered until its rider cast a healing magic upon them, a charm that shimmered with a sudden wave of calming emotion that I felt rather than saw. Briefly the dragonfly chittered in pain, its mouth segments working in agonized frenzy, and then it used those mandibles to tear at the wall gnawing away holes like those worms leave in parchment but deeper and deeper in seconds.

We choked momentarily on the stench of burning feathers from where more of the flame stuff had caught the wings of the hippogriff, which whinnied in pain like a stallion and screamed like a diving eagle before tearing at the fortress with beak and talons so that what had looked like masonry fell away and revealed raw pale jelly quivering flesh beneath.

Its rider took up the calming spell in a descant and the flicker of flames among the beast's feathers snuffed out.

My own mount, Garm the Dog, barked in triumphant anger and leaped higher than I had imagined he could, his back feet gaining purchase on the shore of Liberty Island and scrabbling a landing on the fortress roof amid a squad of the black uniformed men with whom I had my own score to settle. He picked up one after another in his jaws, biting off heads and limbs and dropping them without further chewing. With a lazy foreleg he pushed first one and then another gun emplacement into the sea.

Leviathan reached up with a tentacle to pluck down the two missile batteries at the further end, then hauled itself up on to the roof at Garm's side. I wondered that even the fortress creature could take its weight, but as I looked I realised that Leviathan was shrinking.

Soon Josette dismounted: Leviathan was hardly bigger than her, and they fought back to back.

I myself reached down with my lance in one hand and my singing Japanese blade in the other and pierced and slashed without ever growing tired until we cleared the roof of black uniforms and there were no more emerging from hatches. I reflected that this would all have been so much harder—more or less impossible—had Emma and I not destroyed dark alchemy and with it most of Burnedover's more powerful weapons.

I also could not help noticing that the Burnedover fighters were also surprisingly easy to kill and fell like limp rags, my sword meeting little resistance in their flesh; these were magically engineered duplicate soldiers who had previously been hard to kill.

And my destruction of the dead gods had helped too: for the first time I felt that we had seized the initiative, that stoic despair might not serve us.

And then I heard a voice thunder my name.

Out to sea, leagues away, stood the creature that was a part of, that was the Atlantic Ocean—not just a tutelary spirit but the sea itself, brother of that smaller sea I had once seen devour Atlantis.

"Mara," it spoke and the world trembled. "Our servant Dagon is dead and undead. That creature you fight was made from his flesh. We consider this an affront."

"Indeed," I said, quietly, knowing that it would hear without my shouting, aware as it was of every curse and whispered prayer that drowning men whisper on clear days or in tempest. How did I know this? Because I had held many conversations with its least sibling, the Lord of Salt, conversations that I have not yet shared with you, like much else. "I did not know this until now. I am sorry that the group of men known as Burnedover, who serve the Enemy of all men, have done this. It will be held to their account."

"See to it," the Ocean spoke, and it was a request and a command. "Cleanse and restore the body of our servant, once worshipped among men, once you have removed the foulness that has given it a similitude of life. We do not have inexhaustible patience for humanity."

I reflected on all that humanity had done that Ocean might have considered an affront and trembled slightly at the idea of what exhausting its patience might mean for what remnant of humanity survived the next days.

Our problem to be dealt with if we won; and, if we lost, a consolation that we would be avenged. A world in which the Enemy and his people gnawed our bones, would have Ocean to reckon with and little time to enjoy their dark feast.

The calming spells with which the House of Art had healed their creatures modulated into a hymn of predicted victory. The creature we fought was no longer defending itself and we had cleared the troops from its upper surface.

Time perhaps to make rendezvous with Emma and her party.

I alighted from Garm, who turned back into his small terrier form, and together we walked towards the hatchway. Josette joined me, a much shrunken though still massive Leviathan padding at her side on small reptilian legs.

She caught my surprised glance, and said, "At some point after we met him, Leviathan became less of a mere brute, somewhat more of a person. Not a great conversationalist, but understands, and, as you see has somehow learned to grow and shrink. A useful attribute: I have no idea how…"

One of you—Memory, I think—fluttered down and whispered in my ear.

"My bird says it was someone he ate."

Most of the House and their creatures continued their attack on the structure, which seemed to shudder and moan. A few set up camp on the roof, to guard the skies against reinforcements. One of them waved long-nailed hands in an elaborate twirl, and suddenly I saw a dome of magical power surrounding the entire structure.

"That will hold off most things," she called down to us. "I don't guarantee against an asteroid strike."

But her voice cut out as we entered the fortress, you and Emma's bird fluttering behind us.

* * *

The sirens went on blaring, but after a while there were no more sounds of feet running upstairs.

"They probably know we are here," said Alexander, "but they have other things on their mind. Distraction is sometimes a matter of confused priorities."

After they had gone a few paces down the corridor, Emma realised something. She looked at Syeed, who was looking back at her. Clearly they had had the same thought.

"I don't want to worry anyone," she said, "but there's a sort of smell, a feel, to this place, I find unpleasantly familiar. And Syeed obviously senses the same thing."

"It's like they slapped chipboard and emulsion paint over raw and bloody flesh," Syeed said. "When they had Emma and me and that dead friend of hers prisoner. This place is alive."

Emma added, "Or possibly undead. Except it's not a Dead God, because Mara's Hunt got all of those and with one this big we'd all be biting our fingers off or flaking away. And it's not a bit of the Time Jump creatures because, well, it isn't. It doesn't feel quite the same. Like, but not."

Caroline piped up. "I know what you mean about recognizing it, but I wasn't with you in Iraq. It's more like–"

"–That thing Aurora turned herself into," Elodie finished her thought. "Inside on the outside and everything sculpted and repurposed. So there's probably some sort of perfect ivory statue somewhere inside these walls."

"I just mentioned distraction," Alexander said.

"I'm sure that's all very interesting," the god Apollo said impatiently, "for people with time on their hands to think about the finer points of magic. But we're here to make war. If this is some sort of creature we should get on with what we're here for and get out as quickly as possible."

"Find where they make their soldiers," Alexander added, "and smash the mould or whatever. Then look and see if there are a bunch of evil mind-twisting babies, and sort those out, if we can."

"Preferably from a distance. With cleansing flame," said Apollo. "It's the only way to be sure."

"Perhaps," Alexander said. "In any case, before our enemies realise we're here and the crucial attack force and Mara and Josette are the incredibly damaging massive diversion."

The corridor forked into two ramps, one of which curved up to the right and the other down, with a precipitous drop between them.

Emma looked round at her companions, then gestured them to come closer—in a living building, the walls might not just have, but be, ears. "I know we've got two things to do, but we don't know for certain that this is the place, so let's not split up. I think we should do down first because that's where most evil lairs I've seen do all the dark magic and mad science they plan but are actually a bit ashamed of. Plus, I know they may have all charged upstairs to fight Mara's monsters, but there are usually guards or at least the odd mad scientist in such places."

She felt she should actually be giving orders, but in such company...

But as they proceeded along the down ramp, they heard a drone of complaints in a voice that Emma and Caroline knew well, only faded and querulous. This was the right direction.

"Colonel Green," Emma said, "or possibly Reverend Black. Or maybe the other way round, by this point. Some people just don't stay dead, but I suppose he was my first."

The feeble voice said, "White. Plain Mister Bob White. I have no need of titles."

Everyone drew guns or swords: Emma prepared a sort of blasting spell. But there were no guards to be seen in the vast industrial space at the bottom of the ramp.

Just a terrible stench, most of it coming from the row upon row of person-sized vats that filled most of the space.

The rest of the stench was coming from a chair—like a dentist's chair only with more drills and arms—and strapped to it what was left of someone who looked much the same as Green or Black, only older and more in focus.

He had soiled himself, but that was not the main reason he stank. There were streaks of dried blood and tears on his face and he was alone and desolate. The scars on his naked torso looked as if untalented but enthusiastic surgeons had been whittling samples from him for decades—he had all his limbs still but they were pipe stems covered in plasters and held together by plastic bandages. His flesh was livid in places, green and purple and yellow and black with what might have been bruises, but was probably rot.

"Guards!" he said in protest as they entered the room, but none appeared. Brünnhilde took a stance just outside the door.

"Someone has to stand watch," she said, "and I see little profit in talking to that scrap of rank flesh. It has no nobility to it and we of the Aesir have no regard for such. I did not speak even to Ivar the Boneless at his end, and he was a great king."

Most of the others hung back too; he was a disgusting sight, and also an enemy for whom they did not wish to be tricked into compassion. Gods, demigods and men—they were warriors and he had perverted their calling into something utterly foul, and was now paying the price in agony.

Emma approached the chair and bent over to let him see her face.

"Emma Jones," he croaked in a voice like a door in a breeze, "fitting, I suppose. You took the head of my first copy, thirty years ago—I felt and saw his rage and his death—and you come for me at the last. When I have lost all faith and all hope."

She asked, because she wanted to know, "How could you think you were a man of God, and weaponise worship to kill so many? And spend your life preaching a religion with no love in it, but serving a master far worse than any god."

"Gods? As you know, girl, there are no gods. Not you and not Jehovah. I took Jesus as my personal saviour and I thought he came to me and I did terrible things in his service. I thought I was one of

342

the elect, but in the end I helped eject the saved from Heaven. I thought I could send the elect to heaven ahead of time, and if others worshipped false dead gods, they deserved annihilation. He came to me so many times and said he was my Lord and Saviour, my Redeemer who lived, and he showed me his wounds and placed my fingers into them, but later he showed me his wrists and side unmarked and said that it was all a lie. Jesus had died on the cross, he said, and if he rose no one had seen him for two thousand years. And then he showed me his true face and laughed scorn at me through many teeth. I thought Jehovah was the one true god and I thought I served him, but he was just another cheat and liar and I felt joy as one of my bodies plunged a knife into his chest to rot and fester there. Unknowing, I served an evil lord, but better that than a petty old fraud who now lies in a ditch somewhere."

He coughed unpleasantly; his breath stank of decayed lung.

"In that you failed," said Sof, walking over to stand by Emma. "As his doctor, I take great pleasure in telling you that I helped him survive your betrayal and he, unlike you, will make a full recovery." She cast a professional eye on him, sniffed his breath, reached down to feel his pulse and made disapproving noises with her tongue against her teeth. "I've seen this before. Amateurs who burn out their bodies with magical austerities until there was no healing in them. What were you doing? Growing copies of yourself from scraps in those vats? And what was in them? Some charlatan's brew?"

Emma stepped away to look at one of the vats. She lifted its cover and hastily slammed it down again, pulling a face at the stench.

"Whatever was in it, nothing is going to grow in it now except mould and filth. It has well and truly gone off."

"I would imagine that destroying what we're calling dark alchemy a few days ago had something to do with that." She smirked slightly. "I am so very pleased with that day's work. We took away your nastiest weapons and stopped you and your master having any new soldiers."

He strained against the chair as if trying to sit up to confront them, but was too weak. His voice was failing too, as if his lungs were withering in his chest.

"The day the weapons crumbled was the day the last soldiers out of the vats were mewling limp things that could not stand. I felt them deliquesce before they died and felt my own body begin to corrode. They were flesh of my flesh. As are the last few troops your friends and their monsters are killing on the roof."

"Sympathetic magic backlash," Sof and Emma explained to each other.

"I die," he said. "I deserve this death. My consolation is that you will all die too. With the rest of us mere humans. When he restores the rule of the strong."

Emma nodded to Sof and turned to the others where they were hanging about the doorway. "I think that concludes this part of our operations."

The husk in the chair coughed as if to get their attention. "Aren't you going to finish me?" he whined.

"Your men stood around and laughed while my friend John died as bad a death as you have earned," Emma said, "and you watched through their eyes and doubtless laughed too. And you unleashed dead gods on the world and thousands, perhaps millions, died that death. You get no mercy stroke from me."

"Nor me," added Sof. "Men like you, fanatics who called themselves Christians, tore me to living fragments. There are worse fates than you have earned."

He cried at last, in humiliation and pain.

"You betrayed your god, you betrayed the entire human race, and you expect mercy…"

"I beg you. In Jesus' name--"

Caroline, standing at Emma's side, stared him down. "She hates you too. Who do you think is leading the monsters that are tearing this place apart? Scarlet Woman of Revelations to you maybe, but actually… Elodie, what do you think?"

Elodie had joined them.

She looked silently at Caroline and Caroline looked silently back at her. Then they both pressed their sidearms to the dying man's forehead and blew his brains out.

It created a surprising amount of mess. Emma realised that she had heard the phrase for years and not realised it was literally true.

"We do the right thing," Caroline said.

"It sucks," Elodie said, "but we do it anyway. Maybe you need us here because we can't be as justly angry as you."

Emma was angry for a moment but kissed them both anyway.

Sof stepped back, reached into her clothes and produced the Stone, stroking it as she would the head of a small much-loved child. It flared with light and the mess of blood, bone and brain, and the stench from the chair and the vats, vanished.

But the body of the old man who had been Burnedover was still dead. His soul was still there, though, even more tattered than his body and crying out still in silent anguish. As they watched, wisps of spirit drifted towards him through the open door and filled in a tiny fraction of the holes: it would take so many more deaths and so much more pain before he could ever be whole.

"They're massacring his clones upstairs," Emma said. "He's dead, but his soul feels every death."

"Less than he earned," Tom said.

"Justice and mercy," said Syeed. "The parts of him are coming together, at least, so the pain is earning him a sort of relief."

Emma, Judge of the Damned, shrugged, resignedly. "Now, I forgive him."

* * *

We found ourselves at the top of a ramp that spiralled down. Fond as I was of Garm, I was quite glad not to have to carry him down a staircase, though it would have been instructive to see how this small version of Leviathan would have coped.

345

"Poor old Dagon," I remarked, "we were there, your father, Star and me. Right at the start of his story, when he was an idiot child, whose fellow villagers magicked him into a half-fish that would help them fill their nets. Yet somehow he outlived and outstayed all the Baals and all the Tanits."

"He escaped Father, but the black uniformed scum got him in the end," Josette said angrily, "and doubtless convinced themselves that they were doing it in my name."

You fluttered ahead of us, but there seemed to be no guards left anywhere in the building.

"Surely we can't have already wiped out the entire garrison," I said. "They fell awfully quickly…"

"Not if their best troops have all been shifted to help with whatever is going on in Heaven."

There were a couple of shots from a room several levels down.

"I hope," Josette said," that that was the noise of Emma and the rest concluding part of our business here. Very few shots, though."

"Not enough for a massacre on either side. More than enough for a single execution."

"Double tap. One to kill, and one to be sure."

The years and the world had changed and hardened her, I thought, with regret.

She smiled a wan smile. "I died on the cross. You killed me. Out of love. You brought me back without meaning to. Judas betrayed me, out of love, my brother, whom I love, for the sake of my father, whom I adored and served, and who let me die in agony because I would not serve him in the way I wanted. You also, out of love, killed your sister, who I also loved. I love the world and I love people: you taught me on the cross, that sometimes you kill out of love. I just try not to."

"As do I," I said.

We had already killed that day. And the logic of the situation was that we should kill more, but…

346

"I don't care what they are," Josette burst out. "We're not doing it. No child is guilty."

I smiled. I had come to the same conclusion the more I thought about it. I trusted her, but you never know anyone with certainty. We all have to pass so many tests.

From the next level below, we heard sounds of struggle, and the sound of hungry babies crying. Emma's bird fluttered down and you followed.

Alexander and Syeed had the god Apollo jammed up against a wall while Tom held a gun steady and pointed at his groin. Emma, her bird now on her shoulder, and Brünnhilde were barring the door while Caroline and Elodie stood well off to the side out of harm's way. Sof was inside the room, checking the cradles in a professional manner This was not the selection I would have made for a mission of this kind, but obviously half of them had self-selected to ensure wise counsels prevailed.

"I will hurt you all," Apollo shouted in anger, "– I will if needed kill you all—if I need to. Those children need to die before they grow a day older. They are monsters. Like their father. Like their kind."

I remembered his ruthlessness with the Shaggy One, who had been his friend. The myth the Greeks made of that tale got almost everything decoratively wrong. they got that savagery right.

"I learned many things when I was stuck in Josette's head," Alexander replied. "And among them was not to be hasty."

Syeed looked Apollo straight in the eye. "You are a false god from the Age of Ignorance, so you cannot be expected to know better. But killing children is haram. Even the child who grew up to be Hitler. Now, some of us can go back in time. As I mentioned earlier to some of the others, I discussed this once with the Sheikh, and we concluded that if you do wrong to tamper with destiny, worse will ensue."

Tom added, "And, god or not, one in each kneecap and one in the balls. It will hurt, though I have no way of knowing how much."

Brünnhilde looked at Josette with fondness in her eyes. "I knew what the All-Father would have said, but fuck that kinslayer. I asked myself what you would do and came along to argue with everyone. And, look, they almost all agree with me."

Elodie just said "But babies--" and Caroline nodded.

Emma looked a little guilty.

"When we first guessed they might be here, I was tempted. I steeled myself, but you know, having Stalin as a clerk has taught me a lot about people thinking they're doing the right thing... As it is, clearly not his babies anyway."

"How can you possibly know that?" Apollo shouted scornfully.

"I'm pretty certain telepathic babies cry in silence," Emma said.

"Some of them are teething," added Sof, from behind her. "I looked in their mouths. At their dentition. Pretty certain they're not all the same kind of people. And not exclusive carnivores."

Apollo was still struggling to get free and adding muscles to himself in a way that meant sooner or later he would succeed. Alexander leaned in and spoke closely into his ear.

"You were in Lucifer's oubliette a long time. People know more about teeth than they did when m'tutor got it wrong about females. If Sof says they're not our sort of people, but not the Enemy's either, she'll know what she's talking about. Unlike most of us ancients, she has bothered to inform herself of all the new learning."

The god stopped struggling and growing, but obviously wasn't convinced.

"The world is much older than we thought," I explained, "and there were many ancestors and cousins before there were people."

"I don't think these can be any sort of copies," Sof said. "No sign of dark alchemy or falling apart from not having it anymore. I think their peoples still exist and he stole these, from somewhere in the far reaches of Shadow. But why? There aren't enough for him to make a meal of."

I sighed. The answer was obvious to me, but not to all these much cleverer people. "It's a trap. He will have dedicated their deaths at our hands as a Ritual of Blood for his intentions. It's a trick he's taught his pawns down the ages; I am surprised he thinks I at least would fall for it again."

Alexander smirked. "That's because he's not used to not having the initiative. Most things have gone his way for years, but in the last few days you and Emma have taken a lot away from him."

Josette, the reduced Leviathan still looming behind her, nodded and raised a hand for everyone's attention. We gave it to her at once.

"We need to get the babies out of here, and then destroy this place. Utterly. It's the transformed corpse of my old friend the God Dagon. Mara and I just promised that to some beings we really cannot afford to offend. Tom, could you fetch a couple of my friends from upstairs?"

Tom flicked away and returned twice, once with Miss Gloria and then with another of the House of Art.

He looked at both of them, intrigued, and Gloria smiled and tousled his hair.

Josette looked at them sternly and with love, as if she might never see these friends again.

"Girls," she said, and the word was a title of nobility in her mouth, "I had hoped to bring you with me on our final desperate raid on Heaven and our final fight with the Enemy, for good or ill. But see, here are twenty babies, children of the other human peoples that we had thought gone and slain by the Enemy's folk, or by us humans, but somewhere in Shadow he stole their children and brought them here to trick us into wrongness. I charge you to care for these babies and return them to their families. And then, if we should lose, do what you can to protect those families. He thinks them—like all of us—as rightfully his people's cattle and prey. Do what you can to disappoint him and to spoil his appetite."

Miss Gloria thought for a second. "We will take them to Morgan's palace to feed and clean them. The hippogriff will take a few hours to heal from her hurts enough for a long flight, but if you can get them upstairs as quickly as possible, we will evacuate them straight away."

She and her silent friend turned elegantly on their heels, and headed up the ramp, muttering something about always being stuck running the creche.

Tom wheeled himself into the nursery which was suddenly full of a flurry of him and then entirely empty.

With no more noise of fighting and no crying infants, the fortress that had been Dagon was suddenly very empty and very quiet. Except for the pulsing of a mighty heart.

Tom reappeared, froze at the sound of the heart, and frowned. "So Dagon's not exactly dead," he said. "But we've promised The Authorities to destroy this place utterly. As a professional assassin, I do see a problem with this. I'm sure rampaging kaiju will get to something vital eventually, but that's going to take a while and is pretty cruel."

The reduced Leviathan reached out a mouth tentacle and tapped Josette on the shoulder. It was clearly not the action of a mere dumb brute. Then, to explain and emphasize its point, it doubled in size so that it touched the ceiling and parts of it hung over the ramp and down into the stair well.

"I think those of us who can move through Shadow, or fly, or jump really well," I said, "need to leave right away."

"Tom," Emma said, more or less at the same time, "could you get everyone back to Liberty Island?"

Again we were surrounded by a flurry of multiple Toms and suddenly Syeed, Alexander, Elodie and Caroline were gone. Sof, I noticed, left under her own steam through Shadow. Apollo, always a show off like all Olympians, stepped out into the void and flew out, blasting a hole in the roof rather than using the hatchway like a normal person.

Brünnhilde yodelled and followed him. You and Emma's bird fluttered after her.

350

Which left me, Emma and Josette, who patted Leviathan on—not really its muzzle but the space above the nearest of its mouths she could reach—and then was gone.

I was about to follow her when Emma reached out a hand.

"One way or another," she said, "this will be over soon."

"Yes, of course. One way or another."

"And then what?"

"If we lose, there is no afterwards, obviously… Otherwise…"

"Do you trust me?"

I thought about it, very briefly, and nodded.

"We have a sort of plan."

"We?"

"An old friend of yours and someone you've only met briefly. I need to talk to Sof but I'm sure she'll agree. It's mostly their plan, but it's a good plan. If we win."

I shrugged—I was not entirely convinced we would win—but nodded again. I trusted Emma. I probably trusted anyone she trusted.

There was a place not far off in Shadow—it turned out—a strut of rock that stretched out to Liberty Island. Emma, Garm and I slipped out and away from the fortress that Dagon had become and joined the others on the shore I had left a mere forty-five minutes or so before.

The House of Art had left already and with them the wyverns, the dragonfly, the hippogriffs and the other winged beasts.

The fortress had great rents in its side that gushed a sort of blood, but seemed to be trying to heal; its flesh twitched and shuddered as salt spray hit it. It was now somehow less out of phase with the actual world. The krakens, sharks, orcas and other sea beasts had ceased to attack it and had pulled out to sea as if waiting for something, as if there were communications going on that we beings of the land were not privy to.

"Run," I shouted and Emma, Josette, and Sof did the same in synch with me, then did so. Another flurry of Toms and all of us found ourselves, with his help or our own speed, sheltering on the other side of the pedestal of the statue.

I did not precisely see what happened next: the noises that followed were graphic enough that I did not wish to. I have had to do many terrible things in a long life but there are some things, things I have not had to do myself that I have been glad to miss.

The sky filled with seagulls, but they kept a safe distance.

Our ears were split with a creaking that seemed loud as thunder and then a moan and a sound of wood and shell being smashed into splinters and then what was less an explosion than a very loud pop as if corks were coming out of thousands of bottles and then suddenly the air at either side of the statue was filled with debris—fragments of the outer wall and inner structure of the fortress, nothing much bigger than a small coin and luckily none of it hitting any of us. The same could not be said of the brief rain of stinking bodily fluids, though only some of it reached us where we sheltered.

Once the shower of rubble and filth was done, we stood up. Sof talked sweetly to the Stone until it flashed us clean. We left our shelter and walked back around to see what was going on.

The gulls shrieked in greedy delight to peck fragments of jellied flesh from the seaward side of the great statue and from Leviathan, who reared up titanic from the wreckage of what he had destroyed from the inside. You and Emma's bird joined them—it is in your nature to be eaters of carrion.

The krakens likewise swam up to pick fragments of Dagon's flesh from the parts of Leviathan that were under water. All of the sea beasts swam up in an orderly line to be fed as if taking a kind of Eucharist; there was nothing of the feeding frenzy from them I had half expected, but rather the stateliness of a ritual dance.

After a while, even you and the gulls started to behave with decorum.

We all stood in silence, heads bowed for two hours even though we had urgent business elsewhere, as befitted witnesses the funeral rites of one of the oldest and kindest of deities and the servant of Powers it behoved us to respect.

After a while, I looked around silently and saw that we had been joined by Jehovah and Lucifer, Polly and the girl Olivia and the faun, who trotted up to Sof and shyly took her hand. Loki and his children arrived too, and the terrier slipped from my side to stand with his brothers and sisters.

Sobekh was there too, his head bowed.

Jehovah broke the silence for a moment with a hoarse whisper. "Saw what was going on, on the girl Polly's video screens, and I said to Star that we ought to pay our respects. Obviously we and the fishgod had our issues down the years…"

But Emma and his daughter glared at him and he respected the silence he had broken.

Eventually the harbour and the island and the further shore were clean and all of the beasts and birds had eaten their fill. Except for Leviathan, who had stood still and passive all this time.

Now it whipped out tentacles from every part of its body and descended into the depths for a long minute. When it emerged it was clutching two things: a vast purple still-beating heart, and a perfect replica of Dagon as I had first seen him—a young man in robes crowned with a fish head—carved in white stone or possibly ivory. Leviathan opened the widest of its mouths, placed the heart whole between several rows of teeth and began to chew.

The sea creatures clustered round attentive: this was no longer some simple brute eating its prey, but a purposeful act, a transfer of sovereignty. Again, we watched in silence, knowing that it was important that we did so though without quite understanding why.

When the heart was consumed, Leviathan took the white image and held it reverentially with four or five mouth tentacles, dropped horizontal and begin to swim out to sea followed by all the sea beasts that had shared in the ritual and by a flight of gulls.

You and Emma's bird started to leave with them, and then came to your senses and returned to my shoulders and Emma's.

You whispered that we should wait, and indeed it was clear that none of us wished yet to break the moment of solemnity.

We continued to stand, heads slightly bowed, until the procession was gone beyond our sight, though whether under the sea or below the horizon I could not tell you.

And then he returned, the vast being that was Ocean.

"You have done well, little men, little women, little gods. You helped save our servant Dagon from his captors and killers, and brought Leviathan, his killer and his successor as servant, to this place at the hour appointed by time and chance. It has much to do, to help clean the seas of the damage humanity has done—shoals of plastic, sheens of oil, rusting canisters of poison and worse. Yet because of your past kindness, it has asked for a boon beyond mere reprieve. It tells me that many of humanity's worst crimes against me are the result of an evil individual, who is not even of your kind. We are minded to grant this boon and assist in the punishment of this individual."

It paused. I looked around for someone to give it the answer it so obviously wished to get before continuing, and realised that it must be my job to answer.

"Your boon would please us greatly," I said.

"We have discussed this with the other Powers of our rank. The firmament, and the waters under and above the earth in Shadow and the currents, planets, rings and clouds of what lies beyond the Mundane sky. Jehovah, your 'heaven' is a bubble you have hung above us. The firmament does not mind the intrusion: its denizens make sweet sounds that please the firmament. We shall expedite your purposes by transferring you to that bubble post haste."

I had always wondered what Newton had seen out in space that had so perturbed and confused him, that he had been unable adequately to describe to Einstein and Hawking.

"That is most terribly kind," I said, because really what else could I possibly say to a being of such vastness.

You will note that spending time in London with Emma and Caroline had taught me a particular useful kind of bourgeois English manners, which, I had observed, served them well in their dealing with Powers. Never let it be said that, after seven thousand or so years, I was incapable of learning new tricks of our trade.

It thundered and I realised that Ocean was laughing.

"Not at all," Ocean said. "It is my duty to be useful. Are we not all servants of the One? Or possibly parts of the One? I and those like me have the privilege of certainty that the One exists, but with that knowledge goes awareness that it would be wilful pride to ask to know more."

"But…" Jehovah started to speak and then fell silent.

His white bird puffed up its neck in protest and was still.

"Yes, little god," said Ocean. "Even you and your children and prophets have served the One, as do we all. Sometimes we envy you small beings the joy of coming to know of the One by reason or inspiration. It humbles us before you."

And Ocean bowed.

What happened next was unclear to me at the time and remains so. Even the sequence of events.

Ocean bowed to us in humility and we were caught up for a time in something like a wave and something like a great comforting hand. I was once caught up in nets and carried to Atlantis by great birds, that were not like you children of the Bird, but rather parts of him, and this was something like and yet at once gentler, faster and involved far greater power used with infinite restraint.

Day of Wrath

And in what might have been moments or hours—time passed but how much I cannot say—we found ourselves standing before the many-storeyed, many-tiered, excessively ornate, actually rather tasteless, facade that surrounds the Heaven of Jehovah.

I have, down the years, disapproved of Judas far more than was ever kind or fair, but I have never questioned his ability as a builder. The reason why Pandemonium in its various versions always looked better than Heaven even though Judas is a far better architect than Hawksmoor, Malevich or Speer is that Lucifer never did more than say "big" and really didn't care that much, whereas Judas had Jehovah for his client and had to accommodate endless whims and never remove anything the client had ever liked. And Judas' problem is that he has never known how to say no to his adopted father.

Tours Cathedral is a hodgepodge because it took so many centuries to build that the locals used to say "when the cathedral is finished" to mean "never" and different builders in different centuries changed the design. The walls and gate of Heaven are much, much worse. Bits of Romanesque, bits of Palladian and some truly awful Pugin ripoffs—whenever Nameless snuck off to do a bit of tourism and listen to himself being worshipped, he would come back full of notions.

And now from every flying buttress, from every gargoyle, from every corbel, spire or belltower there dangled a badly injured angel trussed like game fowl in a butcher's shop window. Their moans of pain were a sort of music: I've never cared for angels, but they do many things well and being beautiful is one of them.

"Before we try to enter the Gate," I asked, "are there any unpleasant surprises we ought to know about? Loki, any luck with the gods of Hind or the Celestial Bureaucracy? Or the lesser pantheons?"

He shook his head ruefully. "Those small gods I could find were busy packing for the farthest reaches of Shadow. Most of them see you as far too close to Jehovah here for them to trust you at all: as far as they are concerned, victory by the Enemy is only marginally worse than a return of things as they were—we'll get no help from them. Elsewhere, I got there too late—a lot of dying milkmaids and nautch dancers in one place and a lot of over-turned desks and inkstones in the other. They're either dead or hostages."

I'd hoped for little from those pantheons, but... Isis had closed the Land of Reeds pretty effectively. The Aesir were gone apart from the few who were here. The Olympians had sent Apollo, who was handy enough in a fight, but clearly here to keep a chair at the table rather than because they planned any further help. Hell and the Mundane world—well, Emma had come herself but had clearly left her realm well-garrisoned.

The force we had was going to have to be enough, but I had no strategy and little enough hope.

Emma caught my eye. She knew me well enough to guess what I was thinking.

"Alexander said earlier that the Enemy has lost the initiative," she said. "We know he has millennia of power from the Rituals, but we have quite a lot of accumulated power ourselves. What we mostly need to do is keep distracting him from his endgame—we win by not losing and by making him waste resources. If it weren't going to take millennia of blood to bring back his people, he would have done it long ago. So we try to wear him down and we try not to die."

Her red bird alighted on her shoulder and cawed harsh agreement.

She was right, of course, though the Enemy had even more unpleasant surprises in store than she guessed—but then, so did we.

The Gate to Heaven is a vast Gothic doorway with doors carved from redwoods—not the mere redwoods of the Mundane Pacific Northwest, but their larger cousins in Shadow. You might expect some decoration, given the way the rest of the facade looks, but clearly for once Judas prevailed. Plain wood, lacquered to a high sheen, and with smaller doors set into the lower tenth of them for day-to-day business.

But that was not what we were here for.

I walked to the base of the doors, took a moment to appreciate the height, weight and sheer scale of them, and then set the smallest finger of my left hand to them and flung them wide open.

There were, I fear, screams as they shook on their hinges and slammed against the gatehouse walls. Whoever had planned that particular ambush had wasted his men's lives by underestimating the force I and my allies could bring to bear. I was, though, surprised at how utterly crushed the remains of the ambush were. I hadn't pushed the doors that hard surely.

But I did not particularly trouble myself with the thought because of the vista that greeted us, a vista which added to the impression that we were expected.

There were, confronting us immediately, a significant force of several thousand more of the Burnedover soldiers, who appeared to be in rude health still and whose grizzled hair, occasional missing limbs and facial scars were those of seasoned veterans. And as we watched, reserves marched up to join them.

Clearly these were not just out of the vat, and in numbers that did not especially concern me given the strength of our small force, but they were so many that they might cause us inconvenience or delay.

Behind them we could see the smashed remains of the choir stalls in which the Blessed had previously sung now arranged into a series of pyres, each of them surmounted by a platform on which trussed classically onto stakes were the missing pantheons, the members of Jehovah's council and a variety of other important hostages, all of them cast into the flesh for the occasion, among them friends who mattered.

Polly muttered to me, "Clever fucking bastard. He's collected the lot—Frankie, Herbert, my daughter, Georgiana, even Mackie. Tell you what though, he's not got my da; slippery to the last, my old dad…"

Behind the centre of this row of pyres was a staircase leading to a platform on which stood Jehovah's gaudy and bejewelled throne. At the bottom of the staircase stood Berin, all human disguise cast aside and looking as uncanny and unseely as Caroline had described him.

In all the years that I had pursued him, he and I had only once as far as I knew been in the same place—the Oxford party at which I had rescued Emma and failed both to save Caroline and to recognize the Enemy disguised as their Politics tutor.

Jehovah whispered, "At least he has not yet taken his seat on my throne."

I wondered how he thought he knew that and why it mattered.

At Berin's feet, wrapped in chains—and I wondered that they could hold her—knelt our sister Lillit, her glistening skin dull, and dull tears streaking her face.

She called out to me and to Sof, her voice clear and bell-like as it echoed in that vast space. And, I realised, to Emma and Caroline.

"Sisters, all five of you, I greet you. Hail—and farewell, because I am almost at my final true end. I know—I have always known in every moment of time since my first death to which I shall shortly return—every word that will be spoken, every gesture that will be made in the seconds as they tick down. You first, Sof…"

I wondered what she meant by Five.

Everything was still in that space. Even Berin was caught in that moment; even the hostages chained to their stakes.

Sof too wept, and, weeping, said, "I know now, sister, the consequences of our choices so long ago. I know where your choice led you, trapped you. I cursed you for so long. I bless you. I forgive you."

I did not weep. "Things are as they are," I said. "You have saved much and destroyed much. How time, chance and destiny work out, how your memory will be judged, remains to be seen."

"But not by me," Lillit laughed, and her laugh was the saddest thing I heard that day.

Caroline said, "I am you. I will remember you."

"More than you guess," Lillit said.

Emma said, "Is there nothing to be done?"

"There are things," Lillit said, "which are foredoomed, beyond magic, beyond cleverness and beyond kind words."

Berin finally spoke.

"Sentimental to the last. You will not be missed. As the Huntress said, you have betrayed me as much as you have helped me, but that's all one now. Now your time has run out and your knowledge has run through the hourglass with it. Your only use is as a sacrifice."

"You are wrong in this, Enemy of All," Sof said, "because two more things happen before you kill me—which is the thing I know but cannot foresee. The first is this…"

And with a flash of purple light, a C Sharp Minor chord and the melodious sound of a gong, Hekkat who was now known as Morgan appeared. And her carrion bird with her.

You, and Jehovah's bird and Emma's bird all exchanged your greetings.

It occurred to me that this was the first time I had seen all five in the same place at the same time since we parted ways on the shore of the new sea where Atlantis had stood.

Morgan said nothing as yet, but stood in silence considering the situation. We caught each other's glance, momentarily, but both knew that we must not say or do anything that would let Berin know we were now together lest it be a weakness he could exploit.

So much had happened in the few days since I had seen her: I was amazed at how much it hurt not to rush to her side and tell her of it. And, if things went badly, how terrible that it was not until now that this was even a possibility.

Then Lillit stood up in spite of the weight of her chains and stared into Berin's eyes with hatred.

"The second is this. I speak my death curse against you. I curse you to failure and to despair. I have always hated you, monster, even when destiny me serve you. Destiny also made me bring your people to their ruin. It made me keep Emma safe as she walked through the Hell of Lucifer, the Night Journey that made her a goddess and the Judge of the Damned. From which she learned forgiveness, but also prudence…"

Berin lost patience. He waved his hand and a small circle opened in the air from which licked a tentative tongue of white flame so bright it hurt the eyes. "Destiny is done with you. And so am I. Burn as your sisters and their friends will burn, and the rest of the gods of Men. This is the sleeping flame born of the moment of creation and I dedicate your death by it to my purpose."

Like a man with a blowtorch, he ran the flame up and down her shining body. She screamed once and then the Quintessence flowed away like quicksilver.

But beneath it, there was no body for him to burn to ashes. As she had told him she would, she had returned to her first and only death at his hands, to die reaching out to her beloved sister Sof. And the greater part of my sister, her wit and compassion and goodness, had already left her to become Caroline.

And through and between the pyres and the feet of the unsmiling and undistracted Burnedover veterans, the Quintessence flowed, a living creature with a purpose of its own. Once it reached the thirty yards between the troops and our party, it paused as if considering its options and then split into two streams, one of which made for Sof and one for Caroline, for its creator and for its former mistress' avatar, and flowed up their bodies under their clothes and up their faces to the crowns of their heads as if exploring acquaintance, and then withdrew itself, a single gold glove on Caroline's left hand, a gold torc around Sof's neck.

Both listened attentively for a moment. A voice none of the rest of us could hear was talking to them. I knew beyond a shadow of a doubt that it was Lillit's explanation of her bequest to them and no one else's business at all.

Except that Caroline spoke, but not to any of us.

"Sister, I shall remember. Everything."

But I did not understand what she meant.

Berin, meanwhile, was paying this no heed at all, but toying with a finger at the tongue of bright white flame, never quite letting it touch him, but teasing it so that it grew ever longer and thicker and wrapped around itself and came more and more out of its hole in the air so that he had to tease it with a finger at the full span of his arm. Able to bear the heat of closeness to it, and flirt with it, but not quite daring to let it touch him.

Suddenly he pointed upwards with the finger that he had teased it with and it shot into the air where it hovered, twenty feet above his head, a second sun. He smirked at us.

"My hostages are gods and immortals, as are many of you. Fire can kill but it can also torment—I would not wish any of you to miss my triumph, the return of my people and the end of the reign of Mankind the Usurper, but I see no reason why you should not be in agony the whiles. In moments my fires will be ready and my sphere of death will shoot out tendrils to light these pyres and then reach out for the rest of you. The Quintessence did not protect Lillit; Sof and Caroline, you know agony better than most. You may use these last minutes to tell your friends how to try to bear the worst and then let it devour you into madness."

Several of us had heard his laugh before. It had nothing of mirth in it.

Suddenly you both fluttered up from my shoulders and high in the air started to wind in a spiral dance, your wingtips almost touching. And then Morgan's bird, the Morrigan that had been many and was now one again, lumbered uncouthly part of the same dance, and the filigree fluttering scarlet Tsassiporath, that had been Lucifer's and was now Emma's, its dance rococo in its twirls and saudades, and the white silent Ghost, that was Jehovah's but had helped heal Josette when she was sick and her strength overtaxed. Ghost flew up the centre of the spiral the others made, then plunged back down that centre. Over and over.

And then you and they sang. I was used to the harshness of your voices and the Morrigan's, and to the cloying sweetness of Tsassipporah, but this was quite other. Clear and touching birdsong like a nightingale in despair at the end of all roses.

Singing, the five of you flew off in different directions a moment and then rushed headlong together, but what looked like a collision was not, because suddenly where you had been was—not your parent as he had been at the heart of Atlantis, bloated, rotting, elephantine, but the Bird in his prime, vast enough that only magic

363

could have kept him in the air, his wing beats like the noise of the hurricane as it uproots whole trees and the föhn as it bears madness and avalanche from the mountains.

He was the Crow, he was the Cock, he was the Cuckoo; he was the Simurgh; he was the Roc. And he was one other bird as well, and his thunderous cawing was laughter in the face of death and at return to life.

"I claimed once to be the champion of life against death," he bellowed. "And I lied, because I was afraid of dying. But then I died, and found it but a little thing. There have been other Phoenixes, but they are gone from the world and I am here, last and to pay for all. These people, whom I had deceived and abused, took in the chicks that I became and cherished them for thousands of years. How can I not return and save them?"

And he plunged into the heart of the sphere of white fire and he enveloped it in his wings and he burned with its fire and the stench of burning feathers was like the burning of incense and gradually the white of the flame dulled to red and then to purple and then to a black as deep as the black of his feathers and the ash that they became as they flamed and fell.

The sphere of flame was snuffed and the burned carcass of the Bird fell upon the back rows of the Burnedover troops, crushing many of them as it fell, though many others broke and ran and destroyed the neat parade-ground array in which they stood, and rather than fall and be trampled some of them charged forwards, firing their weapons at us but unprepared and uncoordinated.

Berin shouted to them, "Hold back, you fools," but in the rage of battle, who was he to them, but some monster they had not knowingly seen before, who held their contracts but not their respect, and I had just pulped their comrades behind the door.

They were white American men and we were few and many of us were women and most of us were brown. They had automatic weapons and we had swords and spears and bows or were unarmed.

And one of us was in a wheelchair and several of us had the appearance of great age.

They did not stand a chance.

Apollo started to fire arrows into the heart of their charge, and for him this was sport, and besides our ally had just died by fire, and so he used his arrows of plague. Wherever his shots hit, men fell writhing and blisters and black buboes grew and burst on their exposed flesh.

Loki addressed his children, the Beasts of Ragnarök. "Jormungandr and Fenris, you are sworn to defend those here who cannot fight—I and your sister will take on that task. If this is not Ragnarök as was prophesied, it will do. You and Garm were born for this."

As he spoke, he drew the weapon Laevetin, whose flickering between sword, staff and mace was fast enough to look like flame, but was not, and struck out at any Burnedover men who came within his reach with results appropriate to whichever aspect of his weapon was dominant as it hit. Hel stood at his side, and her glance was deadly to any of the enemy at whom she pointed.

Garm and Fenris howled and charged at the reserves as they came up to the enemy's left flank before they could wheel and encircle us; their brother hissed and did likewise on the right.

The Dog and the Wolf trampled as they ran, picking up random unlucky soldiers in their teeth and worrying at them until their necks broke. The serpent struck over and over and gulped huge mouthfuls.

Sobekh stood back and at first seemed to do nothing, until I noticed row after row of small grey and brown mice run underfoot and up trousers and into the mouths of the fallen but not yet dead to choke and nibble.

Apollo noticed this and commented, "Had I known, reptile, that my former worshippers could do that, I would not have been so ready to gift them to you."

Sobekh said nothing, but smirked, toothily.

Tom produced a gun as big as the ones they were firing and tossed it to Syeed, who dropped to a crouch so as to show as small a profile as possible and started firing single deadly shots.

Tom meanwhile jumped, chair and all, from platform to platform on top of the pyres, freeing one victim on each and trusting them to show initiative and free their companions. He only had to return to one or two platforms where the first god or saint he freed seized the opportunity to try to flee or was peculiarly unhandy. For the most part, they freed their fellows who either helped them or picked up dropped weapons from the soldiers crushed under the smouldering ruins of the bird and joined in the firefight.

Many of them started shooting at Berin himself, without effect—shots that came near him ricocheted. Still, I could see him flinch as he retreated up the steps towards the throne, all the while shouting orders that his army simply ignored.

I stepped forward with my long sword and my spear and slashed and thrust faster than their eyes could readily see. Brünnhilde did likewise with a great battle axe while Josette danced among their bullets deflecting them with an invisible shield of force; she had had her fill of killing earlier. Alexander walked up and down the enemy ranks methodically—almost mechanically—stabbing: his sword arm moving almost faster than I could see.

The Quintessence flared above and behind Sof and Caroline like a great fan that protected those who were not fighting, and bullets that struck it either fell spent before our feet or flared and faded into nothingness. It is worth remembering that the Fifth Thing has the qualities of the other four—in this instance both the impenetrability of the Adamant and the voracious appetite for annihilation of the Alkahest, That Which Devours.

I wondered for a moment why Emma was not involving herself more in the actual fighting but instead stood there quietly chanting to herself, but then I saw Sof and then Morgan do the same and realised that for every soldier I or Brünnhilde decapitated or Alexander stabbed or Apollo infected, another ten would fall, and then I realised what Emma and the others were saying over and over, and willing to be the case.

I had a moment of concern for the young woman Olivia, who was in the middle of this and defenceless—I looked across and saw that her father was shielding her with his limited resources of power.

She was staring at the carnage with unflinching shock and horror.

And as the Burnedover soldiers, all of them copies of the man Elodie and Caroline had killed earlier, died, their corpses fell away to mulch, bones and dust. There is little breeze in the courts of Heaven, but enough from the stir of battle that there was little to be seen.

"Sympathetic Magic Backlash," the explanation of White's decay Sof and Emma had given each other, now became the deadliest of spells. We all took it up as our battle cry—some spells work even for those with little natural talent for magic—and the more we chanted it the more it became the case.

Yet even as rank after rank died where they stood, and even though their weapons had no effect on us, they never broke, they continued to march and fire and die in perfect dogged silence. Were they fighting ordinary regulars, they would have been terrifying and invincible. They had taken and held Heaven, and defeated the Angelic Host and strung it up helpless.

We destroyed them to the last man, and they were fighting for the utter destruction of humanity, but I would not have you think we killed them in scorn and disrespect.

Normally in such a defeat you see the shades of the dead rise up, but these had no souls or rather were mere wisps of the man from whom they had been grown.

Whether those little puffs of soul that were all that marked their passing rejoined what little was left of him I know not but hope so. Utter extinction happens and is a terrible thing, and not the least of Burnedover's collective crimes, but though they had done it to so many with their dead gods, I still would not wish it on them.

As I have remarked before, in my eyes Death pays all debts, but that, of course, is the privileged perspective of one who has killed so many and has never died myself. I know that many of those whom I know and love take a different view.

We had to remove that army before Berin recovered from his momentary panic and drew further on the vast reservoir of magic he had accumulated from millennia of people working the Rituals: it was the grimmest of tasks, but necessary. However he planned to bring his people back obviously demanded even more power than he already had—his intention to deceive us into slaughtering babies, his plan to subject so many gods and saints to endless torment, these should have produced that power. But instead he had squandered power on producing that primordial flame and the Bird had appeared and snuffed it out, taking that magic into his own self for the death that was a part of his purpose.

Because though the Bird knew he would die the true death, he also knew that he was the Phoenix. In his first life, he had tried to avoid that fate and had become monstrous. Now he had embraced it and hoped for yet another chance.

While most of those freed from the pyres either fled or tried to take part in the fighting, I saw Mary the mother of Josette walk over to the Bird's remains and look at them carefully. The flames had left the feathers of his tail intact and she bent and raised them. I guessed what she was looking for, even though I did not see her pick them up and cradle them in her mantle.

When we see her next, you need to thank her: she thought to rescue and protect you in the middle of a desperate fight. Yes, I know that you don't remember this; you don't remember anything from before you hatched. Perhaps someday you and your hatchmates will.

But, as I say, the fight was desperate even though we were winning it, because we had to keep momentum and destroy

Burnedover utterly, so that no scrap was left from which it could be reborn. These were the early generations of White's copies: we could not assume that their decay could not in some way be reversed.

They did not ask us for quarter. They did not retreat. They continued to try to advance even as we killed them, even as Apollo's plagues spread among them, even as the decay Emma's spell encouraged felled them in rows.

I had not counted the host and its reserves when first we arrived: it seemed a pointless exercise in a situation with only two possible outcomes. But now there were only two hundred, and moments later ninety, and then forty…

I left the last score to my companions, and do not know who killed the last one, because I was rushing to and up the high staircase to the dais on which stood Jehovah's throne. I wondered that Berin had not taken his seat on it, the moment his forces seized Heaven, but I suppose it was as important to him that we see his victory as that he win.

I suppose this because I have observed the like in other bad men, but I do not claim to understand it.

For some such similar reason he took his time mounting the stairs, even though his freed victims were shooting at him, even though his army was being cut to ribbons. It was as if he wanted to let us almost stop him, but then fail.

Amid the noise of battle, I heard Jehovah shout to me, "Don't try to stop him." Assuming my old apprentice knew his business, I stopped where I was, on the thirteenth step. Berin looked back, saw that I was no longer pursuing, looked puzzled for a second and then proceeded up the last few steps.

He stood there smiling, and then called down to us.

"What was it that Daniel prophesied? The abomination of desolation seated in the high place? That prophesy at least I come to fulfil."

And he sneered at us, his jaw of many rows of teeth fixed in rictus, and he sat himself down comfortably as if it were some ordinary chair.

It was not simply the bands of steel that appeared from the armrests and the back, snapped shut and bound him securely by wrists, waist and neck. It was the multicoloured smoke that gushed from the jewels with which the throne was decorated, smoke that started to resolve itself into the shapes of the men and angels whom Jehovah had imprisoned there for betraying or deceiving him.

The first to solidify into an angry shell of its former self was the former Patriarch of Alexandria, Cyril, who had organized the dismemberment of my beloved sister Sof in the life where she was Hypatia and made the mistake of lying about it to Jehovah. He had let himself be suborned and then caught, and Berin had burned his brain out somehow.

His anger and his spite were still there, though none of that fine intellect. Between them, Jehovah and Berin had reduced him to a beast that guarded Jehovah's throne as a dog whipped and starved might guard a warehouse. And indeed I worried that Cyril and the other guardians might tear out Berin's throat and leave his spirit free to attack us from elsewhere, perhaps housed in another body.

Most of his defeats had been down to unlikely chances or to good people acting in ways that bad people would not act, making choices that he would not have. We could not rely on this forever, and his body being destroyed before his purposes bore fruit was an eventuality he must have considered and for which he would have obvious counter-moves.

I did not know, for example, that he had always inhabited the same body. He would have had no qualms about growing at least a few copies of his own. He would have hated hiding in a human body, but would have regarded that distaste as secondary to his purpose. And now he was close to success, even though we were inflicting some defeats on him, I could not assume anything.

Besides, I am human enough that taking one opportunity finally to punch Cyril in the face—even zombie brain-burned Cyril—was a reward in itself. Most of the jewels had been angels—the renegades Emma had overcome were not the only defectors or plotters down the years; it's worth remembering that all angels are mercenaries even though most of them are true to their hire and play along to the mythology and Jehovah's ego. So I kept Berin safe from them. I took the haft of my spear and beat them away from him. He was pinioned and I thought him helpless because I trusted the solidity of Jehovah's traps.

And doing so, thinking so, I almost brought disaster on us all.

Because he broke his bonds while I was distracted, though he tore gashes down to the bone in his hands on his forearms and his hands on the broken metal as he did so and lost a lot of blood and was in too much of a hurry to pause and heal himself, and he reached out to the point of my spear and placed one of his hands over my hand that was nearest to it and seized my other hand in a bloody grip and pulled the point of my spear once between his ribs to pierce his heart and a second time to slash open his belly deep into the bloody mess of his guts.

And, without whimpering even slightly, he whispered in my ear, "Huntress, why should I steal stored booby-trapped power from Jehovah's throne when there is a far greater reservoir of it in you? All those workers of my Rituals that I tithed of their stolen power— that power is as nothing to what you took from them when you punished them with death. And you have been such a miser with that power these last seven thousand years; you have hardly squandered a death. I thank you; my people who will be born from your death thank you. Now, despair and die."

When I killed Josh on the cross, who was now Josette, I had felt some small fraction of power leave me, that brought about her resurrection, but that was nothing to this. Berin reached into me and tore me apart: I felt my hair grow matted and white and sparse; I felt the teeth grow loose and worn down to nubs in my mouth; I felt the skin of my face stretch tight and crease and crack; I felt the muscles in my limbs wither and grow slack and my bones turn to powder in the sack of my flesh.

I said earlier that I have never died and that is true. I have however known what it is like to start to die, with my dying enemy laughing in my ear and drawing his victory out of my agonized flesh.

I looked down at the ruin of his lower torso and saw the wound stretch itself further and further as the small clawed hands of evil babies started to reach to me through the tatters of his guts. I heard them munching on his flesh as they came; I heard their whispering scorn in my mind.

"The ring of flesh has burst," he whispered, "and the sleepers wake and all is undone."

Except, though I know this happened, and I came close to death and ruining us all, suddenly it was not so. Suddenly, impossibly, it was the moment before Berin tore himself free of his bonds, and Tom was at my side in his wheelchair and he smacked Berin across the forehead with a leather sap, and on the backswing knocked my spear from my hands and out of Berin's reach.

"I think we lost," I said. "I think I almost died."

"That happened," Tom said. "I saw it. And then I jumped. Now it did not."

I was distracted a little for a moment. Cyril had struggled back to his feet and so I had the chance to punch him in the face again. This time it discouraged him and he shambled away, almost immediately falling headlong down the staircase. He started to rise, but Sobekh, grown vast, wandered across, picked him up between his paws and gulped him down.

The god looked up at me, apologetically. "Zombies don't count, right? But he harmed your sister?"

I waved him permission; he wasn't going to make a habit of it.

Berin came back to his senses to find Tom peering into his eyes.

"I probably gave you a nasty concussion there, sir," Tom said. "If I were you, I'd get it looked at by a medical professional."

372

"What happened?" Berin shrieked in disbelief. "I tricked you. I won. My people started to come back. And then—"

"You won," I agreed. "Fair and square, as we humans say. Unfortunately, it's not a game and we humans cheat. Young Tom here recently learned to jump in time as well as in space, and so what just happened was all undone. As, you will recall, the prophesy stated it would be. Prophesy is a bitch. You should probably not have been so quick to silence my sister in the middle of her death curse. As it is, and as she told you, failure and despair."

That inhuman face crumpled, and the monster cried like a little child.

I felt almost sorry for him as I snapped his restored bonds and led him down the staircase to face our judgement.

Victor's justice.

And as at all such moments. the players were moving around the board and power was shifting and alliances were being formed and reformed. My and Emma's usual close allies were standing closer together and—entirely separately—Jehovah with a clap of his hands had summoned his usual council of advisers to stand around him.

He fixed his children with a loving smirk and then a glare as they persisted in standing with Emma, Sof, Caroline and Polly and an increasing number of my former companions who had been hostages.

Lucifer and his daughter stood somewhat apart, still guarded by his other children; Loki wandered over and joined them.

The Gods of Hind and the Celestial Bureaucracy had already put down their guns and departed without ceremony. They had, it seemed, no desire to get further involved or to spend any more time in the Heaven of Jehovah, leaving behind a representative each— the elephant Ganesh and Guanyin, goddess of mercy—a fairly strong indicator that they expected us to do any dirty work that needed doing and take a moral high ground of plausible deniability about it.

Apollo stepped forward towards me and was forthright about it. "Why isn't that creature already dead, Huntress? You've hunted him ineffectually for thousands of years and you just watched him slaughter your sister…"

"Who died," Emma cut him off, "reminding me that she had enabled me to learn both prudence and forgiveness. I, for one, don't choose to forget her last words."

"Surely prudence would dictate—" suggested Lucifer and left the words hanging. He always had a sense of the room.

"He's a prisoner," Brünnhilde said, "taken by trickery. At the very least, he should be given weapons and a chance to fight our champion."

Elodie shook her head, distressed. "Caroline and I put the man White out of his misery when most of you were prepared to leave him to rot. It didn't feel good. I think if we kill him, it may make us feel better for a bit, but…"

"Plus," her beloved added, "to him, we're the monsters. He's alone. He always has been. We won. Time for mercy and compassion. As is written."

"We're all talking," Caroline said, "as if death were in any way relevant. I know most of you have never actually died, but several of us have. And we're still here."

"And before anyone asks," Emma interjected, glaring very pointedly at Jehovah and Lucifer, "no, I'm not setting up some private torture chamber specially for him. The Dukes are very bad people, and I keep them where they can't do much harm even to each other, but Hell doesn't do punishment any more. Unless you count me being sarcastic at them in parole hearings."

Jehovah looked sulky. "What about that oubliette under Pandemonium?"

Apollo looked daggers at him. "I spent a couple of millennia in that pit. We of Olympus have not forgotten." And pointedly turned his back.

Emma intervened. "Aserath and I filled it in. Too much of a temptation…"

Jehovah moved from sulky to grumpy. "I don't know how I let you talk me into it. Bloody rest home… And by the way, young Emma, I'll be wanting the Heavenly Choir back sometime soon."

"I think that's rather up to them. You don't actually need them now. Judas has built them rather a nifty concert hall, and they've updated their repertoire rather…"

"Not the point," Jehovah growled irritably, and pointed again at Berin. "Extended death by torture followed by eternal torment. Why don't you all see that? His people stuck a knife in me that ate me from the inside. And I'm supposed to just forget about it."

Syeed coughed. "The Merciful, the Compassionate…"

"You helped change my bedpan for several months, so I'll ignore that. Prophet, have a word. He'll listen to you."

Mohammed, who along with the rest of the Council had clustered around their master, looked a little embarrassed. "He does have a point, Lord."

Jehovah looked around for support. He found very little.

The girl Olivia, Lucifer's daughter, took a deep breath and stepped forward. "I think you've all got a bit of a fucking nerve, actually."

I wanted to hear what she had to say, so I glared everyone into silence.

"I mean, sure, supervillain, master plan, all of that. But I just stood here and watched you massacre an entire army in what, half an hour. And you're the good guys? Dad's old friend that I just spent a few embarrassing hours being leered at by? He's supposed to be God? And it's all a scam anyway. You play these fucking games, and there's war and slavery and global warming and—"

"I think I fixed global warming a day or so ago, actually," Emma interrupted.

Olivia scoffed, "Oh really? How? By more fucking magic, I suppose?"

"Actually, yes. I had to unfreeze Shadow, so... Magical homeostasis, you see."

Olivia could see she meant it and looked round at the rest of us.

"I sorted out the Dead Gods thing," I said, "and in any case most of us were trapped outside time for thirty years."

She didn't look terribly convinced. I imagine that, living with her father, she had got tired of even plausible excuses.

"Well, OK then. You two women seem to get things done. And I gather Polly over there saved London from being worse than it was. But I just found out that my dad ran a torture camp for thousands of years for him, over there, with the beard, Mr. Patriarchy. And that army you just destroyed—they were all fine and dandy running the American empire until they turned round and bit you."

She wasn't wrong.

"I listened to you and Dad catching up and making up, and it turns out that about half of human history was you two faffing around building a power base to fight him over there. Only it didn't work, did it? You fought stupid little wars with each other while he quietly took over your army and threw you out of your powerbase. And he only didn't win because some guy learned to time jump. Pretty pathetic, don't you think? I love you, because you're my dad, but, well, you've got to admit you're wankers."

And Jehovah stood there and took it, which made me think a little better of him than I had in recent centuries. Or maybe he just fancied her.

Gautama, who had found a broom somewhere and was quietly sweeping the last few remains of the dead army into a very small pile, looked over and bowed in a non-committal manner.

I kept a firm grip on the subject of all this, who was shaking with silent mirth.

I asked him why.

"Because this is all so typical. You're all locked in your own tiny skulls. You can't agree on anything. No wonder I almost beat you all; just me, against billions of you. Imagine what even a few more of me would have done to you."

Josette wandered over and looked very deeply into his eyes.

"That's not quite the whole story, though, is it? You like to tell yourself stories about your people, but I'm not locked in my skull and I can see everything you know and don't want to know…"

Berin stiffened in my grasp.

Josette went on. "Not really a single mind with a single purpose, were they? They had their rivalries and their little wars. Over who could breed the best and strongest human cattle. And the eruption that broke their control, that wasn't just random bad luck, was it? It was a single angry child throwing the wrong magic tantrum. And when Lillit helped the cattle escape into Shadow, that turned to eating each other, that wasn't wholly a new thing was it?"

I could see what she was trying to do. I'd seen her do it to Zeus.

She pressed on. "Let's talk about that unfortunate woman, your mother."

I was concerned about how Berin might try and stop her delicate torturing kindness; I put a knife to his throat and whispered in his ear, "Don't even think about it."

"You really are quite damaged, aren't you?" she said with genuine sorrowful compassion in her voice. "I'm not sure I could heal you even if you wanted me to. Mother?"

Mary had taken a seat on a step halfway up the staircase and was whispering to you and the other hatchlings—at a glance I could see that there were several more than five and idly wondered who else would get a companion in this turn of the world.

And, as always, what longer game was being played.

"Beyond my skill, dear, I'm afraid."

I could see Jehovah trying to make up his mind to do something violent even if no one agreed with him and doubted whether anyone cared enough to stop him. My own attitude was that letting Berin live a long untroubled life with the knowledge of absolute failure was one of the cruellest things we could do.

Which, to be absolutely clear, did not in my eyes make it a bad thing at all.

Then something happened which I had not expected at all.

Emma's face changed subtly, as if someone else were looking through her eyes.

Caroline, who had clearly seen this a time or two too many, covered her eyes and muttered something that I couldn't quite catch but sounded like "Oh god, more bloody music, I bet."

Emma walked over to me, bowed, said, "Huntress," clicked her heels and pulled a monocle out of nowhere and inserted it in her left eye.

I had known that Berthe was another of Sof's avatars, but had not expected to see her again, thinking her entirely dissolved into Emma.

She guessed what I was thinking. "I let myself go. It was like a warm bath forever. Only, it gets noisy in there. When she does magic, it's like you're in an old apartment block and asleep only the pipes start banging. And there's someone in the next room humming their way through counterpoint and after a bit you're awake and you go next door and it's all equations and fugues, but you chat mind to mind. And then Emma wanders through and you say hi. And she's glad really, that I'm in here, but I still don't want the flesh back. Too much work to finish."

"Work?" I asked, because that was a thing I could understand.

"There are things that need doing only I can do. Berin here knows what those things are, don't you? That's why he had stormtroopers kick me to death. Unnecessarily, because back in the 1920s I only had music to work with, whereas now…" and briefly she was Emma, "Berthe can draw on my resources of power, and our little friend as well."

Jehovah had been dithering, but finally made his move towards the steps up to the throne. Mary stood up, glared and put out a pre-emptively forbidding hand.

"Don't embarrass yourself, dear."

Josette put a firm hand on his shoulder. Jehovah looked around for support and again found none; even Lucifer thought a moment and then shook his head.

Once Jehovah had clearly stepped back and done as he was told, Mary sat back down and continued to pet you and your siblings. When Emma—or Berthe—set foot on the steps, Mary smiled and gave her a thumbs up.

It was definitely Emma who looked around seeking approval. "My friends have a plan," she said.

I had already agreed: I wasn't sure who else she'd canvassed, but from the smiles and nods she was getting from everyone except Jehovah and Apollo it probably didn't matter.

By the time she had sat down on Jehovah's no longer booby-trapped throne, it was clearly Berthe back in charge for the moment.

The sphere of white energy emerged from her forehead.

It emitted a high clear chord that somehow contained within it low strings, a trumpet call and a single reverberating stroke of a bass drum.

It attracted everyone's attention; it also did something that someone should have taken it upon themselves to do at least ten minutes earlier, which is that it freed and restored all of the captive angels, who rose up from the other side of Heaven's vast facade like the pigeons of St. Mark's Piazza when the clocks strike four, and hovered above us like a trompe l'oeil ceiling of ever-receding blue black and gold skies.

They were not our major concern.

Berthe struck an attitude.

"Berin killed from the beginning," she declaimed in what I am told is called Sprechgesang over a low rustling in strings I could not see, and whether it was Emma's power or hers we were all transfixed until she was done, "and if I could consult his first victims I would… but then there were the first gods he met. A little pantheon who did no harm. Gods worshipped for the magic they knew; that magic was being of use, and the worship produced power, and that power was shared and not hoarded. And they tried and failed to help him and he killed one of them and drew power from that act, and they withdrew rather than die at his hand. And they became story. Or were always story. And other stories grew around theirs until they were lost."

Emma had told me of the performance Morgan had commissioned and the version of my story it ended with, but she had not the skill to make me hear the music of Berthe's opera, or assumed I would not be interested, or did not want to bother Berthe. In any case, with the help of the being that also lived in Emma, I heard fragments of reprise now. As did everyone else—men, women, gods, angels and creatures.

It was partly Emma's will that fixed us and partly Berthe's music that seduced and salved and instructed us and partly the inexorable proceedings of equations and fugues that underpinned the new world. We were fixed in place mostly because we suddenly wanted to be and needed to be.

I trusted Emma on this and trusted Berthe. I even trusted the strange mathematical being.

A low male voice over hushed bowed strings, but also some plucked instrument and a delicate percussive sound like a stream running over pebbles, intoned, "Thus it was, thus it is, thus it will be," and then "What was forgotten is remembered, what was lost is regained, what was harmed will be healed," and then "Perfect knowledge, perfect justice, perfect love."

There were other voices in the mix, human voices captured and remixed, singing in many tongues. There were the instruments of the European symphony orchestra, but there were other sounds as well—as passive travellers in Emma's head and readers in her vast memory palace of experience and judgement, Berthe and her collaborator the white light had absorbed so much—music of other continents, strange electronic squawks and all under the control of a single creative will and an alien interpreter prepared to subordinate itself totally to that will.

I wish that I could tell you eloquently of which instruments I heard in what combinations and what order, as Emma could, perhaps, or Berthe if she chose, but I have no skill in such matters. I am merely one who used to hunt and used to think myself alone, who protects and saves all that I can. And I felt myself protected and saved by that music.

Berthe was as talented as her avatars; her eclectic strange music was as intense and strange and great a working as any of Emma's or Sof's.

I saw among the freed worthies of Heaven Jehovah's choir master, whom I had last seen in Prague at the first night of his opera about the damned libertine. And he wept for joy at what we were hearing and in sorrow that someone else had found these worlds to conquer.

The Wolf, the Dog, the Horse and the Serpent wept for it spoke to their mixed nature; their parent wept for this was persuasion beyond the power of his silver tongue; Gautama managed not to weep for he had achieved mastery even of such emotions, but he nodded along to the universality and wisdom of it.

The freed angels wept because it reached beyond humanity.

Jehovah wept, for it was the culmination of all the music he had ever loved. He had been to so many first nights to be among the first connoisseurs of some surprising novelty or product of genius, and here this was telling him, telling all of us that we could, that we must, change who we are and what we do.

And that all he had tried and largely failed to do—that no longer mattered, because his good intentions, and his massive vanity, were forgiven and redeemed.

And I smiled because I trusted Emma and I trusted Berthe and it was a good plan.

All of us were secondary though, because the real immediate audience of that music was Berin.

Who wept. And was changed.

He wept for himself, and millennia of lonely hatred, and for his people whom he had failed. He thought himself other and better, yet all of his life had been spent among the humans he thought he hated and despised and here was one of his victims reaching out to him and reaching the heart he did not know he had.

The child reared by wolves howls with the pack. Even his thoughts were in human language. Last of his people, he could never have lived among them. The milk of the mother he tortured and slaughtered had changed him more than he wanted to know.

And this music dragged him back to stare up helpless and comforted at her loving, bignosed forehead and sloping features.

He wept for his lost people. He wept for himself. He wept for all that he had lost but also for all his victims betrayed, misled, tormented, slaughtered, annihilated.

It was a story. It was a myth. It was a truth. It came from the heart of what it is to be human: it went to all hearts.

"Thus it was," a voice intoned.

It told us of Hemul, one of five gods who served, protected and were of use, until they met with misfortune.

Hemul, as we were told by voices but also by an accompanying stringed instrument that said as much as the words, became story to warn humanity of the wolf in the fold, that we never forget there was one among us who did not wish us well, but he also dwelled in story to learn among its many branches the thing he needed.

Ysh was dead, killed in horror by Berin. Beautiful rash loving young Ysh. He was the first god king lover to be slaughtered, but he was not the last.

Osiris was killed by Set and his limbs and organs scattered, but Isis wandered up and down the River and reassembled him.

Orpheus went to Hades to bring back his snake-slain wife. And he failed, but stories of failure were as important as stories of success.

Inanna was stripped of her finery and her beauty as she descended into Hell, but she returned.

As did Proserpine. But not Balder.

Lazarus came forth. Josh died and rose as Josette.

All of this was in Berthe's music, shown and catalogued and analysed and rendered at once glorious and curative. Each story had its own music and all of those musics twined around each other in a fugue of many voices that also portrayed Hemul's growing understanding of resurrection and rebirth.

Sof came back into the world and Caroline.

Morgan forgave the Morrigan and was in turn made whole again.

The Bird rose and was sacrificially consumed and was reborn again.

How could that be portrayed in music that must surely have been composed before it happened? It is a mystery; all I know, what I learned in that time, is that the great Arts, the great Workings, exist in Eternity, are parts of how we apprehend or become the One.

I have often mocked Plato, but that is because I knew him, and begrudged his human weakness.

And before our eyes Hemul recreated himself out of Story and brought Ysh back from Death. Had they even existed before this moment? Was Berthe's first opera a rehearsal of forgotten truth translated from scratchings in baked clay or was it a fable that she had invented?

It did not, it does not, matter.

Remember, it portrayed how I became the Huntress, the avenger of a young god slaughtered by Berin, yet that story as she told it was not my story, but a beautiful invention as false in one sense as it was true in another.

Yet there they were, two young gods in glorified flesh, dancing and singing before us—the wise Hemul and his brother lover Ysh, who had tried rashly to heal Berin by bringing him into that love, that dance and had been brutally killed for his pains.

The music portrayed that dance to yearning woodwind measures, that rashness with horns and trumpets, that slaughter with a frenzy of trombones and drums and that return from death with soaring shimmering exultant strings.

"*Thus it is,*" sang that voice.

In my grip, Berin groaned at the sight as if something were drawn out of him, as perhaps it was. Ysh or someone or many someones had been slaughtered to give Berin power. And what had been stolen was now redressed.

I felt a pressure of sadness lift from my heart that I had never known was there and looked around at all my friends and allies and saw that same lightness in their eyes.

I looked at Morgan and saw a smile of delighted promise. Because the dance of the two men became ever closer and the music ever more slow and sensual and heat spread through the audience and lovers stared at each other with open lust and all sorts of others stared at each other in pairs and trios and quartets in lascivious speculation and mounting tension. And the strings soared and twined and the horns and trumpets rose out of them and drums and struck brass built a frenzy that was suddenly released as the three goddesses, Larala, Ashtra and Asapha returned into time and the world from wherever they had been and gathered the two spent men into their embrace that started a slower reiteration of the music in a dance which the two men gradually joined and gained a second wind. This new dance was statelier, less frenzied, but richer and more intense and it built and built until it suddenly came to a halt and silence held us all in its grip and Berin was suddenly held in the fixed glance of the five gods.

And they sang. They reached out their hands and hearts.

To Berin.
"*Beloved. Dark half. Soul that is many souls.*
Full of hate and crime.
You the Destroyer the Monster the Beast in the Night.

In defeat accept love.
There is no place for you in the world.
Not for you. Not for your many souls.
Yet Join Us.
We have waited so long.
In ecstasy. In knowledge.
In Number, in Music, in Magic, in all the workings and refinings of
the Mind.
In the light that contains and conquers darkness.
In the One."

He started to walk forward and I let him go. And as he walked towards the Five, he unravelled. Into points of light. Into a sigh that was consummation. And with him, all of his monstrous kind, and all their nightmare crimes.

Darkness, lost in light. Giving it texture.

He was gone. That was enough. Was watching him disappear from the world enough for me? Was quiet gladness that he and his were gone from the world, from Shadow, forgiveness enough? I do not know.

The Five were suddenly vast shadows looking down at us.

"Apart so long," they sang, "together at last in song, in dance, in love. In the One."

And they departed from our sight, unravelling into points of light as Berin had, into a sigh that was clearly that other kind of consummation. It was a sadness. It was a joy.

They were gone, and I cannot be wholly sure even now that they were ever there except as part of Berthe's music.

Which had finished with the Five and with Berin but was not done with us.

The lower strings became more and more urgent. This was new music, but it contained fragments of other things—rags and ragas, the call to prayer, a cantor elaborating the Nishmat, "the soul of every *living thing,"* Tibetan chants, the phrase *"diesen kuss der ganzen welt"* from the Ode to Joy.

And suddenly we all chose to accept a compulsion to sing. It was as if we were all offered a choice and all freely chose the only right thing. That is how it was for us at that moment: that perhaps lingers, or perhaps it is that in a post-Berin world we find the right thing easier because we are so aware of how many bad decisions we made, of how close we came.

"Thus it will be," we intoned along with the music, *"Must it be?"* we asked ourselves, men and women and beasts, angels and gods. *"It must be,"* we sang and it was like an oath. And it was not just sung there in the broken halls of Heaven.

We knew, beyond the possibility of knowing, that it was taken up, that it was sung and sworn, among the groves of former Hell and the hall of Valhalla that was now Olympus and by ratkings in the undercroft of Shadow. By stockbrokers and their ghoul clerks in the City of London. By carpetweavers in Isfahan and the men who dig for diamonds in Namibia, by priests and houngans and quite ordinary civilians who found an internet feed from the camera Polly had put in her lapel and never turned off.

And we saw such things, such glorious things that we could hardly refuse to make them happen. I do not know what others saw. This is what I saw in the music as we sang along to it and swore our oaths.

I saw Berthe walk slowly down from the throne, and be Emma again.

I saw Jehovah crawl the stairs to his throne on penitential knees and then flex those muscles and smash it into kindling, letting the power it stored go where it will. I saw him and Lucifer serving bowls of soup or rice in any city where there was famine; I saw them both digging children from the rubble of an orphanage in an earthquake-smashed California or digging channels for lava in Indonesia.

Both had birds, your siblings, perched on their shoulders singing Berthe's music to them, as a reminder.

I saw Olivia grudgingly start to forgive her father and his best friend for all they had done and failed to do. And joyfully share their work.

I saw Aserath waving her elegant hands and planting groves and orchards throughout Shadow and thence into the hearts of Mundane cities and the empty fields of the world.

I saw Tom snatching people from dangers that would have killed them seconds before they died. "Whispering death," malefactors had once called him; now he had another name.

For all these things would be needed. The world was wounded and needed those who would help heal and minimize harm.

Some of the many dead, blessed and damned alike, would be done with the flesh and chose to wander the world as unhoused spirits; Aspara and Eithne would recruit enough dryads to help guard the new forests. Others would choose hell-flesh that did not tire or age or bear children and whose odour was undetectable save by goblins.

Some of our friends would choose quiet domestic lives. Elodie and Syeed would set up house in her Mayfair flat, so that Tom always had a place to eat and sleep between rescues. The faun would move in as well when Polly found his perkiness irritating.

She would continue to guard and protect London from her lair. After a while she would manage to persuade the dead loves of her past to re-embody and return to her—or at least French Frankie and Young Herbert. The McHeath of her younger days whom she had always yearned for would take one look at the Tutelar she had become and return to doxies he could bully and boss.

Her home would become something of a clubhouse for old dead spies—my friend Georgiana and her colleague Gibbon. Polly had never mentioned—because she is capable of tact—that Crowley sometimes worked for her; he too would sometimes look in for a drink or a handout, and leave quickly when her other friends mocked him. After a while he would go live with the ghouls, who appreciated him, even when he refused their offers of food.

Josette would continue to act as chief therapist and convenor of the increasingly democratic and decentralised Just City to which more and more of the lost and damaged and rejected would flock for succour. Her brother would join her there and build to his heart's content and according to his own desires. After a while the Just City would become the best looking city in Shadow.

Which in due course would reduce Olympus that was once Valhalla to a mere suburb and attract those to it who needed refuge without their having yet to have died. Because the veils between life and death, between the Mundane and Shadow, would grow ever more permeable.

Emma would stick to her duties in for Hell for as long as she was needed, essentially until she had talked the last of the former Dukes into accepting the error of their ways. Explanations of how their crimes had served Berin would work more often than not.

With Aserath off spreading fertility, more and more of what organizing former Hell needed would fall to Theophania and Dawn, who would grow close.

Eventually the last business of the old Hell would be done with and Emma would retire to Oxford to join Sof. I would never quite understand what they and Berthe and the white sphere were doing until it was complete -a grand unification of magic and alchemy, of music and mathematics. There was, they would theorise, a substance beyond the Quintessence—perhaps not merely a Sixth Thing but more. Yet it would not be reached by alchemy alone...

When Lillit was done, most of her memories have passed to Caroline—that knowledge of the workings of time and chance as it actually happened would in due course make Caroline the greatest of the world's chroniclers but also offer a route to the success of their project which will be the culmination of all their arts and their last and most ambitious act of healing—the retrieval of all those lost to annihilation devoured by Dead Gods.

All of the issues between Emma and Caroline about the aeons of memory lurking behind their eyes would disappear once they were equal in this.

So much to share, so much to forget.

So much love. So much joy.

And I?

The world will not yet be safe. There will still be menaces in the world and in Shadow. Not everyone will have good intentions. As always, I will travel the roads and pathways and tracks and keep them safe—but not alone. Morgan who was once Hekkat will travel with me and you, Thought and Memory, and your brother the Morrigan, and my pack, the Beasts of Ragnarök, and a rag tag under my leadership—Alexander and his lover Knox, Loki Silvertongue and the fat theologian.

We will seek out miscreants and we will dissuade them, as I have always preferred to do.

Through story.

Because our future will be one of Perfect Knowledge, Perfect Justice, Perfect Love.

Caught forever in great Workings that lead us forever closer to knowing, in Number, in Music, in Magic, in all the Workings of the Mind, loving and knowing and becoming the One.

Some Things About Roz Kaveney

She has been a professional writer since her twenties but published her first novel—a non fantasy novel about trans street life *Tiny Pieces of Skull* (which had taken 28 years to find a publisher but then won a Lambda in 2016.)

She published *Rhapsody of Blood: Rituals* and her first collection of poetry, *Dialectic of the Flesh*, at the age of 63. Asked why, she says, "Well, I was quite busy."

Friends say it's hard to be out with Roz in Central London and not find yourself being randomly greeted by other people she knows. Some say this happens in New York, too, on the rare occasions when she goes there. This is because Roz's circle of acquaintance includes everyone from politicians to poets, art historians to dominatrixes, at least one serial killer to at least one Poet Laureate.

She helped negotiate changes to the law that helped trans people—Roz is a proud trans woman—change their legal status; she helped block a law that would have imposed stringent sexual censorship in UK bookstores.

She once rescued a flatmate from a Chicago mob hit.

She and Neil Gaiman once sold a two-book deal on the basis of a proposal they improvised in a meeting at which the publisher had turned their original idea down.

She discovered in the British Library an unknown verse play by a major Victorian poet; later, she told this story to a leading contemporary novelist, who based an award-winning novel on it.

She knows that British Intelligence has a file on her—she's seen the letter in which an Oxford don denounced her to them as a subversive. She does not know what the don meant…

She co-founded both Feminists against Censorship and The

Midnight Rose Collective. Look them up.

She's contributed to reference books that vary from *The Cambridge Guide to Women Writing in English* to *The Encyclopaedia of Fantasy.*

She was deputy Chair of Liberty (The National Council for Civil Liberties), and active in the Oxford Union debating society, the Gay Liberation Front and Chain Reaction, a dyke SM disco she helped run in the 80s.

She's been on television talking about sex, alternate worlds and who should have won the Booker Prize in 1953 if it had existed then; she's been on radio talking about fan fiction and film music.

She was a contributor to the legendary Alan Moore anti-Clause 28 comic book *AARGH! (Action Against Rampant Government Homophobia)*.

As a journalist, she's written about everything from the Alternative Miss World competition to the crimes of the Vatican.

Her acclaimed books on popular culture include *Reading The Vampire Slayer; From Alien To The Matrix; Teen Dreams;* and *Superheroes.*

"I was reared Catholic but got over it, was born male but got over it, stopped sleeping with boys about the time I stopped being one and am much happier than I was when I was younger."

She likes baroque opera, romantic string quartets, the music of Kurt Weill and Bruce Springsteen, the singing of Ella Fitzgerald, Ricki Lee Jones and Amanda Palmer.

She makes adequate chili, perfectly decent scrambled eggs, and a good cassoulet if she's got a couple of days.

She will write you a goodish sonnet in about five minutes if she's in the mood—sestinas usually take an hour.

When she grows up, she wants to be awesome.

For more about Roz, visit her Glamourous Rags website at:

glamourousrags.dymphna.net/index.html

Milton Keynes UK
Ingram Content Group UK Ltd.
UKHW011838041023
429946UK00001B/2